PRAISE FOR THE PEMBERLEY CHRONICLES SERIES

"Collins is a   n… If Austen
were alive today, I think

—*Austenprose*

"Consistent characters, lively dialogue, and a vivid narrative style… a very readable and believable tale."

—*Book News*

"*Perfect* for the purist at heart."

—*Jane Austen Sequel Examiner*

"Masterfully written and historically interesting."

—*Everything Victorian*

"A superb book… fascinating reading."

—*A Bibliophile's Bookshelf*

"The Pemberley Chronicles books have an elegance to them…I reread them over and over for comfort."

—*A Curious Statistical Anomaly*

"Stays true to the witty and romantic attributes of Austen's original."

—*Luxury Reading*

"Rebecca Ann Collins stays so close to the style and spirit of Jane Austen. Witty and heartfelt, her series is a must for any Austen fan."

—*Libby's Library News*

"There is so much to love in this series. The characters are engaging and the writing is spot on… I love how Rebecca Ann Collins emulates Jane Austen's writing style but makes it her own. It lends an authenticity to this series."

—*Books Like Breathing*

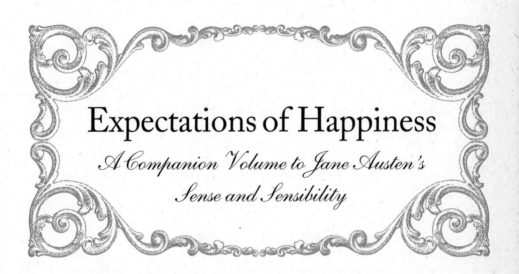

Expectations of Happiness

A Companion Volume to Jane Austen's
Sense and Sensibility

DEVISED AND COMPILED BY

Rebecca Ann Collins

sourcebooks
landmark

Published by Sourcebooks Landmark, an imprint of Sourcebooks, Inc.
P.O. Box 4410, Naperville, Illinois 60567-4410
(630) 961-3900
FAX: (630) 961-2168
www.sourcebooks.com

Library of Congress Cataloging-in-Publication Data is on file with the publisher.

Printed and bound in the United States of America
VP 10 9 8 7 6 5 4 3 2 1

Dedicated to those friends of our youth,

with whom we shared the

"sanguine expectations of happiness"

that filled our dreams.

"…That sanguine expectation of happiness, that is happiness itself…"

—*Sense and Sensibility,* Jane Austen, 1811

An Introduction...

ORIGINALLY PUBLISHED IN 1811, *Sense and Sensibility*, more so than any of Jane Austen's other novels, leaves open the option for a sequel.

In the final chapter of the book, while she tidies up the various strands of the story, Austen allows sufficient room for certain developments, which may be credibly used to continue the narrative without distorting the original concept of her characters.

Elinor Dashwood and Edward Ferrars, the author has assured us, have a union of hearts and minds that is the accepted foundation for a happy marriage. In contrast, the marriage of Marianne Dashwood and Colonel Brandon, encouraged by Mrs Dashwood, following upon the end of a most unhappy affair between Marianne and Mr John Willoughby, does not engender in readers the same feeling of sanguinity.

On first reading the novel many years ago, soon after I had read *Pride and Prejudice*, I was struck by this difference. Re-reading it more recently, after writing The Pemberley Chronicles series, I was further intrigued by the language of the author as she described the Brandons' marriage. Marianne, we are told, "instead of falling a sacrifice to an irresistible passion" as she had expected, "found herself at nineteen submitting to new attachments, entering on new duties, placed in a new home, a wife, the mistress of a family, and the patroness of a village." Colonel Brandon, who is twice her age, "was now as happy as all those who best loved him believed he deserved to be... consoled for every past affliction" by the regard and company of his wife, Marianne. Plausible, but not, one must admit, a particularly inspiring portrait of marital bliss.

The prospect is not improved when one realises (and here we have Miss Austen's word for it) that Willoughby still roams the countryside, unhappily wed, regretting his loss of Marianne and hating Colonel Brandon. There are even hints that his dishonourable conduct has been forgiven by those who were most injured by it—including Marianne.

And then, there is Margaret, the youngest Miss Dashwood, thirteen years old in the original novel, precocious, bright, and keen to learn—she deserved to be permitted to discover her own "expectations of happiness" in a freer environment than before. I took particular pleasure in giving Margaret that opportunity, by drawing the story of this family forward into the next dynamic decade of the nineteenth century.

Unlike *Pride and Prejudice*, in *Sense and Sensibility* we are not supported and surrounded by the weight of tradition and the social structures of a place like Pemberley providing the framework for the novel.

The story of the Dashwood sisters is, by contrast, that of a family of modest means, living quietly in the country, coping with the varying circumstances and challenges that life throws up. My interest was mainly in the way these characters mature and play out their individual roles, as they seek to substantiate those simple expectations of happiness that we all cherish.

RAC / November 2010.

For the benefit of those readers who wish to be reminded of the characters and their relationships to one another, an aide-mémoire is provided in the appendix.

Prologue

Summer 1819

THE DINNER PARTY AT Barton Park was exactly as Sir John Middleton had ordered it should be. The table was laid with the best porcelain, silver, and crystal, and the guests were presented with several courses of excellent fish, flesh, and fowl, accompanied by the finest wines in Sir John's well-stocked cellar. Lady Middleton had reminded him that it was her mother, Mrs Jennings's, birthday on Saturday, and Sir John had decided to please both his wife and his mother-in-law with an appropriately jolly celebration. Being a keen sportsman, no doubt Sir John may have been familiar with the notion of killing two birds with one stone, but, being also a kindly sort of man, it is unlikely he would have made mention of it on this occasion.

Mrs Jennings, an elderly, fat, cheerful woman with a tendency to talk loud and long, had been delighted to have a party given for her birthday, at which both her daughters, Lady Middleton and Mrs Palmer, sat on either side of her at table. She was able to indulge her love of gossip and jokes, while her sons-in-law sat at the other end, where Sir John ate, drank, and talked and Mr Palmer listened, thus humouring each other. It was the sort of diversion Sir John enjoyed hugely, and it was the type of occasion that allowed him to indulge his preference for food, wine, and company without feeling any sense of guilt, for he had ensured that a good time would be had by his family and guests as well.

There were not as many guests on this occasion as he would have liked, because, as he explained to each arriving visitor, it was almost the end of summer and many of the young men and ladies were already engaged for dances, picnics, and the like and had not been available at short notice.

"But that must not mean that we will be any less merry," he declared, encouraging everyone to enjoy themselves, as food and drink appeared in such variety and quantities as would satisfy even the keenest connoisseur and the heartiest appetite.

Since they could all eat well, even if they were not all particularly good at clever conversation, there would be no complaints from the guests, thought Mrs Dashwood, who had been conveyed to the manor house from her cottage in a curricle sent by Sir John. He was her cousin, whose kindness in making Barton Cottage available to them some nine years ago had rescued her and her three daughters from the embarrassment of being evicted from Norland Park, their home in Sussex, on the death of her husband, Mr Henry Dashwood.

Her stepson, Mr John Dashwood, and his wife, Fanny, had arrived, eager to take possession of Norland as soon as the funeral was over, and were it not for the generosity of Sir John's offer of the cottage, they would have been in very dire straits indeed.

Once settled at Barton Cottage in the county of Devon, Mrs Dashwood and her three daughters, Elinor, Marianne, and Margaret, had found themselves drawn into the ample circle of the Middletons' hospitality. While it had meant that they would never want for company or entertainment, it had not always been agreeable and had occasionally brought complaints from Miss Marianne that they suffered from an excess of both.

Since then, of course, two of Mrs Dashwood's daughters had been married: Elinor to Mr Edward Ferrars, now parson of the living of Delaford in Dorsetshire, and Marianne was married to Colonel Brandon and presided over the mansion house at Delaford herself.

The youngest sister, Margaret, had continued to live with her mother until the age of sixteen, when she had insisted that her thirst for knowledge could no longer be assuaged by books alone and she felt compelled to seek a fuller education. With the recommendation of her brother-in-law, the Reverend Edward

Ferrars, she had enrolled at a ladies' seminary outside of Oxford, where she studied with great dedication to improve her mind and her skills, in the hope of becoming a travel writer, thus felicitously combining her desire to travel with her literary aspirations.

Mrs Dashwood, who had been very close to her two elder daughters, travelled often to Delaford to see them, but seemed not to miss, quite as much, young Margaret, who maintained an irregular sort of correspondence with her mother and sisters, sufficient to provide the kind of news of her progress that her relatives demanded.

"Margaret writes that she is almost at the end of her course of study of English poetry and is writing an essay on the work of Mr Wordsworth," Mrs Dashwood replied rather proudly to an enquiry about her daughter from Mrs Jennings, whose knowledge of both English poetry in general and the work of Mr Wordsworth in particular was inadequate to permit her to say more than, "Is she indeed? My very word—did you hear that, Sir John?"

To which her son-in-law replied, "Hear what, madam?" and when Mrs Dashwood repeated her original information about Margaret, he merely grinned broadly and added, "Is she indeed? Excellent, excellent! I always said she was a smart young thing!" before returning to refill his glass. Mrs Jennings, whose enquiry had been directed at Miss Margaret's love life rather than her academic pursuits, also lost interest and turned away to chat with her daughter Charlotte Palmer, who had plenty of gossip from London to tell regarding the latest exploits of the Prince Regent and his courtiers.

And in such a manner was the party proceeding, until one young lady— the daughter of a near neighbour—was persuaded to take her place at the pianoforte, which she did with some enthusiasm, providing two or three jolly songs in quick succession for their entertainment. Sir John, who liked nothing better than a good "sing-along," set about gathering a small circle around the instrument, urging everyone to join in, intending by this means to increase the general merriment of the party to make up for its lack of numbers.

It was at this point in the proceedings that Lady Middleton, who had been standing by the coffee table at the far end of the room, fell suddenly to the floor. Her sister, Mrs Palmer, first gasped, then screamed loudly enough to stop the performers in midsong.

No one seemed to know what to do next. Mrs Palmer continued to scream,

Mrs Jennings looked stupefied, and Mrs Dashwood bent over the collapsed form of Lady Middleton, making soothing sounds and trying to rouse her with her fan.

"I do believe the room is too hot," she cried and proceeded to wave her fan about, while Sir John seemed to be stunned into silence. Only the consistently imperturbable and reputedly droll Mr Palmer, who had not been persuaded to join the singers and had continued to smoke his pipe by the fire, appeared to understand the need for some action. Ordering the servants to go for the doctor, he gave instructions for Lady Middleton to be laid upon a couch and asked his wife, Charlotte, to loosen her sister's clothing and fetch the smelling salts, while he ushered the rest of the company out of the drawing room, declaring that there was need for more air.

The doctor arrived and went directly to Lady Middleton's side, where Mrs Palmer sat weeping and wringing her hands, while Mrs Dashwood continued to wield her fan assiduously but to little effect. The doctor was attentive and thorough but, alas, it was too late; the patient had suffered a severe seizure and it seemed her heart had failed.

Lady Middleton was pronounced dead.

Sometime later the doctor went away, leaving Sir John still stunned and bewildered, Mrs Jennings and Charlotte Palmer both distraught, trying to console one another, and Mrs Dashwood in a quandary, for once, not of her own making.

She felt she had to do what she could to help, yet knew not what to do; she couldn't go back to Barton Cottage at that hour—it was long past midnight— and she wanted desperately to contact her daughters at Delaford, but had no means to do so. As the hours passed, feeling awkward, still dressed as she was in her evening gown, Mrs Dashwood went into the kitchen and found the staff in various stages of shock and grief, apparently unable to comprehend the death of their mistress. With some difficulty, a sobbing maid was persuaded to prepare a tea tray and take it in to the morning room, where Mr Palmer stood at the window, regarding the early dawn sky. Somewhat tentatively, Mrs Dashwood approached him and asked if it would be possible to have a message sent to her daughter Mrs Edward Ferrars at the Delaford parsonage in the neighbouring county of Dorset. Familiar with Mr Palmer's reserved and often abrupt manner, she was quite taken aback when he acknowledged her, bowing politely, thanked her for ordering the tea, and then declared that of course it could be done and if she would write a note, he would have it conveyed to Delaford immediately.

"Of course you wish to inform your daughters, Mrs Dashwood; I will have it sent directly. Furthermore, should you wish to return to Barton Cottage at any time, my carriage is available to take you home. You have been awake all night, attending on Mrs Jennings and my wife; you must be very tired, I am sure you must wish to rest."

Mrs Dashwood, pleasantly surprised by his consideration, expressed her gratitude and, assuring him she was in no hurry to leave, moved to sit at a side table and compose her message to Elinor. Giving few details, but conveying the shock and sorrow she felt, she wrote:

Clearly, everyone has been shocked by Lady Middleton's untimely death. Poor Sir John—he seems stunned; he said not a word and has not left his room since. As for Mrs Jennings and Mrs Palmer, I cannot imagine how they will console one another, they are both utterly bereft. Only Mr Palmer seems able to cope and it's a good thing he is able, because there is no one else to handle the arrangements for the funeral. I confess I am as disabled as the rest, for I cannot take it in and do not know what I can do to assist my cousin at this time. I long for your advice, my dear daughters, and beg you to come to me as soon as possible.

Urging Elinor to convey the news to Marianne and Colonel Brandon as well, Mrs Dashwood begged her daughters to come at once to Barton Cottage, where they were all welcome to stay until the funeral.

❧

It was almost late afternoon when Elinor and Edward Ferrars arrived at Barton Cottage. Mrs Dashwood was first surprised and then disappointed that Marianne was not with them and would not be attending the funeral.

"Marianne sends her condolences, Mama, but unfortunately, she is unwell and cannot travel; however, Colonel Brandon has been informed and promises to be here by nightfall. He insisted that we take the carriage; he will follow on horseback," Elinor explained.

Her mother was not happy; Sir John had been exceedingly kind and generous to them all and had taken a particular interest in Marianne when she had fallen seriously ill following her disastrous love affair with John Willoughby. No one had been happier than Sir John when she had finally married his good friend Colonel Brandon.

"I had hoped Marianne would have understood that Sir John is all the family we have—the only relative we may turn to, since it is unlikely that the selfish attitude of John and Fanny Dashwood will ever change. We have every reason to be grateful to him and to show him some kindness and sympathy in his time of grief," she complained.

While Elinor agreed with her mother on the matter of Sir John's generosity, she was uncertain about the depth of his grief; she had not noticed any signs of deep affection between the Middletons. His wife had spent most of her time spoiling her children and gossiping with her mother and sister, while her husband pursued his favourite pastimes with his friends. However, Elinor knew her mother's sensibility well and did not wish to provoke her, so said nothing of that, trying instead to console her with the news that Edward had dispatched an express to Margaret's address in Oxfordshire breaking the news, and it was possible she would arrive in time for the funeral.

Later that afternoon, Colonel Brandon arrived at the cottage and together with Edward went up to Barton Park to support his old friend Sir John and remained there for most of the evening. When Edward returned, he reported that Sir John's spirits had improved a little. "He seemed better able to cope with the arrangements that have to be made and was exceedingly gratified to have Colonel Brandon's company," said Edward, adding that Mr Palmer was being very useful and appeared to have everything in hand. "He seems such an odd sort of fellow, yet he is clearly a man of practical common sense and good understanding," he said.

"He certainly is," replied Elinor, who recalled well and recounted for her husband and mother the kindness of Mr Palmer, when Marianne had lain gravely ill at Cleveland House and only Mr Palmer had offered to stay and support Elinor until her mother arrived to help nurse the patient. "He was most kind, and I confess I was surprised, because we had grown accustomed to regarding him as withdrawn and proud, but when it mattered most, he was none of those things."

When Mrs Dashwood added her own recent experience, Elinor felt obliged to remark that Mr Palmer's reputation had probably suffered more as a consequence of his marriage to a silly woman like Charlotte, whose incessant prattling drove him to distraction, than any evidence of ill nature on his part.

At this the ladies laughed, but as the Reverend Edward Ferrars saw it, this was another example of why one should not leap to conclusions about people's characters—whether for good or ill; but he did not get far with his homily, because there was a knock at the door and the maid opened it to admit none other than Mr Palmer himself.

Silenced by surprise at seeing him and the coincidence of his arrival at that very moment, in the middle of their conversation about him, they were barely able to greet Mr Palmer, until Edward invited him into the sitting room. Clearly, he had walked from the manor house.

Mrs Dashwood rushed away to order tea. Edward stood beside the fireplace and Elinor sat facing their visitor, quite unable to comprehend the reason for his visit. Not in all the years that the Dashwoods had lived at Barton Cottage had Mr Palmer visited them on his own. What had brought him there that night? As he sat rather awkwardly in a high-backed chair by the fire, the chair that used to be her father's, Elinor wondered what had happened at Barton Park to cause him to call on them in this way.

It was after several minutes, and only when Mrs Dashwood returned and the maid bearing the tea tray had set it down and left the room, closing the door behind her, that he seemed sufficiently comfortable to explain his visit. He had come to ask a favour, he said, clearly speaking with great reluctance. His wife, Mrs Palmer, was so bereft at the sudden death of her sister, she had been unable to rise from her bed, much less come downstairs and attend to the normal matters of the household, and as for his mother-in-law, Mrs Jennings, she was in no fit state to be of any assistance to Sir John. He wondered if Mrs Dashwood could be prevailed upon, adding rather lamely, "I am very reluctant to ask you, ma'am, since it must surely appear unreasonable to expect that you—"

But before he could conclude his sentence, Mrs Dashwood had risen and offered to go with him directly to Barton Park.

"Mr Palmer, pray do not say another word; of course I am willing to help. Hasn't Sir John been kindness itself to me and my daughters when we needed help, and have we not enjoyed the hospitality of Sir John and Lady Middleton on occasions too numerous to mention? Why would I not be ready to offer help at such a time as this? Elinor and Edward are here and they can attend to matters at the cottage. I can be ready in an hour." Mr Palmer's expression was instantly transformed from one of grim austerity to pleasant relief as he thanked both mother and daughter for their generosity, twice over, before declaring that he would send the carriage to transport Mrs Dashwood and her things to Barton Park—within the hour.

He finished his tea and left soon afterward, and Mrs Dashwood rushed upstairs to pack her things, leaving Elinor and Edward shaking their heads at the strange turn of events. It had been an astonishing day.

But more was to follow. On the morrow, Elinor and Edward were preparing to walk over to Barton Park to call on Sir John, when an open pony cart arrived at the cottage bringing Margaret Dashwood. She explained that on receiving the news, she had travelled post to Exeter and taken the hack to Barton Cottage. "It was not very comfortable, but it was the only thing available," she explained, pointing to the effects of the ride upon her clothes and hair.

While there was no real surprise in her arrival, for she had been expected, she had barely been seated twenty minutes and taken a cup of tea when she rose and declared that she wished to accompany her sister and brother-in-law to call on Sir John Middleton, because she could not stay for the funeral and would presently be returning to Oxford.

Elinor was outraged. "What? Having come all this way, why can you not attend the funeral? Think what it will seem like to Sir John, Margaret; he is Mama's cousin and was more than kind to us when Papa died and we needed help."

Margaret shook her head. "I know all that, Elinor, and I am not ungrateful, but I cannot attend the funeral—it is not a question of time, it's just that I have no wish to meet all Sir John's fine friends who will no doubt travel down from London for the occasion," she said.

"And why ever not? Why should their presence at the funeral trouble you?" Elinor demanded to know, but Margaret would only say that there may be some among them whom she did not care to meet.

"I cannot say more now; perhaps when things are more settled, I may be able to explain, but please believe me, Elinor, it is in all our interests that I wish not to be seen at the funeral. I will call on Sir John and Mrs Jennings today and spend as much time with them as you think fit, but I must leave on Friday. I have arranged to travel on the overnight coach."

Elinor recalled that her young sister had always been very determined, and it would seem that she was even more so now. But the fact that Margaret would give no reasonable explanation for her actions disturbed and confused her.

When Margaret had gone upstairs to change out of her travelling clothes, Elinor confided in Edward. "What do you suppose lies behind this, Edward? Do you think Margaret has some kind of understanding with one of the gentlemen she expects to be at the funeral and does not wish it to be generally known? Unless that is the case, I can find no explanation for her conduct; Margaret is not usually unkind or insensitive."

"Indeed, she is not, and I would not say she is being so on this occasion, my dear; she has travelled a great distance to be here and intends to spend time with the bereaved family, which is a kindness in itself," Edward replied, being as usual cautious in making judgments. "As to your other proposition, I cannot be sure. I agree that it seems your sister has a very strong desire to avoid meeting a particular person or persons likely to attend Lady Middleton's funeral, but whether there is a matter of any understanding, I have seen no evidence of it."

"Then why can she not tell me who it is? If it is someone she does not wish to meet, we may be able to arrange that she doesn't meet him—or her, as the case may be. Why all this secrecy?" she complained.

Edward was hard put to find an answer that would satisfy his wife, but being very fond of Margaret himself, he did try. "Perhaps, my dear, it is not something she wishes to speak of at this moment. She may not wish to reveal the identity of the person; I recall that she did say she may be able to talk about it when it was settled."

Elinor grasped at the notion. "You may well be right, Edward, it is likely there is someone Margaret is in love with, but does not wish everyone—particularly people like Sir John Middleton and Mrs Jennings—to discover the association. You know how Mrs Jennings scents out a romantic involvement and then talks endlessly about it to anyone who will listen. I can well believe Margaret would hate that." When Edward merely nodded, she continued, "Of course, that must be it. Poor Margaret, she saw at firsthand the teasing that Marianne and I endured—no doubt she hopes to avoid it until it is quite settled and then she will reveal everything and surprise us all."

Presently, Edward and the two ladies walked over to Barton Park, where they were somewhat surprised to find Mrs Dashwood ably managing the household, a feat she had often been unable to cope with at Norland, surrendering it gladly to her eldest daughter.

Meanwhile, Sir John Middleton, with the support of Colonel Brandon and plenty of good wine, was bravely meeting and greeting the many neighbours, friends, and confreres who were arriving every hour to condole with him. In spite of being kept very busy with these duties, Sir John did find time to thank Margaret Dashwood, expressing his great pleasure at seeing her. "I appreciate very much your thoughtfulness in coming, my dear, and I am sorry that your sister Marianne is unable to join us. Brandon tells me she is unwell—she always was a delicate flower, I suppose," he said with a sigh, adding more brightly, "Miss Margaret, it was two Christmases ago that we all met in London, and since then you have grown exceedingly pretty and elegant, my dear. I am sure your mama is prodigiously proud of you." Margaret, who had been a little wary of meeting him, blushed at the compliments but was glad she had come.

Toward evening, when the house began to fill with more visitors, some from London and others from Bath, Margaret slipped away upstairs to spend some time with Mrs Jennings, who sat in her room, attended by her daughter, Charlotte. Finding the usually cheerful woman in a state of severe dejection, Margaret sat with her and tried to draw her into conversation, but to no avail. The usually loquacious and jolly Mrs Jennings appeared to have been stricken dumb with shock.

Later, Margaret went to talk to her mother and was amazed to find her bustling about with household activities, consulting the housekeeper and cook on the meals to be prepared for their visitors, organising arrangements for guests who were staying at the manor house, and ensuring that the maids and footmen were going to be correctly attired and knew their duties on the day of the funeral. To see her mother carrying out all these tasks, with hardly any sign of the muddle and confusion that had beset her at Norland, was as amusing as it was surprising to her daughter.

This did mean that, apart from an affectionate embrace and some quiet, tearful words, mother and daughter had little time together. Mrs Dashwood was saddened to learn that Margaret would not be staying to attend the funeral of Lady Middleton, but accepted her explanation that she needed to return to Oxford, assuming it had something to do with her continuing work at the seminary.

❧

Returning later that evening to Barton Cottage, they dined and Edward retired to read by the fire, while Elinor followed her sister upstairs to the spare room, where Margaret was preparing for bed. Seated in front of the mirror, she brushed and braided her hair, which was a pretty honey-gold colour that glowed in the firelight.

Elinor, seeing her thus, was struck by the singular loveliness of her young sister. Following the marriages of her two older sisters, Margaret had grown up very quickly; she was now a very independent young lady, and as she recalled the bright, precocious little girl at Norland some years ago, Elinor struggled to contain her feelings.

She went to her and, standing behind her, looked into the mirror; their eyes met and they smiled. It felt as though they had moved back in time and were as they had been, arriving at Barton Cottage following the death of their father, having left their idyllic childhood behind at Norland. Elinor remembered the many times when she had brushed and braided her lovely hair when Margaret, finding it difficult to cope alone with the consequences of the death of their father, would seek out her elder sister and tearfully confide in her. Her childish fears had been simple but nonetheless important to her, and Elinor had always tried to understand and explain them away.

This time, Elinor was concerned that her efforts to help had been unsuccessful, because Margaret was unwilling to confide in her. Even as they looked at each other in the mirror, Elinor knew that Margaret was not going to explain why she had decided not to attend Lady Middleton's funeral.

She tried, asking gently, "Will you not tell me, dearest Margaret, what is troubling you? I can see there is something—I know it, I can read it in your eyes." Then, persisting with a nagging doubt that had assailed her mind, she asked, "Is there someone who will be at the funeral that you do not wish to meet?"

Margaret looked surprised at the question, then smiled and said, "Dear Elinor, believe me, it is nothing of any consequence, nothing you need worry about, I promise. If it were, I should tell you and ask your advice, as I have always done."

"And you do not need my advice now? Is there nothing I can do to help?" Elinor's eyes searched her young sister's face, but Margaret shook her head and said, "No, but I do love you for asking."

So saying, she stood up and embraced Elinor, and they stood together for a long moment before breaking away to say good night.

Turning at the door to look at her, Elinor knew there was something troubling her sister; she longed to know and to help her, but had to be content that it was not the right time.

END OF PROLOGUE

EXPECTATIONS OF HAPPINESS

Part One

Chapter One

THE FUNERAL OF LADY Middleton and all the attendant formalities being completed, Elinor and Edward Ferrars prepared to return to the parsonage at Delaford.

Staying one last night at Barton Cottage, they had hoped to have Mrs Dashwood with them. Elinor had decided that it would be a good opportunity to consult her mother about her plans for the future. Would she wish to continue at Barton Cottage, now that Lady Middleton was no more and Mrs Jennings was most likely to move to live with her daughter, Mrs Palmer, at Cleveland? Mrs Dashwood was not on intimate terms with any of the other neighbouring families and might find the solitude depressing, Elinor believed.

Talking it over with Edward the previous night, she had been convinced that it was unlikely her mother would choose to stay. "I should be more at ease in my mind if I knew what Mama preferred, rather than propose a solution," she had said, and her husband had suggested that it was possible her mother may be amenable to a proposition. "Perhaps your mother would consider a move to Delaford, seeing it is in the next county, where either or both of her two elder daughters could offer her a comfortable home?" he had said, adding, "Undoubtedly, Marianne would have the advantage over us, with a far more spacious establishment at the manor house; but were she to wish for a different environment or quieter society, then she would always be welcome at the parsonage."

Elinor agreed and thanked her husband, pointing out that she could see no problem of space or comfort at the parsonage, which had been recently extended and refurbished for their use; although she wondered whether her mother would find some difficulty with the presence of her two young grand-sons. "I wonder how she will cope with our boys; Harry and John *are* lively, though they are not boisterous or troublesome children. Do you think she may have a problem getting accustomed to them?" she asked.

Edward was quick to reassure her. "I doubt it, my dear. Your mother is a kind, warmhearted woman; she loves both her grandchildren. I cannot believe she will find them a hindrance to a comfortable life with us. But, as I said, should she prefer it, she may decide to divide her time between the manor house and the parsonage. They are at no great distance from each other and she may, if she chooses, move quite conveniently between them."

Elinor smiled, but her husband could sense her anxiety and did his best to calm her fears. "You need have no qualms about asking her, my love; in the end, your mother will make up her mind and we will accommodate her wishes. There has never been any friction between us; you must not suppose that there will be any on this matter."

Elinor, having discussed the subject with her husband, was ready to make the offer to her mother and wanted only some few hours of her time to do so. But they were to discover that, in the meantime, Mrs Dashwood had agreed to a request from her cousin, Sir John Middleton, to stay on at Barton Park for a while longer. Colonel Brandon, arriving at the cottage to wish them a safe journey and send a message to Marianne, brought the surprising news.

"Sir John is very grateful to Mrs Dashwood for her kindness in agreeing to remain awhile at Barton Park," he said, explaining the situation. "I understand Mr and Mrs Palmer must return to Cleveland House today and Mrs Jennings is as yet unfit to travel, nor are the Palmers able to accommodate her needs at this time—they are expecting some of Mr Palmer's relatives to stay. This has placed Sir John in an exceedingly difficult situation. He was at a complete loss as to how to cope with matters concerning the running of his household and the care of his mother-in-law, who would be entirely alone," Colonel Brandon reported. "Mrs Dashwood's agreement to remain at Barton Park has consider-ably alleviated his problem."

He spoke with a degree of gravitas that ensured that Elinor would not laugh, but it left both Edward and Elinor at a loss for words. Never had it been supposed among members of their family that Mrs Dashwood would emerge as a saviour in the cause of domestic management. Her rather muddled ways of running her own household at Norland, her inability to maintain accurate accounts, her total lack of understanding of the need for economy—extending even to complete ignorance of the prices of various commonplace household goods—made the thought of her running the establishment at Barton Park seem a risible proposition.

Yet, it appeared that Colonel Brandon, generally a sensible and reasonable man, was taking it quite seriously and seemed to have no difficulty with the idea. "Do you mean, Colonel Brandon, that Mama has agreed to remain at Barton Park indefinitely, taking charge of the household arrangements for Sir John?" Elinor asked, and it was clear to her husband from the tone of her voice that she found the notion unconvincing.

Colonel Brandon took a while to absorb the point of her question and when he responded said quietly, "I am not privy to Mrs Dashwood's understanding of the situation, Elinor; I have not spoken with her on the subject. I know only what Sir John has told me. It seems they had a discussion after dinner last night, when he made his request for her help, and again this morning, before the Palmers departed, and have reached a mutually satisfactory agreement. Mrs Dashwood wishes me to assure you she is content to remain and help her cousin and Mrs Jennings through this difficult time and has asked that I convey her love to you and the children. I also have this note from her for you," he said, handing over Mrs Dashwood's letter.

There were many other questions to which Elinor wanted answers, but she knew the colonel was unlikely to have them. Clearly his sympathies were with his longtime friend Sir John, and he was not willing to query the basis of an arrangement that could offer some relief to him in the awkward situation in which he found himself. He assured them also that they could use his carriage to return to Delaford, while he would follow on horseback not long afterward.

Handing over a sealed envelope addressed to his wife, which he begged Elinor to convey to her sister, he left them to return to Barton Park.

The conversation that followed between Edward and Elinor revealed as much of their own deep understanding of each other as it did of their tolerance of the frequently odd and occasionally bizarre behaviour of both her mother and Sir John Middleton.

Mrs Dashwood's letter was brief.

Dearest Elinor, she wrote:

> *As I am sure Colonel Brandon will explain, Sir John has asked if I could stay on at Barton Park for a while, and in view of the dire situation in which they are placed, with Mrs Jennings being so poorly, I feel it is the least I can do to help.*
>
> *I know you were hoping that we could have a talk about future plans, but I fear that will have to wait. I shall write as soon as I can find some time—which may not be soon, for there seems to be a great deal to be done here. Apart from Mrs Williams, the housekeeper, there is no one who seems to understand what needs be done, and even she waits upon my instructions at every turn.*

It was clear to Edward that his wife was uneasy with her mother's decision to remain at Barton Park; he tried to forestall her expressions of concern with some comforting speculation.

"Perhaps, my dear, your mother means only to demonstrate her appreciation for the generosity of Sir John Middleton, by assisting him. It is a particularly difficult time for Sir John, especially with Mrs Jennings being unwell, and no doubt your mama wishes to help."

Elinor turned and he could see tears in her eyes. "Edward, dearest, of course Mama is grateful and wants to help Sir John, but I have considerable reservations about this decision. Mama, as you well know, is not some well-organised manager, experienced in running a large household; she has little knowledge of the requirements of Barton Park and is unfamiliar with the staff. She has probably agreed on impulse with only the best intentions, but, Edward, if this were to lead to friction and muddle, I fear she will have done more harm than good."

Edward felt this was a somewhat harsh judgement and said so, but his wife would not be comforted and they talked late into the night, trying to comprehend the reasons for Mrs Dashwood's action and wondering how things might turn out.

"How do you suppose Marianne will feel about it?" he asked.

"Marianne will probably accept it without argument; she, like Mama, is given to sudden impulses; they both love to make grand gestures without first working out the consequences. But I doubt if Margaret will," Elinor predicted, before putting out the candle and pulling up the eider down. She was both weary and worried. "Oh Edward, this is such a mess. I had hoped that Mama would be here and we could reach some agreement as to her future, and now here we are, with so many uncertainties, leaving with no resolution at all. I cannot help feeling quite apprehensive about this situation."

"Come now, dearest, there's no need to be so dispirited," said Edward, trying to provide some consolation. "At the very least, we can be assured that your mama is happy with the decision she has made, and we know it is a temporary arrangement to assist her cousin over a difficult patch. I am quite certain that within the month, we will see her back home and possibly even settled at Delaford."

"Do you really believe that?" she asked, solemnly regarding his face. "I am not as certain as you are, but I know you mean to comfort me and I shall pray you are right," she said and snuggled down beside him, enjoying the reassuring warmth of his presence.

For Elinor, one thing had changed materially with her marriage: While she could feel some anxiety about the conduct of her mother or sisters, she no longer spent lonely, sleepless nights pondering the whys and wherefores of every difficult situation they faced. The intimacy they shared, together with Edward's willingness to listen, analyse, and occasionally argue away her fears, had rendered her life considerably more tranquil than before, while the warmth of his affection had brought genuine contentment.

What had begun as a dutiful visit to attend the funeral of Lady Middleton had, without warning, given rise to an uncomfortable situation that could become a continuing source of aggravation. Her husband, aware there was little he could do to change the circumstances, put a comforting arm around her and was pleased to be rewarded with an affectionate if somewhat sleepy response.

Chapter Two

S INCE COMING TO LIVE at the parsonage in the parish of Delaford, the living gifted to Edward by Colonel Brandon, Elinor had become acquainted with a number of families, some of whom, by dint of their long residence in the district, felt able to dispense information and advice on just about anyone and anything under the sun.

While, as the wife of the Reverend Edward Ferrars, Elinor wished to maintain good relations with all of his parishioners, there were those among them in whose company she was more—and others with whom she was distinctly less—comfortable.

Among the former group was Dr Bradley King—doctor not of medicine but of philosophy—lately retired from one of the Oxford Colleges, his wife, and daughter. Dr King had been a tutor to Edward Ferrars at Oxford, and when the pair met again by chance in Dorchester, both men had been delighted to discover that they were living within a few miles of each other. Upon being invited to meet Dr King's family, Edward and Elinor had been easily drawn into their very friendly circle, in which, after the obligatory praise of their historic cottage situated on a site overlooking the confluence of two rivers, their discourse was all of subjects that interested and enthused them both.

Like Edward Ferrars, Dr King was a man of learning and culture, with a special fascination for medieval archaeology, while Mrs King, who insisted that

Elinor must call her Helen, found in her new acquaintance a rare companion who could share her love of reading and music, and enjoy thoughtful conversations during long walks in the woods. Not surprisingly, the two couples had, over the next few years, become firm friends.

The Kings' daughter, Dorothea, was a pretty, amiable young woman with a penchant for everything French—despite her passionate dislike of the former emperor, Napoleon. Her mother had confided to Elinor that this abhorrence of Bonaparte was chiefly based upon the circumstance that a young guardsman she had admired had gone to fight in France and been so grievously wounded in the war against Bonaparte that he had returned embittered and unable to propose marriage to the young lady he had courted through the previous summer.

Helen King and Elinor Ferrars, both coming into the county recently, and having few other intimate friends, soon formed a natural bond; although Mrs King was almost ten years older than Elinor, neither felt the difference in their ages impeded the development of a warm friendship between them.

On returning to Delaford, Elinor went first to the manor house, where she found Marianne still keeping mainly to her apartments upstairs, where she would read and draw and entertain herself by attempting to copy the works of artists she admired, in a studio specially fitted out for her at her husband's behest. Elinor handed over Colonel Brandon's letter, which Marianne put aside unopened and continued with her drawing. She was somewhat less communicative than usual, asking only a few perfunctory questions about Lady Middleton's sudden demise and showing no interest at all in her funeral. "I suppose the Palmers were there; had I been well enough, I may have been better able to put up with Charlotte Palmer, but believe me, Elinor, I was in no state to endure her witless chatter."

Surprised at the sharpness of her sister's remark, Elinor believed she was still feeling unwell, and chose not to mention her concerns about their mother's decision to remain at Barton Park. Marianne herself made no comment on the matter and, urging her sister to take good care of herself, Elinor left to visit her friend Mrs King.

She meant to acquaint her with some of the extraordinary things that had occurred at Barton Park and her own disquiet on the matter. She was sure Helen King, who was of a practical disposition, would have a sensible explanation that would help allay her anxiety.

But, while Mrs King did indeed welcome her friend warmly, she appeared rather distressed herself and, after they'd taken tea, suggested a walk out on the path that ran along the edge of the bluff upon which their cottage was situated. It afforded not only a most picturesque view of the valley and river below, but guaranteed the privacy that both women clearly desired.

Mrs King spoke first, explaining that she had been worried all week about her daughter. Dorothea had met her young guardsman again at a dinner party in the home of mutual friends. The young man, now sadly retired from his regiment and unable, on account of his injuries, to obtain other work, had treated her rather coldly, and Dorothea had been very distressed, Mrs King confided. "She still loves him, Elinor, and though Dr King and I have tried tactfully and gently to suggest that all may not be lost—they are both quite young and the young man may yet overcome his disability—Dorothea is not hopeful. We worry that she, while unlikely to go into a melancholy decline—it is not in her nature—has nonetheless decided that love and marriage are out of her reach, and, Elinor, she is only twenty-three!" she cried.

Understanding her friend's concern, Elinor confessed that she had once held similar fears for her young sister Marianne, now Mrs Brandon, when she was but seventeen. But she was happy to report that things had taken a turn for the better, when Marianne had decided, some months after a particularly unhappy experience, to accept Colonel Brandon.

"As you can see, they are now quite happily settled at Delaford," she added. Elinor had not mentioned the man concerned by name at all, referring instead to a disappointment in love sustained at an impressionable age, from which Marianne, being passionate and sincere as well as very young at the time, had suffered very badly. Which was why Elinor was astonished to hear Mrs King say in a confidential sort of voice that yes, she *had* heard about young Mrs Brandon's unhappy love affair with a certain Mr Willoughby of Somersetshire.

Turning immediately to face her companion, Elinor, startled and disconcerted, asked how she had come by that information, to be told that it was generally known among some of the ladies in the district. Her own informant had been a Miss Henrietta Clift, who claimed to know both Mr Willoughby and his late aunt, Mrs Smith, the former owner of Allenham, a fine estate in the county of Devon. Miss Clift, said Mrs King, had claimed therefore to be well acquainted with the facts of the case.

Unwilling to allow the subject of her sister's past to be trawled further, Elinor stated with great conviction that all of their friends and family had been delighted when Marianne had accepted Colonel Brandon, who was universally liked and respected, and Mrs King concurred, adding that she was sure Mrs Brandon must have completely recovered from her youthful infatuation.

Their conversation continued thereafter along different, less contentious lines, but it left Elinor disturbed and troubled. She had no knowledge at all of this Miss Henrietta Clift and wondered by what means she had acquired the information she seemed to have passed on to others in the district. Furthermore, she knew not if Miss Clift was well regarded by Helen King and was therefore constrained in her ability to question or contradict her motives and assertions. Yet, she felt keenly the need to do so, for it would not do to have her sister's reputation gossiped about in and around Delaford.

Determined, however, not to reveal her disquiet to her friend, lest it signify a level of concern it did not warrant, Elinor remained silent on the matter until she returned to the parsonage, where with their two sons out walking in the park with their governess, she had more time to worry before her husband arrived home.

Unaccustomed to finding his wife in a state of agitation—for Elinor, of all the women he knew, was by far the least likely to give way to such moods—Edward Ferrars was concerned, more so because he was privy to some information with which he had not wished to trouble her, fearing that she may be unduly upset. He wondered whether the same news may have reached her by some other route and sought to discover the cause of her concern. When they had dined and the maid had cleared the table, he asked, "Elinor, dearest, has there been any news from Barton Park? Have you heard from your mother?"

Elinor looked up and indicated that she would prefer to continue this conversation in the parlour, into which they withdrew with their tea tray. Edward set about drawing the fire into a good blaze, while his wife poured out tea, and as soon as they were seated, she said, "I have had no further news from my mother, but Helen King said something that has disturbed me, Edward. I cannot explain it and I have been worrying about it ever since," and when he looked at her, clearly puzzled, she continued quickly, "She says that many of the women in the district are already aware of the affair of Willoughby and Marianne. How can this be? Indeed, a Miss Henrietta Clift, who I suspect is the main source of the tale, has claimed that she has had the information from Willoughby himself and his late aunt, Mrs Smith of Allenham, whom she knew intimately. Edward, should this be gossiped about around the district, should it reach either Colonel Brandon or Marianne, can you imagine the damage it will do?"

The arrival of their two sons with their dog, all determined to attract maximum attention, meant that Edward had not the opportunity to answer her query, for which he was somewhat grateful, for it would give him sufficient time to contemplate and decide if he should acquaint his wife with the information he had heard that afternoon. He loved her dearly and was loathe to add to her troubles, but at the same time it seemed to him, in the light of what she had just said, that it was imperative Elinor should know all the facts.

After young Harry and John had been bathed and sent to bed, Elinor returned to the subject, and Edward decided he had to speak. She was wondering aloud who Henrietta Clift might be and how she had come by the information, when Edward said quietly, "I believe they are relatives of his—Mr Willoughby's—and have recently moved to live here."

Elinor, who was braiding her hair in front of her mirror, swung round. "What? How do you know this?" she asked in a voice that betrayed her anxiety, and her husband came to her side and said in a quiet, matter-of-fact tone, "I am sorry, my love. I have been meaning to tell you, but I did not wish to add to your present worries. The family has been living in Somerset for some time, but have recently moved to Wareham—not within my parish, but near enough. I was introduced to Mr and Mrs Clift yesterday and heard them mention in conversation that their cousin, a Mr Willoughby, had a place in Somersetshire and was a particular friend of their elder daughter. I knew then it had to be the same man, but I was reluctant to ask too many questions."

Elinor's countenance was pale as she gazed at him. "Did they say if he was in the area—I mean, did they mention if he came into Somerset often?" she asked, adding, "I had understood that he lives mainly in London." Edward nodded and took her hands in his before saying, "Please do not upset yourself, my love, it may not mean anything at all, but I believe he is in Somerset already and intends to spend the rest of the season in the county. The Clifts were looking forward to his visiting them soon."

Elinor covered her face with her hands, and nothing he said would comfort her. Ever since he had become acquainted with the Dashwoods—initially when his sister, Fanny, had married John Dashwood, and later when he had met the family again at Norland, their family home in Sussex—Edward had become aware of Elinor's strong sense of responsibility toward her younger sister, Marianne, and to a lesser degree, her mother. The intensity of her concern had at first surprised him, but he had soon realised that it was a consequence of the value she placed on sound judgment and understanding, qualities in which they were somewhat lacking, and she possessed in full measure. This had been amply demonstrated during the period of Marianne's amorous liaison with Mr Willoughby and its inevitable unhappy consequences. While Mrs Dashwood had indulged and defended both Marianne and Willoughby, Elinor alone had counselled caution. As he had come to admire and love her dearly, Edward had noted many examples of Elinor's selfless devotion to her family and in particular Marianne, of whom she seemed especially protective.

Once again, he was witnessing her excessive unease and on this occasion decided to question whether it was warranted. When she was a little calmer, he asked gently, "While I do understand your general concern, my love, I wonder whether you are not being unduly pessimistic about Mr Willoughby. Do you not think your sister, after almost seven years of marriage, is far less likely to be affected by recollections of her youthful association with him? After all, everyone knows she is now happily married to Colonel Brandon…"

He was not ready for Elinor's interruption. "Is she? Do you know that for certain, Edward?" she asked. Shocked, Edward was silent for a moment before he found his voice and said, "Is she not? Have you any evidence that their marriage is not happy? For I have seen none."

This time, Elinor struggled to respond, unable or perhaps unwilling to put into words the niggling doubts that had troubled her over the last year as she watched her sister grow restless and bored with her role as Lady of the Manor at Delaford.

As her husband listened, amazed by the extent of her distress, she detailed her concerns. Some she had held without speaking of them to anyone, from the very first months of Colonel Brandon's courtship of Marianne and their mother's enthusiastic encouragement of it.

"Even as I admired and valued the qualities that everyone applauded in Colonel Brandon, I could not help wondering whether these would suffice to hold Marianne's interest and loyalty; knowing her as I do, aware of her addiction to a high level of romantic love and excessive emotion, I doubted if she would be satisfied with the rather gentlemanly courtliness and practicality of Colonel Brandon, whom she had already dismissed as being far too old to understand, much less match, her kind of sensibility," she said. "She was grateful to him, of course, and appreciated his kindness, but that was when she was still recovering from the misery that had overwhelmed her after Willoughby's betrayal. It was easy, in that mood, for Marianne to turn to someone like the colonel, who represented the very opposite of Willoughby. But even as I saw the affection between them grow, I feared that it might not be strong enough for Marianne. It seemed more like the agreeable warmth between good friends rather than the ardour of lovers," Elinor explained.

"And yet you said nothing?" Edward could scarcely credit it.

She nodded. "Because nothing I said would have made a jot of difference to my mother, who saw Colonel Brandon as the only man who could save Marianne from wasting away. He had become her new hero; having had her favourite dethroned, she had placed Colonel Brandon on a pedestal as some kind of noble knight, who had remained in the background, loving Marianne throughout her affair with Willoughby, knowing all the time that he was not a man to be trusted, stepping in to rescue and preserve her at the end. Can you imagine how she would have welcomed any dissenting opinion from me? As for saying anything to Marianne, I did not dare. I, who had defended Colonel Brandon against criticism and ridicule from Marianne and Willoughby often enough, what would she say if I decided to caution her against accepting him too hastily? She could claim that she had come around to seeing in him the very things I had always valued. There was nothing I could do, save pray that it would work out well in the end," she said.

"And you are not confident that it has?" her husband asked, and her answer astonished him.

"Sadly I am not; indeed I would go further—I fear that while in the most obvious sense, they may appear happily married, there are some things that have caused me much anxiety. They have no children, and I know that causes Marianne and my mother much pain; I can see it in my sister's eyes when our boys are around. She would have loved to have had children on whom to lavish the kind of warmth and affection she has so much of. What must make matters even worse is the fact that Colonel Brandon pays a great deal of attention to Eliza Williams's daughter, who is really Willoughby's illegitimate child. It is a further grievance that Marianne must carry. Can you not imagine how she must feel?"

Edward agreed that it was indeed a most unhappy situation, but pointed out quite reasonably that all these circumstances were known to her sister and their mother before Marianne accepted Colonel Brandon—with Mrs Dashwood's blessing. Elinor conceded that this was true, but contended that neither her mother nor Marianne had paid much attention to it at the time.

"The child had just been born, and Miss Williams, who Mrs Jennings had assured everybody was Colonel Brandon's natural daughter, was just a name. No one had met her—we knew nothing of her, nor did they expect to meet her in the future," she explained.

"Apart from that obvious and continuing problem, are there other reasons that cause you to doubt your sister's contentment?" Edward asked, trying not to pry, yet wanting desperately to alleviate his wife's anguish. To his astonishment, she admitted that indeed there were.

"I do believe that Marianne is bored; she has little to do at the manor house, which is exceedingly well staffed and efficiently run; she does not become deeply involved in parish or council matters, preferring to leave those to the colonel, and in addition, he has, during the last two years, had to make several visits to his estates in Ireland, leaving her mostly alone. Marianne doesn't make friends easily; she is wary of people whom she doesn't know well, and since Margaret went away to study at the seminary in Oxford, she has not even the consolation of her company. Oh, Edward, forgive me, I should not burden you with what may seem like my silly fears, but I cannot help worrying, especially now that you say that Willoughby is back in Somerset and visiting relatives but a few miles from Delaford."

He would not let her continue. "Elinor, dearest, of course these are not silly fears, I know you well enough to believe that they are legitimate concerns that trouble you and of course you must tell me about them; but you cannot be suggesting that there is any danger for Marianne from Willoughby? Was he not thoroughly exposed as a dissembler? Did not your sister and all her family and friends come to understand what a blackguard he was?"

Elinor nodded. "Oh yes, they did, and heaped a great deal of opprobrium upon him at first; but, as the months and years have passed, I have noticed that he has undergone a degree of gradual rehabilitation—certainly in my mother's eyes and perhaps in Marianne's as well, although she has not spoken of it to me, except just once or twice while she was still recovering from her illness. But I believe Marianne and my mother have come to blame Willoughby's domineering aunt Mrs Smith, who, by his account, was solely responsible for his betrayal of Marianne. He blamed his new, wealthy fiancée, Miss Grey, for his vile treatment of my sister when they met in town. I believe that Mama and Marianne wish to ignore that he knew all the time, while he was courting Marianne in Devonshire, that Mrs Smith would never countenance a match between them. As for his appalling behaviour towards Eliza Williams, it is as though they wish to turn a blind eye to it."

Edward was shocked, not only because his own values were affronted by what he had heard, but because until today, Elinor had not spoken of her fears to him. He felt deeply for her, because clearly she had concealed her fears out of loyalty to her family.

However, the news he had brought of the arrival of Willoughby in the neighbouring county of Somerset, and his imminent visit to relatives near Delaford in Dorset, had brought all her anxieties to the surface.

Chapter Three

MARGARET DASHWOOD HAD LIVED most of her young life in the shadow of her two elder sisters, Elinor and Marianne.

A bright, articulate little girl with a degree of intellectual curiosity almost approaching precociousness, she had long been interested in study and travel. While the modest pecuniary circumstances of their family had seriously circumscribed her ability to follow her dreams of journeying to exotic places, she had succeeded in improving her mind and her knowledge by extensive reading over many years. She had also the example of her sisters, Elinor in particular, for whom learning had a very special value.

Following the marriages of her sisters, Margaret, dissatisfied with the type of education she could achieve at home, had begged to be allowed to attend what she called "a proper school with real teachers," but in vain, until Elinor's husband, Edward Ferrars, became involved. Through the good offices of a friend at Oxford, he had obtained for Margaret a place as a scholar in a ladies' seminary situated just outside the university town. Edward had always appreciated young Margaret's intelligence, and she would be forever grateful to her brother-in-law for the opportunity that opened for her the doors to an entirely new life.

Margaret applied herself so assiduously to her studies and acquitted herself so well at the seminary that she soon caught the attention of the ladies who ran the establishment. They saw in her a potential teacher and sent her on a scholarship to a school in France to improve her knowledge of French language and literature. During her sojourn there, not only did Margaret improve her skill in the French language but she added to her list of friends a young woman named Claire Jones, some five years older than herself, of French and Welsh descent. Being a fluent French speaker, and a woman of some sophistication, Miss Jones was not only of considerable assistance to Margaret in learning the language and culture of France, but the two also became good companions as they studied and travelled together. Despite the difference in their backgrounds and upbringing—Miss Jones was considerably more worldly-wise than her young friend—they found they had many interests in common, and on returning to England, they shared accommodation in a small country cottage they leased, within walking distance from the seminary, where Margaret began her employment as a teacher, while Miss Jones obtained work reading proofs for an academic publisher in Oxford. It was a situation that suited both young women well, providing each with as much congenial company or solitude as they desired.

It was to the cottage and her friend Claire Jones that Margaret returned following her visit to Barton Park. Still feeling disconsolate that she had upset her sister Elinor by not attending Lady Middleton's funeral, nor providing her with a logical explanation for not doing so, Margaret found a sympathetic listener in Miss Jones, who had toasted muffins and a large pot of tea ready before the fire, when Margaret, having changed out of her travelling clothes, came downstairs.

"I can see that you are not happy, Margaret," Claire began. "It cannot have been as bad as that. I had not thought that Lady Middleton was such a favourite of yours."

The lightness of her tone implied that she did not expect to be taken seriously, which was probably why Margaret was at first reluctant to reveal the reason for her discomposure. She tried at first to respond lightly, denying that she would miss Lady Middleton at all, although she had the grace to add, "No doubt her children will miss her; she was devoted to them and inclined to spoil them. As for Sir John, he certainly seemed very shocked by her sudden demise, but I doubt that his grief will last beyond the next shooting season. I gathered that his stewards were already planning for their next shoot."

Claire smiled and nodded. "And yet I see you looking particularly down-cast; was the funeral a dreary one? Country parsons have a reputation for droning on…"

Margaret interrupted her to say briefly, "I did not attend the funeral, Claire; I never intended to. I went to Barton Park to please my mother and sister and to demonstrate my gratitude for the hospitality Sir John had extended to us when Papa died and Fanny took over Norland Park, leaving us practically homeless. But I did not wish to attend the funeral."

"Why ever not?" asked Claire, puzzled at this admission; her friend had said not a word of this before departing for Dorsetshire.

Margaret accepted a cup of tea and a muffin and settled herself into a corner of the deep sofa, tucking her bare feet under her skirts, before saying quietly, "There was someone I did not wish to meet, who was certain to be there. I decided, well before I reached Barton Park, that I would not attend the funeral; it would be simpler than trying to avoid him amidst all the relatives and friends."

Her friend's curiosity knew no bounds. There was no way in which Margaret, having tossed in such a lure, could avoid further explanation. Claire insisted, and as she pressed and persuaded, the story had to be told.

As Margaret told it, she made light of the circumstances, trying not to add more gravity to the tale than it deserved, but Claire was not fooled. Determined to discover what had so troubled her friend that she, having travelled to Dorset, had merely called on the family at Barton Park and left the following day in order to avoid a meeting with someone, Claire would not be denied. And Margaret soon realised that she could not avoid providing an explanation for her unusual behaviour.

Which is how the story came to be told of a gentleman named Andrew Barton, a cousin of Sir John Middleton, whom she had met at the London residence of the Middletons two years ago. The second son of a titled family, with an income of over five thousand a year and houses in both London and Bath, he had been touted as an eminently eligible suitor for her, promoted as such by both Sir John and his indomitable mother-in-law, Mrs Jennings.

Claire was smiling as she listened. "But you did not agree?" she queried, and was unsurprised when Margaret replied, "I most certainly did not."

"Why? Was he plain? Were his manners revolting?" her friend joked.

"Neither was the case—he is reasonably good-looking, and his manners are impeccable, if you like that sort of thing, although I admit I find all that bowing and scraping irritating. But, Claire, I have absolutely no interest in marrying anyone like him—indeed I have no interest in marrying anyone at this time. I have far too much to do before I settle into dull domesticity—if I ever do. Doubtless he would expect any wife of his to set up house in one of his elegant residences and play the lady of leisure—hostessing coffee parties and soirees and things. Can you imagine me in that role?"

Claire laughed merrily. "I confess I cannot. Has Mr Andrew Barton addressed himself to you—I mean, has he proposed?"

"He has not, thank goodness; although I did fear on one occasion, when we were dancing together in London, that he was about to do so. Thereafter, when I have met him at Barton Park, I have made every effort to avoid giving him any encouragement. I do not intend to give him the opportunity to propose or do anything of the sort, because there would be a big to-do if he were to speak to my mother and get her blessing as well. I know that Sir John has suggested that he should speak to Mama—he thinks she likes him. I begged him last summer to desist, but neither he nor Mrs Jennings have any idea how I feel; they think I am being silly—passing up such a chance to be so advantageously married! Besides, I have another objection to him, which I think you should hear," she declared and, as her friend looked all agog for a new revelation, Margaret added, "Mr Barton is a most devoted follower of the Prince of Wales."

At that Claire burst into laughter and clapped her hands. "Oh, my dear friend, now *that* I cannot forgive. He may or may not be plain or handsome, stylish or simple, rich or poor—none of these things would rule him out in my eyes—but a devout follower of the Prince of Wales! I sympathise with you completely; nothing can be so totally objectionable in a prospective suitor as being a supporter of the Regent!"

Margaret put down her cup, snuggled into the cushions, and heaved a sigh of relief. "Thank you, Claire, I knew you would understand. I just could not explain to Elinor and Edward, or to my mother—they simply would not see it as you do, although I will admit that Edward is frequently critical of the Regent and his courtiers. But I cannot see that having any influence upon Mama and Sir John and Mrs Jennings, who will probably point out that Andrew Barton is nothing like the Regent and he is Sir John's cousin!"

Despite the levity in her tone, Margaret was being completely serious; she, like many other men and women of intelligence, had long formed an adverse opinion about the Prince of Wales. It was based mainly upon the accounts of extravagance and riotous behaviour at court since his appointment in the year 1811 as Regent of Britain to rule the kingdom in place of his deranged, though much loved father, George the Third.

The Prince Regent—though educated in the classics, well versed in the arts, and a keen sportsman—appeared not to have any notion of the living conditions of the majority of his subjects. Their trials and tribulations seemed not to concern him, and he was frequently astonished when they complained at the profligate waste of public money that went to accommodate the style and taste of the prince and his courtiers.

In addition, the Regent and his merry men were equally renowned for their cavalier disregard for decorum in their private lives; the prince made no secret that he detested his wife—the rather plain and unloved Princess Caroline of Brunswick—from whom he separated, having formed an attachment to a certain Mrs Fitzherbert. Their quite open liaison continued for many years, setting the worst possible example to others in court circles and causing a great scandal among the populace to which the prince seemed completely immune.

Claire Jones, who had spent the first part of the Regency in France, had only heard accounts of these happenings until her return to England, when she, having spent some time in London, was soon exposed to the very worst excesses of the Regency Court.

With the end of the Napoleonic wars, the Regent felt free to indulge in even greater levels of extravagance, with triumphal declarations and self-congratulatory celebrations, spending even more of the nation's wealth and squandering what was left of his own goodwill.

It had been a wonderfully fruitful period for satirists, but they needed to be careful, for it was still a time when one could be jailed for sedition. Claire and Margaret had met again in London, where the Dashwoods had been invited to spend Christmas with the Middletons, and the two friends had spent much of that season together before repairing to their haven of peace and common sense in Oxfordshire. They had shared a mutual disdain for the behaviour of the Regency Court, and despite the best efforts of the Middletons, who had several useful social contacts to whom they offered to introduce them, the young ladies had preferred to leave London and return to the country.

Mrs Jennings, in particular, had bemoaned the fact that young women these days had no notion of how best to advance their prospects of getting a good husband. "Two pretty girls, turning their backs on London and returning to the wilds of Oxfordshire! If they had stayed with me, I'd have had them both engaged before the end of the season," she had boasted. Claire was entirely in sympathy with Margaret's reservations about Mr Andrew Barton, as she explained, "I had no wish to give him any encouragement at all, which is why I had to leave before the funeral, and of course, I upset everyone—except Sir John, bless him!"

Claire was still not entirely convinced that such drastic action had been necessary. "Do you believe he would have approached you at the funeral? Would he not have thought it indelicate?" she asked.

"Not if Sir John had already suggested that he speak with Mama. I could not risk it; I decided to absent myself and thwart their plans. After all, if I wasn't there, he could hardly make the offer to my mother!"

"Hardly," Claire retorted, and both young women laughed as Margaret, feeling somewhat happier than she had done an hour or two ago, relaxed and proceeded to tell her friend of other, pleasanter plans she was making for their next vacation.

"I do believe it would be nice to travel to the south of France this autumn—do you not agree?" she suggested, and found her friend in complete agreement.

Having grown up mainly in France with her mother, Claire was accustomed to a far freer culture, with less intrusive social scrutiny than existed in rural English communities, of which she complained constantly.

"Oh yes indeed, I should enjoy that very much. My friend Mr Wilcox visits the south of France often and claims it is a paradise on earth. Not only is it beautiful in scenic terms, there is so much to see and experience, and one can do it with the greatest ease, since one is not harried by nosey, gossiping women at every turn, as we are here. The French really do mind their own business," she said and smiling, added "I think, my dear Margaret, the south of France in autumn will be the very thing after a long English summer."

Margaret was pleased; "I had hoped you would say that. I have read about these places and always longed to visit them. I am sure we will not be disappointed," she said and soon they were drawn into discussions of places to stay and sites to visit, which kept them agreeably occupied all evening.

Chapter Four

DELAFORD MANOR WAS BY any measure a valuable property, with several established tenancies, plenty of excellent pasture, and some of the finest woods in this part of the country. While these qualities were appreciated by those who knew and understood such matters, to the lady of the manor, Mrs Brandon, they were not immediately apparent.

For Marianne, Norland Park was the standard by which all estates were to be judged, and while admitting that Colonel Brandon's could be considered valuable when viewed in a commercial light, she found nothing here to compare with her memories of "dear Norland," where she had spent all of her early life. It was the place she would always associate with the varied experiences of childhood, of growing up and discovering the pleasures of painting and poetry, of romantic music and literature.

The trees at Norland Park were, as she remembered them, more majestic, the sweeping grounds more extensive, the prospect of distant hills and downs more exquisitely appealing in the morning mist, than anything the West Country could offer. Together, they had provided the appropriate background for the exercise of her romantic imagination, and indeed, their appeal had only increased with the passing years.

As for the house, while Colonel Brandon's manor house was an edifice of solid construction in russet brick, with generous accommodation and many comfortably furnished rooms, it had neither the architectural style nor the nostalgic charm of Norland. There she had learned from childhood to admire and love every prospect and discover the fascination of each well-appointed room. Norland possessed for Marianne, as it did for her mother, Mrs Dashwood, a grace that no other place could match. Certainly Delaford, for all its advantages, could never surpass it.

She said nothing of this to anyone, especially not to her devoted husband, but these perceptions rankled as she tried to settle into life as the mistress of Delaford Manor—a role for which she had had little preparation.

Marianne had enjoyed immensely the feeling of being cherished and adored by a man who loved her dearly. Colonel Brandon had been there, strong, reliable, and loving, as she had emerged from the nightmare of Willoughby's betrayal, emotionally ravaged and physically exhausted after a near-fatal bout of fever. He had offered her his devotion and a comfortable marriage—a safe haven, which she had entered with gratitude and affection, though without the hopes of rapture such as she had imagined with Willoughby.

And in the years following their wedding, her husband continued to be loving, kind, and devoted to her, and there was not one thing she could complain of in his treatment of her or in the comfort and style of life afforded her at Delaford. Over the years, nothing very much had changed, which probably explained why Marianne, her beauty now fully recovered, who tended to view her life as though she were a character in a novel, had begun to feel rather bored with her role as the mistress of Delaford Manor.

Wearied by the unvarying pace of her existence, she had been wondering how she would occupy her time as summer ended and Colonel Brandon travelled to Ireland to attend to his estates there.

He had persuaded her on one occasion—quite early in their life together—to accompany him, but the cold and damp had not suited her delicate constitution at all; she had become unwell, and they had had to return early to England as a consequence. Much medication and several weeks at Lyme Regis, taking the sea air, had been needed to restore both her health and her spirits.

Thereafter, Colonel Brandon had always gone alone, reluctantly leaving Marianne to occupy herself at Delaford. It was usually a very pleasant time of year, with the harvests being gathered in and village fairs and festivals being organised around the county for Harvest Home. Aware that his wife did not take a great interest in these public activities, he had provided her with everything she could need to pursue all of her hobbies and did not expect that boredom would pose a problem for her.

In previous years, Mrs Dashwood would arrive to spend a few weeks at Delaford and keep her daughter company, affording Marianne some respite from the tedium of life alone at the manor; but this year, following the death of Lady Middleton, Mrs Dashwood was otherwise engaged.

Visiting the parsonage, Colonel Brandon drew Elinor's attention to the date of his departure for Ireland and asked especially that she attend on her sister as often as her parish duties would allow, since Mrs Dashwood was not available to visit. Elinor assured him she would do so with pleasure. She retained, as well as her sisterly affection, a strong sense of family responsibility toward Marianne.

When Elinor had visited her sister after the funeral of Lady Middleton, she had noticed that she was not in good spirits and had tried to discover the reason for it, but Marianne had successfully avoided answering any questions, save in the most superficial way. She had confessed that she had grown tired of reading and had begun writing a diary. "I intend to record everything I do and feel each day, for at least a year, after which I shall read it over and decide if it is worthwhile to continue the exercise," she had declared, causing Elinor to smile and say, "Indeed? That should keep you busy," only to have her sister interrupt abruptly, "I wonder you should say that, Elinor, you must know how little I have to do each day that is of any real interest to me; I should be surprised if I could fill half a page."

Following this odd exchange, Elinor had come away believing her young sister was bored, but she had as yet no appreciation of the depth of her discontent. Sometime later, however, after the colonel had left for Ireland, Elinor visited her sister again, taking with her a letter from their mother in which she declared her resolve to remain at Barton Park for a further month at least, attending upon the ailing Mrs Jennings and assisting her cousin, Sir John Middleton, with his household.

I really feel it is not possible for me to leave at this time, when Mrs Jennings is still quite unable to even contemplate travelling alone to London or Cleveland. Indeed, it would appear that the Palmers are not at

Cleveland, having decided to take their summer holiday at Ramsgate this year. That would mean Mrs Jennings would be quite alone, and I cannot imagine what she would do all day.

—Mrs Dashwood wrote.

As for my poor cousin, Sir John, he seems quite unable to decide on how anything is to be organised in the household. I understand Lady Middleton was a most meticulous mistress. The housekeeper relies almost entirely on me for instructions regarding provisions and menus, and I have to wonder how they will get on without me. One must hope they are all honest and will not take advantage of my poor cousin.

Elinor was astonished that Mrs Dashwood could be relied upon to organise an establishment the size and status of Barton Park, but she was even more disconcerted by the news that her mother appeared to have no plans to join them at Delaford as she had hoped. She was concerned too that Marianne would be exceedingly disappointed at the news; Marianne was much closer to her mother than were either Elinor or Margaret. Indeed, so alike were they in manner and disposition, they could, but for the difference in their ages, have been sisters.

Elinor had expected that Mrs Dashwood would return within the month, which seemed now to be very unlikely, and she, worried that Marianne would resent her mother's absence, had a suggestion. "I know you miss Mama a great deal, my dear, so Edward and I wondered if you would like to join us when we travel to Weymouth for a fortnight. It should be a pleasant change; Edward is looking forward to meeting with a colleague who was at Oxford with him, which will give us time to see something of the town and the surrounding country. We hope to stay outside the town; our friends Dr and Mrs King have recommended a small hotel and they say there are many historic sites within easy distance..."

Elinor's enthusiastic recital of prospective pleasures was interrupted when Marianne said quietly, "That is kind of you, Elinor, and I have no doubt Weymouth will have many delights, but I'm afraid I shall not be free to join your party. I shall be busy entertaining Mr and Mrs Robert Ferrars, who have plans to visit friends in Dawlish and expect to spend a few days with me at Delaford."

Elinor was speechless for several minutes. Robert Ferrars, her brother-in-law, had married Lucy Steele, a young woman whose deception of both Elinor and Edward had been quite unpardonable. Lucy had become secretly engaged to a young Edward Ferrars and had pretended to be deeply in love with him for many years, before she had abruptly thrown him over for his brother, Robert, for blatantly mercenary reasons.

All this was well known to Marianne, yet it appeared she had invited the couple—for whom none of them had any regard—without so much as a word to Elinor. When she could speak, she asked, "And when did this come about?" Marianne replied, "Not very long ago; I had a note from Lucy telling me of their plans to visit us en route to Dawlish, and I invited them to spend a few days at Delaford. I knew Colonel Brandon would be in Ireland and hoped they might be company for me."

Elinor was shocked. "Company for you? Marianne, surely you cannot be serious? Since when have you sought the company of Robert and Lucy?" She knew—from her own experience of conversations with Lucy and Robert and from everything that Marianne had said in the past of their superficiality, their complete lack of taste and judgment, except in ensuring their own advancement over all else—that they were the last people in whose company her sister would take any pleasure.

But Marianne bridled at the suggestion and claimed in her defence that she was certain their company would afford her greater pleasure than being alone at Delaford for several weeks.

"It is all very well for you, Elinor; Edward is there at your side every day, and you engage with a dozen different groups of people in your parish work—you do not lack company," Marianne claimed. "My situation is entirely different. I must find company where I can, and besides, Robert is Edward's brother—I cannot see that it is such a dreadful imposition upon you if I invite them to Delaford. When I did, Lucy wrote almost at once to say they would be delighted—they have not visited in two years or more. I believe they expect to call on Edward and you at the parsonage, too; they are sure to be disappointed to find you gone away to Weymouth."

Astonished by her insouciance, Elinor replied, "I doubt their disappointment will be long lived, Marianne; you cannot have forgotten Lucy's past behaviour to both Edward and me, surely. You may well find them relieved to discover that we are away. I confess, for my part, I am rather glad to be missing them."

Marianne's lighthearted response confounded her sister. "Oh, Elinor, surely it's a long time ago now. I would have thought that you would be feeling quite charitable towards Lucy for having jilted Edward; after all, it allowed him to come back to you with honour!"

This remark so discomposed Elinor, she rose, preparing to leave, fighting back tears. She could not comprehend Marianne's attitude and felt quite unable to deal with the situation. It was not often that Elinor, whose ability to govern her feelings had stood her in good stead for most of her life, had faced such a circumstance. There had been other occasions when Marianne's words had wounded her feelings, but that had been many years ago, when she'd had the excuse of temporary derangement following Willoughby's cruel conduct. Then, they had all treated Marianne with indulgence and tender concern, excusing any and every *faux pas* as a consequence of her misery. But surely, Elinor thought, there was nothing similar now that would mitigate such an unfeeling remark.

Seeing Elinor's discomposure, Marianne rose too and grasped her hand, as if she wished to apologise, but even as she did so, she smiled and seemed not to realise how deeply her remark had hurt her sister. She attempted to make light of it, claiming she had spoken in jest, but clearly Elinor was not comforted and left soon afterward.

Walking home in a light drizzle that added to her discomfort, she could not help the tears that flooded her eyes. Marianne may have forgotten, but Elinor could not. The shabby episode of Lucy and Robert's behaviour, in which they had deliberately deceived both Edward and herself while courting the favour of Mrs Ferrars by assiduous flattery, had left her feeling a degree of generic shame for those members of her sex for whom self-interest was the sole motivator. That Edward's exemplary character counted for less with his mother than the hypocrisy of his selfish brother and his duplicitous wife had left her feeling sore. But worse now to learn that all that meant nothing to Marianne, with whom she had shared her feelings at the time. It was, for Elinor, an unconscionable betrayal by a sister she loved.

When she reached the parsonage, she was further disconcerted to find Edward waiting for her in the sitting room. She had hoped to have some time alone to regain her composure, but it was not to be. She hurried in, greeting him quickly, putting down her things in the hall, and proceeded directly upstairs to change out of her damp shoes and coat and compose herself, before asking for afternoon tea to be served. Returning to the sitting room, she found her husband regarding her with some concern.

"Elinor dearest, you look so worried, I can see you are troubled about something. What is it, my dear? Is Marianne unwell?" he asked with the kind of warm sympathy that she valued so much, yet she was determined that he would not be told of the true cause of her distress. Her sister's remarks would hurt him almost as much as they had wounded her. Instead, she informed him that Marianne was expecting visitors at Delaford and would not be able to accompany them on their visit to Weymouth.

"Is that all?" he said, smiling, as the tea tray was brought in and placed upon the table. "Well, of course I am sorry your sister cannot join us, and I know that is disappointing, but it is unlikely to spoil our enjoyment. We should have plenty to occupy our time. I met Dr King in the village this morning, and he has told me of two more places that are worth visiting. I understand Milton Abbey is not to be missed; it was a famous Benedictine monastery until the dissolution under Henry the Eighth, he says, and he also recommends the walk along the cliffs from Weymouth to the village of Osmington. They took the walk last year, and he claims it affords some remarkable views of the coast." Clearly Edward believed that the delights of Weymouth would soon compensate for Marianne's absence.

As Elinor busied herself pouring out tea, he continued with more information about Weymouth and its environs gleaned from Dr King. Edward had not suspected that her distress was due to anything more serious than disappointment with Marianne's inability to join their party; he had not even asked who her visitors were, making it easier for Elinor to avoid mentioning Robert Ferrars and his wife, Lucy—a couple for whom she had neither affection nor respect.

Perhaps, she thought, Edward need not learn of the visit of his brother and his wife until after they had returned from their own holiday in Weymouth, and by then it would be old news and of little consequence.

Elinor was by nature both generous and magnanimous and was willing to allow that Marianne, in a mood of boredom and loneliness, with her husband away in Ireland, had spoken thoughtlessly, without intending to wound. Her remarks would in time be forgiven.

It was somewhat more difficult, however, for her to overlook the fact that her sister, in full knowledge of the reprehensible conduct of both Lucy and Robert Ferrars, could have blithely invited them to stay at Delaford, even before she knew that Elinor and Edward would be away at the time. "Is it possible that Marianne has grown so self-absorbed, so insensitive to our feelings—Edward's and mine—that she did not think what it would mean to us to have to meet and perhaps even entertain them here?" she asked herself, but again, determined not to let it spoil the pleasure of their own holiday, she pushed it out of her mind as she began preparations for their journey.

She looked forward to the holiday she hoped would be a change from the routines of parish work. Both Edward and she worked hard and conscientiously in the community he served, and though Elinor had tried to involve her sister in some of their activities, such as the church choir or the Christmas play, her participation had been desultory and haphazard at best. It was yet another aspect of Marianne's behaviour that had puzzled Elinor, for which she could find no answer.

Chapter Five

AN UNEXPECTED VISIT FROM her stepbrother, John Dashwood, on the afternoon before they were due to depart on their journey to Weymouth, gave Elinor more reasons for satisfaction that they were soon to be going away.

Greeting her with his usual lack of warmth, he claimed he had called on Sir John Middleton to pay his respects, and had been very surprised to find Mrs Dashwood still at Barton Park. He wondered if Elinor could enlighten him as to her mother's reasons for being there and her plans for the future.

Taken aback by his sudden interest in her mother's forthcoming plans, Elinor took some delight in denying him the information he sought. "I am sorry, John, but Mama has not made any decisions about her future plans yet; for the present, she has agreed to help her cousin Sir John Middleton care for his mother-in-law, Mrs Jennings. She has been very poorly since Lady Middleton's death, and is unable to travel to join her daughter, Mrs Palmer, whose family is presently at Ramsgate. As to what Mama will do thereafter," she shrugged her shoulders and added, "you will need to ask her; she has certainly not confided in me."

John Dashwood seemed very put out. "Ah!" said he, and continued in a voice that suggested he was less than satisfied with her answer, "I had very much hoped you might know, Elinor. You see, Fanny was wondering about Barton

Cottage; there is a person, a former housekeeper of her mother's, who is in need of a place to stay, and Fanny thinks that Barton Cottage might be the very thing—especially since the rent is reasonable—if Mrs Dashwood were to vacate it. She particularly asked that I ascertain what plans Mrs Dashwood may have, and it is rather awkward that I cannot take back an answer. Perhaps Marianne may know... I could call on her at Delaford Manor later today," he mused.

His motives being exposed clearly now, Elinor felt a particular pleasure that she had not been able to satisfy him. She had no wish to be disagreeable, but, assisting Fanny and her mother, Mrs Ferrars, to accommodate a retired housekeeper, whom they no longer wished to shelter, was not high on Elinor's list of priorities.

Knowing she was adding to his discomfort, she said, "Marianne knows no more than I do of Mama's plans, but, at least on the question of Barton Cottage, I can certainly assure you that Mama has no intention whatsoever of quitting it. While she is happy to spend some part of her time with Marianne and me, she greatly values her independence and has said on many occasions that she so enjoys the cottage, she will never give it up."

Looking decidedly crestfallen, John Dashwood had to admit defeat and stayed only to finish his tea. A weak, selfish man who was continually pandering to the high notion that his wife and mother-in-law had of themselves and their place in society, his paltry treatment of his stepmother and stepsisters after their father's death had greatly reduced him in Elinor's estimation. The further humiliation they had been allowed to suffer at the hands of his wife, Fanny, had consolidated her contempt for all of them—save Edward, Fanny's brother, in whom she had found a man of many virtues and a gentle temperament quite unlike his relatives.

Elinor was sure Edward would enjoy the tale of John Dashwood's disappointment with which she hoped to entertain him on their journey to Weymouth.

❧

Their fortnight away proved to be a great success.

Though principally a seaside resort, Weymouth offered many other possibilities for the enterprising traveller, and since neither Edward nor Elinor wished merely to sit in the sun on the beach, they found several interesting things to do.

Edward's friend, Dr Trelawney, a retired Oxford don, was writing a book about the many ancient abbeys and churches, mostly in a sad state of disrepair, that were scattered around the county. He encouraged them to accompany him on his visits and proved to be a most knowledgeable guide. On his recommendation, too, in the second week of their stay, they moved from their hotel in Melcombe to comfortable lodgings in the charming village of Sutton Poyntz. Their hosts were a friendly pair of sisters, who welcomed them warmly and opened up their best room for their use. The Misses Jane and Elfrida Dunkley attended to their every need with the particular care one usually reserves for very dear friends.

The weather was kind for most of their stay, and even when it was not, the company was excellent, for Dr Trelawney introduced them to his family and invited them to dine at his home, while Mrs Trelawney, a woman of many talents and a fine sense of humour, was excellent company for Elinor. The four of them spent their days in travel and exploration and their evenings in intelligent and diverting discourse.

The fortnight passed far too quickly, and when it was time to return to Delaford, Elinor could not help the sigh that escaped her lips as she packed their trunk. Thanks to Dr Trelawney, who was travelling in his own vehicle to Dorchester, their homeward journey was more swiftly and comfortably accomplished, and they reached the parsonage on Saturday afternoon. Having taken tea and dealt with the demands of her two sons, who were eager to be told everything about Weymouth at once, Elinor went upstairs to rest, while Edward went to open up the church and read his accumulated mail.

It was in her bedroom that she found, propped up on her dressing table, a hand-delivered note from Marianne. Opening it up immediately, Elinor read it quickly through. She was concerned because their last meeting had not been a propitious one.

Marianne wrote:

Dearest Elinor,

I trust Edward and you are safely home after a restful holiday at Weymouth.

This is only a brief note, written in a great hurry. It has been such a busy time with Robert and Lucy here this last week, although they have not spent all their time at Delaford Manor. They've been visiting friends in the area too, and we have had some of them here to tea, which was good fun.

We have gone twice into Dorchester and once to Wareham to see the deep pool, which is such a beautiful sight—Robert and Lucy had heard it was not to be missed, and they did not believe that I had not been there before, having lived in Dorset these many years.

Truly, Elinor, Robert and Lucy are much improved since we saw them last, I have so enjoyed having them to stay.

On Saturday, we are to join a party of Robert's friends to drive into Somerset; I do so long to see Somerset, which I know to be especially beautiful at this time of year.

Thereafter the letter ended abruptly, with the words:

Lucy and Robert are back—I can hear their carriage in the drive. I must go downstairs directly.
  Your loving sister,
  Marianne

Elinor's response to her sister's note was one of intense anxiety and bewilderment. She was bewildered by Marianne's cavalier acceptance of Robert and Lucy as "much improved" when she knew that neither had shown, in the years since her marriage to Edward, that they had changed either in inclination or demeanour. He had, for the most part, remained selfish and supercilious, while she had made no attempt at all to improve her disposition or her understanding, continuing to indulge in the type of shallow, mindless gossip that was her stock in trade. Neither by an improvement of mind or manners or by any worthwhile accomplishments had they distinguished themselves from what they had been when Elinor had first met them several years ago.

Marianne's mention of a journey into Somerset with them had increased Elinor's apprehension. For it was there, she had recently learned, that Willoughby was spending the summer. Questions flooded her mind—what if he were to encounter their party? How would it be if they were to meet? Recalling Willoughby's infamous protestations of love, she wondered, would he approach Marianne? Knowing Marianne's predisposition, Elinor was concerned that in the company of two people as irresponsible as Robert and Lucy Ferrars, her sister might not be able to resist the type of impulsive behaviour that had, on previous occasions, led to embarrassment and distress.

When her husband returned, she was in two minds as to whether she should tell him of her fears; to do so, she would have to reveal her knowledge of the visit of Robert and Lucy, but she was forestalled when he announced that he'd had a letter from his brother Robert.

He held up a note. "It seems they've been here while we were away, staying at Delaford Manor and visiting friends in the area! Isn't that a surprise?" and then seeing that Elinor was clearly not particularly surprised, asked, "Have you heard already?"

Marianne's note, lying on the bedside table, provided a clue, and he assumed she had just heard the news from her sister, but Elinor could no longer carry on the deception; she had to reveal the fact that she had known of the visit well before they left for Weymouth. She was very contrite. "I'm sorry, dearest, I can give you no logical explanation, except that I was so completely disconcerted by Marianne's revelation that she had invited them to stay. I could not understand it; she has never liked Lucy and has nothing in common with her. Besides, Marianne has not the patience to put up with Lucy as I do. I found her change of heart inexplicable; it upset me and I just decided not to trouble you with the news. I am sorry."

Edward was his usual gentle, understanding self, if a little confused by her confession. He simply shrugged his shoulders and said, "It matters little, my love, it would have made no difference to our plans—no doubt they had plenty to occupy them… Robert says they enjoyed their stay—their friends the Percevals live not far from Delaford and they spent most of their time with them. He says they were sorry to have missed us, but he is probably just being civil."

Elinor handed him her sister's note and watched him as he read it.

"Hmm, it certainly looks like Marianne has been enjoying the company too," he said and was surprised when Elinor said softly, "That is exactly what concerns me; these friends of Robert's that she speaks of, who are they and why was she going into Somerset with them?"

Edward raised his eyebrows. "You believe there is still some danger lurking in Somerset for Marianne?" he asked.

"I do. You told me that Willoughby was spending the summer there. It probably sounds silly, and perhaps I am being over-anxious, but, Edward, you did not see Marianne when she was in love with Willoughby. I can only describe it as being besotted; she believed he was a prince among men who could do no wrong and would never betray her. She was unwilling to allow that she could be wrong in her estimation of him, and I don't know if Marianne is strong enough to resist him now. Were they to meet again, at a time when the colonel is away and she is bored and susceptible to flattery, one cannot predict what consequences might follow."

Edward, who had been considering the possibility that his wife was being overprotective of her sister, hearing the apprehension in her voice, began to take her concerns more seriously. His brother had mentioned the Percevals—Edward recalled them vaguely as a wealthy family of young men and women whose main pastimes were entertainment and fun.

"Are you certain, Elinor? Marianne has been married for some years now; is it not more likely that she will be able to deal with any such meeting—were it to occur—with greater confidence than before?" he asked, keen to reassure her.

But Elinor was not comforted. "I wish I could be as confident as you are, dearest, but I'm afraid I cannot." She recalled how easily Marianne, having recovered from her illness and expressed deep remorse for her undisciplined displays of affection for Willoughby and contempt for the opinions of others of their acquaintance, had persuaded herself that she had forgiven him. Convinced that Willoughby genuinely loved her, she had been prepared to lay the guilt for his behaviour principally upon his aunt and Miss Grey, the wealthy, unloved wife he had acquired. Remembering with great clarity Marianne's response to her account of Willoughby's visit and his protestations of remorse, Elinor could not regard with any degree of complaisance the prospect of a meeting between them. In her mind it was fraught with danger to her sister and ought be avoided.

If Elinor could have known Marianne's own thoughts and the content of her conversations with Lucy Ferrars, it is likely that she would have been a good deal more concerned.

～❦～

Once Robert and Lucy Ferrars had departed for Dawlish, Marianne had little to occupy her. Seated at her desk, at the window in the studio she used but rarely for the purpose for which it had been intended, she looked out on the familiar prospect of the grounds of Delaford Manor. It was not one that inspired her at all, being simply a view of green lawns and stands of old trees that she found singularly unexciting. It had neither the romantic quality of her memories of Norland Park, nor the immediate appeal of Somerset, which she had enjoyed more recently on her visit to that county with Lucy and Robert and their friends the Percevals.

Thoughts of Exmoor and the Somerset woodlands quickly aroused pictures in her mind, and she turned to the diary she had recently begun to keep, to record her thoughts and observations.

After a few prosaic entries of ordinary activities on the manor, it made interesting reading...

Lucy and Robert Ferrars are here; and though I knew little of Robert, and had not a very high opinion of Lucy, on account of her dealings with Edward and Elinor in the past, I confess that I have enjoyed their company on this visit. I cannot say that either has acquired a better understanding of art or music—they appeared equally bored by both—but they have lots of stories to tell of London life and are constantly engaged with friends all over the country. Lucy declares that she is glad to have a good ladies' maid, since they are always travelling about, leaving at a moment's notice to visit friends. She claims she would be lost without her maid, and she is clearly very happy with Robert's friends.

One such family, the Percevals, live here in Dorset not ten miles from Delaford, and when I was introduced to them, they were astonished that we had not met before, seeing I had lived in Dorset for several years.

They are a large, engaging family of six or seven, with two young girls and a boy still at home, while two older sons are in the navy and their eldest girl is married and settled in Somersetshire. Mr Perceval is a retired ship's captain who took up a business as a chandler and is said to have made his money victualling the navy during the wars with France. Mrs Perceval is a quiet woman with a partiality for odd-looking lace caps. However, the Percevals are all very cheerful and hospitable and very polite to me at all times.

I am to accompany them on a visit to Somerset next Saturday; I have heard so much of the beauty of Somerset—I look forward to seeing it.

Some days later, she had written in glowing terms of their visit to Somerset.

Our journey to Somerset was unforgettable. I did recall some of what I had been told—it was many years ago, but as we drove through the lovely landscape, I remembered it all as one does a dream. Oh why is Dorset so dull, so lacking in features that inspire me, compared to this enchanting county?

We drove first through acres of farmland and orchard, with wildflowers in profusion everywhere, and stopped to climb a little hill overlooking a valley through which flowed one of the many rivers of Somerset. The Percevals' daughter lives in the peaceful little town of Langport, on the east bank of one such river; her husband is the rector there of a very old church. The Rectory overlooks the river and has a view of the distant hills. What a joy it must be to awaken to such a prospect each morning!

They welcomed us and treated us to luncheon, after which Robert insisted that we must drive forth and take a look at Exmoor—which was rather chilling, being all dark and mysterious. The Percevals were all for staying on and exploring, but Lucy and Robert thought that was not a good idea. Lucy claimed her shoes were not suitable for exploring Exmoor, and we had to agree, for they did look rather too dainty for walking on the moor.

The Perceval girls have vowed to go back again—the mystery of the moor has gripped their imagination, as it has mine. I have read a great deal about the moors and their appeal to poetic souls, but have never actually walked upon one before. It could be a very exciting experience.

On our return to Delaford, Robert went out again with friends, leaving Lucy and me together for the evening, and she took the opportunity to ask if I had heard anything of Mr Willoughby in the last year or two. She was careful to beg my pardon for asking first, but said she thought I must have heard that he was at present living at his place in Somerset. When I looked surprised, even as I tried not to appear interested, she revealed that it was now generally known in town that Willoughby and his wife, Sophia, lived mostly apart. When she was in London, he moved to the country and vice versa. I did not wish to appear curious, but I had to ask if that meant that she came down to Somerset when he went up to

London, but Lucy said, "Oh no, she has an extensive property in Essex, which she inherited from her mother, and that is her family home."

I confess I did not wish to ask any more questions, but Lucy, probably because she has so little to offer as conversation, continued with various bits of information. It appears Mrs Smith, his aunt, died, but Willoughby did not inherit all of her estate because she never forgave him for his misdemeanours in the matter of Eliza Williams, and Lucy says Willoughby still believes it was Colonel Brandon who advised his aunt of that episode in his past.

When she said this, I was so astonished I protested that it could not be true—it cannot have been my husband—but Lucy herself is convinced it was—she claims that Lady Middleton told her Colonel Brandon was so incensed when he discovered Eliza and her child had been abandoned by Willoughby, he wrote to Mrs Smith apprising her of the circumstances. Lucy declares that Lady Middleton had it from her mother, Mrs Jennings, who was very close to Colonel Brandon.

And thereby hangs a tale...

END OF PART ONE

EXPECTATIONS OF HAPPINESS

Part Two

Chapter Six

Autumn 1819

MARGARET DASHWOOD AND HER friend Claire Jones had planned to leave for their holiday in Europe before the end of summer; but, as often happens with the best-laid plans, their departure was delayed by the necessities of business, when Miss Jones's employer discovered an urgent assignment that could not be postponed. However, the setback did allow Margaret a fortnight in which she could visit her mother and sisters before leaving for France and acquaint them with her plans.

Margaret had pleasanter memories of Devonshire than Marianne; having spent the latter part of her childhood there, she took much pleasure in visiting and looked forward to seeing the park and woods again. She had intended to stay with her mother at Barton Cottage, but finding her still in charge of the household at Barton Park, accepted Sir John Middleton's invitation to stay at the manor house.

Mrs Dashwood was delighted to see her youngest daughter looking so well, and so was Sir John, who was sufficiently recovered from his wife's death to tease Margaret at dinner about a certain gentleman, who had missed her when he was down at Barton Park some weeks ago. When Margaret pretended not to know whom he meant, Sir John was supported by her mother.

"Sir John means Mr Andrew Barton, my dear; he was here for dear Lady

Middleton's funeral and stayed on for a few days to call on friends in the neighbourhood. He particularly asked after you and was disappointed to learn that you had been down, but had to return to Oxford to keep an important appointment," explained Mrs Dashwood, trying tactfully to indicate that she had provided her daughter with a plausible excuse. Margaret looked at her mother and nodded gratefully, appreciating her help, but it appeared that Sir John and Mrs Jennings were not to be satisfied so easily.

The latter was determined to discover what had caused Margaret to leave before the funeral. "Come now, Miss Margaret, what was this important appointment, hmmm? It cannot have been work surely; was it another beau?" she quizzed, fixing Margaret with her penetrating gaze, and when Margaret said quite spiritedly, "It most certainly was not, Mrs Jennings, I assure you," her son-in-law chimed in, "I'm very glad to hear it, Miss Margaret, because if that were the case, poor Barton would be quite desolated." He then looked directly at Margaret and declared, "You must know the young fellow is hopelessly in love with you. He has told me, more than once since you met last December, that he has not met another young lady who has so enchanted him, and I assure you he is quite serious; he means to propose to you at the earliest opportunity. Considering that he can have the pick of the young ladies in London, that is a very particular compliment, wouldn't you agree? I have told your mama that he is an excellent match for you, if you will have him; he has at least five thousand a year and two fine houses in London and Bath, with the prospect of a share in a great estate in the north of England when his father dies, which may not be long, considering he is almost eighty and suffers badly from the gout and a few other ailments besides."

As Margaret listened, Mrs Dashwood observed her daughter, hoping to see some flicker of interest on her countenance, and Mrs Jennings sat literally open mouthed, agog for some response. But, to their general disappointment, she shook her head. "I am sorry, Sir John, I have no wish to marry Mr Barton—"

"Why ever not?" interrupted Mrs Jennings, loudly. "He is as handsome a man as ever I saw, with a fine upstanding figure and such charming manners. If I had an unmarried daughter, I'd have been perfectly willing to let him marry her—as I said to your mama the other day, he is a jolly good catch for anyone…"

"I have no doubt he is, Mrs Jennings, and I do not mean to disparage Mr Barton, I do assure you, but I am not interested in marriage to anyone at this time," Margaret explained. "Besides I have just contracted to complete another year's teaching at the seminary—and considering they sent me away to study in Europe at their expense, I cannot possibly let them down."

Despite the various sounds of disapprobation emanating from Sir John and his mother-in-law, it was clear to everyone at the table that Margaret was unlikely to be moved by any of their arguments. Mrs Dashwood had said no more then, but afterward, when they were alone in her room, Margaret could not escape her mother's inquisition. "I don't mean to push you, my dear, but are you sure you are not making a hasty decision about Mr Barton? He is a respectable man and from an excellent family, you know. Are you not willing to consider?" she asked, and Margaret replied gently but with the kind of determination her mother recognised, "I am not, Mama, believe me, I have no wish to marry him or anyone else."

"And there is no one else? No one you have given your word to? No young French gentleman?" At this Margaret laughed merrily. "No, Mama, none. I promise you," she said, and Mrs Dashwood had to be satisfied, although, as she said later to Sir John and Mrs Jennings, "I really cannot make her out at all."

Two days later, Margaret left to travel to Delaford to visit her sisters, going first to the parsonage where Elinor and Edward welcomed her warmly and demanded to be told how she had spent her time since they'd last met. Comfortably ensconced in the parlour, enjoying tea and muffins with home-made jam, she spent the afternoon regaling them with stories of her work at the seminary and the plans she and Claire Jones had made for their tour of Provence in the autumn.

On that topic, there was indeed much to talk about: Edward had visited the south of France some years ago and said he thought Aix-en-Provence was a most interesting area, "with so many ancient Roman antiquities, early Christian monasteries and abbeys—one could see as many as would fill all of one's time, if that was your wish," he said. He did, however, recommend that they try to visit Lyon, which he described as "one of the pleasantest towns in France." Margaret assured him that both places were on their itinerary, and indeed, Miss Jones had a friend, a regular visitor to the area, who would act as their guide. "He is a tutor at one of the colleges in Oxford and has promised to show us all the best places, which means we shall not be at the mercy of itinerant tour guides," she said, and Elinor, who had never travelled outside of England and was rather wary, said she was very glad to hear it.

"Our friends Dr and Mrs King have travelled often in Europe and tell some amazing stories of local guides who are generally not to be trusted and will often tell the gullible traveller tall tales of miraculous relics of saints and healing springs, which have no foundation in fact at all. You are fortunate to be spared that sort of hazard. However, I shall look forward to receiving a letter or two with some account of your travels and the wonderful places you visit. You must promise to be very careful, Margaret, I know Mama will be worrying about you, and so will I," she said, but Margaret laughed at her fears. "Have no fear, Elinor, I am sure I shall be quite safe; besides, Mama is far more worried about trying to marry me off to that impossible cousin of Sir John's—Mr Barton, whom we met at the Middletons' house in London. They spent most of yesterday singing his praises to me—not only is he rich and handsome, he has houses in Bath and London, his aging father has an estate somewhere in the North Country, and Mama believes he is a 'respectable' man!"

Edward laughed. "And is he not?" he asked, almost in jest. Margaret snorted in a most unladylike manner. "Indeed, he is not—I have no evidence of his own conduct, but he is a great admirer of the Regent and has many friends in that dubious circle. I cannot imagine that any man who keeps such company can be called 'respectable.' He once declared proudly—hoping to impress me, no doubt—that if he had wished to do so, he could obtain a place at court, as though that were some pinnacle of achievement Ugh! Can you imagine?"

Elinor, hearing the scorn in her sister's voice, asked, "And was it Mr Barton you wished to avoid at Lady Middleton's funeral? Was that why you wouldn't stay?"

Margaret said softly, "Yes it was; I couldn't tell you then, Elinor, I thought you would laugh at me; but now I am quite certain that had I stayed, he would have proposed. Sir John confirmed it yesterday, and then, no doubt he would have asked Mama and they would have all driven me quite mad. Even Mrs Jennings was determined that I should know what a fine catch he was! She claims she would gladly let him marry a daughter of hers, if she had one to spare! Well, she is welcome to him."

Elinor and Edward laughed and Elinor said, "Mrs Jennings is very fortu-nate in both her sons-in-law—Sir John is not the brightest of men but he is generous and respectable, and Mr Palmer, for all his so-called drollery and reserve, is essentially a very sensible gentleman."

"And neither of them have anything in common with Prince George!" said Edward, and Margaret, believing she had found an ally in her brother-in-law, said, "For which I think we must all give thanks. The lurid tales one hears of the antics of the Regent and his band of merry men are quite outrageous."

That night, after they'd enjoyed a very pleasant meal and Margaret had entertained them with more stories of her work at the seminary, Elinor took her up to her room, and as the sisters talked, she found herself confiding in Margaret her apprehensions about Marianne and the return to Somerset of Mr Willoughby. Margaret, who had never been as impressed with Willoughby's pretensions as her sister and mother had been, was not surprised. "I do recall that Mama was most reluctant to condemn him, and when she heard of his remorse and the tale he had told you of being ordered by his elderly aunt and his bride-to-be to write those cruel letters to Marianne, she was quite ready to believe him and forgive at least some of his horrid behaviour," she said.

Elinor asked gently, "And were you not?" to which Margaret was swift to respond, "Indeed I was not. How could anyone, after what he had done, after the deception he had practised upon all of us and particularly after poor Marianne had almost died as a consequence? I did not know then about his dreadful betrayal of Eliza Williams, of which I learnt much later from Mrs Jennings. But Mama and Marianne knew of this, and yet they were ready to believe his story, which I took to be a pack of lies."

Shocked, her sister said, "Margaret, my dear, you could not have known that."

"Perhaps not in every detail, but think on this, Elinor, everything he did and said to Marianne was based on a lie; he was prepared to put not just her heart but her reputation and her life in jeopardy by his selfish actions—just as he did with Miss Williams. Do you not recall how ready he was to lead her into excessive behaviour, which I know you disapproved of—I heard you try to persuade her to be more restrained and wary, but she believed she could trust him and would not take your advice? It was only Marianne's good luck that protected her from being led deeper into the mire, when Willoughby's aunt uncovered his conduct by sheer chance and sent him packing."

Elinor could scarcely believe her ears. Margaret had been not much more than a child at the time, yet she had clearly seen what was happening and had comprehended the danger her sister had faced. Growing up and seeing more of the world than either Marianne or Elinor herself had been exposed to, Margaret was now far more clear-sighted than either of them, and she did not mince her words. Perhaps it should have surprised Elinor that this young girl had more common sense than either her mother or Marianne, but knowing them all as she did, it did not. It gave her the chance to confide her own troubling thoughts and fears about Marianne as the two sisters talked late into the night.

Margaret could see that Elinor was deeply disturbed and asked, "Do you believe it is only the lack of any deep interest and a general boredom with life at Delaford that has brought about this malaise in Marianne? If that is true, can we not suggest some scheme, some good cause that might usefully engage her mind?"

Elinor looked forlorn. "If only it were possible; I have tried not once or twice but often to encourage her participation in the parish school, where I could use her talents in music and her love of poetry to benefit the children. I have suggested that she help with the church choir, and Edward has talked of the campaigns that he and Dr King are working on to collect petitions for the abolition of slavery—Mr Wilberforce has asked local communities to lend their support—and we thought Marianne might wish to be involved, but to no avail. She seems unable to summon up sufficient interest in any of these causes. I even went so far as to suggest to Colonel Brandon that he might wish to persuade her to join us when we attended a meeting at the church hall in Dorchester to draw attention to the plight of the climbing boys—the little boys who are apprenticed to chimney sweeps and made to undertake dangerous work when they are only five or six years old—but he seemed unwilling, too. I'm afraid I have failed utterly to do anything for her..." and here Elinor's feelings got the better of her and tears coursed down her cheeks, causing Margaret to put her arms around her. "Elinor, you must not blame yourself; you've done all you can, and if Marianne will not be persuaded, you are not at fault," she said firmly, but she knew that her sister would not be comforted. Elinor's strong sense of responsibility would not let her slough off her concerns easily, despite the fact that Marianne was now a married woman; she would never forget how a few years ago, they had almost lost her.

The following afternoon, Margaret left Elinor and Edward to pursue their various parochial and family activities and set out to walk to Delaford Manor.

As she made her way there, she pondered over the conversations she'd had with Elinor about Marianne and Willoughby, and it made her uneasy. Marianne was not very much older than herself, yet, from what she had learned from Elinor, it would seem that her sister still hankered after some romantic idyll, for which marriage to Colonel Brandon and her status as mistress of Delaford Manor had been no substitute.

Arriving at the manor house, Margaret was shown into a large room upstairs, with windows looking out over the surrounding park and drive. There she found her sister, reclining upon a gracious chaise-lounge replete with several satin cushions, a rug over her knees, clearly deep in a reverie—much like a lady in a French painting she had once seen. Marianne greeted her with a lovely smile but did not rise, making it necessary for Margaret to go to her and embrace her as they exchanged greetings. Clearly she was expecting her, Margaret thought—there were plates and cups and things on a low table laid out for afternoon tea—and yet Marianne appeared in no hurry to order refreshments, until Margaret, thirsty from her walk, asked if she might have a cup of tea. While the maid hurried to get it, Marianne revealed that she was expecting some visitors. The Misses Perceval, to whom she had been introduced by Robert and Lucy Ferrars, were visiting friends in the area and had sent a note that morning promising to call and she had asked them to stay to tea, she explained.

Margaret, not wishing to reveal that she had heard of the Percevals from Elinor, for fear that Marianne might suspect she had been the subject of discussion and resent it, merely nodded and said she was sorry she wasn't better dressed to meet the visitors, having just walked across from the parsonage, but Marianne waved away her worries. "They are not likely to notice such things—they are very modern young ladies. I'm sure you will like them very well, Margaret," she said, causing Margaret to wonder what Marianne meant by "modern young ladies."

When the two ladies arrived some little time later, Margaret was even more confused, for she could see little in the Misses Perceval—Maria and Eugenie—that could be termed "modern" to her way of thinking; as to the possibility of her liking them very well, as her sister had predicted she would, there was neither the time nor the inclination on either side to do more than meet and greet each other. The Misses Perceval showed not the slightest interest in

Margaret. They had arrived to invite Marianne to join them on an expedition to Glastonbury.

There was no mistaking Marianne's excitement as she heard of their plans, and by the time Margaret rose to leave, since she had promised to be back at the parsonage by six, it was quite clear that Marianne had agreed upon a day and arrangements were afoot for the journey. Glastonbury was in Somerset, and Elinor had told her that Willoughby was spending the summer there. The notion that Marianne was going to Glastonbury with the Percevals left Margaret experiencing a frisson of unease as she walked home in the late evening light that poured through the great old trees, making huge indigo shadows on the grass.

Approaching the parsonage, she saw her sister and brother-in-law walking in the shrubbery, close in conversation, and wondered if she should avoid adding to their disquiet by revealing what she knew of Marianne's plans. She feared that Elinor might panic and decide to visit Marianne and counsel her against going, increasing her resentment.

However, after she'd had time to think some more, while she bathed and dressed for dinner, she decided that Elinor had to know, if only that she could be prepared for any consequences that might flow from it in the future. But, she decided, she would beg her not to approach Marianne, thus avoiding a possible rift between the sisters.

Having prepared herself for the task, Margaret went down to dinner to find her sister looking unusually worried, and even Edward appeared not his usual calm self. While neither of them said anything during dinner with the servants around, once they had withdrawn to the parlour and Edward had taken to his chair by the fire with a book, Elinor joined Margaret on the sofa and invited her to come upstairs with her, confirming the impression that she had some grave news to impart.

Seated in the alcove of a small, well-lit room that Elinor reserved for her reading and sewing, Margaret heard a tale that added considerably to her concerns about Marianne's expedition to Glastonbury. It seemed that while she was away at Delaford Manor, Elinor and Edward had been visited by their friend Mrs King, who had brought them some information that greatly increased Elinor's anxiety. Mrs King, who'd had some previous knowledge of Marianne's unfortunate affair with Willoughby, had heard that Mr Willoughby was in Dorset, staying with his cousins the Clifts. Her informant, a Miss Henrietta

Clift, had declared that Willoughby had become bored with being on his own at his place in Somerset and had been delighted to accept the hospitality of the Clifts and, being an active sort of fellow, he was said to be organising a party to Glastonbury that weekend.

Elinor took Margaret's hand and said, "At least, that means he will be out of the county for a couple of days with his cousins and I need not worry about the possibility that he may encounter Marianne in town. Besides, she doesn't go into Dorchester alone, so there may be no immediate danger, but I cannot help worrying about her. I fear for her, as long as he is in the neighbourhood."

Poor Margaret was in such a quandary; events had changed so swiftly, she had no idea how to act. If Willoughby's party was going to Glastonbury that week, and Marianne's friends were taking her there also—it was almost inevitable that they would meet; yet how could she tell Elinor, and if she did, what good would it do? It was unlikely that Elinor could stop her sister; indeed she could not even attempt it without revealing what she knew about both Marianne's and Willoughby's plans. To reveal that information would certainly open them up to accusations that they were spying on Marianne, which Margaret, who knew her sister's disposition well, was certain would fix her resolution to defy Elinor's advice. It was a dreadful dilemma.

The need for Edward to accompany Dr Bradley King to a meeting of the anti-slavery campaign in Bridgwater in the county of Somerset, where some of the earliest petitions had begun, kept Elinor at home over the next two days, attending to sundry parish duties. Fearing that Margaret would be bored, she suggested that they ask Marianne to dinner on the Saturday.

"It would be just the three of us, and with Colonel Brandon away in Ireland, I'm sure she would enjoy the company, especially since you are soon to be going away to France. Don't you agree?" she asked, and Margaret tried to sound cheerful as she said, "She might, but then she may have visitors at the manor house. Perhaps we should send a note?" Elinor agreed and then had a better idea. "We could walk over to the manor house and ask her; I have a couple of her books I'd like to return, so we may make a virtue of necessity, especially as it's such a fine afternoon."

There was no escape now. Margaret realised she had to go along with the scheme else Elinor would become suspicious. Putting on their bonnets, they set out walking through the copse that separated the grounds of the parsonage from the more extensive park that surrounded Delaford Manor, where the trees, still in full summer leaf, afforded them shade from the warm afternoon sun. As they emerged from the wood and took the path leading to the side entrance of the manor house, they saw a carriage leaving the main gates and turning onto the road that led out of the property toward the village and thence to Dorchester.

It was a fine vehicle, drawn by a pair of handsome horses, and Margaret recognised it immediately as the carriage in which the Misses Perceval had arrived while she was visiting Marianne a few days ago. "I wonder who that can be…" Elinor mused. "I can't say I have seen that carriage in this area before. You were right, Margaret, Marianne has had visitors." Margaret said nothing, not wanting to upset her sister, but when they reached the manor house, the news could not be avoided.

The servant who let them into the hall informed them that her mistress had just left, but a few minutes ago, with the Misses Perceval.

"Left?" said Elinor, as though she could not comprehend the word. "Left to go where?" The girl apologised and said she wasn't exactly sure, but she thought they were planning to visit Glastonbury on the morrow, and Mrs Brandon had said she would be staying over at the Percevals' and would return home on Sunday.

Elinor said in a strained voice, "Glastonbury—in Somerset?" as though she had not heard right, and when the maid replied, "Yes, ma'am," Margaret saw her sister turn pale, as she looked at her, disbelieving, and reached for her hand.

"Will you not come in and take some tea, ma'am?" the girl asked, and Elinor shook her head and made to leave. Margaret could see from her countenance that she was thoroughly discomposed and very close to tears. As they walked back, Elinor grasped her sister's hand and held it very tight, but she said little. It was as though the shock had unsettled her and she was unsure what to do or say.

Then as they approached the parsonage, she spoke, "Oh Margaret, what is to be done? I am at a loss… I do not know what to think… these Perceval girls… I know nothing of them, except they are friends of Robert and Lucy, and I don't know if that is much of a recommendation."

"It is no great endorsement of their good sense," said Margaret, and then realising that such a remark would only increase her sister's discomfort, she added quickly, "but at least they have no connection to Willoughby."

"That is true," said Elinor in a dull voice, "but they are young and bent on having fun; who knows where they might go and whom they might meet? If they are all going to Glastonbury—on the same day—it seems inevitable that the parties will meet. Oh dear God, I pray they do not, because if they do, I know enough of Willoughby's recklessness to believe that he will feel no compunction at all about presenting himself to Marianne again, and I cannot bear to think that he will again have the opportunity to use the power he once had over her, to entice her into an association that can only end in tears."

Margaret was incredulous. "Elinor, you cannot really believe that—surely even if Willoughby cannot be relied upon to act with honour, Marianne will not be as vulnerable as she was those many years ago. Surely she is older and—"

Her sister interrupted her. "Wiser? Were you about to say older and wiser, Margaret? Because if you were, then I have bad news for you. Our sister was hurt, badly hurt by what happened between her and Willoughby some years ago, and yes, she did agree that he had been wrong to deceive her and all of us at the time, but as you pointed out when we spoke earlier of this matter, both Marianne and Mama were ready, nay eager, to find reasons to forgive him, to lay the blame for his conduct at the feet of his aunt or his wife—so who can tell if Marianne may not see him in a different light now. Oh dear, I wish Edward were here..." She sounded so forlorn, Margaret said, "I can stay another day or two—at least until Edward returns on Sunday night. I had meant to take the coach on Monday morning, but I will send an express instead, telling Claire I have been delayed. It will not signify, we are due to leave for Plymouth on Friday and sail on Saturday morning for Marseilles."

Elinor was very touched and hugged her young sister, marvelling at how mature she had become. "Thank you, Margaret, you are very kind; Edward will be home on Sunday night, but I don't think I will trouble him with these matters—he will be tired from the journey. But I *am* happy to have you with me to help me think things through; else I cannot imagine what I should have done."

They dined alone that evening, and afterward, Margaret tried to cheer her sister up by playing some of their favourite music on the pianoforte, but it was easy to see that Elinor, while she made a valiant attempt to be cheerful, could not shake off the fears that assailed her.

Chapter Seven

MEANWHILE, MARIANNE, OBLIVIOUS OF the concerns of both her sisters and in complete ignorance of the presence of Mr Willoughby in the neighbourhood, prepared to enjoy the expedition to Glastonbury.

Marianne never did anything by halves; it was in her nature to commit as much enthusiasm as she could muster to any activity or emotion that possessed her. The library at Delaford, though it had nothing like the impressive collection she'd had available to her at Norland, did have a considerable array of publications, most of which had been accumulated by Colonel Brandon's parents. His mother, in particular, had been a keen reader of historical and travel tales; consequently, while there may have been a paucity of romantic novels and poetry of the type that had captivated Marianne in her younger days, there were sufficient books, maps, and journals to satisfy the appetite of the adventurous traveller.

These had never interested Marianne much before, but, since hearing of the Percevals' planned expedition to Glastonbury, she had spent many hours opening up the old cabinets and taking out a large number of books in which she hoped to find some interesting information that she could share with her new friends. She did not expect that the two Misses Perceval would have done much reading about Somerset or Glastonbury; they were far more interested in discussing what they would wear and how much food and lemonade they would need to help them survive the rigours of the day.

Perusing the books and journals, Marianne was disappointed that while most gave adequate accounts of the towns and villages of Somerset, and others noted the many ruined abbeys and monasteries in the county, only one work provided her with a satisfactory description of Glastonbury, with its ancient history going back to the seventh century and suggestions that it was a site linked to the romantic tales of King Arthur and his knights of the Round Table. She also found references in both fiction and poetry to the Arthurian legends and read them avidly. Absorbed for the first time by something outside of what she considered to be her somewhat humdrum life at Delaford, Marianne read eagerly and made copious notes.

Determined to discover more, she sent a note to Margaret at the parsonage, requesting that she should seek information in the libraries to which she had access in Oxford. Clearly the excitement generated by her forthcoming journey to Glastonbury had driven all Margaret's travel plans out of her mind; Marianne had quite forgotten that her sister was leaving for France at the end of the week.

Arriving at the home of the Percevals on Friday afternoon, Marianne was pleasantly surprised. The house was a spacious and comfortable if rather nondescript residence, with few of the distinguishing features of places like Norland or even Barton Park, but it had been furnished with some style, and the Perceval family paid her a great deal of courtesy, ensuring she was comfortable and complimenting her on her appearance, her hair, her gown, and her singing, and persuading her to entertain them after dinner, which Marianne did gladly. Though she did not count them her equals in either elegance or erudition, she clearly appreciated their praise, which transported her once more to the days when she, talented and beautiful, had been the centre of attention in their social circle.

The Percevals, as a family, were a somewhat diverse lot; the parents appeared to be old-fashioned people such as one might meet in any English country community, hospitable and good-natured, but not greatly interested in matters that did not directly concern their lives, while their children seemed to be of a different bent altogether. Their elder brother, it was said, had enlisted in the navy, inspired by Admiral Nelson, and his family were excessively proud of him on this account, but no one was certain if he had or had not seen action in the war with Bonaparte. At the end of that conflict, he had attached himself quite firmly to the social circle of the officers and their followers in London and rarely ventured into the West Country. As for the two youngest—Misses Maria and Eugenie Perceval—they had little formal education but had acquired sufficient information from their string of governesses to engage in wide-ranging social chatter and would profess themselves keenly interested in anything new or fashionable.

Marianne's account of the history and legends of Glastonbury had been heard without interruption for scarcely ten minutes, before the mention of the romance of Guinevere and Lancelot distracted them from the realm of history and plunged the conversation into a romantic fantasy. Each of the girls had her own personal preference as to how King Arthur should have dealt with the matter of his betrayal by his dearest friend and his loving wife—and there was no bringing them back to mundane matters of archaeological evidence and historical fact. Despite her devotion to the philosophy of passionate love, Marianne was irritated by their inability to concentrate upon her recital of the story of Glastonbury. Deciding to hold back on some of the more interesting information she had discovered, she hoped there would be someone in their party who would appreciate it more than Maria and Eugenie, once they had actually visited the site.

After supper, the two sisters escorted her to her bedroom, smiled roguishly, and wished her "sweet dreams," and when Marianne looked a little bemused, they giggled and said, "Well, don't you want to dream of one of those handsome Knights of the Round Table sweeping you up onto a beautiful white horse? We certainly do!" and fled down the corridor, giggling uncontrollably as they went.

Waking early the following day to a crisp autumn morning, Marianne experienced a distinct feeling of excitement stirring in her. For the first time in her life, she was away from home—alone, without any member of her family beside her to watch or to counsel. She had an intoxicating sense of freedom as she dressed and went down to breakfast. She found only Mr and Mrs Perceval in the breakfast room and learned from them that Maria and Eugenie had been up and about even earlier, had breakfasted already, and taken the carriage round to collect two more members of their picnic party from a house just two miles away.

"The four young Hawthornes are joining our party, Mrs Brandon," Mrs Perceval revealed as she buttered her toast. "Their father is a most distinguished gentleman, a former commander under Lord Nelson," she proclaimed, adding, "I think our son Stephen once served under him, but alas, Commander Hawthorne suffered an injury that renders walking or sitting for long periods most painful, so he is unable to join us, but I am sure you will find the two girls and their brothers very agreeable companions. They are very fond of society, and the girls have been out a few years, although neither is as yet engaged to be married."

Marianne heard all this information, agreed that she was sure she would, and went on to say what a good day it was for the expedition, seeing the weather was so fine, but her hosts had returned to their breakfast and made no reply. She then finished hers and was about to excuse herself and leave the room when the carriage arrived, with Maria and Eugenie and their guests—the two Misses Hawthorne, Hannah and Harriet. Their brothers, they said, were riding and would arrive soon. They appeared a little older than the Perceval girls, but, to Marianne's eyes, seemed to have a very similar disposition to their friends, in that they were eager, keen, and wild for fun. No sooner were they introduced to Marianne, they began to quiz her about Glastonbury—"Mrs Brandon, we hear you are a veritable font of knowledge on Glastonbury and King Arthur's Knights of the Round Table! Maria and Eugenie have been telling us about it, but pray do tell us more..." they pleaded, and Marianne, who had been a little put out by the lack of attention from the Misses Perceval, was pleased to be able to oblige, as they waited for the rest of their party to assemble.

When the two gentlemen—Andrew and Joseph Hawthorne—arrived, they were introduced, and though formally courteous and correct, they paid very little attention to Marianne thereafter and seemed completely dedicated to the task of teasing and entertaining Maria and Eugenie Perceval. Marianne was quite glad that they would be travelling in two vehicles—she with Mr and Mrs Perceval, a cousin of Mrs Perceval named Miss Peabody, a maid, and a manservant in the large carriage, while the rest of the party were to pack into the smaller brougham.

This arrangement had clearly been planned so all the young people could be together and maximise opportunities for fun. Marianne, who thought them all a little lacking in understanding and well below her level of erudition, did not regret that she had been placed with the older members of the party. She did not expect that they would have much to say to her, and this would afford her time to think and enjoy the sights and sounds they would encounter, as the carriages rolled out onto the main road to Somerset. There was something profoundly stirring about the thought of going to Glastonbury, and she wanted the time alone to experience the excitement.

As the horses drew the vehicle over the old stone bridge with three high arches that carried the road into town, Marianne could not resist a feeling of exhilaration, as though she was on an adventure into the unknown. Though she had been married some seven years, she was still a very young woman and, having no children, felt none of the physical strain or the emotional pressure that customarily constrained women in her situation. Her tastes and inclinations had remained much the same as they had been when she was seventeen, save for the fact that she claimed to have extended them by further reading over the intervening years. However, her reading had not become more discriminating; rather it had, being more extensive, allowed her to indulge even more deeply in the type of literature that had always brought her the greatest satisfaction. Her life, sheltered by the circumstances of her marriage to Colonel Brandon, whose affection and care had cherished and protected her from every possible peril and aggravation, had afforded few opportunities for learning from experience, unless it was of comfort and pleasure.

As they drove through the villages and ancient market towns of Somerset, Marianne absorbed the beauty of the surrounding countryside, while her companions' talk of family and friends was of little interest to her. Content to let her thoughts wander, as the movement of the carriage gently rocked her body, she was only roused from her reverie when they stopped to water the horses at Yeovil, where the entire party alighted and went across to sample the refreshment at the coaching inn.

Back on the road, her hosts were solicitous and keen to assure themselves that Marianne was enjoying the journey. "Are you familiar with this part of the country, Mrs Brandon?" asked Mr Perceval, and when she said she was not, but was prepared to be enthusiastic about everything she had seen thus far, he sat opposite her and proceeded, strangely, to tell her all about his travels in

Scotland. "The Scottish highlands are a magnificent experience, I can assure you, Mrs Brandon, and there is nothing here in the West Country to rival the great mountains of Scotland. Mind you, I travelled there as a young man, I daresay I would not be confident that I could do it now. But, when friends in Somerset and Oxfordshire boast of the beauty of the Cotswolds or the Mendip Hills, I find I must restrain myself, for while they are pretty enough, they are as nothing when compared to the grandeur of the Grampians."

Marianne, who had never been to Scotland, smiled and acknowledged that she had been told the Scottish highlands were remarkably beautiful, but added quickly that from her somewhat limited experience, based upon a family holiday spent in the Cotswolds, she could say she had found them very pleasing and was looking forward to her first sight of the Mendip Hills and Glastonbury Tor.

"Ah, Glastonbury Tor," said Mr Perceval, and she feared he was about to launch into another instructive discourse on the subject, when she was spared by Mrs Perceval drawing her husband's attention to some particular site they were passing, causing him to return to the other side of the vehicle. Marianne continued looking out and absorbing the beauty of the woods, where the leaves were just turning to russet and gold, as she sank once more into silent contemplation.

Upon reaching their destination, a small hostelry outside Glastonbury, they alighted and found the rest of the party, the young Percevals and their friends, who'd arrived ahead of them, gathered within. On seeing their parents, the Perceval girls claimed they were all quite famished and wanted only to unpack their picnic baskets and eat! Astonished that having had a large breakfast but a few hours ago, they could be so hungry, Marianne wondered aloud whether they could not take a little walk in the direction of Glastonbury first, only to be met with cries of alarm from the Perceval girls. "Oh no, that would be impossible… I simply could not walk all that way and back without some food—I shall faint for certain…" causing Mrs Perceval to declare with a sigh that, "Young people have such hearty appetites—they are never satisfied," and since Mr Perceval had already settled into a chair with a jug of ale, it looked as though the last word had been said on the matter. The appearance of the Hawthorne sisters, Harriet and Hannah, proclaiming that they had "found just the most perfect place for our picnic," set the seal upon it.

Resigned to the fact that everyone apart from herself seemed keener on satisfying their appetites than getting a glimpse of Glastonbury, Marianne said no more and went out to assist the girls, who were already ordering the manservant to unpack their things and carry the hampers to the picnic spot. She could not deny that Harriet and Hannah had indeed found a near perfect place, in a small grove of trees, beside a clear running stream. In such agreeable surroundings, with ample food and drink, the party required little more to satisfy them, and consequently, there was hardly any conversation for the next hour or so, during which time large quantities of food and drink were consumed. Amazed at the quantity and variety of food being eaten, Marianne was not surprised to note that Mr Perceval and Miss Peabody were already surrendering to the soporific ambience of the afternoon, and Mrs Perceval looked so comfortably settled, she was unlikely to be easily persuaded to leave her seat. The young Hawthornes and Percevals were themselves so occupied with entertaining each other that it looked as though they were in no mood to move.

Bored and determined not to lose the opportunity to see something of the site for which she had prepared herself with so much anticipation, Marianne rose and, leaving her companions in various states of relaxation, took the path that led up a small hill behind the inn, from where, the innkeeper had advised them, "one could get a very good view of Glastonbury Tor."

She didn't know what to expect, but when she first saw the dramatic dark mount, with its tower rising like a stark sentinel above the fabled Avalon marshes and heath lands, all bathed in the red-gold afternoon light, Marianne gasped. It was a breathtaking sight, atmospheric and magical, like nothing she had seen before, and all the tales of ancient times with kings and knights and deeds of derring-do came flooding back. As she stood there, trying to absorb its impact, she heard a voice behind her say, "If you climb the Tor and stand on its summit, you can overlook three counties," and Marianne froze, unable to move, because she knew that voice, she knew it well; it was, it had to be, the voice of Mr Willoughby.

Often, in times past, she had wondered if she would ever see him again and, if she did, how she would cope with the situation. She had toyed with the notion that it would be easy, now she was married and quite out of his reach, to greet him with cold courtesy. She had believed that a mere formal bow would suffice to indicate politely but firmly that he meant nothing to her, that he was no more than a stranger. However, at this moment, not knowing if he was even aware who she was, for she had her back to him and wore a cloak and bonnet that almost completely hid her person, Marianne was unable even to turn and face the man who had addressed her. Indeed, she could not be certain that it was to her he had spoken, for, she thought, there may well have been some other person with him.

As myriad thoughts reeled through her mind, she stood still, until he, taking a few more steps, reached her side and said, "It is not as difficult a climb as it might seem from here—even for a lady; it is steep, but well worth the effort," thus making it plain that his words had indeed been directed at her.

Marianne could no longer avoid it; she turned and looked up into his face, and the consternation reflected upon it told her that he had not known it was she. Indeed, she, in recognising his voice, had been momentarily advantaged and better prepared for this encounter, while he was clearly deeply shaken. When he could speak, which was in a few seconds, though it seemed an eternity, he said, "Marianne—I beg your pardon, Mrs Brandon—I had no idea it was you. There is a party here from Somerton, who are visiting Glastonbury... I met them briefly at the inn and seeing you from behind, standing there, I assumed it was one of the ladies... else I should never have taken the liberty... please forgive me..." at which point words seemed to fail him, and as he stopped, she said in a voice that she struggled to keep from trembling, "Mr Willoughby, there is no need to apologise; I can see you were mistaken." And in a gesture that at once astonished and delighted him, she held out her hand, which he grasped and held for a moment before raising it to his lips.

Marianne withdrew her hand swiftly and tucked it inside the deep pockets of her cloak before saying, "I too am with a party of friends who mean to visit Glastonbury this afternoon. I left them in the woods below the inn and made my way here to get a glimpse of the view—the landlord recommended it; but it is time I returned, or they may begin to worry that I have got myself lost."

At this, with the smooth gallantry she remembered so well, he warned her of the danger of sliding and falling on the rough footpath as they descended the hill, which remark immediately recalled to her mind the very first time they had met at Barton Park, and a blush rose in her cheeks. He offered her his arm, which she may well have found quite helpful, yet Marianne, realising that she must not be seen with him by the Percevals and their friends, who would proceed to ask a thousand questions, politely declined his assistance, claimed she was able to manage the descent on her own, and preceded him downhill.

She found the rest of the party making preparations to return to their carriages. "Ah, there you are, Mrs Brandon, we were beginning to wonder if we should send out a search party to find you," said Mr Perceval, and his wife demanded to know where she had been. Marianne obliged quickly, seeing it was easier to answer the question, else it would be asked again and again, relentlessly. "I wasn't far away; I walked up the hill behind the inn and took a look at Glastonbury Tor in the distance—it is a most impressive sight, indeed," she said.

By this time the younger members of the party had all climbed into the brougham and were about to drive out of the yard, which brought the conversation to an end, as Mr Perceval urged his wife and her cousin Miss Peabody to hasten, if they were to have any chance of seeing Glastonbury before sundown. When they were all seated and the carriage was moving out, Marianne turned and looked toward the inn, and there she saw Willoughby standing at one of the windows, a glass in his hand, watching them; as she caught his eye, he lifted a hand in a casual gesture, looking for all the world like an indifferent acquaintance waving them farewell. His insouciance startled her; yet knowing him, she should not have been, for it was exactly what she could have expected him to do.

As they travelled toward Glastonbury, Marianne's thoughts were filled with the afternoon's encounter and the image of the man who had filled her life, to the exclusion of all else, but a few years ago. She was surprised at how little he had changed in appearance; he looked perhaps a very little older but not, she decided, in any way coarser in his features or less graceful in his figure, and his confident air and gallant manner were as they had ever been. The contemplation of these matters gave her an unexpected degree of pleasure, making it difficult for her to drag her mind away when they arrived at their destination.

Marianne had looked forward to Glastonbury with such avid interest, and yet, suddenly, she felt drained of energy and enthusiasm as they alighted from their vehicles. She decided it was because her present companions were so dull in their responses to what lay before them—the timeless site, its mysterious ruins inspiring a string of myths and legends reaching back into the earliest period of Christianity in Britain. It had been one of the most significant centres of religious practice and pilgrimage since the tenth century, during the time of the great Abbot of Glastonbury—later Saint Dunstan. As Marianne stood before the massive piles of stone, sunk in the soil of an ancient land over which the setting sun cast huge purple shadows, she was conscious of being in a sacred place, which was deeply moving to her romantic soul.

Meanwhile, the Misses Perceval tramped about the place with very little comprehension of where they were or what significance might be ascribed to each ancient ruin, and Marianne, who had hoped to give them the benefit of her research into the site, felt a sudden sense of lassitude at the thought of trying to convince them of its antiquity and historical significance. Consequently, she moved from one monumental pile to the next, studying them intently, recalling all the things she had read but making no effort to share her feelings with the young men and ladies, who appeared to be far more interested in teasing each other with secrets and jokes and references to Lancelot and Guinevere.

As the sunlight faded and a cool breeze invaded the ancient site, Mrs Perceval, tiring from her exertions, retired to their carriage, while the younger members of the party flitted around like late butterflies—to no particular purpose, except to exclaim from time to time, "Oh do come and look at this," each time their eyes fell upon some carving or inscription. However, when the others gathered round, there was not much more said, except to ooh and aah and speculate at how very old it must be. Marianne found it all very unedifying. She was almost relieved when it was decided that it was time to get back in their vehicles and make for the inn. Miss Peabody agreed at once, claiming she was simply dying for a cup of tea.

Their carriage reached the inn first and the ladies—Mrs Perceval, Miss Peabody, and Marianne—went upstairs to refresh themselves, while awaiting the brougham bearing the rest of their party. They were surprised, on coming down to tea half an hour later, to find no sign of the others. Mr Perceval, who had been taking some liquid refreshment in the bar, came out to greet the ladies, and when it was pointed out to him that the vehicle bearing the younger members of their party had not arrived, he seemed puzzled and quite unable to comprehend what might have happened or, indeed, what needed to be done.

While Mr and Mrs Perceval were standing in the hall, the latter looking rather troubled, Marianne and Miss Peabody had seated themselves in the parlour from where they could see and hear what was going on. Miss Peabody poured out the tea, claiming she was very tired and would like nothing better than a bit of dinner and a good night's sleep. Marianne was about to agree, when suddenly, another voice was heard in the hall, addressing Mr Perceval. "I could not help overhearing your conversation, sir," it said. "The rest of your party may have been delayed by some minor mishap—a lame horse or a broken axle, perhaps. It may not be safe for the young people to be stranded out there after dark. May I suggest that I ride out along the road to Glastonbury, taking your manservant with me, and if there has been a problem, we could take your carriage and bring the stranded travellers back with us?" Marianne knew at once it was Willoughby, but said nothing to Miss Peabody, who was eager to listen and discover what was afoot.

Both Mr and Mrs Perceval responded with great appreciation to Willoughby's offer of assistance, and Marianne heard him say, with all of his usual charm, that he would not consider it any trouble at all—he understood their concern and it was indeed a pleasure to be of assistance. As he went out into the yard with Mr Perceval to find Wilson, the manservant, Mrs Perceval entered the parlour, declaring that there was a very fine gentleman indeed and were they not truly fortunate he was at hand to offer his help? Marianne and Miss Peabody nodded, and the latter poured out more tea for herself and Mrs Perceval.

Shortly afterwards, Willoughby and the Percevals' servant were heard riding out to search for the brougham on the road to Glastonbury, and Mr Perceval entered the parlour with more praise for the exceedingly helpful Mr Willoughby, whom he had fortuitously met in the bar of the inn that very evening, he said.

"I must say that Mr Willoughby is such a decent young fellow; upon my word, am I glad that I responded kindly to him this evening when he came over and introduced himself. I don't stand much on ceremony, you see; he seemed a good sort of fellow, and when he said he had a place here in Somerset, I knew he was a gentleman and acknowledged him, which was a jolly good thing because as you see, he's offered to go out on the road and look for the brougham, which is more than I could have done. It's jolly decent of him, I must say. He's taken Wilson with him, and I daresay they'll find them stranded somewhere—Willoughby thinks it must be a lame horse..." He rattled on even though no one was listening, while Mrs Perceval seated herself next to Miss Peabody on the sofa and sipped her tea.

It was clear she was still anxious about the girls. "I do hope Mr Perceval is right and they are all safe. I am terrified of accidents, and I do not know what I shall say to the Hawthornes if anything has happened to their girls," she said over and over again, until Marianne began to wish she had never come on this expedition.

Chapter Eight

A S THE SKY DARKENED outside and the candles were lit in the inn, it was decided that they would take some dinner while waiting for news. The host was setting a table for them, when there came the sound of horses' hooves in the yard, followed by boots in the hall, and Mr Willoughby strode in.

"They are safe," he announced brightly, bringing a great cheer from Mr Perceval and a cry of relief from his lady. "We found them stranded not two miles up the road. It is as I thought, a horse has thrown a shoe and pulled the vehicle into the ditch, which has damaged a wheel—but there's no injury to any of the passengers, except, with the wind coming off the marshes, they were beginning to feel the cold. Naturally the young gentlemen were reluctant to leave the ladies alone and go for help—no doubt they expected someone would come looking for them."

"No doubt, no doubt," echoed Mr Perceval, "and I thank you, Mr Willoughby, for your kindness in offering to look for them. But how shall we arrange to transport them? We are too large a party to pack into my carriage together…" Once again Mr Perceval, for all his boast of travelling in the Grampians, appeared not to have any practical common sense, and again, it was Willoughby who said, in a quiet but decisive voice, "If you will allow me, sir, to make a suggestion that may resolve your problem, I have taken the liberty of asking your man to take your carriage to collect the young ladies and gentlemen and convey them hither. In view of their state of discomfort, I thought it was best to have that done without delay," with which Mr Perceval agreed directly.

Willoughby continued, "When they arrive, may I suggest that you and Mrs Perceval should join the four young ladies and return to your home, while the two young gentlemen remain here with the rest of your party," he said, bowing in the direction of Marianne and Miss Peabody, as though he had never met them before and had no idea who they were. Whereupon Mr Perceval proceeded to introduce the two ladies, and Mr Willoughby bowed deeply again to each of them. Continuing to explain his plan, he added, "My own place is but a few miles from here—I shall ride there directly and return with my carriage, in which I am sure we can arrange to convey them safely to your home." He sounded so confident, the Percevals, clearly delighted that he had taken the problem out of their hands, were effusively grateful. Mrs Perceval began to say, "But, Mr Willoughby, we cannot possibly put you to so much trouble. It will be dark and riding around these country roads could be quite hazardous…" but he interrupted her protestations with a wave of the hand. "Mrs Perceval, as I have said before to Mr Perceval, it is no trouble to me, and I am perfectly familiar with the roads in Somersetshire, I assure you."

Then, looking at them directly, he added, "There is no other way, unless the ladies choose to stay overnight here, which, while it may be quite safe, is unlikely to be very comfortable. It is only a small establishment, and I am not certain the facilities and services will be to your satisfaction. However, if that is your preference, I will ask the landlord if he has a room for the two ladies." Then, seeing the look of consternation on the faces of Mrs Brandon and Miss Peabody, who were both thoroughly disconcerted at the prospect of having to stay overnight at the inn, without the help of a ladies' maid and no nightclothes to change into, Willoughby smiled and said, "I think, sir, the ladies have made their wishes clear; I have no doubt that after a long day out of doors, they would appreciate a good night's sleep in their own beds." At which both women nodded vigorously, and Mrs Perceval added that it certainly would not be seemly to leave the two ladies alone at the inn overnight.

Listening to Willoughby, Marianne, who had remained silent throughout this discourse, was amazed at the ease with which he had promoted himself to everyone as their saviour—the man with the best solution to their problem, the good Samaritan who would extricate them from the predicament in which they had found themselves. Indeed, she decided, he had not changed at all. Not long afterward, he took his leave of them and left the inn, and they heard him ride out of the yard.

Marianne was tired and hungry but could not eat as they waited for the carriage to return with the young Percevals and Hawthornes. She had no fears for them; Willoughby had assured them they were safe. Rather, she was contemplating what was to follow—the prospect of being conveyed in Mr Willoughby's carriage with only Miss Peabody for company. As he had outlined his plan, she had listened passively, unable and unwilling to make any comment, so as not to arouse any suspicion that they had once known one another intimately. It was best, she thought, to say nothing and accept his help as the Percevals clearly wanted to do, because for her, there was no alternative.

Sometime later, the Percevals' carriage arrived and the six young people tumbled out, looking somewhat the worse for wear; the girls complaining of cold and demanding hot food, the young men cursing the lame horse, while making directly for the bar. Mr and Mrs Perceval, though keen to get away, had to ensure they were all satisfied before they piled into the carriage and left. Messrs Andrew and Joseph Hawthorne, determined not to be left behind, had persuaded their tired hosts to leave Wilson, the Percevals' manservant, to watch over Miss Peabody and Mrs Brandon while they awaited the return of Mr Willoughby, thereby providing Marianne with a clear contrast between their selfishness and Willoughby's concern for their comfort and his keenness to help.

They did not have very long to wait after the Percevals had left. Willoughby was as good as his word and arrived within the hour with a very comfortable, enclosed carriage drawn by two handsome horses, complete with a driver and an outrider. He apologised if he had kept the ladies waiting, seemed a little surprised that the rest of the party had all managed to accommodate themselves in the Percevals' carriage, invited Wilson to climb onto the box beside the driver, and helped Miss Peabody and Mrs Brandon into his vehicle with care, ensuring they were provided with rugs to keep them warm on the journey, before entering it and seating himself opposite Marianne. He did it all with such élan, Marianne thought, it was as if he spent every day of the week rescuing stranded travellers and returning them safely to their homes.

And all the while, she was struck by the fact that he had assiduously avoided revealing any previous connection between them, treating her with the same effortless but formal courtesy he extended to all the others. Only in the very first moment of recognition, when they had confronted each other as they stood looking out across at Glastonbury Tor, had he been clearly shaken; however, it appeared he had recovered quickly from the shock and was as determined as she was to maintain a perfectly plausible demeanour for the benefit of the rest of the party. For this she was particularly grateful.

As the carriage rolled out of the yard and onto the road, she hoped it would continue thus, so that she might consider this chance encounter a providential opportunity that had proved to both of them that they were now able to regard their past association with a degree of equanimity; certainly in her case, without bitterness or pain.

Some part of their journey had passed when Marianne noticed that Miss Peabody had fallen asleep and her head was lolling heavily to one side. She tried to use a cushion to prop her up, but Willoughby, seeing the problem, rose and, taking out a rolled-up rug from under the seat, arranged it so as to provide Miss Peabody with some support. Marianne thanked him and he said he was sure they were both very tired—it must have been a long day. He hoped, however, that it had been an enjoyable experience, he said. Marianne admitted that it certainly was that, but added that she was sorry they had not made better use of the day.

"I had hoped we would have more time at Glastonbury, rather than spend most of it at the inn and the picnic; I was keen to see more of the ruins and learn some more of the history of the place. I had read a good deal about it, but I fear my companions were not sufficiently interested…" she broke off, conscious suddenly of his keen attention and fearing she had said too much. But Willoughby was the soul of tact and discretion; maintaining the pretence that he had throughout the evening, he asked, as though she were a complete stranger, "Have you never visited Glastonbury before?" And when she answered, "No, nor am I familiar with Somersetshire," he responded with a level of natural politeness that she could not fault, "And yet you live just across the border in Dorset. Mrs Brandon, I am sorry to hear that. There are many beautiful places and much to admire and love in Somerset. I hope you will find time to visit again, and you must certainly see more of Glastonbury, which is a place of special significance. For my part, I spent much of my childhood here and know it well. To my way of thinking it is one of the finest counties in England; there is so much history here—sites that go back to Roman times, and a wealth of Saxon history, dating back to the seventh century—so many great abbeys and churches, I cannot begin to tell you. Mrs Brandon, if you have an interest in the history of England, then Somerset has much that will interest you," he said.

Marianne nodded and confessed that while she did not have a great knowledge of it, she was keenly interested in history. He needed very little encouragement then to relate several tales of Somerset and the history of the West Country, which he said he had known from childhood, and as she listened, she recalled again their first meeting in Devonshire all those years ago, and how easily they had been able to slip into conversation on their favourite topics. She wondered if he remembered too and was sure he did—but she was afraid to say anything that might make it seem as though she was trying to remind him of those days. Which was why she remained mostly silent, as Willoughby spoke with rising enthusiasm of the attractions of his county, quoting writers and poets and leaving her in no doubt that he remembered well her enthusiasms. Quite clearly, while he was maintaining the pretence of having met her that afternoon, his memory of her was very clear. Yet determined not to be the first to breach the unspoken bar, partly because she had no idea how she would deal with the consequences, Marianne let him continue as though they were strangers, indifferent acquaintances, thrown together by chance.

Their journey ended when the carriage reached the lane into which they drove and the manservant Wilson was heard directing the driver to the Percevals' house. When the vehicle stopped, Wilson leapt down from the box to open the door, and Willoughby helped the ladies out and escorted them to the entrance, where a sleepy maid opened the front door and waited to assist them. Clearly the rest of the party had long gone to bed.

Miss Peabody, roused from sleep and obviously waiting only to fall asleep again as soon as possible, thanked Mr Willoughby rather perfunctorily and left it to Marianne to convey more fully their appreciation for all he had done to assist their party that day. She could not say it without a degree of heartfelt gratitude, which, for her personally, included his particular care not to embarrass her in any way at all. "I thank you very much, Mr Willoughby, for your very kind assistance to our party; I cannot think how we should have found our way home without your help. I am sure I speak for all of the party," she said, and as she extended her hand, he took it and, raising it to his lips, replied, "It was entirely my pleasure, Mrs Brandon," before wishing her good night as he left to return to his carriage. She stood at the door and heard him exchange some words with Wilson regarding the stranded carriage and horses, before driving off into the night.

As Marianne followed the maid up to her room, many thoughts assailed her. It had been a day like no other in her experience; not only had she been shocked to hear Willoughby's voice addressing her and turned to see him regarding her with an even greater degree of surprise than she had felt, but then, what had been a chance encounter had developed into a series of incidents and meetings that had opened up a veritable Pandora's box of memories, which she had hoped had long been set aside.

At each point in the evening, she had feared that something she said or he did might shatter the fragile pretence they had both maintained, without ever saying a word; but nothing untoward had occurred, and for this she was exceedingly grateful to him. She could not decide whether it was kindness, simple courtesy, or his own convenience that had caused him to spare her any embarrassment, and expected that she would lie awake through the night, puzzling over it. But, contrary to her expectations, once she had changed into her nightclothes and crept between the sheets, sheer weariness overwhelmed her and she fell fast asleep.

❦

Marianne awoke the following morning surprised that she had slept so soundly. It was Sunday, and when the maid brought in her tea, she asked the time and was amazed at the lateness of the hour. The girl assured her that no one had risen early that day, except Miss Peabody, who had gone to church.

Feeling a little reassured by this information, Marianne dressed and went down to breakfast, to find only Mr and Mrs Perceval at the table. They greeted her, asked if she had slept well, and proceeded with their breakfast. It was past ten o'clock when the Misses Hawthorne appeared and word was sent to the kitchen for more tea and fresh toast. The Percevals' daughters were as yet asleep when a vehicle drew up at the gate and voices were heard outside. A maid opened the door to admit Miss Peabody, who entered the breakfast room and informed Mr and Mrs Perceval that Mr Willoughby was waiting in the parlour. He had passed her as she walked back from church, she said, and had stopped to give her a ride home. He was waiting to speak with Mr Perceval, she said as she sat down to breakfast, still singing the praises of Mr Willoughby and his great goodness.

"He is a most courteous and charitable gentleman; he has had the two horses stabled at his place and awaits your instructions regarding the repairs to the carriage," she added, pouring out her tea. Mrs Perceval exclaimed at the gentleman's kindness, and her husband was no less astonished. "My very word, that is jolly decent of him, to have gone to all that trouble," he said as he left the table and hurried into the parlour to greet his visitor.

Marianne could hear him as he proceeded to thank Willoughby, and then there was Willoughby's response in that unmistakable voice—soft-spoken, without fuss, claiming that he had only done what any good neighbour would have done—he could not have left the poor horses stranded without feed or water, so he'd sent a farrier and one of his grooms to look to their needs. There were further discussions about the repairs to the Percevals' vehicle, and not long afterward, they heard the front door close and Mr Perceval re-entered the break-fast room to announce that Mr Willoughby would be back in about an hour to drive Mrs Brandon and the Misses Hawthorne to their respective homes, which Mr Perceval considered a huge favour, since their own carriage was unavailable.

"It is very good of him to offer, and I hope it will suit you, Mrs Brandon—I know you wish to be back at Delaford this afternoon. As for Miss Harriet and Miss Hannah, I know your mama will not mind, because Mrs Brandon will be there with you, and of course your brothers can ride with you as you go. I realise that Mr Willoughby is not known to your family, but I am sure there can be no objection—he seems a jolly decent fellow. I cannot begin to thank him for all he has done, I cannot imagine how we should have got on without his help," he said, and sat down to have more breakfast.

The Misses Hawthorne made no objection to the arrangement, and Marianne could hardly have protested, so she said nothing at all, although she was more than a little shaken at the thought that once the Hawthornes had been conveyed to their home—a few streets away—Willoughby would be driving her all the way to Delaford. For the first time, they would be alone together, and she could not deny some feelings of unease.

Chapter Nine

MEANWHILE, AT THE PARSONAGE in Delaford, Elinor had awakened to a Sunday morning like no other. Edward was away, and the curate from another parish would be arriving to conduct the morning service at ten. It would be a grave discourtesy if she did not attend and invite him to morning tea afterward. Yet, it was one day when presenting herself at church was not her priority; rather, she was keen to discover if Marianne was back at the manor house after her expedition to Glastonbury. Going into Margaret's room, she found her awake, sitting up in bed, taking tea. When Elinor explained her problem, Margaret declared that she had no particular desire to go to church and could quite easily walk over to the manor house and inquire if their sister was at home.

"Would you? Oh Margaret, what would I do without you?" cried Elinor, and Margaret felt deeply sorry to see how disturbed her sister was about Marianne.

"Elinor, of course I shall; but you must not take this so much to heart, you cannot worry about everything Marianne does or does not do, you will make yourself ill. Let me discover if she is home, and if she is, I'll persuade her to come back with me to the parsonage and tell us all about the Percevals and the trip to Glastonbury. Wouldn't you like that?" asked Margaret.

"Indeed I would; that would mean Marianne is quite safe—at least as far as we can tell. It will be such a relief to know that nothing untoward has occurred.

I know I ought not to worry but, Margaret, I cannot trust Willoughby and, sadly, I have not sufficient confidence in our sister to believe that she will resist him. With Colonel Brandon away for some weeks in Ireland, I cannot help but fear for her."

Margaret, realising that the best thing she could do for her sister was to ascertain if Marianne was safely back from Glastonbury, went down to breakfast, and, having seen Elinor leave to attend church, set off to walk across the woodland to Delaford Manor. It was an unusually still morning, with soft swirls of mist drifting gently through the trees, and as she walked, Margaret could not resist the feeling of nostalgia for her childhood, when she, as the youngest in the family, had been allowed a good deal of freedom in organising her life. She'd had very little supervision and even less responsibility as their mother, concerned with their father's health and, later, the well-being of her two elder daughters, had largely left Margaret to her own devices, which meant she had spent many hours wandering through the meadows and woods of the Norland Estate.

And it had done her no harm at all, she thought, as she crossed the lane that ran along the boundary of the manor and entered the garden, where a large lilac tree was just coming into bloom. The lilac reminded her of the cottage in Oxfordshire and the need to go down to the post office in the village and send a message to her friend Claire, advising that her return would be delayed.

As she walked up the drive, a young man on horseback rode past her and delivered a message to the maid who opened the door. By the time Margaret reached the entrance, the maid, Molly, had seen her and was waiting at the door for her. When she asked, "Is Mrs Brandon home from Somerset?" the girl replied, "No, ma'am, and the man who brought this said Mrs Brandon had been delayed on account of an accident to the vehicle in which they were travelling. I hope it is not bad news, ma'am," the girl cried, clearly concerned for her mistress.

Margaret snatched the note from the maid. Seeing it was not addressed to anyone in particular—just directed to Delaford Manor—and since Colonel Brandon was away, Margaret assumed it would not signify if she opened it. As she tore it open, she saw written in a bold hand the information that Mr Perceval regretted to advise that Mrs Brandon's return to Delaford would be delayed until later that afternoon, because a minor accident had damaged his carriage. It continued:

Be assured however, that arrangements have been made for all our guests to be conveyed safely to their homes later today, through the kind offices of a very generous neighbour—Mr Willoughby of Somersetshire.

Margaret stood in the hall, stunned, until Molly asked, "Is the mistress all right, ma'am? Does it say when she will be back?" Conscious of the need to reassure the girl, who would undoubtedly convey the information to the rest of the staff at the manor house, Margaret hastily said, "Oh yes, Molly, it seems the Percevals' carriage has been damaged in an accident and they have arranged to have their guests, including Mrs Brandon, conveyed to their homes by a neighbour. She should be here this afternoon. I shall return to the parsonage now and give the news to Mrs Ferrars; but, Molly, when my sister does return, would you please make sure that she sends a message over to the parsonage to let us know she is home safe and well? Mrs Ferrars will be waiting anxiously for the news."

Having received assurances from the maid, Margaret tucked Mr Perceval's note into her pocket and set off for the village, where she sent an express off to her friend Claire Jones advising that she would be returning on the Tuesday morning coach from Dorchester. It was quite clear to Margaret that Elinor would need company at least until she was sure all was well with their sister; she was likely to be even more apprehensive, now that it had been revealed, contrary to their expectations, that Mr Willoughby may have been one of the party that went to Glastonbury. Either that or he was a friend of the Percevals, who had been called upon to assist them with transporting their guests. What Elinor would make of it Margaret was uncertain; whatever it was, she was sure her sister would have even less peace of mind than before.

Returning to the parsonage, she found Elinor in the parlour, entertaining the curate to tea. He was a thin, febrile-looking young man with a strangely deep voice and a great fondness for Elinor's fruit cake. Margaret was impatient for him to be gone. When at last he departed, having delayed his exit as long as possible while he thanked Mrs Ferrars for her kind hospitality, Margaret rushed downstairs and indicated to her sister that she had important news.

Elinor was calm, cheerful even, as she gathered the tea things onto the tray and carried them into the kitchen. "Was Marianne home? Did you see her?" she asked, and when Margaret shook her head and indicated by rolling her eyes that she thought they ought be going outdoors for a talk, Elinor's expression changed.

"Why, Margaret, what has happened?" she asked, and as they went out and walked in the direction of the shrubbery, Margaret handed her the note and said, "That note from Mr Perceval was delivered just as I arrived at the front door of the manor house—you can read what it says."

Elinor gasped as she read it and clutched at her sister's arm. "Oh Margaret, this is dreadful news—it is surely the very worst thing—the Percevals clearly know nothing of their previous association and have calmly delivered Marianne into Willoughby's care! I cannot think of anything worse! Whatever is to be done now?" she cried, and there were tears welling in her eyes. It was clear that Elinor now thought the very worst had happened, and unless Margaret could convince her otherwise, she would surely feel the need to race off to the manor house to ascertain if Marianne was safe. Margaret did not believe that any good would come of such action and set out to advise her sister that it would be best to await some message from Marianne.

"I did ask, very particularly, that a message should be sent to you as soon as Marianne arrived, so that we may know she was safely home. I think we should wait at least until some news is received. It is entirely possible that all will be well and Mr Willoughby will simply convey her to Delaford Manor and that will be an end of it," she said, but even before she had finished speaking, she could see that Elinor was unconvinced. Her countenance made it clear before she spoke, "You cannot possibly know that, Margaret, not if you know what Willoughby is, not after you have heard him speak and understood the depth of his perceived grievances. Not only does he claim that Marianne is the great love of his life, whose loss means he will never know happiness again, he also carries a grudge—a most terrible hatred against Colonel Brandon, whom he blames for all his misery, which gives him two reasons for wanting to use such an unexpected opportunity. And though he did appear to accept that he had done great wrong by deceiving Marianne, he is also completely selfish and I cannot believe that he will let such a chance slip."

Though Margaret had not known it at the time, she had learned from both her mother and Elinor of Willoughby's visit to Cleveland House. Despite her strong condemnation of his actions, Elinor had shown a degree of compassion that had surprised Margaret at the time, but with the passage of years following the marriages of Elinor and Marianne, she had moved out of the intimate circle of their family in Dorset, and Margaret had lost interest in Willoughby's brief but intense affair with her sister. Elinor's remarks raked up the memory, but she could not feel as perturbed as her sister, who doubtless still carried some weight of responsibility for Marianne. Still, Margaret begged Elinor not to allow her concern for their sister to besiege her mind to the extent that it would make her ill with worry.

"I understand your concern, Elinor, but surely it is unlikely that in the course of one such encounter—a journey of perhaps an hour or two at the most—he could cause Marianne to subvert..." she began cautiously, but Elinor did not let her finish.

"Do not forget that in the course of a few minutes, when he rescued her after her fall and carried her home to the cottage in the rain, she had been completely captivated, to the extent that Willoughby became the epitome of what she expected of a man. I know that she is several years older and she is a married woman now, but our sister has not quite given up on those romantic notions yet, nor has she attained a level of maturity that would let her turn her back on them," she said. Elinor's distress seemed intractable; Margaret had almost given up on persuading her to adopt a less woeful outlook, when the doorbell rang and the maid opened it and found outside a servant from the manor house. He had, he told the girl, a message from Mrs Brandon for her sister Mrs Ferrars. Hearing his words, Margaret and Elinor rushed to the door. He was to say, he said, that Mrs Brandon was back safe and well from Somerset. She was, however, very tired from her journey and had gone directly to bed. Elinor and Margaret looked at one another, thanked the servant, and instructed him to tell Mrs Brandon that her sisters would call on her tomorrow. They then returned to the parlour, embraced, and wept with relief.

When Edward Ferrars returned home a few hours later, he found his wife and sister-in-law enjoying tea and toasted muffins with the two boys in the parlour and eager to hear all his news. Elinor had already decided that she would not involve her husband in what might or might not be a problem with Marianne and Willoughby. In any event, she had argued, they could not know whether there was a problem until they had seen Marianne on the following day. Margaret had agreed that 'twere best not to worry Edward with any of it. She knew that her brother-in-law, busy with matters of the parish and his own family, would probably find it an imposition to be burdened with such a question at this time, particularly since they could provide very little evidence of a problem. Like most men, she thought, Edward would attribute it to their excessive anxiety about Marianne.

At dinner that night, therefore, their conversation was almost entirely about the successful meetings of the anti-slavery campaign that Edward had attended together with Dr Bradley King. He was quite elated with the success of their lobbying, which had elicited interest at a high political level in the Parliament, and was genuinely hopeful that Mr Wilberforce would win the day and get a bill passed, banning slavery in Britain and her colonies.

"If we could only get as many people interested in our campaign as Shelley and Byron are attracting to the cause of the Greeks, we could do a great deal better," he said, but added quickly, "but I am very hopeful, if only because Wilberforce is such a persuasive speaker and his sincere belief in the cause is so clear. He cannot fail."

"There is a great deal of conversation about it, but do you really believe that Parliament will pass a law to stop the loathsome traffic?" Margaret asked. She had heard much talk on the subject in Oxfordshire, but was far less confident that action would follow. "I understand that many wealthy British business enterprises are profiting from the use of slaves in the Caribbean colonies, and they are none too keen to stop the practice."

Edward agreed, "Indeed, you are right, Margaret, there is a strong lobby of businessmen in the colonies and here in Britain, too, whose enterprises do well out of slave labour in the cotton fields and fruit orchards of America and the Caribbean islands, but I am assured the tide is turning. Many more people are speaking out against it, and we have at last got the churches involved," he said hopefully.

"And so they should be," said Elinor, who had not entered the conversation earlier and appeared rather lost in thought. Margaret was certain her sister was still troubled about Marianne—despite her assurances that she was not.

Later that night, as she packed her trunk in preparation for her departure on Tuesday, there was a soft knock on her door and Elinor entered. "Edward has gone to bed; he is very tired after the journey from Bridgwater, and he has to be awake early for matins tomorrow," she whispered as she came to sit on Margaret's bed. "I am so grateful that you stayed, Margaret; I hope when we see Marianne tomorrow, everything will become clearer. It will be obvious if she is out of sorts and upset—I do hope she is not—and perhaps she will tell us about the meeting with Willoughby and we can judge from her demeanour if she has been affected by it or not."

"Do you expect that she will tell us?" Margaret asked, not entirely confident that their sister would reveal that Willoughby had been one of the party. But Elinor had no doubts at all. "Indeed, I do believe she will. It would surely be a way of asserting her complete indifference to him and demonstrating to all of us that he means no more to her than a casual acquaintance, whom she has met again by mere chance. Do you not think she will?" Margaret was silent for a while before she answered the question, "I hope she will; as you say, it will demonstrate clearly that he means nothing to her and that means you need no longer fear for her as you do."

"But you are not convinced that she will?" Elinor's anxiety was obvious. Margaret was loath to add to her sister's pain, but she had to speak the truth. "Sadly I am not, Elinor. I should like to think that Marianne will tell us about her meeting with Willoughby and how he came to convey her and the other guests to their homes, and perhaps she will tell us what they spoke of on the journey, since it is unlikely that they travelled in complete silence. But I am not at all certain she will," she said and was saddened to see the look on Elinor's face as she spoke.

"If that is the case, it can only mean that she is unwilling to talk about him to us because she is either uneasy or still feels some affection for him, and we will not be able to mention him either, for remember, we are not supposed to know about Willoughby's presence at Glastonbury at all."

Margaret nodded. "Indeed, since we cannot admit that we have read Mr Perceval's note, we are not to know the identity of the kind neighbour who conveyed her home to Delaford. I fear, Elinor, we are in a quandary here—mostly of our own making," she said with a wry smile.

Neither had any answer to the problem they faced, and as it was late, they decided to leave the matter until the morrow. "Let us hope things will not be as difficult as we imagine; it is quite possible that Marianne will be open and cheerful and tell us all about it in such an offhand manner as to reassure us of her complete indifference to the charms of Mr Willoughby," said Margaret, and though she smiled as she said it, neither she nor Elinor felt at all optimistic as they went to bed that night.

It was around ten o'clock on the following day when Elinor and Margaret arrived at the manor house, expecting to find their sister either still upstairs or having a late breakfast. Instead, they found Marianne dressed and busy with one of the maids, arranging flowers for the main drawing room, which had been opened up and aired as though visitors were expected. She looked remarkably cheerful and greeted them with a degree of warmth that both sisters found quite a contrast to their earlier meetings. Margaret found it particularly interesting following on the rather languid mood in which she had found her on her previous visit. What, she wondered, had brought on this extraordinary breakout of energy and good cheer?

Making a point of declaring their intentions openly, Elinor and Margaret began by revealing that they had arrived on Friday just in time to see her driving away in the Percevals' carriage and to be told by the servant that they were going on an expedition to Glastonbury. When Marianne did not appear at all surprised, Margaret added the information that she had called at the manor house on Sunday morning and been advised that a message had been received about an accident to the Percevals' vehicle, and since she was leaving on the morrow and would be away in France for the next four weeks, she had been anxious to see Marianne and be assured that all was well. "Which is why I made Elinor come with me. I wanted to be certain you were safe and well, and I see that is exactly how you are," she concluded.

To which her sister replied, "Indeed I am, and you need not have worried at all, Margaret, the Percevals were very kind and helpful and looked after all their guests, making quite sure we had every comfort."

"And you were returned home safely?" Elinor added in a matter-of-fact sort of voice, trying very hard not to give anything away. "Of course," said Marianne, without missing a beat, as she completed an arrangement of roses, which she then carried to a chiffonier, where she took awhile placing it to advantage so its beauty was reflected in a large ornate mirror that hung opposite. This gave her time to compose her countenance, until she turned and said, "There, I think that's the last of the vases, Molly," and asked the maid to clear away the debris and have a tea tray prepared and brought into the sitting room.

As they followed her to the sitting room, a light, pretty room with sunlight streaming in at the windows, she said, "I do prefer this room for most of the day and the main drawing room after dinner; we hardly use the other rooms, they are far too ornate for my taste. Don't you agree?" and Elinor, who had not given much thought to the interior decor of the manor house, was at a loss for words, but Margaret responded quickly, "Indeed, I agree. I like this room—it is very like our sitting room at Barton Cottage. Did you have it recently redecorated?" To which her sister blushed and replied, "How did you guess? I could not bear the original heavy velvet curtains and gilt accessories, and soon after we were married, Colonel Brandon said I could have it all refurbished to my taste, which is what you see here. It did cost quite a lot, but Colonel Brandon said it was no matter."

The maid brought in the tea tray, and as they partook of tea and cake, Elinor had to ask, "Aren't you going to tell us all about Glastonbury? I have never been."

"Nor have I," added Margaret, and it was as though their words had opened the floodgates of a dam, for Marianne, hardly stopping to take breath, poured out all the information she had ever gathered about the ancient site for the benefit of her sisters. Every detail—from its Saxon origins, its early Christian heritage, to the Arthurian links and the romantic tales of Lancelot and Guinevere—were all retold with an enthusiasm that bewildered them. She revealed that she would have been ready and willing to climb to the summit of the mystical Glastonbury Tor, but the Percevals and their guests, the Hawthorne family, were far keener on their picnic in the woods, and indeed, she let slip that she had been somewhat disappointed at their lack of appreciation of the significance of the historical site. "One could wish for somewhat more imaginative and informed company when visiting such a place; it would make the endeavour more worthwhile, do you not agree?" she asked, and they had to agree. Margaret even added that she was glad that on their visit to Provence, they would have the guidance of an erudite friend who knew the area intimately and would inform them of all the significant facts.

To this Marianne replied that Margaret was fortunate indeed, because she was sure that would vastly improve her enjoyment of the places they visited. "I could have wished for someone similar, who could at least share my interest in the place. But I suppose I must not complain too much—it was kind of the Percevals to invite me. They had very little knowledge of the history of Glastonbury, and now I have been once, I shall certainly look forward to another opportunity to visit the site, seeing it's only in the next county and at such a short distance from here, and the next time I am determined to climb the Tor and enjoy the view, which I understand overlooks three counties, at least," she declared.

"Does it really?" Elinor was intrigued to know who in their party had climbed the mount and seen the view. Marianne hesitated but a moment before she responded, "The innkeeper told us—clearly he is a man from the village and was able to give us a lot of local information. He said climbing the Tor either at dawn or twilight would be the best possible experience—but of course, we were too late for one and could not stay for the other."

By the time they had heard all about Glastonbury, and a great deal more about the Percevals and their friends the Hawthornes, the maid had returned to take away the tea tray and Marianne changed the conversation, asking about Edward's health and Margaret's holiday plans, and it was plain to her sisters that she had no intention of saying anything to them about the chance meeting with Willoughby—or his good neighbourly act of kindness in conveying the stranded members of their party to their homes.

So dismayed was Elinor by this lack of candour, for she had believed quite reasonably that if the meeting had held no particular significance for Marianne, she would have recounted it without reserve, that she felt she could stay no longer, or she would betray her concern. She also wanted time to talk to Margaret before she left the following day. Presently, she rose and warmly thanked Marianne for her hospitality, said she was very glad she'd had an enjoyable excursion even if it had not come up to expectations, and the sisters left.

As they walked back though the woods, at first Elinor was tight-lipped, as though reluctant or unable to bring up the matter that was clearly foremost in both their minds. Then Margaret spoke, saying, "I cannot believe that she would recount all that trivial information about people we do not know at all—after all, who on earth are these Hawthornes?—while saying nothing about Willoughby driving her home!"

Elinor's voice shook and tears filled her eyes. "Margaret, it is exactly as you suspected last night—you did say that you were not confident that Marianne would tell us of her meeting with Willoughby; I know I believed she would, but obviously that was just my naive hope that he no longer meant anything to her. Quite clearly he does."

Margaret turned to her sister. "You cannot believe that, Elinor; why, it may be that Marianne feels a little awkward to mention him. She knows what we think of him; she may not wish to remind us of him; it does not necessarily mean that she cares for him." But Elinor was adamant.

"Why else would she conceal the fact that they met, that he is clearly a friend of the Percevals and conveniently offered to transport their guests—including Marianne—after their carriage was damaged? There is nothing awkward in such an incident—she could have related it quite naturally and shown us how little he mattered to her after several years. It would have set my mind at rest—but her total silence has roused all my fears."

Margaret did try to provide other, probable explanations for Marianne's behaviour, but Elinor had a stronger recollection than Margaret of the period in which Willoughby had first met and courted their sister when their relationship had been cloaked in secrecy, leaving her family in complete ignorance of his intentions and her expectations.

Elinor explained, "You were probably too young to understand at the time, but I did protest often to Mama that Marianne and Willoughby were constantly behaving as though their engagement was a *fait accompli*. But, though they behaved as though that were the case, neither of them said a word, and when he departed suddenly for London and became engaged to Miss Grey with her fifty thousand pounds, none of us had been given any explanation. Everyone else, including Colonel Brandon and Mrs Jennings, knew before we did. Marianne was humiliated and heartbroken, and all because we—Mama and I—had allowed the situation to develop and continue without ever asking a single question, as we were entitled to do."

Margaret, who did recall some of the confusion and despair that had followed the sudden departure of Willoughby that summer, and had learnt more about it later, asked, "And you fear that a similar situation may be developing again? Surely, you cannot believe that Marianne will allow herself to be deceived twice—by the same man?" She was incredulous, but Elinor, who had by then composed herself and dried her tears, said, "That is precisely what I fear, because while Marianne is unlikely to be deceived by some stranger of whom she knows little, she is clearly more vulnerable with Willoughby—only because she believes she knows him well. And she will make allowance for any of his misdemeanours because she sees in him a man after her own heart—well read, passionate, ready to match all her enthusiasms. Oh Margaret, I am so afraid for her, I shall have to go to Barton Park and see Mama and ask her to come back to Delaford."

Margaret was apprehensive. "Do you suppose she will? How will she explain her knowledge of this? Will it not make Marianne very angry were she to discover that you had known of her meeting with Willoughby and had told Mama about it?"

Elinor tried to think fast enough to formulate an answer. "She need not know—Mama can simply return and stay with her until Colonel Brandon returns from Ireland; she can make some excuse, say she is tired with looking after Mrs Jennings and running the household at Barton Park, or that she needs some company herself... no matter, I will think of something."

"Will Mama agree to come?" asked Margaret.

"She must—there is no one else whom Marianne trusts." Elinor was determined. "At least if Mama is staying with her, Willoughby will not be able to call on her with impunity."

Margaret was sceptical. "You cannot believe that he intends to call on her at the manor house?" But Elinor had no doubts. "Why else do you suppose she was up and about filling vases with flowers and opening up the main drawing room—while Colonel Brandon is away? She did not mention that any other visitors were expected, so it can only be that she expects Willoughby to call."

"But would he dare?" asked Margaret, still dubious, to which her sister replied, "Margaret, he is the type of man who would dare anything if he thought it was in his interest. Doubtless he is aware that Colonel Brandon is away in Ireland and he is quite safe to call—if he can find some excuse. If the Percevals are friends of his, he may use them; truly I do not put it past him. As we have seen before, he can be reckless and quite devoid of any decorum, and now, estranged from his wife, he has nothing to lose."

Margaret could see that Elinor was determined to do something about the situation she saw developing around their sister, and it seemed to her that nothing she could say was going to change that. She was leaving the following day and would be away from England for four weeks; it was, she thought, far better that she leave her sister to make her decision and act as she thought fit.

But even as she decided that 'twere best not to press the matter further, she was far from confident that Elinor's plan to involve their mother would succeed.

It was a most unsatisfactory way to leave, and yet there was little Margaret could do to affect the course that either of her sisters would follow in the days and weeks to come.

Chapter Ten

W HEN ELINOR AND MARGARET parted on Tuesday, both
sisters seemed reluctant to speak of Marianne's predicament, since
neither could predict how matters would turn out.

Margaret's mind turned now to the preparations she must make for her
departure for France; her friend Claire had promised to have most of their
arrangements in place, so she had only her personal packing to do. She looked
forward to their journey with the greatest anticipation.

Elinor, on the other hand, faced a far less pleasurable prospect; having
to visit her mother and persuade her of the urgent need to return with her to
Delaford, whilst not revealing all she knew about Marianne's situation, was
daunting indeed. Besides that, what explanation would she give her husband?
Should she tell him about Marianne's excursion to Glastonbury? Would he not
wonder why she had not spoken earlier? Unaccustomed to concealment, yet
uncomfortable with the prospect of detailing the events of the last week to her
husband, lest he should question her involvement, she was at a loss as to what
to do.

The decision to appeal to her mother had been born of a sense of despera-
tion, a feeling that Marianne must not be let down again by those whose duty it
was to protect her. Recollections of what had occurred in the past, the manner
in which Mrs Dashwood had initially argued against the need to question

Marianne and Willoughby about their possible engagement and then dismissed Elinor's fears that there appeared to be no firm intention on his part, returned to haunt her as she considered the implications of Marianne's silence.

That her sister had found it necessary to conceal the fact that Willoughby had been present, that he had been sufficiently confident of acceptance to offer his services to the Percevals to transport their stranded guests, and that Marianne had accepted his help but could not bring herself to reveal this to her sisters, all pointed to a circumstance reminiscent of the days when they had first met Willoughby. He had courted Marianne assiduously, cultivating all her tastes, promoting her enthusiasms, and soliciting the favour of her family, yet he had said not one word to confirm his intentions, leaving Marianne betrayed and humiliated, and her family the object of ridicule and pity.

Determined that it must not happen again, Elinor went to see her friend Mrs King, in whom she confided some of her fears. That Mrs King knew something of Marianne's unhappy affair, which fact Elinor had earlier regarded as an unfortunate consequence of gossip in the village, proved now to be quite providential. It meant that she could account for her concerns to her friend without the need for extensive explanations.

She found Mrs King occupied in her garden, cutting back the last of her summer blooms and bemoaning the fact that her roses had not done as well this season. Delighted to see her friend, she greeted Elinor and invited her indoors to take tea. As Elinor gave a brief account of the situation, Mrs King appeared as deeply concerned as she was. However, being of a particularly practical disposition, Mrs King was inclined to advise some caution.

"Elinor, before you rush to take any action, which may cause your mother considerable anxiety and even lead to a possible rift between you and your sister, let me ask if you are certain that this man, Mr Willoughby, after some seven or eight years, still entertains the same feelings he claimed he had for your sister. I ask only because one needs to remember that after so many years have passed, during which time they have both been married, too, there is the likelihood that there may have been some diminution of his ardour. Can you be sure that he will endeavour to pursue her as he did before?"

Elinor answered her carefully, but with conviction. "Helen, you are quite right to ask, and I agree I must be cautious, but while I cannot say with any certainty that Willoughby's feelings for Marianne are as sincere or as deep as he claimed at the time, I do know that his resentment against Colonel Brandon was great, and those feelings are unlikely to have diminished over the years. They have an earlier history of grievances between them, too, which had nothing to do with my sister. When Marianne accepted Colonel Brandon's offer of marriage, Willoughby was both bitter and furious. He came to see me and made his hatred of Colonel Brandon very plain indeed."

"Do you believe then that quite apart from his feelings for your sister, he may be motivated by a desire for revenge, by trying to take her away from Colonel Brandon?" Mrs King's countenance was very grave and Elinor's answer did nothing to assuage her anxiety.

"I cannot say if he wants to 'take her away' as you suggest, and I do not think even Marianne will be silly enough to countenance anything so foolish, but I do believe Willoughby is both selfish and opportunistic, and if he could engage my sister in what she may deem to be a harmless friendship, but will inevitably be seen as a secret liaison between them, it will ruin her reputation, destroy her marriage, and humiliate Colonel Brandon. I can rate it no higher, but that will certainly be sweet revenge for Willoughby." Try as she might, Elinor could not restrain her tears, and Mrs King decided that the situation was serious enough to warrant firm action.

Consoling her friend, she said, "And do you suppose that your mother, if she comes to Delaford, will be able to prevent this from happening? What does Mr Ferrars say? Does he agree?"

Elinor had then to reveal, with some degree of embarrassment, that she had not told her husband all of the details and he was unaware of her plan to go to Barton Park. "Edward has been very busy with parish work and the petitions concerning the abolition of slavery; I have not had the heart to trouble him with this. Moreover, he does not know Willoughby as I do and is unlikely to think that my sister could be drawn back into an association with him. Edward rarely speaks ill of anyone and will not believe the danger that she is in. I had hoped to convince my mother and bring her back to Delaford, making some plausible excuse so she could spend some time with Marianne. They have always been close," she explained, wondering even as she spoke, whether her friend would consider her foolish for worrying as she did. But Mrs King did not. A kind and sensible woman, she took Elinor's concerns quite seriously and agreed to help her.

"Leave it to me, Elinor, I shall think of a plan. Meanwhile, say nothing to your sister or your mother. Let us hope it may not be necessary, but if it is, we will go to Barton Park, you and I."

❧

On the following day, an invitation arrived at the parsonage asking Edward and Elinor to dinner with Dr and Mrs Bradley King. It was both an unexpected pleasure and, for Elinor, a great relief, since it signalled that Helen King had devised a plan.

They arrived at the Kings' home to find two other guests present; they were two gentlemen from Oxford, one a distinguished scholar and the other a well-known theologian. Both men were involved in the campaign of Mr Wilberforce to abolish slavery in all its forms in Britain and her colonies. They were there to invite Dr Bradley King to speak at a gathering of like-minded scholars and churchmen at one of the colleges and were happy to have Edward Ferrars attend as well. Mrs King had seen that this would afford them an opportunity to put her plan into action. When they withdrew to the drawing room, she revealed it to Elinor. "If Dr King and Mr Ferrars go to Oxford with them, we could make the journey to Barton Park to visit your mother on the same day, with no need for any concealment. What could be more natural?" she said, and Elinor could have hugged her. Taking both her hands, she said, "Oh Helen, that would be wonderful. Edward need not be concerned at all—we could visit my mother, stay overnight at Barton Cottage, and return with her on the day following. Nothing could be simpler."

And so it was arranged. Elinor was relieved not to have to detail her troubled thoughts about Marianne to her husband, who agreed that it was a perfectly good scheme for Elinor and Mrs King to travel to Devonshire and visit Mrs Dashwood.

"I imagine she will be delighted to see you, my dear, after enduring the company of just Sir John and Mrs Jennings for several weeks; I am sure it will be a most pleasant surprise," he said as they prepared for bed, and Elinor had not the heart to disabuse him. What she had to tell her mother was unlikely to be pleasant, and Elinor was certain it would not be welcome news to Mrs Dashwood.

❧

Meanwhile, back at Delaford Manor, Marianne had spent the evening in her bedroom, writing in her diary. When she had begun it, a few weeks ago, she had not expected that there would be much to write each day; she regarded her life as being rather ordinary and often boring. Some of the earlier entries reflected this attitude.

Nothing very exciting happens here; unless one were to regard a commotion in the lower meadow, when some pigs escaped from their enclosure and got into an argument with the cattle, as a stirring adventure. I suppose it was matter of life and death for the pigs, which would have come off worse if the men hadn't rescued them and shut them up in their sty. Silly things!

Two days later, she wrote:

A letter from Mama brought news that she is enjoying her stay at Barton Park. Evidently she is in sole charge of the household because Sir John is too busy with business matters and Mrs Jennings is still too depressed to take an interest. Mama says she has been back to the cottage just the once since Lady M's funeral, and that was only to collect some warm clothes. Sir John's housekeeper has assigned a maid to attend to her needs, which must mean Mama is very well looked after at Barton Park.

However, within the last fortnight, several incidents that had happened ensured that the pages of her diary were filling up with accounts of events and people she never could have anticipated. Looking over the last few days, she read her entries with some degree of amusement.

Margaret is here in Dorset, staying with Elinor and Edward at the parsonage. She came over to see me and met the Perceval girls, Maria and Eugenie, who came to tea and invited me to join them on an excursion to Somerset, in particular to Glastonbury. I have, quite fortuitously, become involved in an acquaintance with the Percevals, thanks to Robert and Lucy Ferrars, but I do not think Margaret liked them very much. They are not particularly well educated, enjoy telling silly jokes, and do not care for reading, which means they could hardly find anything to say to Margaret, who has become quite a scholar now! But they are very good-natured and amiable and lots of fun, which is in short supply here, so I have to confess that I am very happy to know them.

One recent consequence of her "fortuitous acquaintance" with the Perceval girls—the excursion to Glastonbury—received special mention in Marianne's diary.

I shall always recall the excursion to Glastonbury as an occasion that promised a great deal of interest and then seemed to provide very little, because hardly anyone in the party apart from me seemed to know or care about the significance of this historic place. The Percevals and their friends the Hawthornes appeared to care not one whit for the ancient tales of King Arthur and his Knights of the Round Table, although they did giggle like schoolgirls over the romance of Lancelot and Guinevere. I was ready to give up on the day altogether, when something quite astonishing happened and someone I had not seen in many years appeared on the scene. I cannot recall the moment I heard his voice without a sense of shock, yet he was completely calm and collected, and even if he thought that I may have been shaken, he did not reveal it and behaved in a very gentlemanly manner, acting as though we were strangers who had just met, making no reference at all to our previous association, which was thoughtful of him, since it might have been quite embarrassing if I had to explain our previous acquaintance to the Percevals and their friends.

Following the chance meeting, which I took to be the last time I would see him there, we met again because of the accident that damaged the Percevals' carriage and left us stranded. His generous offer to convey some of the party to their homes meant that I was once again in his company for some two hours, during which we talked but without once intruding upon our personal lives, as though he was trying quite deliberately to make me understand that he had accepted that our lives had diverged forever and this meeting was of two different people who might meet as new acquaintances. It is an idea with which I find I am quite comfortable.

Had her sister Elinor seen Marianne's diary, it is certain *she* would not have been comfortable at all. Indeed, had she known what had followed upon the events recorded there, her sense of anxiety would undoubtedly have been increased considerably.

Two days after the excursion to Glastonbury, Marianne had been upstairs in her room, in one of those moods that she had found herself slipping into recently—a mood in which she would allow her mind to wander freely into the past, in a manner that she had quite deliberately avoided before. Since the evening when Mr Willoughby had brought her safely home from the Percevals, she had permitted herself to think of him often, but always having assured herself that the Willoughby she was contemplating was the man she had met again recently, at Glastonbury; the man who had behaved with great civility and decorum, who had conveyed her to Delaford, without making reference to their past acquaintance, to her husband or family.

"Quite clearly," she had told herself, "he wishes me to understand that he has no wish to resurrect the past that brought us so much sorrow and wants to deal with present circumstances as he finds them. Perhaps it is not too much to hope that we can be friends." She had been toying with the notion when her maid had come in to announce that a visitor had arrived and she had shown him into the sitting room. On being asked who it was, the girl said only that it was the gentleman from Somerset and he hadn't given his name.

Marianne seemed unable to think clearly for a moment or two, but soon recollected that she must not appear discomposed before the servant, and asked that the girl have a tea tray prepared and brought into the sitting room. When she went down, she found Willoughby standing by the fireplace, looking quite at ease, as though it was the most normal thing in the world that he should be there. She was puzzled; how did he know that Colonel Brandon was from home? He would not have risked meeting him, surely? She wondered and was concerned that she may have unwittingly said something that had given him a clue.

But when they met, his words told her otherwise. "Mrs Brandon, I am excessively relieved to see you are well and have suffered no harm from the ordeal of waiting several hours in uncomfortable surroundings. I called at the Percevals and discovered they were all well but for Mrs Perceval, who has a bad cold as a consequence of the exposure she suffered, and keeps to her room; I was concerned that it may have made you unwell, too."

Marianne assured him that she had suffered not at all from the ordeal, and indeed, she was very sorry to hear about Mrs Perceval's illness. Even before she could ask him, Willoughby responded that he would be happy to convey her sympathies to the Percevals when he dined with them that evening.

"They have kindly asked me to dine, which is far more agreeable to me than dining alone, which would be my fate were I to return immediately to Somerset. Indeed, they asked me to convey this invitation to you," he said, taking an unsealed note out of his pocket and holding it out to her. Marianne blushed as she took it and turned away to the window to read the contents—Maria Perceval had written asking her to dine with them and suggesting that, since it may be late and with Colonel Brandon away from Delaford, she may prefer to stay overnight. She added that Mr Willoughby had offered to convey her from Delaford to their house that evening, if she was agreeable.

It was with some difficulty that Marianne turned to face her visitor and say in a voice that she hoped was sufficiently credible, "I am sorry, but I am engaged to dine at the parsonage with my sister and brother-in-law this evening; if you could wait, I will write a note to the Percevals explaining why I cannot accept," and she rushed upstairs, her cheeks burning, knowing that her excuse was a lie, that in her heart she would have liked to accept the invitation, yet aware that she could not. She wrote a brief, polite note to Miss Maria Perceval and took it downstairs. Willoughby put it in his pocket and sat down to take tea.

Apart from a comment about the attractive aspect of the room in which they were seated, which she took to be a clear indication that he recalled the room at Barton Cottage she had replicated here, he behaved exactly as he had done before: speaking of the Percevals and what a very hospitable and pleasant family they were. He made no reference to her sister and brother-in-law, nor did he attempt to engage her in any familiarity, but she knew he must have discovered from the Percevals that her husband was away in Ireland. It had probably emboldened him to suggest that he could convey her to the Percevals' place for dinner, she thought, reflecting that it was very much as Willoughby would have behaved when they had first met those many years ago. He retained the qualities of quick thinking and decisive action that had recommended him to her at their first meeting, when after her fall, he had picked her up in his arms without fuss and carried her home in the drenching rain.

He did not stay long after finishing his tea, but before he left, he thanked her, said again how glad he was to find her well, and hoped they would meet again. He said it as though he knew it would be so, she thought as he bowed and said goodbye. Marianne said nothing except to thank him for his concern and to assure him she was very well. But once he had gone, she went slowly upstairs to her room and her mind was filled with a multitude of thoughts, all of which were the very opposite of what she had said.

~❦~

Elinor and Mrs King travelled to Barton Park on what was a pretty autumn morning, with a pleasant westerly breeze pushing the clouds ahead of them. They arrived at the house to be told that Mrs Dashwood was busy upstairs with two of the servants, who were engaged in clearing out what had been Mrs Jennings's rooms. When Elinor looked surprised, the housekeeper informed her that Mrs Jennings had left that very morning with her son-in-law, Sir John Middleton, to join the Palmers in London.

The news pleased Elinor; this was a most fortunate circumstance indeed, thought she, since it would enable her to speak privately with her mother and convince her to return to Delaford with them, since it would pose no inconvenience at all to Sir John. There should be little doubt that Mrs Williams the housekeeper could maintain the household while the master was away in London.

Leaving Mrs King in the sitting room, Elinor went upstairs and found her mother busier than she had ever seen her in their own home. The rooms and all their fine furniture were being cleaned and aired—fresh linen and accessories were ready to hand and fresh flowers were being arranged in two large glass vases, which Elinor recalled seeing in one of the rooms downstairs. Perhaps they were expecting another visitor, she thought. After greeting her daughter affectionately, but with some degree of impatience at not having been notified of her arrival, Mrs Dashwood informed her that Sir John had taken his mother-in-law to London to join the Palmers. They would travel thence to Brighton, where it was hoped the sea air would help her feel much better. As for Sir John, she said, he had been missing his friends in town and would probably spend a few weeks at his house in London. Mrs Dashwood then continued working as she talked, laying out new doilies on the dressing table, ordering the maids to remove the old linings in the chest of drawers and replace them with fresh ones and hang fresh lavender in the linen press.

Seeing all this activity, Elinor had to ask, "Who is it for?" expecting to hear that some relative of the Middletons was to stay. Her astonishment was beyond imagining when her mother replied, "It's for me, dear, it's my new accommodation; Sir John said I should have this suite of rooms, since it is unlikely that Mrs Jennings will return to stay for long periods of time. She may come with the Palmers when they visit, I suppose, but there are two other rooms that would be quite suitable for a short stay. Sir John thinks these rooms, which are very nice with such a pretty prospect, would be wasted if they are shut away. There's work to be done—Mrs Jennings has used them for many years. I'll be making some changes. I think I'll have some new curtains made up—I am not very fond of that colour—although that may have to wait until after Christmas."

Elinor listened with increasing amazement, as her mother chattered on as though this was the most exciting thing that had happened in her life. Bright and energetic, like some young woman with a new home, Mrs Dashwood was settling in at Barton Park, preparing to occupy a luxurious suite of rooms from where she presumably expected to carry on her duties as a glorified manager of her cousin's household. It was an idea her daughter found difficult to take seriously.

Recalling her duty to her friend Mrs King, who had been sitting patiently downstairs, Elinor informed her mother that they had come on a very important errand and it concerned her sister Marianne. This brought a flicker of interest. "What is the problem? Is she unwell?" she asked quickly, looking a little concerned, but when Elinor said she was not, her mother looked relieved and returned to rearranging her toiletries.

"Marianne is quite well, but there is something you should know, Mama," Elinor began, but Mrs Dashwood waved her away. "Well, my dear, you can tell me all about it later. I am glad to hear she is not ill, but I must get on with this now. Do make my excuses to your friend and say I shall join you for dinner later. Meanwhile, why do you not take some refreshment and then perhaps, you could take her for a stroll in the park. Will you stay the night?" she asked as an afterthought, and when Elinor said she thought they could stay at the cottage, her mother looked appalled and said, "Oh no, my dear, not at the cottage—that would not do. Why, no one has been there to air the bedrooms or anything for several weeks—there's only Thomas and his wife there anyway. What would Sir John say? He'd be most upset to think we sent you off to sleep at the cottage. No, no, you must stay here. The maids will make up a couple of beds in two of the smaller rooms for you. You will be much more comfortable here. It will all be done when you get back from your walk." It was more than Elinor could do to keep a straight face—this she had never anticipated. Finding her mother so completely immersed in her own role at Barton Park was extraordinary; still worse, how on earth was she going to convince her of the need to return to Delaford?

Going downstairs, she apologised to Mrs King and was grateful that the housekeeper had seen fit to send in refreshments. Elinor partook of a cup of tea, but her thoughts were filled with the new circumstances she faced. Glad of the good weather and with the grounds at their best in early autumn, it wasn't too difficult to interest Mrs King in a walk through the groves of Barton Park. As they walked, Elinor, in a most uncharacteristic manner, related most of her conversation with her mother. "Helen, I am at a loss to understand my mother; she appears reluctant to be concerned with any matters outside her own life here at Barton Park—where she is clearly comfortable and pleased with her role in Sir John's household," she complained. "It is quite astonishing; I am not at all certain she will consent to come with us to Delaford. Indeed, I doubt that she will even share my concern for Marianne."

Helen King tried to assuage her friend's anxiety with argument; surely, she said, Mrs Dashwood would consider the situation of her daughter, her happiness, and possible damage to her reputation to be matters of serious concern. She tried to persuade Elinor that when her mother heard all of the circumstances, including the possibility that Willoughby may try to meet Marianne again and that Marianne may be susceptible to his approaches, she would surely begin to take it seriously. But Elinor was not hopeful. She recalled clearly what little disquiet her mother had shown in the past, declaring that she trusted her daughter and Mr Willoughby implicitly and would not intervene to question them. She was, she had stated, perfectly satisfied that they loved each other and that was proof enough for her. She had berated Elinor for doubting her sister and suspecting Willoughby of deception.

Recalling all this, she explained her fears to her friend, "I should very much like to believe as you do, Helen, that Mama will regard this matter as important enough to require her intervention in my sister's life, but I cannot be certain. Should she refuse to return with us to Delaford, I do not know what I shall do. I cannot confront Marianne—I have neither the right, nor the evidence to warrant such action—whereas Mama could, just by being there, make a practical difference to the situation. She needs no excuse to visit Marianne and spend some time with her. Marianne may not welcome it, but she can hardly object."

When they returned to the house some time later, everything had been prepared as promised; their rooms were ready and a maid had been assigned to assist them with their toilette and dressing for dinner. Mrs King was very impressed, but poor Elinor's heart sank. Quite clearly her mother was so immersed in her role at Barton Park, it would take much more than the account of a chance meeting between Marianne and Willoughby to drag her away to Delaford.

When they came down to dinner, Mrs Dashwood greeted Mrs King graciously, apologised for not having met her earlier, asked if her room was comfortable, and added that it was a pity Sir John Middleton was away, as he would have enjoyed meeting her—as he always enjoyed meeting new people and making new friends. Throughout the excellent meal and afterwards, she chatted on about Barton Park and its owner as though she felt it was her responsibility to convince Mrs King of the generosity and kindness of her cousin. Tales of the happy parties and picnics he hosted and the lavish hospitality that his guests always enjoyed were retold with the added aside that of course this was all before the sad demise of dear Lady Middleton, some months ago. There had been no parties since then, except a shooting party for some friends in the neighbourhood, she said.

A query from Mrs King about Sir John's spirits and how he was coping with his loss brought a paean of praise about how brave he had been and how he devoted time to the two children, who were now, "poor little darlings, mainly in the care of their nurse."

"They do miss their mama, I'm sure, but Nurse Wallace is very good and I do my best to keep them happy," she said. "I have suggested to Sir John that it is time they had a young governess who could start them off on learning their letters and numbers and perhaps trying out the pianoforte, too. I always say it's never too early—all my girls started learning early, and as you can see they have done very well indeed," Mrs Dashwood declared, and Mrs King had to agree that she was right.

Throughout the evening Elinor's hopes sank lower. It seemed to her that her mother had sloughed off her own maternal responsibilities and, having taken up a new, more enterprising role at Barton Park, was unlikely to want to revert to that of anxious mother of adult daughters again.

When she did go to her mother's room, after Mrs King had retired to bed, and tried to lay before her the concerns she had about Marianne, Elinor was proved right. Mrs Dashwood, having listened to her elder daughter's account, showed very little interest in the question of Marianne's situation at Delaford, pointing out that she had plenty to keep her occupied because Colonel Brandon had provided her with everything she needed to carry on all her hobbies and interests and there could be no cause for any complaint at all.

As for the question of Willoughby living in Somerset for part of the year and regularly visiting his relatives in Dorset, Mrs Dashwood well nigh ridiculed Elinor's concerns: "But of course he lives in Somerset, dear, we always knew that—he has a property there, and since he married Miss Grey, he now has the money to enable him to keep a second establishment in the country, and a very fine place it is too, I understand. Sir John told me all about it last year. Marianne must have known that—I know Colonel Brandon certainly does; but surely that is not something we can worry over. Elinor, my dear, I know your disposition is cautious and wary—you love to doubt wherever you find a reason—but I do not. I am different and I trust Marianne—of course she loved Willoughby, who did not? We all did—although I grant you, you did express some reservations; but it was a long time ago, they are both much older and they are both married."

Elinor tried to argue with her mother, "Do you really believe that will influence them, do you think it will restrain Willoughby—should he see an opportunity—from trying to re-engage her feelings for him? Remember that he hates Colonel Brandon with a passion and may well be tempted to use this as a means of avenging himself upon the man whom he blames for all his misfortune." But Mrs Dashwood would not be persuaded.

"Elinor, you have been reading too many novels, I think," she protested. "Why, I cannot believe you really think so ill of your sister. Did not Willoughby claim to you, when you met at Cleveland, that she was the love of his life? Why would he wish to destroy her? Even if I allow that we cannot count on Willoughby's sincerity, then surely you must believe that Marianne is quite without virtue, if you think she can so easily be tempted into a liaison that could destroy her marriage and every advantage she has at Delaford. Can you honestly tell me that you believe your sister is capable of such folly?"

It was an argument Elinor knew she could not win; clearly her mother would not countenance any interference in Marianne's life. Sadly, with tears in her eyes, she said, "I can only pray that you are right, Mama," as she left the room and returned to her bed, feeling more helpless than she had been before they had set off for Barton Park.

⁓

Meanwhile, at Delaford, Marianne received a visit from the Perceval sisters, who came accompanied by Mr Willoughby in his open carriage. They came, they said, to ask if she was well and had suffered no distress after the expedition to Glastonbury. On this occasion, Willoughby had brought with him a very pretty sketch of the site at Glastonbury, with the ruined abbey perfectly rendered in watercolours by a local artist, against a distant view of Glastonbury Tor. He presented it to Marianne as a souvenir of her visit, and she was delighted with it, accepting it after some small show of reluctance. Later, he found a moment, while the two Perceval sisters were examining some of the artefacts in the library, to invite her to join them on another excursion, this time to the historic city of Bath.

Having given her some information about the city, he claimed to be organising a party to visit Bath, he said, and the Perceval family and their friends the Hawthornes were coming too; it was to be in a fortnight's time. Marianne asked for time to consider, which he gladly agreed to, and promised to call to hear her answer. But she, exercising some caution, said she would send him her answer by post, whereupon Willoughby gave her his card with the address of his country house in Somerset.

After her visitors had taken tea and left, Marianne took her souvenir of Glastonbury up to her room. She had at first decided it would look well in her studio, but upon further reflection, it looked too lovely to be hidden away up there, she thought, and propped it up on her dressing table. It was a charming piece of work, capturing the ambient atmosphere of the ancient ruins, and the more she looked at it, the more she recalled how Willoughby was wont to indulge her with similar gestures when they had first met at Barton Park. Each time he had brought her some little gift, it would help to confirm in her mind that she was special to him. She had been excited then by the promise of those thoughtful gestures and the warm feelings they had aroused in her, just as she was now.

Marianne was still in two minds about the excursion, though; she wanted to go, but was a little concerned. It was almost the middle of October, and Colonel Brandon was due back soon. While she had convinced herself that there was no harm in her joining a party of friends on an excursion to Bath, she was not entirely comfortable with the thought of explaining the presence of Mr Willoughby in the party to her husband. By the time she fell asleep that night, Marianne had not made up her mind.

The following morning was cold, and rain threatened. She was at breakfast when the post was brought in and there was a letter from Colonel Brandon. She opened it eagerly—it might tell her when he would be back. Following the usual affectionate enquiries about her health and happiness, he informed her that he would be delayed in Ireland by business that had to be concluded before the onset of winter. It would mean he would be home by the middle of November, he wrote, and while apologising for the delay, added that he had arranged that on his next visit, in the spring, she could accompany him and they could spend some time in Dublin, which he assured her was a fine city that she would like very much.

Marianne would never know what had prompted her decision; whether it was the colonel's letter, the annoyance of a further delay in his return, or just the inclement weather that affected her mood. Whichever it was, the prospect of spending a few days in the salubrious city of Bath seemed far more attractive than a week of wet weather at Delaford. She rose from the breakfast table, returned to her room, and on impulse, wrote a note to Willoughby, thanking him for the sketch of Glastonbury and saying she would be happy to join their party on the excursion to Bath. She called for the small carriage to take her into the village and posted the letter herself. And so, upon a whim, the die was cast.

END OF PART TWO

EXPECTATIONS OF HAPPINESS

Part Three

Chapter Eleven

ARRIVING AT THE PORT of Marseilles on a damp, foggy morning, Margaret wondered how anyone could suggest that this weather was preferable to autumn in England. They had left Plymouth in bright sunshine and the voyage had been pleasant enough—except for some high rolling seas as they crossed the dreaded Bay of Biscay—but once in the Mediterranean, conditions had seemed to improve until last night, when it had started to rain. Several passengers had declared that this was most unusual—it never rained here at this time of year, they'd said.

"Just our luck," Claire Jones had observed ruefully as they stood at the ship's rail, looking out at the dreary scene. "Trust us to sail into unusual weather." Margaret had been silent, not wishing to throw a wet blanket (now there was an appropriate image, she thought) over the start of their holiday. They had both looked forward to this so much—she was reluctant to say anything that would spoil it right at the very beginning. They had gone out on deck, relieved that the rain had eased to a light drizzle, allowing them to disembark; but they still had some time to wait, while all manner of creaks and groans went up around them as the vessel was carefully manoeuvred into place at the dockside and the ladders lowered.

Claire was looking out for her friend Mr Wilcox, who was meeting them. She had sent him all the details of place, time, name of vessel, etc., and was confident he would be there. "Nicholas is very reliable—he will be there rain or shine, have no fear," she declared, and Margaret prayed she was right, because neither of them had any knowledge of Marseilles and its busy environs, and if he did not appear, they would be quite lost. Margaret had travelled in northern France—Paris she knew well and loved—but the south was a mystery to her. When they had first thought about Provence, it had seemed like fun, and Claire had told her that Mr Nicholas Wilcox, her friend, who tutored for one of the colleges in Oxford, travelled regularly to the south of France and knew Provence well. Mr Wilcox had travelled ahead and made all the arrangements and reservations for them—and here they were, on a damp morning, in Marseilles.

"There he is!" cried Claire, pointing to a cluster of people on the wharf, standing at some distance from the vessel. "I told you he was dependable, dear old Nicholas, I knew he would come." She waved vigorously and called out his name, and suddenly, he seemed to recognise her under her hat and shawl and waved back. Margaret was greatly relieved; thank God for Mr Wilcox, she thought as they made their way carefully down the ladder, while various passengers called out cautionary words of advice from the deck above. It was good to be on terra firma again, thought Margaret; she had not suffered sea sickness, as had many other passengers, but she disliked crowds and was happy to be off the boat.

They moved away from the quay, and Mr Wilcox approached; with him was another man, somewhat older, tall, good-looking and rather more formally attired than his companion. He was introduced to the ladies by Mr Wilcox as "Mr Daniel Brooke, my very good friend and colleague from Oxford, who is a regular visitor to Provence." Mr Brooke bowed and greeted the ladies and suggested in a quiet voice that they should be shown into the vehicle that waited for them, so they would be out of the continuing drizzle, while Wilcox and he collected their luggage. Both Margaret and Claire thought this was a very good idea indeed.

As they waited for the men to return, Claire said, "I wonder who he is; Nicholas hasn't mentioned him before. He is very handsome, is he not, Margaret?" Margaret had to agree, but added that he did seem rather quiet. "Almost reserved compared to your Mr Wilcox. I cannot believe that he is here on holiday; his countenance looks far too grave for one who is pleasure bound," she said, and her friend laughed, "Oh Margaret, isn't that just like you! You've made your mind up about the poor man, just because he looks more serious than Nicholas!"

"Well no, I have not," Margaret protested. "He may well be a perfectly happy man; perhaps he has just woken up with a headache or maybe it's the bleak weather that makes him seem melancholy, I cannot tell. But do you not agree that he looks a little sombre, like he has weighty matters on his mind? Perhaps he is here to study something grave and historical," she mused.

Miss Jones was unconvinced. "It must be the writer in you, Margaret; you detect character traits within minutes of meeting people. I do recall that you told me very soon after you met Nicholas that he seemed to be a young man with a naturally cheerful disposition, with the look of someone who would take on any task if fun could be guaranteed."

Margaret laughed out loud. "I did and was I not proved right? Just look at him, he is undaunted, admit it." And Miss Jones had to confess she was right. The two gentlemen were seen returning with the ladies' luggage, and their conversation ceased as their trunks were stacked on the back of the carriage, and presently, they drove away from the dockside toward the town, where Mr Wilcox had made reservations for the ladies at a small hotel.

"We thought you would like to stay overnight in Marseilles and travel to Aix-en-Provence tomorrow. There are a few interesting places to be seen here, before one moves north," Mr Wilcox said, and his friend explained, "Particularly if the recent history of France interests you, although it is a very ancient sea port. Bonaparte, escaping from Elba in 1815, landed not far from here and began his march up toward Waterloo, collecting quite a big army as he went."

Claire laughed, "Not a particularly successful campaign, was it?" and Mr Brooke nodded and almost smiled as he responded, "No indeed; he had hoped at least to recapture some part of his lost empire, but..."

"The Duke of Wellington had something quite different in mind," Margaret completed his sentence. That made him laugh for the first time since they had met, and she noticed what a difference it made to his countenance, as his eyes brightened and he asked, "I understand you are a teacher, Miss Dashwood, are you a student of history as well?"

Margaret was a little taken aback, but answered promptly, "I am indeed and of all things ancient and intriguing—they do fascinate me. I have made many promises to my pupils to return with tales of historical places and people sufficient to fill their notebooks and their dreams." Mr Brooke seemed to approve, "Then you will definitely enjoy your time in Provence, which is replete with things ancient and fascinating. But Marseilles is also the home of the revolutionary French national anthem—'La Marseillaise,'" and seeing Margaret's eyes widen with interest, he added, "It is an old part of France and, by its very situation on the borders of Italy and Switzerland, lies right in the path of many historic changes since the third century before the birth of Christ."

Claire Jones noted that Margaret was absorbing everything he said. "You are very fortunate, Margaret, Mr Brooke's knowledge of Provence is clearly extensive and you might learn a great deal from him," she said smiling, before adding, "Margaret plans to be a writer, Mr Brooke, she will certainly benefit from your special knowledge." At this information, Mr Brooke looked at Margaret and nodded, but said nothing, and when she asked, "Have you made a special study of this part of the country, Mr Brooke?" she thought he seemed to close up a little, as though unwilling to answer the question directly. His friend Wilcox was more forthcoming though. "He certainly has; Daniel travels to this area regularly and has been spending a part of his sabbatical year here. I do believe he intends to publish some learned tome about the history of Provence."

"Do you?" asked Claire, curious as usual, and again, Margaret thought she noted a flicker of what might have been resentment cross his countenance; clearly he wasn't prepared for such probing questions from two women who were complete strangers to him. However, he did answer her quite politely, "I do have some plans, Miss Jones, but I am not certain if, with my work at the college, I will ever have sufficient time to bring them to a satisfactory conclusion." It was almost as though he wanted to conclude the discussion and move their conversation on to other matters, and Margaret thought he looked rather relieved when their vehicle stopped in front of the hotel, where the ladies were to stay the night. They alighted and found to their delight that it was a rather informal little place, maintained by a cheerful family that rushed out to assist with their luggage and escort them indoors.

It was then, as Mr Brooke gave instructions to the driver of the carriage, that they discovered their travelling companion spoke excellent French, not of the scholarly variety one learned from French mistresses at ladies' seminaries, but the common or garden vernacular of the Provençal district. Margaret and Claire were quite astonished, but Nicholas Wilcox seemed to regard it as nothing extraordinary, since, as he had pointed out to them before, Brooke spent almost all his vacations in this part of France. Margaret remarked that they were very fortunate indeed to have him in their party, and Claire agreed, adding, "I do wonder what it is that makes him so passionately attached to this particular part of the country; it must have a very special attraction for him."

The gentlemen had lodgings elsewhere in town and, having ascertained that the arrangements were to their satisfaction, left the ladies to settle in. Their hosts had prepared what must have been a late breakfast, but was so substantial, with a variety of rolls, cold meat, cheeses, fruit, conserves, and coffee, that it filled them as well as a complete luncheon would have done. Thereafter, they retired to their rooms—which as it turned out was one big room with two very comfortable beds with a large painted screen between them. Both ladies were so weary with days spent at sea in cramped quarters with swaying bunks, they changed out of their travelling gowns and fell into bed and slept for many hours, with no sense of time, until one of the children knocked on the door and announced that the gentlemen were downstairs.

"Good Lord, it's past four o'clock—we've been asleep for hours and hours!" Margaret exclaimed, leaping out of bed. "Whatever will they think?" but Claire was unconcerned and sent a message down by the girl that the ladies would be down directly. They looked out of the window and found that it had stopped raining and the sky was clear and blue above the town. It was almost half an hour later that they descended the stairs and found just Mr Brooke waiting patiently for them in the parlour. He informed them that Nicholas had gone ahead to get tickets for an entertainment, which he thought they might see before dinner. "Nicholas thought you might enjoy the show—it's a conjurer with a reputation for performing some very intriguing tricks," he explained, with a smile. "I must warn you ladies that the audience can be quite noisy and outspoken," he said, as they went out together and walked down to the old playhouse where Mr Wilcox awaited them.

It was a very memorable performance indeed, with the conjurer putting on some quite amazing illusions and the audience expressing its opinion quite audibly throughout, until the last episode of the vanishing lady. Clearly keeping his best trick to the last, the conjurer left them all confounded and arguing as they left the theatre. How had it been achieved? What had they missed? Where was she hidden? Claire and Margaret argued all the way to the cafe, where they had dinner, after which the gentlemen accompanied them to their lodgings, still arguing, and there they parted for the night, having agreed to meet after breakfast on the morrow.

"Well, that was a most satisfactory first day of our holiday, was it not?" asked Claire as they changed into their nightclothes and prepared for bed, and Margaret agreed completely that it could not have been better. Despite starting off with a damp and dreary morning, the day had improved steadily, concluding with a most entertaining and convivial evening.

As she fell into a deep sleep, Margaret thought how very pleasant it had been to have arrived in a new place one had never visited, met people one had never met before, and to find them all so thoroughly agreeable.

❦

Margaret was awake almost at dawn; it was impossible to sleep late, because of the cacophony of cries from the gulls and other birds around the area. Looking out of the window, she declared, "Now that is certainly the kind of dawn one expects to wake up to in the south of France. Claire, do come and look at this sky," she called to her sleepy companion, who was barely awake. Tumbling out of bed, Claire joined her at the window, and they looked out together on a sky that appeared to have been painted in tones of gold and rose against a dark indigo back cloth, which lightened as they watched into smoky blue-grey and finally, almost reluctantly, blushed deeply pink as the sun came through. The morning had broken perfectly; both women had been silent as it happened and they looked at one another and smiled, before returning to their beds. It was too early for breakfast, but a knock on the door heralded a maid with a pot of hot coffee, two large cups, and lots of cream and sugar.

Later they dressed and went down to breakfast, after which their companions arrived to take them to the infamous "Gulf of Napoleon" and some other places of interest before Mr Wilcox asked if they were ready to move on to Aix-en-Provence, where, at his friend's recommendation, Nicholas had taken rooms for the ladies in a private house rather than a hotel. It was possible, he explained, to find quite good accommodation since this was the end of summer, and Daniel Brooke believed that it would be safer for ladies alone, since they would have the security of a family around them, rather than strangers. Both Claire and Margaret said that sounded like a very good idea, and Margaret thought it was very kind of Mr Brooke to be concerned for their safety and said so.

That afternoon, they collected their luggage, paid their bill, reluctantly said their goodbyes to the family that had looked after them so well, and journeyed on to Aix-en-Provence. As they approached the town, Margaret told them her brother-in-law Edward Ferrars had visited it a few years ago and had said it was quite definitely not to be missed. At the mention of his name, Mr Brooke, who had been silent for most of the journey so far, except to point out geographical features on their route, asked, "Did you say Edward Ferrars? Do you mean the Reverend Edward Ferrars, who took orders some years ago?"

"Indeed I do," she replied, "he is married to my eldest sister Elinor and is the parson at Delaford, which is a living on the estate of my other brother-in-law, Colonel Brandon. Do you know Edward?"

Daniel Brooke shook his head. "I cannot claim to know Mr Ferrars well, but I have met him on several occasions at Oxford, where he undertook theological studies before taking orders, under the tutelage of a very good friend of mine—a theologian of some repute, Dr Francis Grantley."

Margaret was delighted with this piece of information; she had certainly heard her brother-in-law speak highly of Dr Grantley, she said, he had been Edward's mentor at Oxford and he had enormous respect for him as a theologian. Their conversation then proceeded along a path that clearly held much interest for Margaret and Mr Brooke, but had little or no significance for their companions, who looked at one another, shrugged their shoulders, and concentrated on the surrounding scenery.

Later, after they had reached their destination and located the house where they were to stay, met their hosts, and deposited their trunks, they went out again to walk about the area, and Mr Brooke offered to show them one of his favourite places—an ancient abbey, where the monks had lived, worked, and prayed since before the Crusades. It wasn't far, he said, and Margaret was keen to go. Her friend, though less keen to spend a part of a soporific afternoon wandering around an old monastery, was persuaded that it was worth seeing and went too. However, while Mr Brooke and Margaret lingered to admire the ancient buildings and ask questions of the caretaker, Miss Jones declared that she was weary and wished to find a seat, which Mr Wilcox found quite easily in a corner of the old lavender garden behind the abbey.

While waiting for the others, Claire expressed some surprise at the way her friend had plunged into a serious discourse on the abbey and other matters with Mr Brooke, but Nicholas Wilcox assured her that Brooke was indeed a very learned and well-read fellow. "He is a genuine scholar, with a much greater brain than mine, and can always be relied upon to provide plenty of interesting information on a wide range of subjects, which is what makes him such a good travelling companion," he said. "As you will discover, he is a veritable fount of knowledge about Provence and all its great historic places. If your friend Miss Dashwood enjoys that sort of thing, she will not be disappointed," he promised, and Miss Jones assured him that Miss Dashwood certainly did enjoy that sort of thing—being quite a scholar herself!

"She seems quite young and far too pretty for a serious blue-stocking," observed Mr Wilcox with a smile, and Claire agreed, adding pointedly, "Indeed, but she is exceedingly sensible, too. She insisted on getting a proper education, and when the school she attended discovered how clever she was, they sent her on a scholarship to France and, on her return to England, employed her as a teacher."

When Margaret and Mr Brooke emerged from the abbey and approached them, Claire saw that Margaret had made notes and sketches of various parts of the historic building and its grounds. She was clearly taking her tour of Provence seriously and, it seemed, Mr Brooke was happy to encourage her interest.

That evening the gentlemen had other appointments, which left the two friends to their own devices. Claire wished to return to their lodgings to rest, but Margaret was keen to wander around the village for an hour or so before returning to bathe and dress for dinner. They cautioned her not to wander too far and she assured them she would not, promising to be back at their lodgings well before dark. Once again, she was touched by the fact that both Mr Brooke and Mr Wilcox had been particular about advising her on the need to take care. She thanked them both and parted from Claire, who went upstairs to rest.

When she returned to their rooms, which were at the top of the house, overlooking a small yard with an orchard beyond, she found her friend fast asleep. Margaret was too excited to sleep; she had seen and learned so much that day, her mind was filled with the sights, sounds, and stories of one little corner of this enchanting place. How much more there must be to see and learn!

Determined that she would remember it all, she sat down at the little table by the window and wrote everything she could recall in her notebook, promising herself that she would do the same on every day they spent here. It was a promise she kept quite faithfully for the rest of their stay.

That night, after dinner, Margaret wrote to her sister a letter filled with the excitement and enthusiasm she felt as they concluded their first full day in Provence.

Dearest Elinor,

You may not receive this for a week or ten days, but I want to write you immediately, because I must tell you what a wonderful day it has been.

First, I know you will want to hear that we had a safe voyage from Plymouth, and yes, we did, except for a couple of perilous hours crossing the Bay. Marseilles was wet and a bit dreary to begin with, but Aix-en-Provence—do tell Edward he was right—is sublime, and we have only been here one day!

Before proceeding to tell you about our lodgings, which are excellent value, and the places we have seen, I must also tell Edward that we have met a gentleman who knew him when he was at Oxford. He is Mr Daniel Brooke—a colleague of Mr Wilcox, Claire's friend, and also of Edward's mentor at Oxford, Dr Francis Grantley. Now is that not an astonishing coincidence? He recalls meeting Edward at Dr Grantley's rooms and asked after him. I wonder if Edward has any recollection of him—he is tall, very lean, and quite distinguished-looking. Claire says he is very handsome, but I think his countenance is rather too grave to be deemed handsome, although when he smiles or is involved in an animated discussion, he loses some of that gravity, and then I will admit he may be called handsome. Apart from his appearance, I have to say he is an exceedingly well-read and learned gentleman—quite the most informed mind I have encountered in my adult life. And yet, he has none of the conceit and loftiness of manner that one sees in so many less-educated men.

Having exhausted her superlatives in relation to Mr Brooke, Margaret proceeded to give her sister and brother-in-law a detailed account of everything she had seen and heard and all she had learned from their travelling companion. Reading it, they would have no doubt that her holiday in Provence was providing Margaret with enjoyment in full measure.

On the following day, they were to go to the town centre, where they had been told a Market Day was held once a week and all the locals brought their crafts and produce and set up stalls around the square. Margaret was looking forward to it and could scarcely wait until after breakfast, when they had arranged to meet the gentlemen again. However, this time, only Mr Wilcox arrived. His friend, he told them, had to attend to some urgent personal business in another part of town and would not join them that day.

Mr Wilcox recommended that they visit the market and enjoy some of the food and wine available there before travelling to a couple of scenic venues in the area. Margaret could not hide her disappointment. Without Mr Brooke, who was going to tell them all about the historic places? She wasn't sure that Mr Wilcox had that kind of knowledge—he was certainly amiable and helpful, but his knowledge of the area was far less impressive than that of his friend, she thought. Nevertheless, Claire Jones and Mr Wilcox seemed to have their minds set upon visiting the markets, and not wishing to interfere with their plans, Margaret agreed—perhaps the market could turn up a gift or two, she said. Her friend teased, "I know you'd rather be gazing at some old crypt in an ancient church, my dear, but we have many more days to do all that—Nicholas tells me that Mr Brooke has a number of historic places on his list, which we must see; so let's enjoy the sunshine and the food and wine, which I'm assured is excellent, today," and Margaret smiled and agreed.

She was not entirely disappointed, because the day proved to be as interesting as Wilcox and Claire had promised it would be, and the food was certainly delectable, but, as they returned to their lodgings for the night, she had to ask, "Is Mr Brooke joining us tomorrow?" She was pleased when Wilcox said, "Indeed he is, and I believe he has a special treat in store for you, Miss Dashwood; he suggests that we engage a local cart and driver and travel to Saint Remy and Glanum—places of which I have very scant knowledge, but Daniel informs me they are important medieval sites, which I believe hold a great fascination for you, Miss Dashwood."

The smile that broke out on her face left her companions in no doubt that this was indeed true. "He did mention Saint Remy yesterday," she said with such obvious delight, it was no surprise that when they were alone, her friend Claire decided that Margaret deserved to be teased, just a little.

They dined early, since Wilcox had warned them they were to make an early start, and as they prepared for bed, Claire remarked, apropos of nothing at all, that she was very glad that Margaret was not finding their new companion too dull or too serious as she had supposed he would be. Margaret, who had not been expecting to be teased, misread the question and declared candidly that indeed, she was herself surprised to discover that beneath the appearance of gravitas Mr Brooke had quite a good sense of humour, even while he was able to provide much detailed knowledge and had an erudite understanding of all the historic places in the area. "I do believe you are enjoying his company, Margaret, are you not?" asked her friend, to which Margaret responded artlessly, "I am indeed, because it is always so much more rewarding to have a conversation with someone who is knowledgeable than with some ignoramus who pretends to know it all, do you not agree?"

"Oh, indeed I do," said Claire, concealing a smile but deciding that she would not press her friend further on the subject of Daniel Brooke.

Claire Jones, being some years older than Margaret and with wider experience of the world, sensed that young Miss Dashwood, while she was well educated and personable, had probably never before met a gentleman who had taken her by surprise, as it were, by his intellectual prowess alone. All her relations and acquaintances appeared to be exceedingly predictable men, whose moderate measure she could take quite quickly. Which is why, Claire thought, Margaret Dashwood had never admitted to being attracted to or in love with anyone. Neither her family circumstances nor her place of employment were particularly conducive to the possibility of meeting such a man, and Margaret was too deeply immersed in her work and too content in herself to be searching for one, as some young women of her age were wont to do.

The appearance of Daniel Brooke and Margaret's swift appreciation of his intellect and personality had set Claire thinking—but she was too sensible to rush into anything without a good deal more thought. She decided therefore to say nothing more, but determined to observe the pair with interest over the forthcoming days. And where better to observe potential lovers than in romantic Provence? she thought, as she watched her young friend, clad in her cotton nightgown, writing furiously in her notebook.

As for Margaret, she was enjoying herself so much, she had not stopped to ponder whether her pleasure rose from the places they visited or the people they met or both; but she had travelled before and knew that she'd never felt such intense exhilaration nor known such complete satisfaction before. She hadn't stopped to consider how much the presence of Daniel Brooke had enhanced her enjoyment, but she did know that without his knowledge and his quiet capacity to fill in the gaps in her information, her own appreciation of the places they had visited would have been the poorer.

Chapter Twelve

IN DORSET, THE BALMY autumn weather held for a few weeks in October before the temperatures plunged as the north winds stripped the trees of their reddening leaves and drove them into the gullies. Looking out on the bleak landscape, Marianne wondered whether her decision to accept Willoughby's invitation had been rather premature—for it looked as though the party may not eventuate at all. It seemed simpler for her to say nothing about it when Elinor called on her, ostensibly to tell her of her visit to Barton Park and convey a message from their mother.

"Mama wished me to remind you that with the colder weather approaching, you are to be careful not to catch cold or a chill; she worries about you," said Elinor, and Marianne laughed as she poured out tea. "Really, Elinor, Mama and you still believe I am ten years old, do you not? Of course I am careful about colds and chills—Mama knows that. But she need not worry so; I believe I am a good deal stronger now than I was five years ago."

Her sister thought instantly that she would feel a good deal happier if she could be as certain that Marianne was as careful about the company she kept as she was about avoiding colds and chills.

Marianne asked after their mother's health and was told that Mrs Dashwood appeared perfectly content looking after the household at Barton Park while Sir John was away in London. Elinor had expected Marianne to query their mother's newfound interest in household management and was surprised that she did not; nor did she ask about Mrs Dashwood's arrangements for Christmas. It had been a tradition since Elinor and Marianne were married that their mother spent Christmas with one or the other of her daughters. This time, nothing had been said and it appeared to Elinor that Marianne seemed disinterested in what their mother decided to do.

However, when Marianne revealed that Colonel Brandon was delaying his return from Ireland, Elinor thought she had a clue to her sister's mood. Perhaps, she thought, Marianne was feeling disappointed; it was almost six weeks since the colonel had left for Ireland. Believing she might enjoy some company, Elinor asked if she would like to come to dinner at the parsonage on Sunday and was very surprised when Marianne thanked her politely and refused, saying in a nonchalant sort of voice, "I shall be away; the Percevals have invited me to join them on a tour of Bath, and since I have never been to Bath, I have accepted," and when Elinor exclaimed, "What? In this weather?" she added, "Well, I am assured that we will not be inconvenienced greatly by the weather on the journey, because we shall be conveyed there and back in two large closed carriages. Besides, we shall be chiefly indoors, since we are invited to stay at the residence of a particular friend of the Percevals." So astounded was Elinor by her calm declaration, she could frame no suitable response. It was as though Marianne was defying her sister to question her right to enjoy herself as she thought fit, in the company of her new friends. She recalled vividly that this was the same attitude Marianne had taken during the time when Willoughby had courted her, and Elinor experienced a cold feeling of unease that had nothing to do with the weather.

Elinor knew she could not mention Willoughby, though she longed to discover if he was to be of the party. Any mention of his name would immediately set up suspicions in her sister's mind regarding her knowledge of their previous encounter at Glastonbury. Elinor wanted desperately to urge Marianne to have a care—to suggest that the Percevals were only recent acquaintances of whom they knew little—but she knew full well that were she to say any such thing, Marianne would react with such hostility as to destroy any chance of Elinor providing her with some sensible advice. Yet, she did persist, at least with practical matters, reminding her of their mother's warning and urging her to wrap up well if the weather continued as inclement on Saturday. To this Marianne said lightly that she would be leaving Delaford on Friday; the Percevals were sending a carriage for her and she assured her sister that she would be very well looked after by them. "I know you do not care for them, Elinor—only because they are friends of Robert and Lucy—but truly, they are a most hospitable and kindly family, and you need have no fears on my account. They are very fond of me and I shall be very well cared for," she declared confidently and with that, Elinor had to be content.

When, on returning to the parsonage, she told her husband of the meeting and her disappointment that Marianne would not be joining them for dinner on Sunday, he, being ignorant of the circumstances causing her concern, appeared far more sanguine. "I know you are distressed, my love, but it is natural that Marianne would rather spend time with her friends who are younger and probably much more amusing than we are, and with the prospect of visiting Bath thrown in—I doubt that I could find it in my heart to blame her. Personally, I cannot understand what people see in Bath—apart from the impressive architecture in the city, which I grant you is remarkable, the baths and pump rooms are just an excuse for a lot of gouty old men to get together while their ladies gossip about each other, while at night, the same people dress up and dine and dance at the assembly rooms. But, if your sister has never visited Bath, it may well be an experience worth having, while one is still young enough to be entertained by it." Elinor laughed, but not with much conviction; she could not help being concerned about Marianne, and unhappily for her, since she had said nothing to Edward about Willoughby's reappearance in her sister's life, she was unable to seek any counsel or comfort from him on that score.

Two days later, Margaret's letter reached her sister and for some time at least it relieved her mind, filled as it was with cheerful news and plenty of interesting information about their sojourn in Provence. It was quite clear that Margaret was enjoying her holiday, and of her well-being Elinor had no cause to worry.

She carried the letter to her husband, who was equally pleased to hear of Margaret's travels and in particular her meeting with Mr Daniel Brooke.

"Do you recall him at Oxford?" asked Elinor, and Edward certainly did.

"Indeed, I do, he was a colleague of Dr Grantley at whose rooms I saw him frequently, but he was not a student of theology. Francis and he shared an interest in sacred music and architecture—Brooke was reading history and knew everything there was to know about ancient abbeys and churches and all that sort of thing, and I do recall he was making a special study of medieval churches in France. He had a folio of sketches which were quite superb. I have not met him since, but I am quite certain Francis Grantley and he must have remained friends, since they are both still at Oxford."

Elinor was pleased. "Then it is no surprise that he has so much information about all those historic places in Provence. Margaret is very lucky to have someone like him in their party—you know how keenly she studies her history." Edward agreed and was about to return the letter, when his wife asked, "And what sort of person is Mr Daniel Brooke—is he an amiable sort of man?"

"Oh perfectly amiable, as I recall," her husband replied. "He was much younger then, of course, around twenty-five or -six perhaps, rather a scholarly, quiet sort of fellow, but very handsome."

Elinor smiled and said, "I see, and that means he must be no less than thirty years old now," with which Edward readily agreed. "Certainly, though he may appear older because of the gravity of his countenance. I was struck by the fact that he appeared more serious than either Francis or me, although we were both older than he was. But I cannot think why we are concerned with his age, Elinor; is there some particular reason for these questions of which I am unaware?" he asked, regarding her with some amusement, but his wife only laughed lightly and said, "Oh no, Edward, none at all—it's just nice to know that Margaret has had the good fortune to meet with such excellent companions on her holidays. I could wish with all my heart that Marianne might be as well served by her new friends."

She went away to reply to Margaret's letter, and in her response told her sister how pleased they were to learn that she was enjoying her holiday in Provence and took care to mention that Edward did remember Mr Daniel Brooke and had described him as a "perfectly amiable, quiet, scholarly sort of fellow," which, Elinor said, sounded as though he were a very pleasant sort of person, and perhaps when they all returned to England, she might like to invite Mr Brooke to visit them at the parsonage. "I am sure Edward and he will enjoy meeting again after all these years," she wrote.

Neither her husband nor her sister would guess that Elinor, in her heart, had begun to be concerned about Margaret's future—indeed, Elinor would scarcely admit it to herself. But she was aware that Margaret's almost total concentration upon her studies and her teaching, and her lack of interest in the usual romantic pastimes of dancing and parties that filled the waking hours of most young persons of her age, might well leave her a stranded spinster.

At twenty-one, with but a tiny dowry to her name, and no hope of a substantial inheritance, Margaret Dashwood had only her looks, her youth, and her intelligence to commend her to a possible suitor, and there were not many likely men in the circles in which she moved. Having rejected the advances of Mr Andrew Barton, whose wealth and social status had not attracted Margaret—indeed, she had regarded them as a significant drawback—Elinor feared that her youngest sister might be left to survive on the emoluments of her teaching position, unless she met and married a suitable gentleman in the next few years. Yet, she knew that Margaret would never marry anyone unless he could share her interests and she could care deeply for him.

Which is why she had found the enthusiastic account of Mr Daniel Brooke in Margaret's letter so thoroughly promising. At least, she thought, as she sealed her letter and sent it off to the post, the week had brought one thing about which she could feel some pleasure and hope—despite the disappointment she had experienced with her mother and the deep sense of foreboding that shrouded her thoughts of Marianne.

❧

On Friday, Marianne waited, packed and ready, for the Percevals' carriage to arrive. She had written a note to her husband in which she had quite deliberately described the excursion to Bath as being planned by the Percevals. In earlier communications, she had mentioned them and made much of the fact that the family was respectable and their daughters were cheerful and of good character. They were, she'd said, invariably amiable and hospitable and she was glad of their company, to which Colonel Brandon had responded that he was happy indeed that she had made some new friends. On this occasion, Marianne believed he would, therefore, be pleased to learn that her new friends were being so obliging and affording her an opportunity to see Bath, which city the colonel had visited but once and never wished to re-visit. Completing her note, she had given instructions that it was to be taken to the post following her departure on Friday afternoon. Her housekeeper was informed she would return home on Monday.

When the Percevals' carriage arrived, bearing Maria and Eugenie, Marianne could not help feeling a rising sense of adventure; she had decided this was the only way she would extract some excitement out of life in Dorset, and looked forward to the experience with a degree of eagerness that she had not felt since she was seventeen.

As they drove out of Delaford, Maria and Eugenie regaled her with their hopes of seeing and meeting a range of interesting and distinguished personages in Bath. "There is to be a great party at one of the assembly rooms on Saturday night, to which we are all invited," Eugenie advised and added, "I hope, Marianne, that you have brought one of your best gowns, for we understand the ladies of Bath are exceedingly fashionable." There was little mention of the city's celebrated architecture, of which Marianne had heard from her brother-in-law, Edward, whose parents had spent several seasons there when he was a boy; instead, they chattered on about what fun they were determined to have and how they must remember to do and say precisely the right thing when introduced to the various important persons they expected to meet.

Marianne heard rather than listened with any interest to their talk; for while they were not inclined to crudely contemplate conquests of men they had not as yet met, they were both involved in a sort of competitive game—of setting their respective caps at some gentleman or other and making little wagers with one another on the result. They were not particularly vicious or nasty, just good-humoured girls with vacant minds, which could not accommodate more than a couple of thoughts together. And on this occasion all those thoughts were of the fun they intended to have in Bath.

They cared little whether Marianne was at all interested in the pursuit of their kind of entertainment, assuming she would find something to occupy her time. It was well, Marianne thought, that Mr Willoughby was going to join their party—else she might be condemned to spend all her time with Mr and Mrs Perceval. It was not a prospect she could anticipate with much pleasure.

Arriving at the Percevals' house, they found a message had been received from the Hawthornes that one of the young ladies was ill with a fever and the other had been reluctantly persuaded to stay at home with her sister, while their brothers would join the party on the morrow. While there was some disappointment expressed by the Misses Perceval, their main ambition to have fun was unlikely to be thwarted by the absence of two young ladies, who might well be regarded as competition. Consequently, their disappointment did not last long, and by the time they sat down to dinner, their spirits were as high as ever.

"I doubt that I shall sleep at all tonight; I am so brimful of expectation," cried Eugenie as she finished her dessert, and her mother spoke up to warn that she should resist the temptation to have a second serving of trifle.

"Take a cup of camomile tea instead, my love, and make sure you have a good night's sleep, else your head will be heavy and your eyes dull, which would be the very worst thing if one wished to appear at one's best," she declared, adding, "Do you not agree, Mrs Brandon?" and Marianne, who had hardly heard a word, had to respond quickly. "Oh yes indeed," she said, adding that "a good night's sleep was very important." This remark set off another interminable argument between the girls and their mother, during which Marianne wished with all her heart that she were twenty miles away, but forced herself to smile indulgently and say nothing. The Percevals, she noted, treated their daughters as if they were little girls who may be spoilt, as long as they were simultaneously warned of the dangers of overindulgence.

After dinner, claiming she was rather tired, Marianne politely refused coffee and retired to her bedroom, where she changed quickly into her nightgown and slipped into bed, content to have the chance to let her own mind wonder at what tomorrow might bring. Unlike the Misses Perceval, she had no plans for fun or conquest, but she could not help thinking of Willoughby and how it might have been, had she not been married to the colonel and he had returned to find her. How might she have responded then? It was an intriguing question.

Nothing in Marianne's life had engrossed her thoughts and feelings as intensely as had her love affair with Willoughby, and though she had not admitted it even to herself, she had never stopped craving the high intensity of emotion she had known during that brief liaison. In him she had found not just a young man of passion and flair, to enhance the appeal of his good looks; he had also been possessed of the ability to engage her heart in everything they did. They talked, read, and sang together so well, she could imagine no other man in whose company she would wish to spend the rest of her life. Like a little girl who lays her head on her pillow after reading a favourite fairy tale, hoping to dream of Prince Charming, Marianne had not entirely emancipated herself of the beguiling dreams she had once cherished. As she went to bed, they returned to fill her mind and she willingly surrendered to them.

In France, the little party of English travellers had spent most of their first week in Aix-en-Provence and its environs. In the village of Saint Remy and the ancient ruins of the Roman town of Glanum in the foothills of the Alpilles mountain range, Margaret had been both delighted and astonished by the beauty of the area and the antiquity of the sites. Absorbing the historical information and the diverse traditions of the region, she had been equally struck by the depth of Daniel Brooke's knowledge, as well as the ease with which he communicated it to the rest of their party, as though he were telling a story, without any element of loftiness or condescension. What rich pleasure it would have been to have had the opportunity to study with such a teacher, Margaret thought.

As the fine weather held, they travelled north to spend a few days touring one of the finest towns in France: Lyon. Margaret recalled that she had read accounts of excited English travellers in the eighteenth century, making the journey by river craft down the Rhône from Lyon to Avignon. When she mentioned it, Mr Brooke seemed both surprised and pleased by her knowledge and took the time to explain the historical significance of both towns, promising that she would be able to see many places of interest in Lyon. When she asked if they could possibly do the return journey by river, he said quietly that he would not recommend it—especially not in late October. "Now, if it were summer that would be an ideal way to travel down to Avignon. There are many pleasure craft that take touring parties down the river; it can be a very pleasant experience, since one has the advantage of an open boat, which enables one to enjoy the prospect on both sides of the river, and much of the country is very pretty indeed," he explained. "However, it would not be as comfortable at this time of year."

When she said she wished it were possible to make such a journey, he mused, "Well, perhaps if you were to return next summer, Miss Dashwood, it might be arranged," and Margaret looked up at his face to see if he was speaking in jest, but he looked entirely serious. "Do you mean that?" she asked, and seeing a look of some uncertainty cross her countenance, he went further. "Indeed I do, Miss Dashwood; I spend much of every summer in this part of France. I have often travelled down the river by boat, and were you to return in summer, it would not be at all difficult to accommodate your wishes." Margaret smiled and said nothing, but decided that it was an offer worth considering.

Arriving in Lyon, the ladies had been pleasantly surprised to find the streets clean, with many excellent inns and rest houses. Having visited Paris often, Margaret said she thought the inns seemed every bit as good and the streets were cleaner and less crowded. So completely satisfied were they with their accommodation and meals, a decision was made by the entire party that they would spend at least two more days exploring Lyon and its surrounding countryside. They had been assured that there was much to see—many places of antiquity and artistic merit which Margaret looked forward to seeing, with a companion who appeared to take particular pleasure in encouraging and satisfying her interest.

It was during these days in Lyon and later at Arles and Nîmes that she began to realise that what had been an invigorating meeting of minds was gradually developing into something far less familiar to her. Excited by his intellect and knowledge and intoxicated by all she was learning from him, she had begun to experience other feelings—some unfamiliar though quite pleasing and others so sharp they caused her some disquiet each time she became aware of them. She had initially noticed that Daniel Brooke addressed her as Miss Dashwood throughout the last fortnight, even though Nicholas Wilcox had used her name soon after they began their holiday. However, recently it seemed that on some occasions, when their friends had wandered away to look at some other attraction and they were alone together, usually when he wished to draw her attention to something of particular interest, he would call her Margaret and would do so quite naturally, just as he would take her hand to assist her up and down steps or in and out of vehicles without fuss or awkwardness. While there had been no trace of familiarity or boldness, there was a sense of friendly intimacy that she enjoyed. She had smiled once or twice to acknowledge it and also to let him see that she did not object, but it had made little difference; when they were all together at a meal or in a carriage—she was Miss Dashwood to him again.

Writing in her notebook at the end of a long and satisfying day, Margaret recorded her changing feelings.

It has been over two weeks now since we arrived in Marseilles, and I cannot believe how swiftly and with what ease I have come to regard

Daniel Brooke as one of the most remarkable men I have met in all my life. It is an experience quite unique to me, for I have rarely spent so much time in the company of one person. (This comes about because Claire and Mr Wilcox are increasingly inclined to spend as much time as they possibly can together. Although she has not said anything to me, it is become clear that they are very much attracted to one another—Nicholas is particularly keen, I believe, and will, if she will only let him, soon become deeply besotted with her.)

As to my own situation, I cannot say what Mr Brooke thinks of me, except he is exceedingly generous with his time and patient in his answers to every question I ask, so that I have to conclude that he is a dedicated teacher who appears to enjoy imparting knowledge. He accords me a degree of respect that I love, letting me state my views without patronising or contradicting me, which, knowing he is a scholar of some distinction, makes me feel very honoured. Apart from my dear brother-in-law, Edward, I have not known any other man of that age (I assume, and Claire agrees, that Daniel Brooke must be at least thirty or thirty-two, perhaps) who exhibits such generosity of spirit in his willingness to share his time and knowledge with others. It is both remarkable and touching, when one considers how little respect is accorded to the intelligence of women by most men about town.

Furthermore, he is kind and concerned, making every allowance for my safety and comfort as we travel about the place, without conceit or condescension. Unaccustomed as I am to such partiality from a gentleman of his age and reputation, I will acknowledge that it is an intensely pleasurable experience, such as I have not known before. Because I am determined to be sensible and not to let myself imagine that a situation exists which plainly does not, I shall not let myself believe that I am falling in love with him. However, I must confess that were I to permit myself to set foot along that path, it would not be difficult at all, for he is indeed a man of very endearing qualities.

Tomorrow we return to Aix-en-Provence, and I wonder what our last week in the south of France will bring. We have been promised a few more days of this wonderful autumn weather before the arrival of the Mistral, and we must make the most of it.

Concluding her entry, Margaret put away her notebook, extinguished the lamp, and went to bed. There had been some talk in the village of the weather changing—it was said the Alpine winds could begin to blow anytime now, and the temperate, salubrious Mediterranean would be assailed by their icy blast. But Margaret felt only the warmth of anticipated happiness.

Chapter Thirteen

THE JOURNEY TO BATH was accomplished with what seemed like the greatest of ease, with their transport and accommodation both meticulously organised by Mr Willoughby.

The Percevals and their servants travelled in their own carriage, and the two Hawthorne boys rode alongside of them, thus allowing Mrs Brandon and Miss Peabody to be conveniently accommodated within Mr Willoughby's vehicle, while his manservant sat on the box. Throughout the journey, Mr Willoughby was assiduous in his efforts to ascertain that the two ladies were comfortable and well informed of all the sites and scenes that were able to be viewed from the windows of their carriage. As they passed through parts of the Somerset countryside, with which he claimed complete familiarity, having spent much of his life in the county, he gave them accounts of historic places where ancient battles had been fought and settlements made, with the aplomb of a historian. Miss Peabody was most impressed—she had no idea Somerset was such an important county, she declared, only to be told, in the politest and most respectful manner by Mr Willoughby, that Somerset was one of the most historically significant counties in England.

Marianne, who'd heard a good deal of the same information on another occasion, had not forgotten, and while she listened with interest, she could not help being favourably impressed by the way in which he would use his knowledge to move and astonish those in his company. Perhaps, she thought, he wishes to make it plain to me that he is not just attempting to influence my opinion of him, else he would not pay so much attention to Miss Peabody's enquiries as well. As they approached Bath and Mr Willoughby was giving them an account of the unique hot springs that gave the city its reputation, Marianne, not wishing to give the impression that she was indifferent to the significance of the historic city, asked, "And when did the Romans discover these hot springs?"—aware from her own reading that the bath houses had been constructed over two or three centuries of Roman occupation. He answered without hesitation, "Ah, but they did not, Mrs Brandon," he said, with a knowing smile. "Indeed they have long claimed to have done so, but scholars of Celtic history will tell you that the hot springs of Somerset were the centre of a Celtic shrine long before the Roman invasion of Britain. The Romans dispatched the defeated Celts to the mountains, occupied the site, and built a temple to the goddess Minerva on the spot." Miss Peabody made sympathetic noises about the poor defeated Celts, but Marianne was fascinated as he went on to tell them more about the depredations of the Romans and their evil Emperor Claudius. It seemed to her that Willoughby had extended his interests and knowledge, making him an even more fascinating person now than the young man she had met those many years ago in Barton Park. She would never have thought him to be a student of history, and yet here he was giving them facts and dates aplenty. In her readiness to credit him with enhanced learning in the intervening years, Marianne had clearly forgotten that even when they first met, Willoughby had proved to be a quick learner when it came to her particular interests and had matched every one of her enthusiasms with great zest and energy. It was a talent he used to good effect, then as now.

As they drove into Bath, he gave instructions to the driver and, turning to Marianne, said quietly, "There are those who believe that King Arthur fought and won a great battle here, before he set up his court at Glastonbury." Then, looking directly into her eyes, he reminded her, "And I am sure you will recall, Mrs Brandon, that it was at Glastonbury the great traditions of chivalry and romance were laid down in England, by King Arthur himself." He spoke as though his words were meant only for her, and sensing this, Marianne dropped her eyes, feeling for the first time that perhaps he *was* trying to remind her of something else they had shared. She was unsure if she wished to follow where he was leading her, but she could not deny the excitement of the moment.

The carriage drew up before an elegant Georgian building in Camden Terrace, where Willoughby had taken several suites of rooms for their entire party for the next three days. Escorting the ladies in, he handled all the arrangements with swift efficiency and had their trunks carried up to their rooms, while he promised to await the arrival of the second carriage, bearing the Percevals. It was travelling somewhat slower than his own, he said, urging the ladies to retire to their rooms and partake of the refreshments he had ordered for them.

Miss Peabody and Marianne found themselves in a handsome sitting room with windows that looked out across a wide street to a park beyond; two bedchambers led out from doors at either end of the sitting room, both appropriately equipped for comfort and convenience. Miss Peabody was amazed at the luxury, claiming she had never been in such a place before and wondering aloud what it must have cost. Marianne, who knew better than to speculate about the cost, simply wandered in and out of the rooms, thinking that Willoughby's new affluence had only enhanced what had been to her one of his most endearing traits—his generosity. Recalling his desire to bring her gifts, including, on one occasion, a specially trained horse, which to Marianne's chagrin, Elinor had insisted they could not afford to keep, Marianne's mind played upon their present circumstances and sought to see them in the best possible light. He was trying to make amends, to demonstrate that he had learnt from his past mistakes, she decided charitably, permitting herself thereby to enjoy, without guilt, his favours and his company, which she had to confess were very pleasing.

A discreet knock at the door and two footmen were admitted bearing trays of refreshments—cold meats, pastries, and fruit, as well as tea for the travellers. Miss Peabody gave a cry of delight and sat down to enjoy the feast, while Marianne still walked about the rooms, amazed by the luxury of it all, and was only persuaded to take some tea when her companion poured out a cup and begged her to try it. "It is an excellent brew, do try it, Mrs Brandon—the finest India, I am certain," she cried, and Marianne obliged, if only to stop her urging.

Some half an hour later, the rest of their party arrived and were similarly accommodated in their rooms, while Mr Willoughby, it was revealed, still playing the perfect host, had set out to get them tickets for a musical entertainment at one of the theatres in the city.

The Percevals could scarcely open their mouths without praising him for his organisation of the excursion to Bath and all he continued to do to make their stay comfortable and memorable. While their daughters concentrated upon the food, as more trays were brought in and laid upon the table, Mr and Mrs Perceval sang the praises of their new friend.

"I must say I have never met such a generous young fellow—so full of courtesy and concern, he cannot do too much to ensure that we are all satisfactorily served," said Mr Perceval, and his wife echoed his sentiments, then added, "My sister, to whom I wrote mentioning Mr Willoughby's kindness to us when we had the problem with the horses at Glastonbury, says he is well liked wherever he is known, he is such a generous and amiable young man. She lives not far from his country house in Somersetshire and says she cannot think what on earth his wife was thinking of when she decided to seek a separation from him. She must be exceedingly hard to please, my sister says."

Quite clearly, the Percevals had no notion of the pecuniary circumstances of their host, whose largesse depended entirely upon the vast fortune his wife had brought him at their marriage.

Hearing their words, Marianne, astounded, could say nothing; presently, she rose and asked to be excused, claiming she wished to rest awhile. The Perceval girls declared that they were far from tired and intended to accompany the young Hawthornes on a tour of the Grand Terrace and Milsom Street shops that afternoon. Mr Willoughby had told them the shopping in Milsom Street was very good, they said. Marianne smiled and said she had no liking for shopping, urged them to enjoy themselves, and retired to her room.

There, it was not fatigue or the prospect of a visit to the theatre that evening that occupied her mind, but the vital snippet of news, so carelessly thrown about by Mrs Perceval, that Willoughby's wife had sought a separation from him. It absolutely consumed her thoughts. Her active imagination would not rest until she had worked out at least half a dozen possible explanations—almost all of which were favourable to him and not to his wife—for the situation in which Willoughby was now placed.

Any one of the resolutions she could think of would provide him with a plausible reason for spending so much of his time in Somersetshire, and putting so much effort into making new friends, for it was surely unthinkable that he would be able to continue within the same circle of acquaintances they had made during the years of their marriage. This would certainly excuse the extravagance with which he courted the Percevals and attempted to ensure their comfort and satisfaction, she thought, in case one had wondered if he was showing off just a little. That aspect, Marianne decided, could now be explained away quite satisfactorily.

Having spent most of the afternoon constructing scenarios that would excuse—nay justify—Willoughby's present behaviour, she did finally fall into a light sleep, from which Miss Peabody came to rouse her when it was time to dress for dinner and prepare to go out to the theatre. She was most excited. "Mr Willoughby called to say he had obtained tickets for an excellent concert; it is all arranged—we are to dine downstairs at seven and leave for the theatre at eight," she announced, with the kind of extraordinary animation one sees in someone to whom such excitement is rare indeed. Marianne could not help pitying Miss Peabody—she was quite certain she must be forty at least, and it did seem she'd had very little enjoyment out of life and grasped every opportunity with fervour.

When they all met in the dining room, Marianne was glad she had brought one of her best gowns—the Perceval girls were attired in satin gowns with elaborate trimmings and had fur-lined capes to protect their bare arms from the cold, and the Hawthorne boys looked very debonair in formal evening dress, which one hardly ever saw in Dorset. Marianne had not known they would be attending a concert, but had decided that it was worth packing an elegant blue velvet gown, which set off her figure and suited her colouring so well, each time she wore it she had received many compliments. This night was no exception, for everyone at the table noted how well she looked, and both Mr Perceval and Mr Willoughby took time to tell her so. Marianne was well pleased.

The concert was well attended and deserved to be, for it was a veritable musical feast—with a chamber group, two pianists, and two singers of considerable talent, all as determined to delight their audience as the audience was to be delighted.

Their seats were in two groups—a complete half row was occupied by the Percevals and Hawthornes; to one side were three more chairs, and once again, it fell to Mr Willoughby to arrange for all his guests to be seated and then to discover that he had the seat between Miss Peabody and Mrs Brandon. Marianne did not wish to speculate whether he had deliberately arranged it so, but was happy to accept that as their host, he must ensure that the rest of the party had their seats first, although it was apparent that their seats were in no way inferior to the others. Miss Peabody, who confessed to being something of an enthusiast when it came to singing, having taken lessons herself, she told them, was absolutely delighted with the placement of their seats and thanked Mr Willoughby many times, at the beginning of the concert, the end, and in between items. She was sure that she'd never had such good seats ever before, she said.

At one point in the entertainment, when there was a short interval, Miss Peabody had to accompany her cousin, Mrs Perceval, to the cloak room, leaving Marianne with Mr Willoughby. As they walked about the room, she was at first reluctant to break the silence, but when he did, asking her opinion of the performances and offering some comments of his own, she found no difficulty in entering into a discussion about some of the items on the programme. However, when he chose a particular duet—Ben Jonson's pretty "Song to Celia"—as the one he favoured most, she knew he had done so to remind her that it was one they had often sung together at Barton Cottage. It had been a favourite with Mrs Dashwood, too.

The room was rather warm, and he invited her to step out onto the adjacent balcony overlooking the garden, where various men and ladies were promenading and talking quite excitedly, and there they stood and watched the passing scene, without saying a word, until they were summoned within to take their seats. It was then, as she made to go indoors, he said, "Mrs Brandon—Marianne—I must speak with you. Please have no fear that I will embarrass or discompose you in any way—nothing could be further from my thoughts—but I must speak with you. Will you permit me, please, to find some time in the course of these three days to speak privately with you?"

Marianne should have been prepared for such an overture, but she was not, having believed that Willoughby was being particular to avoid any reference to their past association. But she was not inclined in her present frame of mind to deny him and so said, with a fair degree of dignity, "Mr Willoughby, as you are aware, our friends the Percevals have no idea that you and I have known one another before our recent meeting at Glastonbury. I should prefer that they continue in this belief, which makes it difficult for me to grant your request. However, if you can arrange it discreetly, without placing me at risk of becoming the subject of gossip, I am willing to hear what you have to say."

His immediate response was one of deep gratitude and complete acquiescence with the terms she had set, as he promised to make such arrangements as were necessary, taking every precaution to shield her from any suspicion. As they returned to their seats, Miss Peabody came to join them, and she was so busy praising everyone and everything she had seen, she failed to notice the change of mood in both her companions. Mr Willoughby and Mrs Brandon remained very quiet for the rest of the evening, and while Mrs Brandon looked a little flushed, the gentleman wore an expression of heightened excitement that, in truth, had nothing at all to do with the excellent quality of the concert.

The following morning was to be spent mainly in sightseeing in the town before luncheon, followed by attendance at a ball at one of the assembly rooms that night. After breakfast, which was served in their rooms, Marianne found Miss Peabody all agog to go downstairs, because the Percevals were going to the Pump Room, where all the best people met to take the waters, she said, and since she had never been in such a place before, she intended to go with them. Marianne confessed that she had not either, but was not keen to join them.

"I have no particular interest in it myself; I'd much rather take a walk along the Royal Crescent, which I am told is one of the finest architectural achievements in England," she declared, and a voice behind her said softly, "Well said, Mrs Brandon, you are well informed, the Pump Room is for invalids who need the waters and others who like to gossip, while the Royal Terrace is not to be missed." It was Willoughby, and he made it clear that he would be exceedingly happy to escort her as she walked, pointing out that it was a particularly fine day for walking.

Seeing that all other members of the party had by now departed on their own expeditions into the city, Willoughby offered Marianne his arm as they set off up the street. At first, she felt a little self-conscious, but soon, he succeeded in putting her at ease with his conversation, which was as usual full of trivial gossip and lighthearted jokes about some of the people they passed on their walk.

Various gracious carriages and dashing little gigs passed them by, while groups of giggling young girls and flirting couples stood ostensibly examining the wares in shop windows. Clearly familiar with the town, Willoughby maintained a quiet stream of conversation, and Marianne was astonished at how little he had altered in manner and style from the young man she had known.

Yet, there *was* something, she could not quite put her finger on it at first, that was different about him. As they walked, pausing to admire first one fine building and then another, he told her of the history of the city, and it did occur to her that Willoughby's manner seemed far less arrogant than it had been before. It was as though he had realised that the brash self-confidence that had characterised his youth, when he would express contempt for others without reservation, would not be acceptable to her. In its place was a more amenable, certainly far less pretentious gentleman, whom she found very agreeable indeed.

As they made the gradual ascent from Queen's Square to the Gravel Walk and thence to the Royal Crescent, Marianne was able, without any difficulty, to convince herself that here was a more mature Willoughby, changed from the somewhat presumptuous young man she had loved several summers ago. Elinor would be surprised indeed were she to meet him now, she thought to herself, recalling that her elder sister had been thoroughly censorious of his reckless impetuousness and the lack of proper decorum in his behaviour, even when she had enjoyed his company.

As for what had followed, with the dreadful episode when he had left Barton Cottage without giving them an honest explanation and had turned up later in London, engaged to the wealthy Miss Grey, Marianne recalled the condemnation that had been heaped upon him by all and sundry; but today, she could find no trace of the cruelty of which he had been accused or the selfishness that was said to have tainted his contrition. She was pondering what her sister would say if she told her they had met and she had judged him to be a changed man, when he, having been silent as they had slowed their steps while negotiating a rising gradient in the pavement, spoke suddenly, interrupting her thoughts.

"Marianne, I must speak with you; I cannot let this opportunity pass, lest I should never get another chance. Shall we go down into that little park? It is quiet and private, but pretty enough to have a natural attraction for you to visit it." She was a little taken aback, but after his remarks the previous evening, she had been expecting some sort of approach, so acquitted herself quite creditably, saying, "It certainly is, and it is sunny as well, which may provide another reason to visit, since there is quite a breeze rising."

He agreed immediately and assisted her down the shallow steps on to the footpath and then down another flight of steps into the park. It was indeed an exquisite little haven, with a fountain playing amidst the prettiest arrangement of plants; they found a quiet bench beside a pool and were seated. Marianne was glad of the rest; her spirits had been roused since the previous evening, and as they had walked she had felt the racing of her heart—due both to the brisk exercise and a sense of anticipation. Now, as she waited for him to speak, she could scarcely control the rising colour in her cheeks and was glad of her wide-brimmed bonnet that hid some of her face from his view. Willoughby spoke softly, tentatively, as though he feared she would refuse to listen.

"Marianne, I have spent many hours in agony over the years past, wondering if I would ever have the chance to speak with you. I know your sister refused to let me hope; she said you were lost to me forever and urged me to forget you and make my own life—but I hoped and prayed that one day, I would have the opportunity to tell you what I felt, how deeply I loved you, and how wretched was my state of guilt and misery, when we were forcibly parted—" at which point, he was interrupted.

"Forcibly parted? What do you mean? By whom were we forcibly parted?" she asked, disbelieving, and he responded, "Did not your sister Mrs Ferrars acquaint you with the details of my wretched fate? I told her everything, while you lay ill at Cleveland House; I had hoped that she, knowing that I had no chance of ever regaining your good opinion, would at least tell you as much of the story as would help you think me less evil than you did at the time." He sounded hurt; she turned and, looking at him for the first time, said in a quiet voice, "Evil! I never thought you were evil—selfish and thoughtless, reckless, inconsiderate of the tender feelings of others perhaps—but never evil."

He picked up her hand and kissed it then, saying softly, "Thank you, Marianne. Even after all these years, it gives me some comfort to hear you say that. Will you let me tell you the rest—the details you did not hear, which I will relate if only in the hope that it will help you understand how my youthful stupidity combined with the cruelty of Fate itself, led to the circumstances that forced us apart? If I'd had the means or the courage, I should never have let it happen, I would have stayed with you, urged you to come away with me, thrown myself upon the mercy of your family and my friends, rather than be driven meekly into an alliance that has brought me nothing but misery. Marianne, please, will you hear me out?"

She nodded. "But not here—we are too easily observed, and I do not wish to become the subject of gossip among the Percevals. It may be carried to Elinor and Edward."

"Of course; that is the very last thing I should wish. Will you allow me to make some arrangement on our return journey?" he asked, and as she nodded, he continued, "But I thank you from the bottom of my heart," and kissed her hand again. Marianne, unable to hide the blush that rose in her cheek, said, "I think I have stayed too long out of doors, we should be getting back."

They walked back almost in silence; as they passed some notable and significant points in the city, he stopped and drew her attention to them and she nodded and noted what she saw, but they were both very aware that something had changed between them. The many attractions of Bath had long faded into irrelevance as neither could avoid thinking of what had been said. No longer would it be possible to pretend that they were casual acquaintances enjoying a sightseeing tour of Bath.

❧

Back at their rooms at Camden Terrace, all was astonishment, for the Percevals had unexpectedly encountered at the Pump Room another family they had met on a visit to Lyme Regis last summer. The Nicolsons consisted of a father, mother, an aunt, and three young persons—a young man and two girls all of about the same age as the Percevals' daughters—and to their great glee, they were found to be staying in a house on the same street and had promised to join their party at the assembly rooms that evening.

Marianne would normally have been somewhat put out by this sudden increase in the numbers in their party, but on this occasion and in the circumstances, she was rather pleased. It would suit her, she thought, to have the Misses Perceval distracted by more young men and ladies of their own age, leaving her to her own devices and under less scrutiny. Miss Peabody too seemed to be quite excited by the prospect of another meeting with the Nicolsons—also an advantage, Marianne thought.

However, she was cautious, and before she parted from Willoughby, she managed to warn him that they should not appear to be too closely engaged in conversation during the evening, lest it should be noticed and talked of. He promised that he would ensure that no such thing occurred, assuring her that he would engage all the young ladies in their party to dance before approaching her.

Marianne smiled, remembering again how very much like the Willoughby she had known was this man; despite the touches of grey at his temples and the fine lines that marked his countenance, he was still the epitome of her romantic hero.

Marianne dressed with great care that evening and was grateful that Miss Peabody, who had spent a most active and exciting morning, seemed too drained of energy to quiz her too deeply about her own expedition into the city. They had retired to their bedrooms to rest and rose in time to bathe and dress for the evening. Miss Peabody went down to dinner, but Marianne asked only for some tea to be brought up to her room; her thoughts were too full of what Willoughby had told her to let her think of food. The Perceval girls were running from one room to the next, discussing what they should wear, while Mrs Perceval was heard appealing for some peace and quiet so she could rest, else she would have to stay home and someone would have to stay with her, which dire threat seemed to bring instant silence.

The carriages arrived to convey them to the assembly rooms, and the gentlemen were assembled in the vestibule when the ladies came downstairs and, while the youthful energy of Maria and Eugenie may have attracted the most attention, there was no doubt which of the ladies drew and held Mr Willoughby's eyes, for Marianne appeared lovelier than she had looked in many a year. Her eyes had a sparkle and her cheeks a bloom that would have surprised her sisters and delighted her mother, for it made her appear several years younger than she was. There was about her also an air of anticipation, an expectation that she was on the brink of something particularly pleasurable, which generally surrounds the very young.

Perhaps it was fortunate that only Mr Willoughby saw and recalled that it was exactly the quality that had excited and attracted him to her when they had first met at Barton Park. The rest of the party were too immersed in their own plans for the evening to notice that Mrs Brandon of Delaford Manor had stepped back in time, transformed that evening into Miss Marianne Dashwood of Barton Cottage.

The ball at the assembly rooms was crowded, and once again, this suited both Willoughby and Marianne, for there was never any lack of activity or company during which they could be singled out for attention. Willoughby was as good as his word; he was particular to ask each of the Misses Perceval to dance and then went away to get them drinks and find them seats, before approaching Marianne for a dance that he knew she would enjoy—one with slow, gracious steps and elegant figures, rather than the bustling, noisy items that had preceded them. Marianne was a little nervous; they had never danced together in public before, though they had often talked of it in times past. She wondered how it would turn out, but Willoughby expertly led her through the dance, smoothly guiding her in and out of the figures, clearly familiar with the movements and the music. They completed it so successfully that there was spontaneous applause when it ended. Willoughby bowed low and escorted his partner to her seat, just as he had done with the others, thanked her, and then moved away, leaving Marianne feeling so utterly exhilarated that she hoped no one else was going to ask her to dance—her legs felt weak and she was sure she would not be able to stand up.

When the music stopped for supper, Willoughby returned to help Marianne and Miss Peabody to a table and brought them drinks and food. After supper, Mrs Perceval was feeling tired, and though the younger members of the party were keen to remain at the dance, Miss Peabody elected to return with her cousin to Camden Place. When she rose to leave the room, Marianne went with her, but at the moment of leaving, she turned and saw Willoughby regarding her with such a look as she knew she had not seen on the face of any other man. It was the look she carried in her heart and took to her bed as she slipped between the sheets and fell asleep.

For most of her life, Marianne, an avid reader of romantic literature, a lover of deeply emotional music, had cast herself in the role of a young woman whose life would be guided primarily by the intensity of her passions.

While his recital of events, calculated to absolve him of guilt, may have strained credulity, nothing that had happened in her life since her affair with him, had convinced Marianne that Willoughby was not the man who could have made her the happiest girl in the world, if callous people and malign forces beyond their control had not intervened to thwart their destiny.

Chapter Fourteen

WHEN MARIANNE AWOKE THE following morning, she had no notion of what the day would bring. During a restless night she had swung between delightful dreams of the previous day, particularly the almost unbearable pleasure of touching hands with Willoughby in the course of the dance—openly, without guilt—then awaking to the misery of confronting the reality of their situation, with no expectation of future happiness together. Between the dreams and the waking there had been aching moments of realisation that he could still excite in her thoughts and feelings that no other man had inspired.

Prudence would decree, and no doubt, she thought, Elinor would agree, that she should abjure these indiscreet musings now and see him no more. And yet she knew she could not, because she had agreed to hear what Willoughby had to say, not just because he had pleaded to be heard, but because in her heart she wanted very much to hear it.

As she lay in bed, reluctant to rise and face the day—they were due to leave Bath after breakfast—she expected that Miss Peabody must by now be packed and ready and would soon be poking her head around the door to urge Marianne to do likewise. Which was why she was surprised when the maid who brought in the breakfast tray informed her that one of the ladies had been taken ill overnight and a doctor had been called. Marianne was astonished; it could not have been Miss Peabody, she would surely have heard if doctors and others had been tramping through their sitting room, she thought, and went to investigate. Finding Maria Perceval in the corridor, she asked if Miss Peabody was unwell and was told it was not Miss Peabody, but her mama, Mrs Perceval, who had been taken ill during the night. "Poor Mama had such a bad turn, she was very sick indeed. The doctor thinks it must have been the fish she had for supper," Maria declared. Marianne was glad she'd had none of the fish. "Is she feeling any better?" she asked anxiously and was told, "A little better, but she is not able to leave her bed. The doctor will return at noon. It means we cannot leave Bath today—but no matter," she added casually, "Eugenie and I are going over to the Nicolsons' for the rest of the day. Miss Peabody will stay here and attend on Mama."

This piece of intelligence worried Marianne, since she had arranged to be back at Delaford on Monday and wondered about the consequences if she could not. But in the next minute, Maria informed her that her father had to leave Bath directly because he had urgent matters of business to attend to, which could not be delayed, and Mr Willoughby had offered to convey him in his carriage instead of Miss Peabody, who would remain with Mrs Perceval. Marianne was relieved, even though it meant she would be travelling with Willoughby and Mr Perceval. At least her return would not be delayed, causing concern at Delaford.

Not long afterward, Mr Willoughby himself appeared at their door to advise that his carriage would be ready to leave whenever she was. He explained that some of their arrangements had changed, due to Mrs Perceval's sudden illness, but assured her that he would see she was safely conveyed to Delaford that evening. Reassured, Marianne now concentrated upon the practicalities of the journey, hastening to pack and be in readiness to leave as early as possible, aware that the autumn evenings were already drawing in and it would be preferable to be back at Delaford Manor before dark.

When she was ready, she went to call on Mrs Perceval and found her looking very pale and unwell, clearly unable to rise and be dressed, much less undertake a journey of several miles. Marianne commiserated with her, wished her a speedy recovery, and went downstairs, where she found Willoughby's carriage waiting at the door. Mr Perceval's luggage had already been stacked, and Willoughby's manservant added hers to the pile and strapped it in. When his master appeared, the man opened the door, admitting first Marianne and then Mr Perceval, before Willoughby climbed in and minutes later they were on their way.

It was not quite the company she had expected—but, she reasoned, it could suit her better to have Mr Perceval rather than Miss Peabody, since he was less likely to attempt to engage her in chatter, for which she was singularly disinclined, nor was he likely to eavesdrop on their conversation. She was proved right when about half an hour into their journey, Mr Perceval, having made it clear that he was still feeling the aftereffects of the party at the assembly rooms, and encouraged by the motion of the vehicle, fell asleep and snored.

Willoughby, who had been sitting opposite her, crossed over to sit beside her and said in a quiet voice, which would not disturb their sleeping companion, "I am sorry if you were troubled by the change in our travel arrangements, but when I realised that Mrs Perceval was unwell and could not make the journey, while her husband urgently needed to return home, I thought it best to offer to convey him in my carriage. Since Miss Peabody was needed to attend upon Mrs Perceval, it was not an inconvenient arrangement after all. What do you think?"

Marianne indicated that she agreed, adding, "It is very good of you to offer to help. I am sure Mr Perceval is grateful. I am too, since I am expected at Delaford this evening and it could pose some problems were I not to return. I should not like the housekeeper to send word to my sister and trouble her and my brother-in-law, which she might do, were my return to be excessively delayed."

Once again, Willoughby promised her solemnly that she need have no such fears; he expected to deliver Mr Perceval to his home by midday or shortly afterward, and then they would travel on to Delaford.

The first part of the journey was accomplished without difficulty, and a grateful Mr Perceval was delivered to his door before one o'clock. Having broken journey to water the horses, they set off again, leaving the main road for a quieter route through some well-wooded country. Marianne had been wondering when and how Willoughby intended to make the "discreet arrangement" he had promised, so he could tell her more of his story. Since leaving Bath, their conversation had all been of the pleasures of Bath and the beauty of the Somerset countryside, which, in view of the presence of Mr Perceval, seemed a sensible thing to do.

They had travelled some distance from the Percevals' home and she could tell from the lengthening shadows that it was probably midafternoon when, quite suddenly, the carriage slowed and pulled up. There were raised voices and the sound of a horse neighing. Willoughby put his head out of the window and asked a question, then opened the door and got out himself. Marianne began to feel anxious—she hoped it was not a problem like the one that had afflicted the Percevals' vehicle on its way back from Glastonbury. There was more talking among the men; she tried to listen but could not make out what was being said.

Soon afterward she heard a horse galloping away and Willoughby returned. Standing in the road, with the door of the carriage open, he said, "There's been a problem with one of the horses; he could be lame. I've sent my man to fetch another vehicle and a couple of fresh horses; he shouldn't be long."

She was worried. "How far does he have to ride to get another vehicle and fresh horses?" she asked, and he smiled and said, "Not far at all—we are within a few miles of my estate." While that gave her some comfort, it also introduced another question. He had never mentioned that the road to Delaford went anywhere near his property. Had he, she wondered, taken another route in order to bring them past Combe Magna? Had he perhaps planned this? Was this the "arrangement" he had made? She could not help wondering, but was reluctant to ask.

Willoughby closed the carriage door and stood outside the vehicle with the driver while they waited, and Marianne drew her cloak around her and hoped it would not be too long, for it was clear that the wind was much colder now and it would be dark in an hour or two. Looking out, she saw that the land on one side of the road was pasture—she could see haystacks and sheep in the distance—while on the other side, the woods came right down to the road, the trees mostly leafless and bare. The sky was grey, although it didn't look like rain, but Marianne wished the man would hurry; she was not at all comfortable with the situation.

She was almost beginning to panic—despite her confidence in Willoughby, she disliked the idea of being stranded here alone with him and the driver—when she heard the sound of horses' hooves on the road. Willoughby's servant had returned with a neat little curricle, and with him came a groom and two fresh horses for the carriage.

Willoughby acted swiftly, helping her out and into the new vehicle, and, making certain she was well protected from the cold with a warm rug tucked around her, he instructed his servant and the groom to attend to the horses and carriage, climbed in, and drove on at quite a fast pace, putting her once more in mind of days past. He was a skilled driver, she recalled, but she was unaccustomed to being driven at such a pace; however, she said nothing, knowing that she was dependent entirely upon his goodwill to get her home. They spoke little, since he was concentrating on the road, but when they turned in at the gates of a property, she turned and looked at him, questioning what was happening. When the vehicle came to a halt, she asked, "Where is this place?" He smiled then and said, "Marianne, welcome to Combe Magna, I have always wanted you to see it. Now, although it was not how I hoped it would be, here we are."

This time, even she had to protest; it was as though reality had finally intruded upon her romantic fantasies. "Willoughby, I cannot do this; I cannot have it said that I was here at your house. Should this information reach my family or be spoken of in the area and is somehow conveyed to Colonel Brandon…" She stopped, unable to go on. It was the first time her husband's name had ever been mentioned by either of them, and even as she said it, she saw the look on his face change. The welcoming smile had disappeared, and he looked as though he had been reminded of some dreadful memory that he had spent years trying to forget. When he did speak, he said quietly, "Marianne, I did not do this to trick you into visiting my home; but as you must realise, we had no alternative—we could not proceed to Delaford in this little vehicle and must wait until my carriage and horses arrive. Then, I promise, I will ensure that you reach Delaford Manor safely. Meanwhile, we can rest awhile and take some refreshment here. There is no harm done. Have no fear, Marianne; no one knows you here, and none of my servants will ever gossip about me and any guest of mine."

He sounded confident; seeing she had no other alternative and realising that she could not continue to sit in the vehicle without drawing undue attention to herself, she alighted and let him lead her indoors, into a pleasant, large reception room, where a fire burned in the grate and the drapes were drawn against the bleak weather outside. It had clearly been prepared under his instructions, and he hurried to get her settled in front of the fire. A footman brought in refreshments and Marianne was persuaded to partake of a drink, on the grounds that it would help her avoid a chill. "I should not wish to be responsible for making you ill. I recall that you have a delicate constitution and I beg you to take care," he said. She smiled then, for the first time since the horse had pulled up in the forest, and said, "I do believe I am a lot stronger now; I have not caught a chill in years." He bowed and said gravely, "I am very glad to hear it, but I still believe you would be well advised to keep warm and take some hot food while we wait for the carriage. Please help yourself," he urged, and she, not wishing to make too much of it, did as he asked.

As they waited for the carriage to arrive, he told her his story.

It was very little different, in fact, to the tale he had told Elinor at Cleveland several years ago, when he had arrived and demanded to know if Marianne was out of danger and insisted on being permitted to relate the circumstances that he claimed had forced him to leave Marianne and marry Miss Grey. But it was as self-serving a narrative as one might expect of a man who had already betrayed one unfortunate young woman, leaving her with an illegitimate child to care for, while courting another on the other side of the country, permitting her to believe that he was free, willing, and able to make her an offer of marriage. As Marianne listened, he gave his account, omitting any mention of Eliza Williams and her child, concentrating upon the injustice perpetrated upon him by his aunt Mrs Smith in denying him his inheritance and compelling him thereby to marry Miss Grey.

While using the same set of facts as a frame to support his appeal to Marianne's heart, which he had already guessed was kindly disposed toward him, he added many embellishments to the picture—telling her over again how deeply he had fallen in love with her, how there had never been another woman for whom he had felt anything like the depth of affection she had inspired in him. He even insisted that, had she not been married so soon afterward to another (demonstrating again his inability to even speak her husband's name), he would have freed himself of the mutual misery of his marriage and sought once more to regain her affection.

When she looked genuinely shocked at this suggestion, he challenged her, "Can you say with conviction that if you had not been married and I was free again and had come to you, you would have refused me? Knowing how well we loved one another, how happy we had been and could be again? I think, my dear Marianne, if you are honest, you must admit that at the very least, you cannot have said no. I should have begged you to consider—even though I know your sister and perhaps even your mother may have denied us, I believe you would have wanted to take that chance." Then seeing her bite her lip, for she could not bring herself to speak, he added, "But it was a vain hope; for in those few months, when I was unable to do anything to break free from the cruel trap in which I found myself, another person, who must have seen his chances improve during that dreadful time, one who loved you also, but not as I loved you, approached you and won your heart. It was for me the very worst news. I told your sister so and it angered her; she urged me to forget you, she said you were lost to me forever and sent me away," and as he spoke with great passion, Marianne could have sworn there were tears in his eyes.

It was with considerable difficulty that she let him continue, knowing that he had neither the right nor any logical reason for asking that she do so. Yet, it was impossible for her not to be moved by his story, the facts of which were already known to her. That he had wanted to impress on her the depth of his love for her, to ask her to believe that he still loved her, that he had dared even to suggest that his affections were deeper and stronger than Colonel Brandon's could have been—in all these claims, Marianne wanted to believe him. Not because she had spent the intervening years longing for his return, for she had long accepted that he was gone out of her life forever, but because she still wanted to believe that he really had been the romantic young cavalier she had fallen in love with when she was seventeen. It had been the strongest, most passionate experience of her young life; nothing, certainly not her subsequent marriage, had surpassed the exquisite excitement of that first love, and Marianne wished to treasure it. Willoughby, by his passionate confession, had given her a chance to do just that.

The sound of the carriage in the drive reminded them that there was still a journey of several miles to travel before she could be returned to Delaford, and Willoughby, who had been standing before her, appealing to her, rushed out of the room into the hall. He returned soon afterward to assist her with her cloak and help her into the carriage, and directed the driver to make for Delaford Manor. They left almost immediately; this time in the warm darkness of the carriage he sat beside her and, having ensured she was comfortably settled in, took her hand in his and held it throughout the journey, as though he had every right to do so.

Marianne was reluctant to say or do anything to discourage him, lest it should alert the servant sitting on the box, but as they drove on she had to admit that she had not really wished to, either. She had drawn some comfort from the intimacy of the contact and hoped that it would convey the sympathy she had felt but had been unable to put into words. When they drove into the grounds of Delaford Manor, she turned to him on impulse and said in a low voice, "Willoughby, I am sorry, truly sorry," whereupon, he kissed her hand and said, "Bless you, Marianne, my dearest, and thank you for letting me speak."

When the carriage stopped at the front porch, Willoughby's man assisted her to alight and unloaded her luggage, whilst his master sat back in the carriage, so as not to be recognised by the staff at Delaford, who had rushed to the door on hearing the vehicle arrive. Marianne went indoors and retired upstairs directly, explaining to her housekeeper that a horse had gone lame and delayed her return journey from the Percevals'.

The housekeeper informed her that Mr and Mrs Ferrars had called earlier that evening to ask if she had returned from Bath. "Should I send a man round to the parsonage with a message, ma'am? They were very concerned that you had been delayed." Marianne agreed that it was a good idea. "Yes, please, Mrs Jenkins, and ask Molly to prepare my bath. It has been a long day and I am very tired indeed; I think I shall bathe and go directly to bed," she said. "Shall I bring you some tea, ma'am?" Mrs Jenkins asked and Marianne replied, "Yes, I should like that, Mrs Jenkins, thank you."

Sleep did not come easily that night, as Marianne, having bathed and partaken of tea, had hoped it would. Instead, she lay awake thinking through the events of the day, reliving every moment, and hearing again the words Willoughby had spoken.

She could not, as she was sure her sisters would urge her to do, dismiss everything he had said from her mind, even though she knew that it had been part of his attempt to excuse the inexcusable, to place before her his own sorrow and ask her to forgive his conduct. That he had blamed everyone else involved in the sordid episode did not resonate with her, keen as she was to see in his changed demeanour signs of genuine contrition and even a new humility, which she deemed was in accord with her expectations of him.

Even as she relived it, and heard again the words he had spoken, she could not resist the intensity of his passionate declaration, nor could she ignore her own warm response to his words and touch. Nothing had moved her as they had done; she knew in her heart that all the care and concern that Colonel Brandon had lavished upon her, the warm affection with which he had cherished and protected her, had not evoked such a deep response.

Marianne, together with her mother and sisters, had been deeply grateful to Colonel Brandon, and their gratitude had been demonstrated through the level of friendly intimacy that had been extended to him whenever he visited them at Cleveland and later at Barton Cottage. He had been permitted to call as often as he thought necessary to assure himself of her health and the well-being of the rest of her family, to assist them in whatever way he felt was appropriate, until it had become apparent that his deep affection for Marianne could not be denied and he had obtained her mother's permission to propose to her.

Marianne recalled the sense of inevitability that had surrounded her acceptance of Colonel Brandon's offer of marriage and the general happiness that preceded their wedding; it was as though the entire family, from Sir John Middleton and Mrs Jennings to Edward, Elinor, and her mother, had all prepared themselves to rejoice with the couple and so they had. Shocked and dismayed by Willoughby's behaviour, they were all so convinced of Colonel Brandon's decency and generosity that there appeared to be no need to ask whether she would be happy with him—no one doubted that she would.

Now, some seven years later, Marianne could not comprehend how swiftly she had changed from her belief that her destiny was only to be moved by irresistible passion to an acceptance that kindness and compassion together with honest affection were sufficient to make a happy marriage. If they were, then how, she asked herself, was it possible for her to be thrown into such moral confusion by the return of the man who had wooed her with ardour and charm, only to betray her when matters of money and social status intervened?

Try as she might, she could not explain or excuse her response to Willoughby's recent advances—which, even as she understood that they were calculated to win her trust, had nonetheless succeeded in moving her closer to a state when she could forgive his past for the intensity of his present feelings. It was a conundrum to which she had no answer.

Although she did not acknowledge it, Marianne was not yet free from the tyranny of her youthful devotion to romanticism; clearly missing the depth of passion she had once demanded in all her attachments, she thought she was rediscovering it in a reformed Willoughby.

Roused from her bed by the maid, who brought in her tea, she awoke with her mind in the same state of confusion. Deciding that she would go for a long walk in the woods and let the fresh air clear her thoughts, Marianne dressed and went down to breakfast.

Chapter Fifteen

IN PROVENCE, CLAIRE JONES and Margaret Dashwood were preparing to return to England, having correctly interpreted the first signs of the Mistral as heralding the arrival of winter into the Mediterranean. They had but four days before it would be time to return to Marseilles and the vessel that would take them back to Plymouth, when Claire surprised her friend with the news that Nicholas and she planned to go away together to a little place in the lower slopes of the Alpilles.

"Nicholas has asked me to marry him," Claire said quietly, and before Margaret, who had long suspected Mr Wilcox of being in love with her friend, could respond, she added, "I am not sure it's what I want, but I am very fond of him and I do not wish to refuse him without discovering if I do want to marry him or not."

Margaret did not know what to say; she had, over the years, become quite accustomed to her friend's liberal views regarding relationships, which she had accepted as part of the sophistication that gave Claire Jones a particular *savoir faire*, which perturbed some of the straitlaced denizens of Dorsetshire. However, Margaret had never been confronted with a situation such as was being proposed now and she found it exceedingly difficult to respond. Determined not to appear prudish, she was nevertheless concerned about her friend's reputation and asked in the most innocuous way if Claire had considered all the consequences of such a scheme.

"Of course I have," she replied. "Should it be talked about back in England, I shall probably be labelled a wanton hussy; but no one will know, Margaret, except the four of us and I know I can trust you not to gossip. As for Daniel Brooke, Nicholas would trust him with his life! No one here cares—they adore lovers and enjoy seeing them together."

Margaret was confused. "I think you already know you love Nicholas, he certainly loves you..." she began, and when Claire nodded, she asked, "Then why must you—?" Anticipating her question, Claire interrupted her. "Because, my dear young friend, I have believed myself in love before and become engaged only to find that I was not. It is not a pleasant prospect. Fortunately, it was easy enough to become disengaged. But this is the first time I have seriously contemplated matrimony and I must discover if I love Nicholas enough to want to settle into marriage at twenty-seven and not regret it."

Seeing Margaret's troubled countenance, she added, "Now, Margaret, you are not going to be all miss-ish and disapprove of me, are you?" to which Margaret could only reply, in as lighthearted a manner as she could muster, "Of course not, but anyone can see he loves you desperately, Claire, so do take care you don't break his heart."

Claire laughed, the long, uninhibited laugh that Margaret enjoyed so much, and said lightly, "I shan't do that, I know he loves me and I am exceedingly fond of him; I just need to know if I love him enough to want to marry him and change my life completely. It would be far worse to discover after marriage that I did not. I see that you, my dear friend, are not concerned that I may do some damage to my own heart. You must be confident of my good sense at least. But seriously, you must not worry about us at all; Nicholas knows the people we will stay with, we shall be quite safe and expect to be back on Monday afternoon," she said and then, seeking to reassure her friend, added, "Meanwhile, Daniel Brooke has promised to look after you and see that you are not bored. He believes there are one or two places you might like to visit before you leave Provence."

Margaret assured her that she would certainly not be bored, and Claire left, having promised to tell her friend everything when she returned, and urged her to enjoy the last of their vacation. "As you know, Daniel is an excellent travelling companion; he will ensure that you are kept occupied and safe."

That evening, Margaret was entirely alone for the first time and retired to her room directly after supper. She was hoping to finish a letter to Elinor and had just settled down to write, when a maid knocked on her door to say she had a visitor in the parlour. Surprised and curious, Margaret went down to find Daniel Brooke seated in front of the fire. He rose as she entered the room and said, a little awkwardly, "About tomorrow—I wondered if you would... I thought it might be best... I wasn't sure if Miss Jones had said..." Clearly he was unsure if she knew that Claire and Nicholas had gone away together, she thought, and to save them both some awkwardness, she said quickly, "Oh yes, she did. I know they are away for a few days, and in truth, Daniel, I do not want you to feel you have to look after me while they're away. I am well able to wander around on my own after all this time. You must not think that you—" but he interrupted her then.

"I was not thinking that at all," he said, and she stopped speaking as he continued. "I thought it might be a good opportunity to pay a visit to the little village in the valley by the lake, which we passed on our way north; there is an abbey church there which is very ancient, and I recall you saying you would have liked to see more of it. I thought, if you wished to go tomorrow, we could. I called tonight, because if you decided to go, it would mean leaving quite early, soon after breakfast—the days are shorter now and the journey would take a few hours."

Margaret was struck by the gentle reasonableness of his tone and suffered pangs of guilt at having spoken as she had done. He must think her ungrateful and silly, she thought, and apologised. "I'm sorry, Daniel, I did not mean to sound unappreciative of your kindness; I do recall the church and the lake—it was a beautiful place, and of course, I should love to go back and see it properly. It was very kind of you to remember, thank you."

Whereupon, he said, "That's good; I'll call for you at nine and do remember to wear something warm—it can get quite cold there, it's much closer to the mountains." She thanked him again, grateful for his concern, and as he moved to the door, he added in a gentler voice, "It wasn't kindness, Margaret; I was perfectly happy to keep you company while the others were away, and the church at Le Lac du Sainte Germaine is a particular favourite of mine."

Margaret smiled and bade him good night. Returning to her room, she decided to leave her letter to Elinor until the following night—there would be more to tell, she thought. Instead, she made a brief note in her diary before she retired to bed that night:

> *I do feel quite wretched about my words to Daniel; it was a stupid thing to say when he was being so kind, offering to spend his time going out to visit the old abbey church at Sainte Germaine with me, which I did want very much to see, and quite unforgivable, especially after Claire had arranged it all. Yet, he is such a good, generous-hearted man, he was at pains to assure me he had taken no offence, but I still feel such a fool. I must be on my best behaviour tomorrow.*

The morning was bright with clear blue skies and no sign of the winds that would presage the onset of winter. Daniel Brooke arrived in a small vehicle that looked like a gig, but had a hard top, which was useful in cold weather. It was smaller and yet looked quite comfortable inside. Margaret smiled when she saw it. He thought she might be concerned about its stability and reassured her, "Don't worry, it's a lot stronger than it looks, and I've used this one before on longer journeys—the owner is a friend of mine." She laughed and said, "I was not worried about its safety; it's just that I have never seen a gig with a hard top before—not in Devon at any rate."

"They're popular in France, the young men around town seem to favour them—and I imagine there would be some in London, too," he said as he helped her in, and she admitted that she had not lived in London in years.

"Apart from a short visit two years ago at Christmas, when the weather was so dreadful that we stayed indoors all day, I cannot recall when we were last in London."

He confessed that he had no liking for the city either. "I find all that carousing and merry-making that goes on is not to my taste. I do need to visit the British Museum regularly for my work, and when it is done, I tend to get away from London as fast as I can."

Mention of the British Museum brought a sparkle to Margaret's eyes. "I should love to visit the Museum; Edward has told us a great deal about it, but none of us has ever been; one must have to be a scholar of some repute, I expect," she said. He smiled at her enthusiasm and said, "Not at all, the museum's charter grants admission 'to all studious and curious persons' and I am sure you qualify on both counts, Margaret," adding in a very matter-of-fact voice, "Well, the next time I am in England and visiting the museum, you can join me." Margaret looked quickly at his face to see if he was teasing her, only to find that he looked perfectly serious. Clearly he had meant what he said.

They drove out of town in a westerly direction, and as there was little traffic, they talked for most of the time; at least, Margaret did most of the talking, asking questions, while Daniel would provide the answers. It was as it had been throughout the autumn: Margaret had enjoyed their conversations, not because he agreed with every idea or applauded every proposition she made, but because he listened with interest and responded as though he understood her meaning. When he did not agree or pointed out that she was mistaken on some matter, she was never discomposed because she was conscious of his respect. He was, she had decided, the very best type of teacher one could hope to have.

She recalled a day on which they had visited an old convent, where for centuries young girls had come to take their vows as nuns. Claire had remarked that she would have been driven insane if she had been shut away in such a place at a tender age, and Margaret had been inclined to agree, until Daniel had pointed out that many had been orphans or illegitimate daughters of noblemen, who would have had no opportunity for the kind of enjoyment that they assumed a young girl of that age should have. "It is much more likely that they would have become drudges at home or been sold into domestic service with only long hours of hard labour and abuse to look forward to," he had said, explaining that at least at the convent the girls were fed, clothed, taught to read, pray, and sing, as well as work, in healthy, salubrious surroundings. "It may not have been the best life a young woman could aspire to, but it was a good deal better than many of them could expect, had they remained where they were born."

Claire had not been entirely convinced, but Margaret had admitted that she, having no knowledge of abbeys and convents, of which there were not many left in England, had been compelled to think differently of them thereafter.

Later, Daniel had explained that the nuns were not all shut away in the convent either. Some of the girls did not necessarily take all their vows to become full-fledged nuns, but were trained to nurse the sick and dying and care for children at the abbey's hospitals and schools. It was then she had asked, "You know so much about them, Daniel; are you of the Roman Catholic faith?" to which he had smiled and said simply, "I am not, but I have long been interested in the history of the church, not for religious reasons but for the work it does in society. Were it not for dedicated men and women in the church, who would care for the poor and the sick, the frail and the elderly? Certainly not the government." Margaret, who'd heard of the horror of poor houses and debtors' prisons in England, had to agree.

In these and other similar conversations, she had begun to discover in Daniel Brooke the thoughtfulness and compassion that she missed in most of the people she met outside her family, particularly the young men, whose lives were constrained only by their capacity for enjoyment and the size of their allowance. Her appreciation of the extent of his knowledge and understanding had increased with each occasion on which they had travelled together and explored the many fascinating places to which he had led them. When Mr Wilcox and Claire had been with them, it had been fun; but even when they had gone their separate ways, Daniel's enthusiasm and wealth of information had kept her mind engrossed. On this day, which she expected would be their last, Margaret hoped she would get the chance to tell him how well she had enjoyed her holiday in Provence and how much of that enjoyment she owed to him. She did not wish to embarrass him, but resolved to wait for a suitable opportunity.

They reached the valley and saw the lake extending northward, bounded on the far side by thickly forested hills, its shore dotted with clumps of juniper and oak bordering bays and rocky inlets that invited one toward the blue water. In the distance they could see boats and light skiffs skimming over the surface of the lake. It was so calm and beautiful in the sunlight, Margaret wanted to leap from the gig and run toward it. But her companion was swift to advise against it, pointing out the unevenness of the ground and the roughness of the terrain. "It would be better to wait until we are a little farther into the valley, where the foreshore of the lake is less wild and better suited to walking; there are easier paths along the lake's edge, and in the fields behind the abbey, there may yet be some wildflowers left, if you are lucky," he explained.

Margaret agreed to be patient, and they drove on until they saw the abbey and beyond it the old inn a few hundred yards along the road. She recalled the picturesque view they had passed as they had journeyed north a fortnight ago. They drove into the courtyard of the inn and as Daniel helped her out, he reminded her to take her wrap, lest the wind should come up without warning;

she was aware of a sense of ease and tranquillity that was unlike any feeling she had experienced before. So accustomed had she become to accepting his advice, so readily did she accede to his requests, it was as though she had known him and understood his character and disposition for many years, yet she had met him but a few short weeks ago. Margaret could not recall another person—neither man nor woman—in whose company she had felt so contented and secure.

They entered the church, with its ancient carved door, and stood in the cool stone-flagged nave looking up at the circular window, its image of the Christ child and his mother, constructed of myriad slivers of translucent stained glass, and she was glad they had come. Candles flickered below the altar and a few women knelt in prayer in the pews—the ambience of devotion filled the ancient space in which they stood. This place, Margaret thought, she would remember all her life.

As they walked through the grounds of the abbey and passed into the old orchard with its gnarled trees, he warned her of the rocks that jutted through the rough tussocks of grass and took her arm to help her avoid them. Beyond the orchard lay the meadows, where he had promised there may yet be some wildflowers left, and indeed there were, in little sheltered patches of soil, pushing out from under fallen branches or clustered beside piles of stones— purple lavender, pink rock roses, and yellow gorse, sturdy survivors of the late autumn cold.

"There, I did tell you there may yet be some wildflowers left, you are a lucky girl," he said softly, and Margaret's eyes filled with tears as she gazed on them, trying to fix this moment in her mind; she could not recall another like it in all her life. When she looked up at him to thank him for bringing her back to this lovely place, she could not speak, for she knew in that moment, that for her everything had changed. She knew she loved him, but she had no knowledge of his feelings, and there was nothing she could do about it. She tried to speak, to make some comment on the scene, but could not find the words.

It was a place of such enchantment, she could have stayed there for hours, but she heard him say, "Perhaps we should get back to the inn and get some food, you will soon be hungry," and she agreed, although food was the last thing on her mind.

When they reached the inn, with its rough stone and wood exterior and its mullioned windows, they noticed more vehicles and horses tethered in the yard. Some of the young men who had been out on the water, had returned and were seated at tables outside, together with a few young women, partaking of food and drink, while a family with several small children were having fun, squabbling over their meal.

Daniel found her a seat at a table inside, beside a window looking out toward the lake, and went to see the innkeeper. Margaret watched as a young couple walked up from the foreshore, clearly in love, reluctant to break apart. As she sat looking at the lake, which was still shining, jewel-like, in the afternoon sun, Margaret wondered at her situation; she asked herself, had she really fallen in love or was this just an ordinary response to being with a thoughtful, handsome man in a setting of heart-wrenching beauty? That, in itself, was for her an unusual experience, but, she argued, "This is not a conclusion I have reached after a logical discussion about what I wish for in someone I love, nor is it the consequence of a man declaring that I am his ideal of a woman he wishes to love—neither is true. Indeed nothing he has said or done may be construed as an indication that he has any tender feelings for me, apart from a kind concern for my well-being. This has come about without my seeking it, almost in spite of myself," she thought.

Indeed, it had happened when she was least expecting it, yet she was completely involved; her mind, her heart, and her body had all responded to him, and for Margaret, who had never been in love before, it was a unique, all-encompassing, and irrevocable experience.

When Daniel returned, he apologised and said he hoped she would not mind, the food was of a rather simple peasant style and he was taken aback when she smiled as though he had promised her a banquet and said, "I think I should love a simple peasant-style meal." He laughed and said, "That's good then, and there is plenty of it, so we shall not go hungry. They are very good folk, they have even attended to the horse."

While they waited for their meal, some of the young men and ladies left on horseback, meaning, no doubt, to explore the trails in the woods above the lake. Others, less inclined to such energetic pursuits, preferred to relax in the warm comfort of the large parlour, with more wine and cheese. Watching them, Margaret enjoyed their contentment as though it were her own.

Their meal was of fresh baked bread and soup with a large, hot, and hearty rustic casserole of meat and root vegetables, with farm-made butter, cheese, wine, and a bowl of fresh fruit. Margaret was not dissembling when she said that it was one of best meals she had eaten and she would remember it and this beautiful place forever. Daniel smiled at her enthusiasm and when they had finished their meal, asked if she was ready to take a walk along the lake's shore. She nodded, rose to join him, and they moved to the door.

At that moment, a gust of wind swept down from the surrounding hills, and the wooden shutters on the windows clattered and clashed, making a great noise. Surprised, they walked onto the porch and saw that the blue sky of the morning was now as grey as charcoal, and big lumpy clouds hid the tops of the wooded hills above the lake. In the time that they had been taking their meal, the weather had changed, and the lake that had been still as a silken sheet was being whipped up into waves, which slapped and broke upon the foreshore. It was certainly no time for a walk. A few guests looked apprehensive and some decided that it was time to be gone, while others stayed on, in no hurry to leave.

Daniel went to consult the innkeeper and returned with the grim news that the wind would probably get worse and was unlikely to abate for several hours, by which time it would be dark. "He says it will blow itself out over-night; I am sorry, Margaret, it seems we shall have to wait it out, it will be far too hazardous to try to drive back into town." If he had expected her to be put out or protest or even to grumble just a little at the inconvenience, he would have been surprised. She did not. Determined that he should not find her wanting, Margaret set out to be perfectly amenable and merely shrugged her shoulders and said that it would certainly not be sensible to travel in the little covered gig in this weather—and he smiled when she added that it would not be very kind to the horse either. She pointed out that there was a great fire burning in the parlour, and declared that she would be perfectly happy to sit it out in there.

If Daniel *was* surprised by her calm response, he did not show it, and having accompanied her into the parlour, where the innkeeper had put more wood on the fire, he went to make arrangements for the stabling of the horse and vehicle. When he returned, he found her comfortably tucked into an old-fashioned divan, while the squabbling family were arguing whether they should leave immediately or take a room upstairs for the night. In the end, they decided to stay the night, and the innkeeper's wife took the children upstairs while their parents remained in the parlour, enjoying the rest of the wine.

It was going to be a long night, and it appeared they had all accepted the practical realities of their predicament; no one sought to bemoan their circumstances or complain, there being nothing to complain of but the volatile mood of Nature itself.

Daniel spent some time at the bar talking with the innkeeper; they were speaking in the local Provençal tongue, which meant Margaret could hear but could not comprehend a word of their conversation. Meanwhile, the innkeeper's wife brought Margaret a thick knitted rug and a mug of hot chocolate laced with brandy, both of which were accepted gladly.

As the evening wore on, the winds grew stronger and rattled the shutters until the old inn felt more like a ship at sea, creaking and shuddering with each gust. The innkeeper offered them more food, most of which they refused, having eaten well, but his offers of cheese, wine, and hot coffee were gratefully accepted. There remained only a few stranded travellers like themselves, dozing in the chairs around the room. Daniel had seated himself in a chair a few feet from the divan where Margaret sat curled up under her rug, a dark shawl around her shoulders, her hair glowing in the firelight, as she watched the sparks fly up the enormous chimney.

"Are you cold?" he asked suddenly, and she replied at once, "No, not at all. It feels just wonderful; I know you will laugh at me for saying that I am enjoying this, but it's true." He did laugh, but said quickly, "Indeed, I will not laugh at you, Margaret, and you do look as though you are enjoying the experience; I suppose it will be an adventure, eh? Something to tell your family and friends back in England—the unexpected stormy night stranded in an old Provençal inn…"

She had to interrupt him and say, "Please don't say that, Daniel—it makes me sound like another silly young traveller from England, with naive notions of adventures in Provence. I did not come to Provence for adventure, I wanted to learn something about the country and I *have* learnt so much, thanks to you; even today has been such a wonderful experience. I wanted to tell you how grateful I am that you have spent so much of your time with us, explaining things and answering all my foolish questions, it is so generous and kind… and I do not want to go away leaving you here thinking that I was ungrateful because I am not, really." She knew that she was saying too much and wanted to stop, but she could not and she rushed on, trying to tell him everything, but he drew his chair closer to hers and said, "There is no need at all for you to be grateful, Margaret. I have enjoyed it too." She stopped speaking then, and the tears she had held back so bravely coursed down her cheeks.

He was concerned and thoughtful; practical, too, producing first a clean handkerchief and then a mug of coffee, and waiting until she was calm, before he spoke. "Margaret, there is no need for gratitude, because I have enjoyed very much showing you Provence, telling you its stories, and answering your questions, which have never been foolish or naive. At no time have I considered you another silly English traveller. You were always so keen to know things, so eager to learn, so easy to teach—it has been my great pleasure. So have no fears on that score at all." She looked at his face, and seeing what was clearly a sincere reassurance, she smiled. Then, in a quiet, serious voice, he said, "However, there is something else you must know before you return home, and it is possible that it may cause you some distress. It concerns not Provence or your travels, but myself, and I cannot send you away in ignorance lest you hear of it from someone else and be angry with me for keeping the truth from you."

This time, he did not smile, nor did she, for she knew in her heart that whatever it was he was going to tell her, it could bring nothing but pain. She wanted to cry out and say, "Please do not tell me, I have no wish to know," but she knew well enough that she had to know and he was going to tell her, because he must have sensed something of her feelings for him and he would not let her return to England in ignorance of the truth. Neither his honour nor her love would permit it.

Margaret wiped her eyes and sat up straight to hear what he had to say. Daniel drew his chair closer and sat facing the fire, and Margaret, looking at him in the firelight, saw signs of strain upon his countenance that she had not noticed before, or if she had, she'd misconstrued as fatigue. This time there could be no mistake: There were deeply etched lines of anxiety, and a look of despair in his eyes. As she listened to his voice—quiet, undramatic, but grave in its import—she understood the reason.

He told a tale of such sadness that she could not restrain the tears as he spoke, explaining that some years ago, when he was a young student, he had, while travelling in this part of France, met and fallen in love with a young French girl: Helène. They had been married in a village church and had lived happily for a few years until their first child had been stillborn. The toll it had taken on his young wife had been severe, and she had spent several months in a special sanatorium where she had been cared for by the nuns. When she had recovered, they had resumed their life together. Their second child had been born healthy, but had lived not even a year, dying suddenly of a respiratory illness. The double tragedy had destroyed Helène's mind, and despite his efforts and those of the doctors and her family, she had never recovered. Her life was now one of a simple child, whose only comfort was to coddle and nurse a rag doll she carried everywhere and took to bed with her.

Being of the Catholic faith, Helène was being cared for by a group of nursing nuns at a convent some miles outside Aix-en-Provence, and he visited her often but could bring her little comfort, since her mind was so confused, she could neither recognise him nor recall any part of their life together. She had grown weak and, as a final cruel blow, had recently been diagnosed with tuberculosis and the nuns had told him they were sending her to a hospice at a convent near Nice for the winter, away from the bitter alpine winds.

Seeing the shock and sorrow on Margaret's face, Daniel spoke gently, "No one except for one or two dear friends at my college in Oxford know of this; I have decided, however, that I must reveal the truth of my circumstances to you, only because—and I beg you, Margaret, to forgive me if I have misunderstood your feelings—because in these last few days I have sensed a certain partiality, almost akin to affection in your demeanour towards me, and though I have tried to avoid giving you any encouragement, I feared that if you left without learning the truth, you may well feel deceived."

Margaret had heard everything he had said without a word, but could hold back no longer. "No, never deceived, Daniel; sad and grieved certainly, but never deceived. I will not permit you to take the blame, although I will confess to mine. You have not misunderstood my feelings, you are right. I have come to regard you with affection, with great affection, and if there has been deception, it is self-deception on my part, because I hoped it could be so. I have nothing to complain of in your conduct, which has always been honourable. I have been foolish, believing that because we seemed to get on so well and found so much to enjoy together, that it was possible for us to be..." and here she had to stop, because the tears came again.

He let her compose herself, before saying, "Margaret, I too have enjoyed the time we have spent together, and were it not for my circumstances, it may well have been possible for me—" but she could not bear to let him say it and interrupted him.

"I must thank you for your honesty and ask you to believe that my sorrow could not have been greater had your wife Helène been my dearest friend. You have behaved toward me with honour, I acknowledge that, but it does not change in any way the esteem and warm affection I feel for you."

He held her close for a few moments, as one might comfort a grieving child, then settled her back under the rug, stoked up the fire to a blaze, and went away to look out of the window at the starless sky and the darkness outside, where the winds had abated a little, but snow was falling over the landscape, transforming it utterly.

᭦

Awakening early, hearing not a sound in the inn, Margaret rose and looked for Daniel; she found him seated on the steps of the front porch. Her hair loosened from its pins made her seem more childlike then ever, and he took her hand and drew her down to sit beside him. They sat there, saying very little, until the sun rose over the hills and its light flooded the valley. For Margaret, the tenderness of the moment was overwhelming. Before rising to go within, they embraced for a brief moment, as if to confirm what had been said the previous night.

The innkeeper's wife had breakfast ready, eggs and bacon with fresh baked bread and steaming coffee. Margaret claimed she wasn't hungry, but Daniel insisted that she eat because, he said, "We have a long journey before us, and it is Sunday." By which she understood that many inns and hostelries might be shut. Margaret did as he asked and made her preparations, and they were ready to depart within the hour. Having settled his account with the innkeeper, Daniel persuaded her to take a walk along the lakeshore. "It would be a pity, having come this far, to leave without walking along the shore; it is something you will not forget, come," he said, holding out his hand. She took it as they walked beside the water. The lake appeared calm again that morning, but the shore was littered with the debris of the turbulent night; broken boughs and tangled twigs lay in their path. How swiftly it had changed, Margaret thought, recalling the serenity of the scene when they had arrived the previous afternoon, when her mind had been filled only with expectations of a perfect day.

His voice broke in gently upon her thoughts. "Will you promise me, Margaret, that you will not leave here unhappy? It has been such a happy four weeks, I could not bear to think that I have caused you sorrow on our last day here." She could not respond immediately, she feared her voice would betray her; she waited, before saying slowly and deliberately, "I cannot possibly leave unhappy, Daniel, because it was here I discovered that I love you dearly. How can that make me unhappy? Is it not the greatest gift we are given, even if it brings with it sadness and tears? I am content too that I have said it, because it means you know my feelings, and if that makes your life a little easier, then I shall be truly happy."

He was silent then, as though he did not know what to say or do, until she put her arms around him and held him close, feeling the racing of his heart against her cheek. Looking up at his face, she read all she wished to know; she had no need of words.

❦

They spoke mainly of other matters on the journey back into town. This time, he asked most of the questions, concerning her family, her work at the seminary, her hopes and plans, which she answered with her characteristic candour. Her accounts of their relations—the Middletons and Palmers and in particular, her tales of the Ferrars family, of Mrs Ferrars and Fanny, of Robert and Lucy— kept him amused for most of the journey. However, when she mentioned her letter to her sister Elinor and told him she had written of his friendship with Dr Grantley, who had been Edward's mentor at Oxford, he became rather serious and said, "You had best be prepared, if your brother-in-law is a friend of Francis Grantley. He is one of the two intimate friends of mine who are aware of the circumstances of my marriage and my wife's condition. Indeed, Francis has, on one occasion, while travelling in France, accompanied me when I visited her at the convent."

Margaret assured him that her brother-in-law Edward Ferrars was not an intimate friend of Dr Grantley, but even if he were, it was unlikely that they would discuss the private affairs of a colleague. Nevertheless, she was grateful for the warning.

"Elinor has suggested that I should invite you to dine at the parsonage when we return to England. Will you accept?" she asked a little tentatively, and he responded directly. "With the greatest of pleasure; I should like very much to meet your sister and Reverend Ferrars. My friend Francis Grantley has a very high opinion of him as a clergyman," he said, and Margaret agreed that her brother-in-law was indeed worthy of admiration. "He works very hard as a parish priest, and I know he supports Mr Wilberforce's campaign against slavery, too," she said.

After they had been silent for a while, she asked, "Will you travel with us to Marseilles on Tuesday?" and he said very gently, "I fear not. I have arranged to accompany Helène and her nurse to Nice, where I expect to remain until after Christmas. It's quite strange, but Christmas is the one occasion that Helène seems to enjoy—she probably recalls childhood memories—and I have always visited her at Christmas." Perhaps anticipating her disappointment, he said, "Nicholas has been told that I have some work in Nice and cannot travel with your party to Marseilles. Besides, do you not think it may be difficult and more painful to maintain a pretence before Nicholas and Miss Jones? Would you not prefer to say good-bye before they return from their tryst?"

"Claire will be much amused to hear it called a tryst," said Margaret, and he asked with a wry smile, "What would you call it? Not just a sightseeing trip to the Alpilles, surely?" Then she laughed too, but added that he was right, perhaps it was best that they should say their farewells before their friends returned; she feared she may betray her feelings, she said, and he nodded, and admitted that it would be difficult, especially as Nicholas and Miss Jones would, in all probability, return engaged to be married. When she said nothing, he took her hand and held it, and though nothing was said, Margaret knew he meant to comfort her.

They reached Aix-en-Provence as darkness fell and said their goodbyes; he put his arms around her and held her close and there was a degree of warmth and affection that, in spite of the words of that morning, took them both by surprise.

She asked if she might write to him and he said, "Certainly you may," and gave her his card with his poste restante address in Nice, adding that he expected to be back in Oxford at the New Year, which gave her some hope. Margaret wanted to ask if she would see him when he returned to England, but held back, fearing that he might feel compromised by any answer he gave. Instead she asked if he would write, too, and was delighted when he said, "Of course," and added, "I would be very happy to do so."

She was about to go indoors when he took out a small package from his pocket and handed it to her. "It's a little souvenir of Provence, which I hope you will like." As she thanked him, he bent and kissed her cheek, and touching her face gently, said, "Thank you, Margaret, I shall look forward to your letters. Now you must go indoors or you will catch cold. The wind here is very strong already." Then he climbed into the vehicle and drove away.

Margaret went slowly up to her room. Opening the package, she found within an exquisitely painted image of the abbey they had visited, with a tiny posy of dried wildflowers from the surrounding meadows glued to the back of its frame. The thoughtful tenderness of the gift touched her heart and brought tears again. Margaret could not recall when she had wept so much and thought, ruefully, that grief must be an inevitable part of love.

She was alone that night and very glad that Claire and Nicholas were only returning the following day. There would be time enough to get busy with packing and hide the tears, she thought.

Indeed, when they did arrive, there was no question of tears, for they were so obviously happy, so certain that they were in love, celebrations were in order. Nicholas Wilcox and Claire Jones announced that they were engaged and planned to marry in the new year, and Margaret, her friend said, had to be her bridesmaid!

"Now my friend, what have you to say to me?" Claire demanded, and Margaret could only smile and throw her arms around her and wish her friend every possible happiness.

END OF PART THREE

EXPECTATIONS OF HAPPINESS

Part Four

Chapter Sixteen

Winter 1819

A T THE PARSONAGE IN Delaford, following a rather quiet autumn,
all was excitement. Preparations were afoot for Christmas, and
into the midst of their traditional activities had come the news that
the Palmers together with Mrs Jennings were to call, en route to Cleveland
in Somersetshire.

Elinor was keen to ensure that they would all be comfortably accommodated
and, to that end, devoted a great deal of time to planning menus and giving
careful instructions to her housekeeper and staff, while Edward wondered aloud
if he could possibly find a subject serious enough to engross Mr Palmer's attention for the duration of their visit. "You must admit, my dear, he is a somewhat
difficult fellow to engage in any form of discourse; apart from the political news,
of which there will not be much seeing as the Parliament is not in session, I
cannot imagine what conversations we shall have," he said gloomily. His wife
was a good deal less worried about Mr Palmer and much more concerned about
keeping up with both Charlotte Palmer and her mother Mrs Jennings. They
were both garrulous women and, coming directly from London, were certain to
have plenty to gossip about, much of which was of no interest to Elinor.

Elinor knew them well. "I think, my love, I'd rather have the problem of
Mr Palmer's reserve than Charlotte's endless chatter," said she, "and when you

have added Mrs Jennings's contribution to the conversation, we shall probably be grateful for Mr Palmer's silences."

Edward agreed that she had a point and went away to work on his sermon, while Elinor took the post from the maid and sat down to read her letters. There was one from Margaret, which she opened up eagerly. Written about ten days before their party had left Provence, it was full of the joy and exhilaration that Margaret was feeling at the time.

> *Dearest Elinor, how I wish you and Edward could be here. It is hard to describe the appeal of this lovely place. There is so much history everywhere, in the ancient abbeys and churches, the old farmhouses with their orchards and meadows full of wildflowers, and the exquisite blue lakes that stretch forever in the foothills of the mountains. It has been a very special pleasure to have as our guides Claire's friend Mr Nicholas Wilcox and his colleague Mr Daniel Brooke, of whom I wrote earlier. They are both familiar with this part of the country, and Mr Brooke has made a study of historic churches and knows everything about them. He is indeed one of the most interesting people I have met, yet is quiet and modest as well. I do believe Edward will enjoy meeting him again.*

Margaret went on to say that she intended to convey Elinor's invitation to Mr Brooke before they left France and hoped that they would have an answer when she joined them for Christmas at the parsonage.

Elinor smiled; clearly Margaret was very impressed with Mr Daniel Brooke, she thought, drawing certain conclusions from her sister's letter that were not as obvious as she would have liked them to be and hoping this new friendship would lead to something more. She was about to turn the page and read on when she heard the doorbell, and the maid admitted her friend Mrs Helen King. Elinor, always happy to see Mrs King, who had become a trusted confidante as well as a sensible companion, rose to greet her and, looking forward to a pleasant conversation, she asked the maid to bring them tea.

She began immediately to talk about Margaret's letter and her imminent return from France, but Mrs King, while evincing some interest, appeared preoccupied, as though she had something on her mind of which she wanted to speak urgently. Elinor stopped almost in midsentence and asked, "Helen, you seem troubled; have you had some bad news?" to which Mrs King could only nod and say, "Indeed I have, Elinor, and I came as soon as I could. You see, I have had a visit this morning from Miss Henrietta Clift."

Elinor's heart leapt. "Mr Willoughby's cousin?"

"Indeed, and she has mentioned two matters that could cause you some anxiety in relation to your sister, Mrs Brandon."

Elinor sat forward in her chair. "What matters?" she asked, her concern already evident upon her countenance. The maid brought in the tea tray and set it on the table, and their conversation ceased until she left the room. "Helen, please tell me, what did Miss Clift say?" Elinor pleaded.

Mrs King accepted her cup of tea, added two lumps of sugar, and began, "Well, the first point is that, according to Miss Clift, Mr Willoughby is said to have made some new friends in the county—no, she did not name your sister, but they are the Perceval family. I recall you said that your sister had been introduced to them recently and they had become good friends; well, now Willoughby is a friend of theirs too, and his cousin, who is probably a little jealous of the Perceval girls, who are much younger than she is, declares that he must be flirting with one or both of them, because he is forever driving around the county with them in his carriage. I understand that he recently made up a party with them and they travelled to Bath; Miss Clift was not invited and appears to be very put out."

"Oh dear God!" Elinor cried and put down her cup hurriedly, as if afraid that she would drop it, and it was clear to Helen King that her friend was seriously troubled by what she had just heard. "Oh Helen, that is the most dreadful news, because my sister Marianne was also one of the party that went to Bath with the Percevals! Yet she said nothing to me about Mr Willoughby joining them. That must surely mean that she has met him and has decided to keep their meeting a secret."

Mrs King's face revealed her feelings. "Then it is as I feared; although I confess I did not think things had gone this far. I wanted to warn you of Willoughby's newfound friendship with the Percevals because I believed it would afford him opportunities to meet Mrs Brandon. If what you say is right, then it seems they have already met."

"Indeed you are right and the damage is probably done," cried Elinor. "I am concerned that she has said nothing of this meeting to me, which is what

I expected her to do, if he no longer meant anything to her. We thought, my youngest sister Margaret and I, that even if Marianne were to meet Willoughby socially—and one isn't always able to avoid such meetings in a small community like ours—then she could quite easily demonstrate her indifference to him by telling us about their meeting openly. However, if she has met him at the Percevals, and I do believe this is not the first time such a meeting has taken place, and has concealed it from us, it must mean that she still harbours some feelings for him and cannot speak of him without betraying herself to us. Do you not think so?"

Mrs King was inclined to agree but tried to alleviate her friend's distress by pointing out that it could also be argued that Mrs Brandon may have been trying to avoid causing the kind of anguish that Elinor was suffering by not revealing her meeting with Willoughby. While this argument seemed reasonable enough, Elinor felt she knew her sister better and was not readily comforted by it. "You said there were two matters, Helen, what was the other?" she asked, apprehensive that worse was to follow.

Mrs King looked quite grave and spoke in a hushed voice, "Dear Elinor, I must ask you not to take this information too much to heart, since, as far as I can tell, it is still only a rumour, but Henrietta Clift says that they have heard from relatives in London that Mrs Willoughby's lawyer has been instructed to seek a judicial separation—on the grounds of adultery."

Elinor burst into tears; this was much worse than she had expected. Helen King rose and went to her side and begged her not to make herself ill with worry. "It is not right that you should become ill as a consequence of the foolish actions of others. Besides, there is no suggestion your sister is involved, in any way," she said. "Come, my dear, I told you it is only a rumour; Miss Clift has not had it confirmed as yet, so it may just be some London gossip, which has followed him all the way to Somerset."

Elinor wiped away her tears. "It may be, and it may be true as well. Knowing Willoughby's past, I am not confident that it *is* just gossip. Do you not see, Helen, that if his wife and he are separated, he will have nothing to lose; he will feel quite free to try to re-engage my sister's feelings. Oh Marianne, what are you doing? Why have you not confided in any of us?" she cried as tears filled her eyes, and poor Mrs King began to feel truly wretched for having brought her friend this dismal news.

"I wish there was something I could suggest," she said in a forlorn voice. "Since your mother will not intervene, is there not someone your sister respects who can counsel her? Perhaps if you were to ask Mr Ferrars..." but Elinor shook her head. "Edward will not interfere, he loves Marianne as I do, but she is no longer just my younger sister, she is Colonel Brandon's wife, and Edward will not feel comfortable trying to advise her on such an intimate matter, unless she were to ask for his guidance, which of course, she is unlikely to do. It is entirely possible that Marianne will resent it too and it may create a rift between them, that would break my heart," she said, and there was such despair in her voice and attitude that it caused the kindly Mrs King to put her arms around her and say, "Dear Elinor, please do not let this make you ill. If you do, I shall not forgive myself for having brought you the news."

Bur Elinor would not let her friend take the blame. Summoning all her reserves of good sense and sound judgment, she said, "Helen, never say that; I am grateful for the information you have brought me, because at the very least it prepares me for what may follow. As you have wisely said, it may not all be true, but if it is, we can at least be ready to deal with whatever happens in the future. I shall talk to Edward, of course, and fortuitously, we are expecting a visit from some relations from London, who may have some further intelligence on the matter of Mr Willoughby's marital situation, all of which should help us prepare ourselves for the consequences. Furthermore, I am hopeful that Colonel Brandon will be returning from Ireland very soon and that will surely put an end to Willoughby's efforts to restore his reputation with Marianne."

Mrs King was relieved indeed to find her friend recovering from her state of wretchedness and strove to encourage her, suggesting that perhaps with the imminent return of Colonel Brandon, Marianne may also discover that a degree of prudence and caution in her social intercourse might be appropriate. Elinor smiled and, out of loyalty to her sister, did not say what she knew to be true, that prudence and caution were not Marianne's strong suit, and were more likely to be honoured in the breach. Elinor could recall vividly the contempt with which her sister had responded to her requests for some prudence and caution during the early days of her friendship with Willoughby.

She had hoped, indeed for some time she had believed, that Marianne, following the anguish she had suffered after Willoughby's betrayal, had begun to comprehend that life, in order to be worthwhile, did not have to be lived on the cusp of disaster. But in the last few months, she had begun to doubt that the lesson learned at seventeen had been fully absorbed. Her sister's disposition was as yet unsettled, and her emotional volatility made her vulnerable to misdirection by someone whose character was stronger or just more appealing to her. That Willoughby still had the power to move her mind and heart, Elinor had no doubt.

After Mrs King had left, Elinor went to her room, where Edward found her in a sombre mood. He had some news which he was sure would please her—a letter had arrived from Ireland: Colonel Brandon was returning some days earlier than expected. Elinor, delighted with the news, decided not to trouble her husband with the tales of Willoughby's depredations that Mrs King had brought, for, as her friend had said, they may only be rumours and in the light of the colonel's return to Delaford might not signify at all. Besides, there was much to be getting on with; the Palmers and Mrs Jennings were expected in a few days.

❧

The Palmers, their two children, their nurse, Mrs Palmer's maid, and Mr Palmer's manservant as well as Mrs Jennings and her maid all arrived in two carriages, and for a while Elinor was afraid that there would be no room to accommodate all of them at the parsonage. Fortunately, before she began to consider sending a note to Marianne, requesting emergency assistance, Mr Palmer said the second vehicle and most of the staff, except for the nurse and his manservant, would be travelling on to Cleveland directly, leaving a smaller party at the parsonage. When Mrs Palmer claimed she would never find anything in her trunks without her maid, her husband, with characteristic disregard for her protestations, said she should not worry because no one would notice the difference. This brought the usual complaint of excessive drollery from his wife, but Elinor intervened to assure Charlotte Palmer that she would be perfectly happy to lend them her own maid for the duration of their stay. Although they stayed but a few days, Mrs Jennings and her daughter managed to recount such an enormous volume of information and gossip that left Elinor in a fever of apprehension.

On the first evening of their stay, Charlotte, who had not stopped talking and making whimsical comments since the moment of her arrival at the parsonage, broke the news that Lucy—Mrs Robert Ferrars—was pregnant again and that Mrs Ferrars, the mother of Robert and Edward, was said to be considering changing her will if it was a boy. Apparently she was determined to ensure that her grandson was adequately provided for.

Elinor glanced at her husband and found Edward looking amused, while Mr Palmer appeared as inscrutable as ever. Mrs Jennings then intervened to add that she thought it was all rather odd that Mrs Ferrars should want to change her will. "I cannot see that it will make any difference to her now, seeing that Edward and Elinor have already presented her with two grandsons," said she, and Edward said in a very quiet voice, "Perhaps it is the fact that we live so far away, down here in Dorset. Maybe my mother has forgotten that she already has two grandsons." This caused Mrs Palmer to shriek with laughter. "Forgotten that she has two grandsons! Oh, dear Mr Ferrars, you are become almost as droll as my Mr Palmer!" she claimed. Whereupon Mr Palmer looked accusingly at Edward as though he'd been robbed of a prize possession and, determined not to be outdone, added, "I believe it is the fact that your boys have never really been 'presented' to Mrs Ferrars that causes her to forget their existence. Edward, you must see to it that your two sons are taken to London and presented with due ceremony to their grandmother, without delay." This proposition caused Edward and Elinor to smile, while Mrs Jennings laughed very loudly and tears rolled down Charlotte's face as she giggled and cried, "Oh Mr Palmer, you are so droll! I ask you, Elinor, have you heard anything like it? Do you see what I mean?"

The next piece of information, however, was not anywhere as amusing as the first, although Mrs Jennings recounted it with a good deal of cheerfulness. "Mr Willoughby—I am sure you all remember him," she said as they proceeded to consume the trifle and syllabub, "and of course, we all know how rich he became after marrying Miss Grey with her fifty thousand pounds—well, he may have to fight to keep his fortune, if his wife has her way. It is being said that Sophia Willoughby has instructed her lawyers to seek a judicial separation with a view to obtaining a divorce on the grounds of adultery." She was very satisfied by the effect her statement had upon the rest of the diners, their silence denoting their sense of shock, as she went on, "Were she to succeed, I understand she may be able to recoup at least half of the money she brought into the marriage. If he does not pay up—and one wonders how much of it he has already squandered—I understand the court can compel him to do so."

Elinor did not wish to reveal her prior knowledge of the story, but Mrs Jennings added for good measure, "Mrs Ferrars, we were speaking of this matter, Charlotte and I, on our journey here, and I said to Charlotte, 'Although we felt very sorry for Miss Marianne when the business with Willoughby ended so badly for her, it is quite clear now that she has had a fortunate escape.' If Sophia Grey could not hold him with her many thousands of pounds, Miss Marianne would not have had a chance. After a few years of marriage and a couple of children, he would have been off on the hunt again. What do you say, Mrs Ferrars, am I not right?"

Poor Elinor could barely speak, so mortified was she by the recollection of that dreadful time, and it was to the credit of the two gentlemen that the topic was changed and she was released from the obligation of having to answer what was clearly a rhetorical question. None of them had any doubt of the answer.

Earlier that evening Edward had been recounting to Mr Palmer some of his efforts on behalf of the abolitionists, and his guest, clearly bored with the gossip that his mother-in-law and wife were indulging in, put a pointed question to his host about the campaign, thereby ensuring some respite at the dinner table from domination by Mrs Jennings. "Is your group committed to complete abolition of slavery?" he asked, to which Edward replied, "Indeed we are, Mr Palmer, and we mean to get as many petitions as possible and submit them to Mr Wilberforce, who continues to press for total abolition in Britain and all her colonies. Unfortunately, the Act passed in 1807—the Slave Trade Act—only prohibits the shipping of slaves from Africa to the colonies in the Caribbean; it does nothing for the poor wretches who are already enslaved there, working for mainly British businessmen and plantation owners. Where do you stand on this question, Mr Palmer?" Edward asked.

Mr Palmer, whose politics were of the Whig persuasion, put down his glass, nodded sagely, and said, "I am with you, Ferrars, it is a most pernicious practice." Edward looked pleased and said so, but since neither Charlotte Palmer nor her mother had very much to say on the subject, they fell silent, while Elinor, who took a lively interest in her husband's work for the campaign, participated eagerly in the discussion that followed. When the ladies rose and withdrew to the parlour, Elinor feared her two companions would return to the subject of Willoughby, but, much to her relief, both women claimed that they were exceedingly tired after their long journey and chose to retire early to their rooms.

~✥~

The Palmers stayed three more days at Delaford parsonage, during which time the ladies expressed a desire to call on Marianne at the manor house. Mr Palmer had already accepted an invitation from Edward to meet his friend Dr Bradley King, leaving just the ladies to make the visit. Elinor went with them, having first sent a message over to her sister to advise her of the impending visitation. She hoped by doing this to give Marianne time to prepare herself for the arrival of two women she had never suffered gladly. On their arrival around midmorning, however, Elinor was relieved to find that her sister and her servants had been busy preparing for their visitors, who were duly invited into the morning room, where their hostess, elegantly gowned and coiffed, greeted them with a degree of affability that Elinor was surprised to witness.

Trays of refreshments were carried in and tea was served in the finest china available at the manor, as Marianne played hostess with aplomb. Elinor could see that Mrs Jennings and her daughter were very impressed.

Earlier, as they had prepared to leave the parsonage, Elinor had steeled herself to make an earnest request that they would not mention Mr Willoughby or the state of his marital affairs in the presence of her sister. To her relief, both Mrs Jennings and Charlotte Palmer had agreed that it would not be appropriate, although the reasons they adduced for their restraint were puzzling. Mrs Jennings had declared that "it would not do to remind the dear girl of the misery he had put her through," while Charlotte had giggled and added that "nor would it be wise to let her think that Willoughby might be free again, if his wife were to succeed in obtaining a divorce!" Shocked though she was by the sentiment, Elinor restrained herself, thanked them for respecting her wishes, and prayed silently that Marianne would, by her general demeanour, demonstrate to the ladies that she was content and happy in her marriage to Colonel Brandon.

And it was exactly what transpired, as they took tea, walked about the house, admired the garden, and talked for an hour or so of very little that was of any consequence. By the time they were ready to return to the parsonage, it appeared as though Marianne had completely convinced Mrs Jennings and Mrs Palmer that she was perfectly content in her role as lady of the manor. As they stood in the hall, about to leave, Mrs Jennings asked, "And when do you expect dear Colonel Brandon home?" to which Marianne replied with a smile, "We expect him any day now, Mrs Jennings, he is returning a week earlier than expected. Indeed, Cook is planning a celebratory dinner to welcome him home." Whereupon Mrs Jennings responded with a great laugh and characteristic vulgarity, that she was sure the colonel would be looking forward to something more than a celebratory dinner on his return, adding with a wink and a nudge to her daughter, "Just ask my Charlotte, she knows all about it, Mr Palmer returned from two weeks shooting in Scotland, and though it is not plain to see as yet, Charlotte is in the family way again. So you mark my words, after six weeks away in Ireland, your dear husband will be looking forward to much more than a good dinner, and you, my dear, may have some happy news for us in the new year."

While Charlotte Palmer and her mother alternately shrieked and roared with laughter, Elinor winced and saw Marianne's face flushed with embarrassment, but neither of her visitors seemed to notice, and they left with more laughter and warnings of the consequences of the imminent return of her husband from Ireland, urging her to enjoy the fun while it lasted.

Elinor's relief was great when the Palmers finally departed, for though they had been little trouble to her in a practical sense, their presence, intruding as it did upon the usual calm and quietude of her home, had prevented discussion of certain matters with Edward. She had wished particularly to tell him of her continuing unease regarding Willoughby's presence in the neighbourhood and his contact with her sister, an unease whose intensity had increased considerably since the revelations from Helen King and Mrs Jennings that his wife intended to apply for a divorce.

On the evening after the Palmers' departure, Elinor sensed that Edward was in a sufficiently amenable mood, with no parish duties and his sermon for Sunday completed well in advance, to let her take up the subject. It was a matter that had concerned her deeply, and yet she had tried not to trouble him with it unless and until there was something seriously worth talking about. Recent events and information appeared to her to provide an opportunity, and she decided to take it.

Once the boys had been read their bedtime story and put to bed, Elinor went to sit beside her husband on the sofa by the fire and he, sensing her need for comfort, put an arm around her and said, "I know how tired you must be, my dear, and yet you never complain of it. I wish I could do more to help. I would if you would only ask." Elinor knew he was thinking that her fatigue was the consequence of managing their rather trying guests over the past few days; she smiled and said, "Thank you, my love, I know you would, but it is not the Palmers and Mrs Jennings who have me in this state; I wish it were, because it would then be just a transitory feeling of weariness, which I confess Charlotte and her mother seem to bring upon me—nothing that a long lavender-scented bath and a good night's sleep would not cure."

Her unexpected response caused her husband to sit up and look at her seriously, "Dearest, what else is it? You are not unwell? Tell me, Elinor, have you been feeling ill and keeping it from me?" She was quick to deny this and reassured him at once. "Not at all, Edward, you know me better than to think that. I am too sensible to conceal an illness, and if I had been feeling unwell, I'd have sent for Doctor Richards and had him prescribe some potion or other—not that they do much good—but I would not neglect it, because I know I need to look after my health for all our sakes."

Edward was obviously relieved. "Thank goodness for that; well then, what is it that is worrying you? Elinor, you are not still anxious about that scoundrel Willoughby, are you? I did note that you looked rather shocked at the news that his wife was seeking a separation, but why are you astonished? Willoughby never cared for Miss Grey, he clearly married her for her fortune, and being the kind of man he is, bereft of all principle, bent only upon his own pleasure, it is not at all surprising that the marriage should fail. Why should that cause you to worry?"

Elinor sat up very straight and looked into his eyes as she spoke; she wanted Edward to understand clearly that her anxiety was not based on her knowledge of Willoughby and his marital problems alone. "Edward, I know that when I have spoken of this matter previously, you have tried, with the best of intentions, to reassure me, to tell me I was being too anxious, that there was no evidence of any danger to my sister from Willoughby's presence in this area, and I have wished that was the case. However, in recent months, indeed since Margaret was here before she went to France, there have been several occasions on which

I have seen and heard things that have filled me with disquiet, and while I have not wanted to trouble you with constant repetition of my concerns, I can ignore them no longer. I need your advice." Edward could see from her countenance that her worries were too serious to be relieved with simple words of comfort.

Elinor continued, "The rumour—and I accept that coming from Mrs Jennings it can rate no higher than that—that Willoughby's wife is attempting to separate from him, indeed is already living apart from him and may seek a divorce, has only added another element to my fears, that of Willoughby's own situation and his lack of responsibility. If he is no longer restrained, even as a mere formality, by the bonds of marriage, what does he have to lose? Why would he not try his best to re-engage Marianne's feelings, knowing that she was so besotted with him once, she was willing to throw everything, including her own reputation, to the winds for him?"

"And what is this evidence that you have seen and heard? Does it involve Marianne?" he asked, and she nodded and with great determination, held back her tears as she told him of what she and Margaret had learned and the information she had gathered from her friend Helen King. She spoke quietly, undramatically, attempting to convey her fears without hysteria, pointing out that it was her uncertainty that Marianne was happy and content in her own marriage that was at the core of her concern. "If I were as certain of her contentment as I am of my own happiness with you, I would not care if Willoughby were living next door, but I fear I cannot, I do not have that certainty."

Edward's expression had changed as she spoke, reflecting his response to her words; he could no longer speak lightly. "Dearest Elinor, I am sorry, I feel I have not taken your anxieties seriously enough, and I fear I have allowed you to carry the burden alone for too long. Perhaps it is because I have wished to believe that Marianne and Brandon are as contented as we are, but I realise from what you have said that things are not always as they seem or as we wish them to be. However, there is little we can achieve by worrying. Perhaps we should visit your mother tomorrow, and if I were to speak seriously with her about this matter and ask for her help, she might be willing to consider returning to stay with Marianne until Brandon returns, which I am reliably informed is to be very soon. In fact, I met his steward the other day when I was walking with Mr Palmer in the Delaford woods, and he claimed that the master was expected back any day now. What do you say to that?"

Elinor, happy to have finally captured his undivided attention on this matter for the first time and convinced him to take it seriously, was content to agree to his plan. She hoped that Edward, for whom Mrs Dashwood had warm affection and respect, might well convince her of the need to return with them to Delaford.

Elinor's fear that Marianne might be unwittingly drawn into the scandal of Willoughby's divorce was a potent one, and it was possible that their mother's presence at Delaford might, by inhibiting Willoughby's visits to Marianne or her meetings with him, help avoid such a debacle. Eager to credit her husband with alleviating her distress, she agreed, "I think that may help, my love, if *you* can convince Mama that Marianne needs her more than Sir John Middleton does," she replied, and they laughed together as he promised to try his very best. By the time they retired to bed, Elinor felt a small part of the burden of care had rolled off her weary shoulders.

Chapter Seventeen

MARIANNE WAS BUSY PREPARING for a visitor when the letter was delivered. Miss Eugenie Perceval was coming to tea, after which the two friends had arranged to drive out to attend a church function, organised by the eldest of the Perceval girls, who was married to the rector of a small parish in Somersetshire. Eugenie was to sing at the concert and had persuaded Marianne to accompany her at the pianoforte, on account of her elder sister Maria being taken ill with a severe cold.

The letter Marianne had received was from Colonel Brandon. She had assumed he was writing to confirm the precise date and time of his arrival; she knew already that he was returning early from Ireland, which was why Marianne did not open the letter immediately, leaving it on her dressing table to be read at leisure when she returned home later that evening. Marianne enjoyed pleasing an audience and looked forward to the concert; it would give her an opportunity to use the performance skills she had acquired and excelled at as a young girl.

She dressed with care, in a stylish lilac silk gown and a cloak of deep blue velvet, and waited for Eugenie. When she heard the carriage turn into the drive, she delayed a few moments before going downstairs into the sitting room, where, to her astonishment, she found Eugenie Perceval and Miss Peabody with none other than Mr Willoughby. Nothing had been said previously of his attendance at the function, and Marianne's face betrayed her surprise, as he rose to greet her with his usual suave charm, while Eugenie hastened to explain that Mr Willoughby had been visiting them and had kindly offered to convey them to the concert in his carriage.

"Papa was pleased because he needed the carriage this afternoon to attend a business function in town, so it was very kind of Mr Willoughby to offer," which caused the gentleman to protest that it was no kindness at all, the pleasure of driving not one but two lovely ladies was all his. Marianne felt a little ill at ease, but the feeling lasted only a very little while, as she discovered the pleasure of their company, pleasure that required little more than basking in Willoughby's alluring flattery while indulging in the most undemanding social chitchat that young Eugenie Perceval could produce. Occasionally, when she said something particularly silly, Willoughby would smile and his eyes would seek Marianne's as if to enjoy a private joke.

The drive was pleasant enough, but Marianne wondered whether Willoughby had deliberately manoeuvred himself into the situation in order that they might be together again; but, she told herself, surely he must have known that with Eugenie and Miss Peabody present, he could say or do little to advance his cause.

While this was indeed a perfectly logical thought, Marianne had perhaps forgotten that Willoughby was a particularly persistent opportunist and would not let such a chance pass him by if he thought he could make something of it.

The arrangements for the function proceeded sufficiently smoothly to let Marianne believe that she had done her friend a favour, for while Miss Perceval had a pleasant enough voice, she would have been seriously disadvantaged without the support of a sympathetic accompanist. The applause that followed their appearance and the demand for an encore proved her right. Marianne had arranged with Eugenie that they would do a simple English ballad if an encore was requested, and when it was, they launched into it with ease and the young performer was rewarded with generous applause.

Afterward, as Marianne sat in an alcove watching the rest of the concert, Mr Willoughby arrived at her side to praise her contribution and declare that without her accompaniment the singer would have been lost indeed. "Miss Eugenie has a very pretty face and an appealing manner, but I do not believe anyone would contradict my contention that her voice lacks strength and range, both of which were amply supplemented by your most excellent accompaniment," he said, noting that she glowed with pleasure at his words.

It was the type of remark that Marianne should have recognised as typical of Willoughby, couched as it was in words that were calculated to win her approval, but she had already begun to credit him with a transformation of character that prevented her from comprehending his true intent. And, without the support of Elinor, who had been at her side throughout the agonising days and weeks after her betrayal by Willoughby, Marianne was increasingly inclined to accept him as he presented himself to her: a man of good intentions, whose past errors were the consequence of misfortune or the malice of others, rather than his own weakness and poor judgment. In her heart she had almost forgiven him, because he had made it clear that he had loved her then and would love her still if she would only let him. To Marianne's romantic nature this was a potent appeal.

Seating himself beside her, as they watched the other performers, whose skill or lack of it was of no consequence, Willoughby had proceeded to use his eloquence and charm to persuade Marianne to accept an invitation to Combe Magna. "I have asked the Percevals and the Hawthornes to dinner next week, and I had hoped that you might join us. Surely, there can be no criticism of your attendance if you should come as one of the Percevals' party. They are your friends and aware that your husband is away in Ireland; they have asked you to join them. What can be more natural?" he had said, but Marianne, as yet unready to abandon the last restraint she had maintained against his pleas, had steadfastly refused.

"I do not believe it would be right; besides, were it to be discovered by my sister Elinor, I should be roundly condemned. She would see it as conduct lacking in both decorum and loyalty," she had said, and he had protested that she should by now have emancipated herself from the narrow confines of her older sister's regulation.

"Indeed she would, but she is a parson's wife and you are an independent person, Marianne, a married woman with a mind of her own. I recall that at seventeen you were more prepared to challenge your sister's strictures upon your actions. I did not expect that at twenty-five you would be less willing to do so. Consider this: You are not being invited to participate in something unseemly or scandalous; attendance at a sedate dinner party in the company of a very respectable family with whom you are friendly cannot be regarded as imprudent by any but the meanest of minds, and since *they* will assume evil in anything at all, their censure is not worth considering. Do you not agree? My dear Marianne, do not tell me that you are so fearful of criticism that you have lost that fire, that exciting spirit I admired and loved so much," he had implored, but she had remained resolute.

On the journey home, Marianne was glad of the company of Eugenie Perceval and her chaperone Miss Peabody in the carriage, for she had been apprehensive that had she been alone, Willoughby would have persisted with his efforts and she had begun to wonder how long her resistance could hold out against his remonstrations. Despite her best intentions, she had found it hard indeed to contradict the persuasive arguments he had adduced, resorting finally to a silence that she hoped would convey her refusal more clearly than words. Claiming to be very tired, she had asked that they proceed first to Delaford Manor, hoping this would indicate to Willoughby that she was unwilling to be persuaded by him. Miss Perceval, grateful for her invaluable help that evening, agreed at once. Sadly, it seemed Marianne, unable to fully understand her own situation, was incapable of withstanding the power Willoughby had over her.

❧

Once upstairs in her bedroom, Marianne undressed, changed into her night-gown, and sent her maid away before opening the letter from Colonel Brandon, expecting to read a loving message which told her how much he missed her and when they would be reunited. Having steadfastly resisted Willoughby's charm all evening, she had prepared herself to respond with warmth and affection to her husband's sentiments, enabling her to feel some degree of satisfaction at having refused Willoughby's invitation. She had confidently expected that the letter would affirm her husband's love, of which she could have no doubt at all, thereby confirming the moral certitude of her own decision.

However, when she read the colonel's letter, it did nothing of the sort. Indeed, within moments of perusing the single page of writing, she had thrown it across the room as she flung herself onto her bed in tears. Colonel Brandon wrote:

> *My dearest Marianne,*
> *It is with a great deal of reluctance and a very heavy heart that I write this, for I have this day received some very unhappy news, which prevents*

me from returning directly to Delaford and you, as I had earlier planned to do.

This morning I received a letter from Eliza Williams, apprising me of the grave situation in which she and her young daughter find themselves. It would appear that she has been tricked into a situation, which has resulted in their losing the cottage I had arranged to lease for them and they are in danger of being evicted or worse, being incarcerated in a debtor's prison, unless someone can be found to pay her debt. As you know, my dear Marianne, there is no one apart from myself who can do this for Eliza, for she is quite alone in the world, being bereft of friends and relations. There is also the matter of her child, who is far from well and is likely to be seriously afflicted by this situation. I know you will understand the need for me to hasten to help them and will not begrudge them my assistance at this difficult time.

Reading this, Marianne had cried out, "Oh, but I do, I most certainly do, because it is almost six weeks that you have been away in Ireland, and I had hoped that my husband's first thought would have been of me, here, alone, waiting for him to return. But no, it seems it is more important that he should race off to save the damsel in distress, who seems unable to manage without his help for two months together." She did not even bother to read the rest of his note, in which he begged her forgiveness, promised to hurry back to her as soon as he had settled Eliza and her child in a place of safety, concluding with his warmest affection, etc.

Marianne had for some time been rather impatient with her husband's continuing concern for Eliza Williams and her child, even though she had at first charitably conceded that he had a duty to protect them. Now, her mind dwelt upon what Mrs Jennings had said of Miss Williams many years ago; that she was a "very, very close relation of Colonel Brandon… so close as to be shocking to the young ladies," adding under her breath for Elinor's ears alone, "Indeed, she is his natural daughter!" It was something Marianne had wheedled out of her sister, and then, she had been prepared to believe it, without prejudice to the colonel, because he had meant nothing to her at the time and Willoughby had been the centre of her world.

Later, she recalled, following the anguish of Willoughby's duplicitous behaviour, Elinor had told her of a long talk she'd had with Colonel Brandon, in which he had told her of a girl, Eliza, who was his cousin, whom he had loved when they were both very young, but had not been permitted to marry. There was a long, tragic tale of her misadventures, which included her abuse by a cruel husband and various other men, leaving her with a daughter born out of wedlock, also named Eliza, who was the very Miss Williams referred to by Mrs Jennings. This Eliza Williams, Colonel Brandon had claimed, had been seduced by Willoughby—a claim Marianne was only willing to believe because Willoughby had admitted as much to her sister Elinor, in the harrowing interview he'd had with her at Cleveland House, while Marianne had been lying desperately ill upstairs.

While accepting Willoughby's part in the destruction of Miss Williams, Marianne had never sought to interrogate Colonel Brandon about his relationship with young Eliza or her mother, either before or after their marriage, being content to regard it as an unhappy episode from his youth, which had no bearing upon their present life. Nor had he attempted to explain any part of the situation to her, presuming perhaps that her sister had done so already, except to make clear that he had a degree of responsibility for the welfare of Miss Williams and her child because of their familial connection.

It was something Marianne had never queried, but if she were to be honest, she would have to admit that, over the years of their marriage, there had been some moments of annoyance, even aggravation, at the frequency with which Miss Williams seemed able to call on the colonel's assistance, often at the most inopportune of times. Yet, he never seemed able to say nay, and was always ready to rush to her side to extricate her from some dire predicament into which she had fallen, most often as a direct consequence of her own wilful actions.

This time, it seemed to Marianne that once again Miss Williams had succeeded in intruding into their lives, spoiling what should have been his homecoming, returning after some six weeks away, to his wife. Sheer vexation allowed Marianne to contemplate that perhaps Mrs Jennings was right after all. Surely, she argued, Mrs Jennings, who knew the colonel very well and had no reason to slander him, would not fabricate such a tale about him?

And Elinor had only the colonel's word that Eliza's mother, his cousin, whom he had, by his own admission, loved dearly, had been seduced by some unknown man who had fathered her daughter. It may quite easily have been the colonel himself, Marianne contended, which would make young Eliza Williams his natural daughter. It would certainly account for a sense of guilt that might well cause him to rush to assist her on every occasion, she argued.

With all these reflections swirling around in her already confused mind, Marianne could hope for very little sleep; what was worse, she awoke the following morning, even before daylight, with a headache and the same feeling of overwhelming misery she had taken to bed the previous night.

Within a few minutes of rising from her bed, she rang the bell to summon her maid and asked for a bath to be prepared and her gown to be laid out. When she had finished her tea, she dressed, went downstairs, and ordered that the small carriage be brought round to the front door. Marianne had decided that she would visit Elinor at the parsonage and show her Colonel Brandon's letter, hoping that her sister and perhaps even her brother-in-law might prove sympathetic.

Unfortunately for Marianne, Edward and Elinor had left early that morning to travel to Barton Park, hoping to persuade Mrs Dashwood to return with them to Delaford. The maid, who answered the door at the parsonage, had no information to give her, except that Mr and Mrs Ferrars had left at an early hour and were not expected to return until the following day.

Finding herself alone with no one to confide in and no sympathetic listeners to hear her complaint, Marianne returned to Delaford Manor in a state of deep dejection. She proceeded to re-read her husband's letter, looking for some indication of when she might expect him to return, but in vain; indeed, he did not even reveal his destination. She had never interested herself in the exact whereabouts of Eliza Williams; she had assumed it to be in London or someplace nearby, and expected that her husband would send her word during the day, by express perhaps, apprising her of any progress he might have made in settling the problems of Miss Williams and her child. At least, she thought, he would send word as to the date of his return.

But as the day wore on and no message was received, she began to fret and wonder, and the more she pondered, the easier it became to blame Colonel Brandon for a whole array of afflictions, all of which she could link to his inordinate desire to pander to the unreasonable demands, as she saw them, of a young woman who was in a position to take advantage of his compassionate nature. The longer she waited without satisfaction, the more her sense of grievance grew, until it occupied her mind entirely and drove out all other reasonable arguments that may have acquitted her husband of fault.

❧

It was late afternoon, and Marianne, weary of waiting for news, had asked for tea to be brought to her in the sitting room, when a brougham drove up to the door. Believing it to be Colonel Brandon or some emissary bringing a message from him, she ran into the hall to find Willoughby in the doorway. Though taken aback, unable to maintain a pretence of formality she did not feel, she took him into the sitting room, where the tears she had restrained all day filled her eyes and Willoughby, astonished at her state, but able to see that she was too vulnerable to protest, abandoned decorum and sat beside her on the sofa and offered her his handkerchief. "My dear Marianne, what has happened? Please tell me what is the matter? Has there been some bad news? Is there something I can do?" he asked.

He had said all the right words; he was concerned for her and eager to help. Marianne could not but pour out the entire unhappy tale, as he held her hand and provided, with gentle words and expressions, all the warmth and sympathy she craved. It seemed to her that Willoughby, in an instant, had sensed the extent of her unhappiness and by every word and gesture had indicated his desire to alleviate her anguish.

It did not seem to matter at that moment that this man had once caused her such humiliation and despair, she had wished she would die. Nor did she recall that his explanations of his actions had, at the time, seemed glib, self-serving, and unconvincing to Elinor and even to her mother, who had once been his staunchest advocate. Now, when she was alone and miserable, he had appeared, just as he had appeared when she had tumbled down the slope, twisting her ankle, in drenching rain at Barton Park, and by his swift action had saved her from the greater danger of pneumonia. She was grateful to him now as she and all her family had been grateful then; she recalled that young Margaret had dubbed him "Marianne's Preserver," a title they had laughingly bestowed upon him throughout that idyllic summer.

When she had finished, having laid bare all her grievances, not so much blaming her husband, but expressing her deep displeasure at Miss Williams's ability to summon him to her side as and when she wished, Willoughby, shrewdly avoiding any overt criticism of Colonel Brandon, stoked the fire of Marianne's resentment by pointing out that some women were notoriously selfish by nature, and when they discovered a generous, kindly man, they would use him for their own ends. "I do not mean to suggest that Miss Williams is such a person, but I have known many friends who have been dragged down by such women, who seem to have some hold over them," he said, as she sobbed and asked, "What shall I do, Willoughby? I know my husband is a kind, generous man and I am convinced he is being used by her. Surely, she must have some power over him; how else can I account for his behaviour? I expected him to return home to me after six weeks away in Ireland, yet here he is rushing off to London because she has got herself into some predicament and demands his help. Can you explain it?"

Willoughby offered up another pristine handkerchief and as she dried her eyes, he adroitly avoided making any criticism against Colonel Brandon, but made it clear that he could not have left her alone for six days, much less six weeks.

His mind was busy devising a plan that would enable him to take advantage of the situation, without appearing to do so. It had come upon him very suddenly, with no warning, and he was as yet unable to work out how best to proceed. All he knew was this was the best opportunity he would ever get to impress upon Marianne that he loved and cared for her and to persuade her to trust him again.

When she, having regained some of her composure, offered him refreshment, he politely refused, making a curious excuse that his horses were tired from a long journey and he had to get them back to Combe Magna before dark; but, he promised, he would return the following day, by midafternoon. He would make enquiries, he said, about Miss Williams's situation and return with some information for her. However, as a precaution, he asked that she send him a message if her husband returned in the meantime, so as not to embarrass them. "I should not wish to cause you any pain, which is very likely to eventuate should I arrive and find him here. It is unlikely that he would appreciate my appearance." Marianne agreed then to send a servant with a message, to meet him at the inn by the bridge that carried the road into Dorchester, if Colonel Brandon had returned overnight, in which case, he was to abandon the visit.

While Marianne went to bed and slept a little better that night with the dubious satisfaction of having garnered the sympathy of Mr Willoughby, her husband had travelled post haste to London and appeared at the door of the house of Sir John Middleton, in a state close to exhaustion. His friend, shocked and astonished at the colonel's condition, hurried to get him indoors and settled in front of the fire in his sitting room with a drink in his hand, before he would let him speak. Sir John, who was an intimate friend of Colonel Brandon, could not imagine what could have caused such a perturbation in the mind of his friend as to bring him to London in such a state.

Fearing that it must have something to do with the health or well-being of his young wife, he asked, "Good Heavens, Brandon, I had thought you were in Ireland. What brings you here at this time of year and in such a parlous condition?" His friend, having gulped down his drink and accepted another, began to provide some of the details of his story; clearly desperate, he said, "I came at once, I had no time to lose; I must have your advice on this matter."

But Sir John insisted that he must eat first before they could discuss what might be done, and even though dinner had long been over, ordered that a place be laid at the table and some hot food be provided for his guest.

After the servants had withdrawn, the colonel, who had been somewhat reticent in their presence, proceeded to give a full account of the circumstances that had brought him to London. Sir John listened with unusual patience. He already had some but not all the knowledge necessary to interpret his friend's actions, but as the tale unfolded, Sir John realised that his friend was enmeshed in a tangle of difficult emotional relationships and practical problems that had to be resolved forthwith, if a far worse tragedy was to be avoided.

"And what have you accomplished so far?" he asked, and was told that Miss Williams and her child had been located and lodged temporarily with a neighbour, whom Colonel Brandon had paid handsomely for the service, but it was not a satisfactory or permanent arrangement. "I am reluctant to leave them there, where those who have used her so callously can continue to find her and lead her astray again. I need to discover some place, well away from London, where she and her child will be safe and where she can find something worthwhile to do, to keep her occupied," he explained.

When his friend looked rather dubious, he added, "I regret to say, Sir John, that Eliza is neither well educated nor accomplished, not because she lacks the ability, but because no one has taught her and no one has given her an opportunity to learn. I have previously suggested that she take up a position as a helper in a school, where her child may learn, while she works to assist the staff, but she will not agree. She feels ashamed of her lack of learning and wishes not to expose herself to ridicule. Sadly, she is also somewhat wilful, which is not unlike her mother used to be, and is difficult to persuade. But I cannot leave her here again, at the mercy of those who will destroy her and her child," he said, sounding desperately unhappy.

"Then what do you propose?" asked Sir John. "Have you thought of taking her into the country perhaps?" but Colonel Brandon shook his head. "I have, but I cannot have her at Delaford, Marianne will not agree; I sense that she is already impatient with me for spending so much time on the welfare of Eliza and her child."

Sir John comprehended the problem. "Perhaps not at Delaford. I can see that Marianne would resent such an arrangement, wives generally do. But what if you were to rent Barton Cottage for them? It is vacant at present," and when the colonel looked puzzled, he explained, "Mrs Dashwood, who as you know is my cousin, has been managing the household at Barton Park for me these last few months and I have invited her to use one of the guest suites; it suits her convenience in the circumstances. This means the cottage is unoccupied at the moment, and if you were to rent it for Miss Williams and her child, it may prove to be a solution that could suit everybody. What do you think?"

Colonel Brandon was so overwhelmed by the generosity of Sir John's offer that his eyes filled with tears. "Do you mean you would have no objection, even though you are aware of her past problems?" he asked, and his friend slapped him on the back. "Really, Brandon, you must take me for a fool. Of course I am aware of her past problems, but I am also well aware that you take your duty to her seriously, and I am happy to help you in this regard. If Eliza can be persuaded to move to Devonshire, where a quiet, decent life is available to her, there is a chance she and her child may yet survive and make something worthwhile of their lives. After all, you cannot spend the rest of your days racing around England rescuing her each time she gets into trouble. I am not surprised that your wife is getting impatient; what did she say on this occasion?"

Colonel Brandon looked rather sheepish as he replied, "I do not know, I have not seen her; I sent her a note explaining the circumstances…"

Sir John thumped the table. "Brandon, you are a greater simpleton than I took you for! Do you mean to say that after spending six weeks away in Ireland, separated from her, you did not even visit your wife at home, before taking off on this mission to rescue Miss Williams?" he thundered, outraged at his friend's naiveté.

"Indeed, I had to, Eliza's letter was a desperate plea for help, and I hoped Marianne would understand—" but his friend cut him short. "Brandon, you are an idiot. I should not be at all surprised if you find your wife in a very bad mood when you return to Delaford, and I would have to say that I would not blame her! Now, if you agree to rent Barton Cottage, then tomorrow, after you have had a good night's sleep, you will collect Miss Williams and her child and bring them over here. Then *you* will leave at once for Barton Park and take a letter from me to Mrs Dashwood, who will give orders for the cottage to be made ready for the new tenants, after which you will go directly to Delaford and your wife and make suitable amends for your conduct, which I must say has been most derelict. I cannot imagine what Marianne will say, but we must hope for your sake that she will forgive you, if you treat her right," he declared with a twinkle in his eye. "Meanwhile, I shall arrange for Miss Williams and her child to be conveyed, in the company of one of the older women on our staff, to Barton Park and thence to the cottage. There is a caretaker there and his wife, who will help with the housework, and Mrs Dashwood will make a maid available to help her settle in," he explained.

He made it sound so simple, Colonel Brandon was speechless for a moment; then he tried to thank his friend, but Sir John would not let him. "Oh, do go up to bed and get some sleep, Brandon, you look all done in and you have a busy day tomorrow," he said and sent for a manservant to show the colonel to his bedroom.

Chapter Eighteen

Mrs Dashwood had not had a very satisfactory day. She dearly loved her son-in-law Edward Ferrars, and even though she found her eldest daughter Elinor to be what country people might call something of a worrywart, she always respected Edward's concerns. This is why she was feeling particularly unhappy at having had to refuse to agree to his request that she return to Delaford and spend some time with Marianne until Colonel Brandon returned from Ireland. Edward had put his arguments clearly and logically, but Mrs Dashwood had not been able to agree. She had decided that Marianne and her husband must work out their problems and had felt that Colonel Brandon would not thank her for becoming involved in their lives. Nor was she convinced that Willoughby posed a threat to the Brandons' marriage.

"I cannot believe that Marianne is in real danger from Willoughby. She may have some romantic notions, but she is unlikely to allow herself to be run away with, Edward, and while I do applaud your kindness in taking such an interest in her well-being while the colonel is away, I do not think my presence at Delaford Manor will help. Besides, Sir John is due back at Barton Park next week; however shall I explain my sudden departure to him without revealing all this business about Marianne and Willoughby, which will only make matters a lot worse?"

Despite their own fears, Edward and Elinor had to agree that it would not do to have Sir John Middleton and others in his circle privy to the re-emergence of Willoughby in Marianne's life. For all his kindness and generosity, Sir John was not renowned for his discretion in such matters. The very thought of the story being picked up by Mrs Jennings and Charlotte, or Robert and Lucy Ferrars, and purveyed among the families, sent a shiver of apprehension down Elinor's spine.

They had, therefore, returned disappointed to Delaford, leaving Mrs Dashwood feeling somewhat downcast. She loved her daughters, but having seen both Elinor and Marianne married to exemplary men of reasonable means and good character, she had emancipated herself from the maternal desire to entangle herself in their lives. She knew Marianne was unhappy that she and the colonel had no children, but that again was something Mrs Dashwood acknowledged was beyond her capacity to assuage and hoped that Colonel Brandon would find other ways in which to engage and occupy his young wife.

Saying farewell to Edward and Elinor, she had felt helpless and had wished she could have said more to alleviate their obvious anxiety, but in the end, deciding there was little more she could have done, she lay back in her favourite chair by the fire in the sitting room and fell fast asleep.

Mrs Dashwood was awakened by the sound of a carriage in the drive and went to the window. She was both astonished and afraid when she saw Colonel Brandon alight from a hired vehicle. Astonished because she had thought he was still in Ireland, and afraid that he was here alone because there was bad news about Marianne; her relief was great when he greeted her affectionately and handed her Sir John Middleton's letter.

Having hastened to get him out of the cold hallway into the comfort of the sitting room, where a fire burned in the grate and refreshments were to hand, Mrs Dashwood urged him to help himself while she sat down to read Sir John's letter. The colonel, unsure of her response to Sir John's suggestion that Eliza Williams and her daughter be accommodated at Barton Cottage, poured himself a drink and sat nervously on the edge of his chair, while she perused the letter once, then looked up at him with a puzzled frown, and read it again, before saying, "Well, Colonel Brandon, it looks like you have been just in time to avert another disaster, and if I understand Sir John, he is of the opinion that it will be better to have Miss Williams and her child here at Barton Cottage, away from the perils of London. He asks if I would mind letting her use the cottage; well, I probably would have been a little put out, except for the fact that Sir John has very kindly offered me the use of the excellent suite of rooms that Mrs Jennings used to have when she stayed here, and I have just had it all arranged to suit my purposes; so I suppose I cannot say that I should have the cottage as well, could I, now? That would be really selfish, would you not agree, Colonel?" she asked with that rather naive simplicity he had always recognised in her.

Colonel Brandon did not know what to say, except to ask if that meant she would not object to having Miss Williams and her child living at Barton Cottage. To which Mrs Dashwood, regarding him with a look of some bewilderment, said, "Why should I object? If Sir John, in his generosity wishes to offer the poor girl a place where she may live a quiet, decent life, away from all that commotion in London, where, if all I hear is true, a young woman without the protection of a husband or family is likely to be in grave danger, then why should I object? Indeed, Colonel, I shall be more than happy to do as Sir John has suggested and have the cottage made ready for them. Sir John writes that he expects to send them down here in a day or two. I will ensure that the cottage is ready and the housekeeper arranges for one of the maids to be made available to help them settle in."

Overwhelmed by the kindness and generosity of both Sir John and Mrs Dashwood, the colonel thanked her profusely, and then made his next request. Sir John had suggested that Colonel Brandon could borrow a horse from the Barton Park stables and ride on to Delaford directly, instead of waiting for the coach on the following day. Mrs Dashwood urged him to partake of a meal first, but the colonel was determined to reach Delaford as soon as possible and make his peace with his wife. Sir John's words of warning had alerted him to a problem he had not anticipated and he wished to put it right. He insisted on leaving directly and Mrs Dashwood did not argue; she sent for the groom and asked him to take the colonel to the stables so he could choose a horse.

Not long afterward, Colonel Brandon, having thanked her again and again, rode away into the gathering darkness, while Mrs Dashwood was left feeling quite pleased that whatever problems had hitherto afflicted Marianne should soon be resolved.

On the day following, Elinor and Edward, having reviewed their wasted journey to Barton Park, were consoling themselves that they had tried their best to find some solution to the problem of Marianne and Willoughby. They could not agree with Mrs Dashwood's placid assessment of the situation, and were very aware of the hazards posed by gossip in the neighbourhood.

They were in the sitting room enjoying a cup of tea, when Elinor brought out Margaret's latest letter. It had been received that morning, and she had been awaiting Edward's return from his parish work to tell him the news. Margaret wrote that she would be arriving to spend Christmas with her sister and brother-in-law at the parsonage. Her letter was all about their last days in Provence and, particularly, the news of her friend Claire Jones's recent engagement to Mr Nicholas Wilcox. Margaret wrote:

They have known one another for years but have remained just friends for all of this time; I am convinced that it was the irresistible ambience of Provence in the autumn that finally pushed them into realising that they were in love. I have asked Claire many times when she knew, but she will only confess that when it did happen, she knew without a doubt that Nicholas, whom we all know to be a dear, good, kind man, was the man with whom she wanted to spend the rest of her life! They are so obviously happy together, one has to believe that they are genuinely deeply in love!

Elinor sighed, "Happy, fortunate Claire! Oh, if only Margaret would also discover that she loved a good, kind man and settle down too, I shouldn't worry so much," she said, and her husband laughed at her. "My dear Elinor, I do not believe young Margaret will be rushed into settling down with a good, kind man, not unless she loves him and believes that he genuinely cares for her. I am convinced that your young sister was deeply affected by what occurred with Marianne and Mr Willoughby, even though she was but a child at the time. It must have been quite a shock to watch a young man, with all the accoutrements of a gentleman, court her beautiful sister all summer, then deceive her family and betray her, because he chose wealth and the trappings of affluent society above love," he said. Elinor listened as he continued, "While she may not have said anything at the time, it is quite likely that Margaret's own attitude to young men was influenced by what happened that year; do you not agree, my dear?" he asked, and Elinor, who had not given the subject much thought, had to admit that it was possible.

"Margaret knew hardly any young men then. Willoughby was perhaps the first new male acquaintance she had made in a year, and no doubt his conduct that summer shocked her. It is possible that you are right, it may well have shaken her trust in young men, because she has never shown any interest in anyone these many years. She loves and respects you and is in awe of Colonel Brandon—chiefly on account of his age, which from her perspective must appear great—but she has rarely mentioned any other man, not until this holiday in Provence, when she has written quite often and with some degree of enthusiasm about Mr Daniel Brooke, who was their guide around the churches and abbeys of Provence. I wonder if he may turn out to be different, someone she could trust."

So engrossed in their conversation had they been, that they had not heard the sound of an approaching horse on the path and it was only when the maid went to answer the doorbell that Elinor was alerted to the arrival of a visitor. Expecting it to be someone with a message from the manor house, Elinor did not rise from her chair until the maid came in with a note, hurriedly written in a shaky hand—it was from her mother. It said, without any preamble, that Colonel Brandon had been in an accident while riding back to Delaford last night. His horse had returned riderless to the stables, and a search party had gone out at dawn, finding the colonel some miles from Barton Park. He had suffered a broken leg and concussion and had been brought back to Barton Park, where he was being attended by the Middletons' doctor. He was still in a lot of pain and was asking for Marianne. Mrs Dashwood urged Elinor and Edward to go directly to the manor house and bring Marianne to Barton Park as soon as possible.

Elinor leapt up and showed the note to her husband, who was quite bewildered. They'd had no idea that Colonel Brandon was back in England, much less that he was at Barton Park and riding back to Delaford on an icy winter's night. "I wonder what he was doing riding around in the kind of weather we have been having this week. He must have been in a great hurry to get here," said Edward, and Elinor was equally confused.

"I cannot understand how he came to be at Barton Park at all; I believe Sir John is still in London," said Elinor, puzzled that Marianne had said nothing about her husband's return. "When we last spoke, she seemed certain that he would be back from Ireland earlier than originally expected, but I've heard nothing since."

"Well, my dear, I suppose we had better go over to the manor house at once, if we are to start for Barton Park before dark. No doubt Marianne would wish to go prepared to spend some days there," said Edward as they made ready to walk across to the manor house with the bad news.

Elinor was nervous; she could not predict how Marianne would respond to the news. Her sister had been behaving quite oddly of late, and she wondered again why neither she nor Edward had been told of Colonel Brandon's return from Ireland. Was it possible, she thought, that he had arrived home and they had quarrelled? Had the matter of Willoughby and Marianne's meeting him been raised? Was that why he had ridden off to Barton Park to consult his friend? Why had the colonel not come to them? He had always treated her as a trusted friend, and she knew he had a high regard for Edward. Myriad possibilities, none of them very logical or satisfactory, occurred to her as she hastened to get her warm cloak, scarf, and hat and give instructions to the nurse about the children, before leaving for the manor house.

Marianne had spent a wretched day waiting for either a message from her husband or a visit from Willoughby. The latter was, she had assumed, the more probable, since it was unlikely that Colonel Brandon would be able to conclude the business of Eliza Williams and her child expeditiously; she knew from past experience that Miss Williams was almost always strongly opposed to any scheme to remove her from her familiar surroundings. It would take the colonel two or three days at least to make suitable arrangements for her before returning to Delaford. She was vexed by the lack of any new message from him.

By early afternoon, she had grown even more disgruntled with Colonel Brandon and longed for Willoughby to arrive, as promised, with what she hoped would be a solution to her dilemma. She had not stopped to consider what he might propose or how she should respond, but believed that he, because he loved her, would put her interest first.

When she heard the carriage coming up the drive, she assumed immediately that it was Willoughby, and taking a quick look in the mirror that hung above the fireplace, she went out into the hall expecting to see him. Instead, she found that the maid had admitted Mr and Mrs Perceval and their elder daughter, Maria, and the expressions on their faces did not suggest that they had come with good news. Confused, Marianne even forgot her usually good manners and asked in a somewhat irritated voice, "Mr and Mrs Perceval, Maria, what on earth brings you here at this time?" It had occurred to her that if Willoughby were to arrive whilst they were there, she would be hard put to explain his presence. But the Percevals were clearly too troubled to be offended by her brusque question and Maria answered politely, "Mrs Brandon, we are sorry to intrude, but we have had some alarming news which we wished to communicate to you as soon as possible."

Marianne's cheeks flushed as she realised her error and said, "Indeed? And what news is that? Please do come into the sitting room and tell me about it." But the Percevals declined her invitation and Mr Perceval spoke quietly, "Mrs Brandon, we do not think it would be wise to discuss it here, if we were to be overheard by any of your staff, it might cause you embarrassment and we think it would be best if you came with us to our home, where we may speak privately. My younger daughter, Eugenie, who knows nothing of this matter, has gone with Miss Peabody to spend a few days with her sister in Somerset."

"Good Heavens!" exclaimed Marianne, astonished by this turn of events and unable to imagine what could have occasioned such a strange response, "but whatever can you have to say that would embarrass me? I am sure we could speak in the sitting room… See, I will shut the door…" but the Percevals shook their heads and Maria stepped up close to Marianne and whispered in her ear, "It concerns Mr John Willoughby."

It was with the greatest difficulty that Marianne restrained herself and said, in a voice that was now as quiet as that of her visitors, who had been reduced to whispering so that the servants would not hear, "I see; well, in that case, please do wait for me in the sitting room, I shall not be long," and she raced up to her room to get her bonnet and wrap, and returned in a few minutes.

Stopping only to tell her maid that she was going out to the Percevals, Marianne then entered their carriage and was gone. Throughout the short journey to the Percevals' place, she was in a fever of impatience, since none of her companions spoke, clearly unwilling to have any of their private conversation overheard by the driver or the groom. She could not help noticing the grim set of Mr Perceval's usually cheerful countenance and his wife's anxious frown. Even Maria said little, except to comment on the worsening weather.

On reaching the house, they went indoors and upstairs to a private sitting room, where they were unlikely to be overheard, and Maria closed the door. Mr Perceval's first question stunned Marianne. "Mrs Brandon, forgive my asking you what must seem a most impertinent question, but how well do you know Mr Willoughby?" Unaware of the reason for his question, Marianne was at a loss to answer it; she wondered what significance it could have for her. But, even as she searched in vain for some way to answer it, Maria intervened to say, "You see, Mrs Brandon, we have had a visit from a man from a private detective agency, who is in the employ of Mr Willoughby's wife, and he is looking for a certain woman who is said to be intimate with Mr Willoughby. He says she has been visiting him frequently at Combe Magna and has recently been seen with him in his carriage. The man from the agency has been following them for some weeks and has seen Mr Willoughby visit this house and your place at Delaford with this person in his carriage. He is keen to obtain information on her whereabouts for his client, Mrs Willoughby, who is applying for a divorce on the grounds of adultery."

Marianne sat transfixed; so shattered was she by the enormity of the situation in which she now found herself, she could say nothing. She could not take in everything she had heard—she did not want to believe it, yet it was unlikely that the Percevals could be making it up! They had no reason to fabricate such a tale.

As she sat pondering what she should or could say, Mrs Perceval entered the conversation for the first time. "Mrs Brandon, we believed Mr Willoughby was an honourable gentleman, especially when he told us of his long association with your family when you all lived in Devon some years ago, before your marriage to Colonel Brandon. He spoke very highly of your mother and your elder sister, Mrs Ferrars, and your cousin Sir John Middleton, whom he claimed to know well. He appeared to be a decent young gentleman of sober habits, else we would not have invited him into our home or let him become acquainted with our daughters. We were aware that he was married, and he told us his wife preferred to spend summer in town or at her mother's property in Essex, which is why he was here on his own, but we had no idea she was suing him for divorce! I am certain you will understand our concern, especially for young

Eugenie—she is an innocent girl with no knowledge of these matters and has had quite a high regard for Mr Willoughby."

Maria took up the tale again and said, "We wondered, Mrs Brandon, if you could enlighten us as to his background, because we fear that with the appearance of the man from the detective agency, our family may get dragged in to any scandal that may follow from his divorce. If he has been entertaining this woman and driving her around in his carriage, Mama fears that Eugenie and I, who have been seen in his carriage on a few occasions, as have you, Mrs Brandon, may well be unwittingly implicated... even if only as witnesses."

Marianne found her voice at last to say, "Surely not! Whenever you have been in his company, it has been with your family or your friends the Hawthornes. I cannot recall ever seeing either of you alone with Mr Willoughby. As for myself, we... that is my family... did know Mr Willoughby, many years ago at Barton Park in Devon, during one summer, before he was married; but we have had no contact with him whatsoever since. I never saw him in seven years or more until we met by chance at Glastonbury, when he offered to transport us home after your carriage was damaged in an accident. As to his wife suing for divorce, this is the first I have heard of it. I do not know her or this other woman with whom he is said to be intimate. I am as shocked as you are by this information."

The looks on the faces of the three Percevals convinced Marianne that they had some difficulty believing her. Quite clearly, while she had continued to believe that he had been protecting her from embarrassment by avoiding any mention of their past association, Willoughby, who had become a frequent visitor to their home over the past few months, had given the Percevals a vastly different account of his acquaintance with her family. By referring to his visits to Barton Cottage and his friendship with Sir John Middleton—dropping names, mentioning her mother, her sister, and her well-respected brother-in-law, Edward Ferrars—as though they were close friends and no doubt conjuring up a picture of benign intimacy with them—he had advanced an image of his own respectability to suit his pernicious purposes. It was a degree of duplicity that left her deeply shocked.

Even as she realised how he had taken them in, she understood with a sickening clarity how easily she had been deceived, yet again, by the easy charm, the casual courtesies, and the show of concern, which were his stock in trade.

Not only had he deceived her, he had left her open to the dishonour of having her home watched by a man from a detective agency employed by his wife, as though she were party to his misdemeanours. Her husband's home had been named as a place he had visited, with this woman with whom he was said to be intimate. It was an outrage! How was this possible?

Suddenly, she remembered that on the day he had arrived at Delaford Manor without warning and stayed but a short while, listening to her complaints about Miss Williams and promising to return the following day, the curtains of his carriage had been closed, as though there was inside a passenger who did not wish to be seen. Marianne's maid Molly had been certain that this was indeed the case, one of the grooms had told her so, she'd said; but Marianne, consumed by her own grievances, had paid no attention. It was clear now that the passenger was probably the woman being sought by the detective and Mrs Willoughby.

Appalled that she had allowed herself to be so deluded and angry that he had once again left her to suffer the ridicule and humiliation of strangers, as he had done before, tears welled in her eyes and coursed down her cheeks. "You must believe me; I knew nothing of this woman or Mr Willoughby's dealings with her. I fear he has deceived us all most shamefully," she sobbed, and the Percevals, disconcerted but nevertheless concerned for her, strove to comfort her, attaching no blame to her. She thanked them, but when they tried to persuade her to stay and take tea, she refused and begged to be taken home. Her husband was due to return at any time, she said, and as the Percevals agreed, Mr Perceval declared, "Let me assure you, Mrs Brandon, that we will not permit Mr Willoughby or anyone else to besmirch your name; my wife and I have only the highest respect for you." They were kind words; Marianne could only hope that they meant what they said.

As she was leaving, Maria Perceval intervened to add that she had always been wary of Mr Willoughby, on account of something the Hawthorne boys had said. They had friends in London who had warned that he was not a man to be trusted because of his reputation for high living, she said, but she had not wished to put it about in the county, without having any proof. Maria Perceval was not much older, nor could she have been deemed to be cleverer than Marianne had been when she had first encountered Willoughby with all his charm; yet she had not been as easily misled by his duplicitous character. It was something Marianne had time to ponder as the Percevals' carriage conveyed her to Delaford Manor.

⤙⤚

When Elinor and Edward arrived at the manor house, they were surprised to find that many of the rooms were in darkness. It was apparent that no one was upstairs, and the servant who answered the doorbell and admitted them informed them that Mrs Brandon had left with the Percevals earlier that afternoon.

"Did she say when she would return?" asked Elinor, to which the servant shrugged his shoulders and replied that the mistress never said what time she would be back and they had assumed she would be dining with the Percevals. "Did she say so?" asked Edward, but the young man said she had not. It seemed the servants at Delaford Manor had begun to take their mistress for granted. Edward and Elinor exchanged glances, electing to wait for Marianne, hoping that she would not be dining with the Percevals after all. Elinor went to speak with the housekeeper and found her in a state of confusion as she complained that ever since the mistress had begun "going here and there with these Percevals and their strange friends" things had not been the same at the manor house. "We are never told when the mistress will be dining at home, and when she is, she eats so little it seems a waste to prepare a decent meal and bring it to table, ma'am."

Unwilling to pry into the domestic affairs at the manor, but keen nevertheless to discover if the staff knew when Colonel Brandon had returned from Ireland, Elinor asked, "And when did your master return? Has he been back long?" at which the housekeeper rolled her eyes and declared, "Been back long, ma'am? The master has not been back at all—he has been in Ireland these last six weeks and then we had word he was coming home earlier than expected. But, a few days ago, the mistress received a letter saying he was going directly to London to sort out some problem, ma'am, and the mistress was not best pleased. Molly said she wept and threw herself on the bed; then the next day the gentleman from Somerset, who is a friend of those Percevals, arrived and Molly heard the mistress weeping again as they talked. I am sorry, ma'am, but I think the master should come home and sort out matters here first. I wish someone would tell him; I have never seen the mistress in such a state before."

221

Astounded by what she had heard, Elinor returned to the sitting room, where Edward had poured out a glass of sherry and invited her to sit by the fire. His calm exterior belied his own concerns for Marianne; it was late afternoon and he wondered how much longer she would be. Elinor sat down beside him and related some of the information she had gleaned from the housekeeper, adding to his anxiety. By the time the clock struck six, they were beginning to get quite desperate, but there was nothing they could do but wait.

It was half past the hour when a vehicle was heard turning into the drive, and the maid rushed in to tell them that it was the Percevals' carriage and the mistress was back. Elinor and Edward went into the hall and as Marianne alighted and came indoors, they could see she was in a dreadful state. Her eyes were red with weeping, and she looked as though she had already been given the bad news they had brought. Wary of upsetting her further, Elinor went to her at once and put her arms around her sister, "Dearest Marianne, thank God you are safe, we have been so worried, waiting for you to return…" she began and was more than a little perturbed when Marianne pushed back from her and asked, "Elinor, Edward? Why are you here? What have you heard? Has someone been round to the parsonage already, peddling a pack of lies?"

"A pack of lies? Marianne, what are you talking about?" Elinor exclaimed, aghast; this she certainly had not expected and it left her bereft of speech. It was Edward who said quietly, "Marianne, we are here because we have received a message from your mother. Colonel Brandon has had an accident," then seeing the look of horror on her face, he continued, "He was riding last night from Barton Park returning to Delaford and was thrown from his horse and suffered a concussion and a broken leg. When the horse returned, the stable hands set out to search for Colonel Brandon and he was taken to Barton Park, where the Middletons' doctor is attending upon him. Mrs Dashwood has written to ask that we take you directly to him; he is in some pain and has asked for you. We have been here for the best part of an hour, waiting on your return."

Marianne's attention had been riveted by her brother-in-law's calm, serious tone. Struck dumb by the news, she reached for the note which Elinor held out to her, and as she read it, there came more tears and she rushed upstairs to her room. Elinor followed awhile later, rather tentatively, for she was unsure whether she would be welcome; she could see that Marianne had suffered some violent affliction even before she was given the news of her husband's accident, but had no notion what it was that had distressed her. She couldn't help wondering if it had something to do with Willoughby and the Percevals, but was reluctant, in ignorance, to say anything that might further exacerbate her sister's distress.

On entering the bedroom, however, she found to her surprise that Marianne had already sent for her maid Molly and a manservant and asked them to pack two trunks, one with her clothes and one for the master, and had given orders for the big carriage to be made ready for the journey to Barton Park. While there were still traces of tears, it was clear that Marianne, shocked by the news of the accident, had decided that she was going to organise herself for the journey that lay ahead and was doing so with a degree of dispatch that belied the state of extreme agitation in which she had been but a few minutes ago.

She even thought to ask if Edward and Elinor had dined already, and when Elinor said they had, she gave orders for tea to be served to them in the sitting room and declared that she would be dressed and ready to leave within the hour.

Chapter Nineteen

THEY TRAVELLED THROUGH THE night, on icy roads with a bitter wind whipping the vehicle to slow their progress and reaching into the carriage to increase their discomfort. It had been difficult work for the horses and their driver on the roads, and it was easy to see how the accident had happened. As the dawn struggled through a mass of low clouds weighed down with the sleet that was falling all around them, the gates of Barton Park loomed up though the mist and their relief was palpable.

During the entire journey, Marianne had alternately wept and sighed and occasionally whispered questions about the time or the weather, as she clung to her sister's hand. Matters that had not impinged upon her conscience before, pressed hard upon it now. Her demeanour reflected her pain as she struggled to cope with the deep sense of guilt that had afflicted her on learning that her husband had been injured while riding through the night to return to her. She had criticised him for going to the aid of Eliza Williams; yet she could now see that he, at least, had stood ready to help the woman and her child, whose dire plight was the direct consequence of Willoughby's misconduct. He was culpable, not Colonel Brandon, yet he had done nothing to alleviate their suffering, never accepting responsibility for his actions nor admitting the guilt of his callous abandonment of a defenceless young girl.

And while Colonel Brandon had been engaged in perfectly legitimate business in Ireland, attending to a family estate, Marianne had blamed him for leaving her alone and bored at Delaford, and in that state of aggravation, she had been willing to trust Willoughby again, despite all that had gone before. Marianne, who twenty-four hours ago had been angry and resentful against Miss Williams, began to see her own behaviour for what it was: self-centred and lacking in compassion. It was a selfishness that Willoughby, for his own reasons, had been quick to encourage. Marianne could see it now; she was mortified and knew not how she would face her family, especially Elinor. How would she reveal what had happened in the past few weeks?

However, at the moment that did not signify; she wanted only to get to her husband's side and ensure that he, who had devoted himself to her when she had been in extremis, knew that she cared. Elinor, well aware that her sister was distressed, asked no questions, content to wait, knowing Marianne would come to her when she was ready.

Mrs Dashwood heard the horses' hooves and carriage wheels crunch the gravel drive and flew to the door. The travellers alighted, weary and anxious, and Marianne fell into her mother's arms, in tears, wanting to be assured of Colonel Brandon's condition. As Edward and Elinor stood looking on, mother and daughter alternately wept and consoled one another. Marianne wanted to go upstairs at once to see her husband, and Mrs Dashwood took her to him, while the servants bustled around to provide for the comfort of the others, who were badly in need of warmth and refreshment.

In a while, Mrs Dashwood returned to Edward and Elinor, who were drinking hot chocolate and trying to keep warm in front of the fire in the sitting room, and proceeded to give them an account of the extraordinary happenings of the last two days. She began by assuring them that Colonel Brandon had recovered consciousness and was sleeping. Marianne, she said, had wished to sit beside his bed in case he awoke.

"I had no idea that Colonel Brandon was in England, much less that he was in London rescuing Miss Williams and her daughter," she said. "Imagine my surprise, then, when he arrived with a letter from Sir John, asking if I would have Barton Cottage readied for them to occupy in a few days. Sir John, generous to a fault, as you can see, hopes to give the unfortunate young woman a chance to make a decent life in the country away from the dreadful goings-on in town. I have a notion of finding her some respectable work she can do, while caring for her child—if we can set up something at the cottage, but that will depend on Colonel Brandon's agreement too…" She was about to get carried away with her usual enthusiasm for her own elaborate plans, but Elinor, eager for news of the colonel's condition, asked for more details and her mother obliged.

"Well, Dr Richards has been twice already and will return tomorrow; he thinks it is a clean break and the leg should heal well, and the concussion is wearing off, but the colonel will need to be very careful. We have to make quite certain that he is not troubled with all this fuss about Miss Williams, so he can heal and recuperate in peace. I know Sir John will agree; I've sent him a message by express, and he is expected home in a day or two. He is bringing with him a surgeon from London to take a look at Colonel Brandon. Meanwhile, he has authorised me to do everything here for the colonel's care and comfort, including preparing for Marianne to stay with us for as long as is necessary."

Listening to her, both Elinor and Edward could scarcely credit the confidence with which Mrs Dashwood seemed to have taken control of arrangements at Barton Park. Despite her love of grand designs and a propensity to dream of plans that she could never finance, here she was, talking with great assurance of getting this or that done and going here and there, as though she had been so occupied all her life, when in fact, she had been all too eager to surrender those responsibilities to her housekeeper at Norland or her eldest daughter at Barton Cottage. Elinor marvelled at the transformation in her mother, but had no rational explanation for it.

They remained another day or two at Barton Park to assure themselves that Colonel Brandon was recovering well, during which time Miss Eliza Williams arrived with her daughter, escorted by two servants from Sir John Middleton's staff. They had travelled post, and reported that the conditions on the roads were very bad indeed. Miss Williams, a young woman whose pretty features were unfortunately tarnished by a petulant expression, was warmly welcomed by Mrs Dashwood and then taken upstairs to see Colonel Brandon, before being pressed to eat and drink. Marianne meanwhile had tactfully retreated to the rooms allotted to Edward and Elinor, where she found her sister at the window seat gazing out at a forbidding sky and wondering aloud if her husband had taken leave of his senses. "Edward insists on tramping around the park in this weather; I cannot convince him that he can catch a nasty cold and a chill will not be far behind," she complained.

Marianne came to sit beside her and after a few minutes' silence said, "Oh, Elinor, what am I to do? I have been such a fool; not just silly, but an evil, wicked fool! I don't know how I can ever face Mama and Colonel Brandon and tell them what I have done." Her voice trembled and Elinor could see tears in her eyes. She took her hands in hers and asked, "Marianne, what on earth are you talking about? What nonsense is this? What do you mean you have been wicked and evil? There is not a single evil bone in your body!"

Her voice was firm, but Marianne was even more so in her determination to be miserable and confess her transgressions. "Oh, yes there is, and I have already acknowledged it and I shall have to tell Mama and Colonel Brandon about it…" she began, but Elinor would not let her continue in that vein. "Listen, Marianne, whatever it is, this is neither the time nor the place to burden either Mama or Colonel Brandon with more anguish; as you can see they are both under a great deal of strain and, in your poor husband's case, much physical pain. It would be selfish and uncaring to add to their troubles with your own problems, no matter how important they may seem. If you are uneasy and you must talk to someone, tell me and I promise to listen with sympathy," at which Marianne exploded, "No, you must not, I do not need any more sympathy; listen if you will and scold me, excoriate and condemn me, but do not sympathise with me anymore. I am convinced now that *that* was the ruin of me: all of you, Edward, you, dear Elinor, Mama, and Colonel Brandon, you all exuded sympathy and concern for me and let me get away with feeling sorry for myself, at how badly I had been deceived by Willoughby. No one told me how foolish, how naively trusting I had been of a man of whom I, on such short acquaintance, knew nothing at all. No one, not even you, would point out that it was mostly my fault."

Elinor, even with some knowledge of Marianne's recent meetings with Willoughby—knowledge she had not shared with her or their mother—could not account for this dramatic rush of contrition. She had to ask, "Marianne, I do not know what it is you speak of. Will you not tell me what this is all about and what Mr Willoughby has to do with it?"

"He has everything to do with it, Elinor; for I have recently met Willoughby with the Percevals and I am so ashamed to admit that I have permitted him to cajole and flatter me into believing him all over again," she cried. "Oh, Elinor, when you know it all, you will agree that I have been a wicked fool. I have been utterly stupid and wilful; I feel I should be severely punished."

And so began a recital of all that had happened in the days and weeks leading up to the arrival of the colonel's letter announcing his early return from Ireland to rescue Miss Williams from her dire situation, arousing Marianne's indignation and Willoughby's opportunistic efforts to turn her against her husband, for whom he clearly harboured a deep dislike.

Marianne never did do anything by halves; she did not spare herself, she told it all, from her first chance meeting with him at Glastonbury, in that most romantic of places, to the last desperate encounter with him in which she had, in a fit of pique, confided in Willoughby, allowing him to see she was annoyed with her husband and so vulnerable to the machinations of a man who would like to be revenged upon him.

"Oh, he was as he has been before, solicitous and concerned; inflamed my resentment against Eliza Williams, suggesting she was selfish and pretended he could help me cope with my aggravation; yet all the time, he had in his carriage waiting at the front porch, hidden from view by the closed curtains, a certain woman—his mistress, whom his wife intends to cite in suing for a divorce!" Marianne, seeing the ashen countenance of her sister as the full import of her words sank in, gripped Elinor's hand and said, "Elinor, how can I ever explain to my husband that I was so stupid as to permit such a thing to happen? No, don't say I could not have known. I should not have permitted Willoughby to enter the house, much less have his carriage standing at the door; he had no business there and I had no right to let him in after his previous behaviour. I should have known that he was not to be trusted. Maria Perceval told me that she had been wary of him; she thought he was not trustworthy. If she, who is not yet nineteen, could see that, why was I so blind? When Colonel Brandon learns of it, will he ever forgive me, will he ever trust me again?" She was weeping and Elinor held her close.

Elinor could no longer bear the distress in her sister's voice, which was rising to hysteria. She spoke gently but very firmly, "Marianne, promise me that you will not speak of these matters to Mama or to Colonel Brandon—not now, at any rate. Let me talk to Edward first and we will see how things turn out before we say anything to anyone else."

Marianne looked astonished. "Do you not think I should tell them? Am I not to confess how wicked and stupid I have been?" she asked, and Elinor shook her head. "Not now; indeed, it may never be necessary to recount it, depending on what happens to Willoughby. If, as you say, he is no longer welcome at the Percevals and comes no more into Dorset, we may not hear of him again. Let us wait and see. As for what you wish to tell your husband, I am sure there are many more important and pleasant subjects you will want to talk about as he recovers. Do you not think so? I would suggest that rather than seek to punish yourself, and in so doing, add to your husband's grief, you look to the future and let other aggrieved persons deal with Mr Willoughby."

Marianne looked troubled; her elder sister, whose judgment and sense of rectitude was always so correct, was asking her not to lay bare her guilt and confess her sins! She was unsure if this was wise. But she trusted Elinor as she had not trusted anyone else in her entire life and was ready, this time, to act according to her counsel.

Edward walked into the room and, seeing the two sisters together, smiled and said, "I've just been spending some time with Colonel Brandon; he claims he is feeling much better. His head does not ache so badly, and he would like to see Elinor. Why do you two not go to him and keep him company? He is likely to get very bored just lying in bed for days together." Elinor rose to go immediately, and Marianne said she would go first to the library and select a book or two which she could read to him. "I know his favourites," she declared as they went out together.

Later that evening, when they were in their own room again, Elinor recounted to her husband most of what Marianne had told her. Edward was surprised and deeply sad for Marianne; but he, like Elinor, felt there was no need at all for Marianne to confess everything to her husband and Mrs Dashwood. Like Elinor, Edward advised caution. "It is better to wait and see what eventuates. Willoughby, pursued by his wife or his mistress or both, may stay away from this part of the country altogether, and we may never encounter him again. It would seem that the Percevals will have nothing more to do with him now that he has been exposed, and if he has no friends here, he will have no excuse to come into Dorset at all."

Looking approvingly at his wife, he said, "You have advised her well, my love; while she did take a great risk in meeting him, fortunately, no real harm was done. I believe Marianne should say nothing that will increase Brandon's anxiety. While it may alleviate her feelings of guilt to confess it all to him, it is likely to destroy his trust in her and harm their marriage. It would be far better that they should concentrate their time and effort on things they both can enjoy together. Indeed, to that end, I have advised Brandon to spend as much time here as he needs to recuperate and then take his wife for a good long holiday in Europe in the spring."

Elinor was delighted. "Marianne would love that; she has never travelled beyond the south of England," she said.

"Well, Brandon claims he has already promised Marianne that they would travel abroad in the spring, by which time Willoughby will have been quite forgotten," said Edward confidently.

Elinor had seen the warmth of the colonel's affection for his wife when they had gone to his room earlier that day and watched Marianne smile when he'd reached for her hand and kissed it as she sat down to read to him. She hoped her sister's romantic heart, having twice learned its lesson chasing spurious passion, would find satisfaction in the kind of generous affection that a man with Colonel Brandon's genuinely good heart could give her.

They were preparing to leave on the following morning when Sir John Middleton arrived with the surgeon from London. Having greeted them all with great affection, he went directly upstairs to see his friend. He found the colonel sitting up in bed with his wife in attendance and declared that he was mighty pleased to see him in one piece.

After the surgeon had examined the colonel's injuries and declared that he was clearly on the road to recovery, Sir John said his piece. "You must stay here as long as you need to make a full recovery, Brandon. Indeed, I should like you to spend Christmas, which is almost upon us, at Barton Park, if that is agreeable to you and Marianne. I am sure the children will enjoy it better if there are lots of guests around, seeing it's their first time without their dear mama; what do you say?" and when Colonel Brandon looked at his wife, he added, "Marianne won't mind—she'll have nothing to do but look after your comfort, and she will have her mama here, too. What more could you ask, eh?"

When the couple smiled and said no more, he assumed that they had accepted his invitation, and went directly down to inform Mrs Dashwood of his plan. There was nothing Sir John disliked more than being bored and alone, and nothing pleased him more than having friends and good company around him. Having the Brandons with them at Christmas would be a good start.

Satisfied that matters at Barton Park were settling down well, even as the level of noise rose with the arrival of the master, Edward and Elinor felt able to say their farewells and return to the quiet and peace of their home at the parsonage at Delaford and their two boys, who had missed them very much. Their Christmas would be quieter but no less happy; they were looking forward to Margaret's arrival very soon.

~~~

The sleet and rain gave way to snow as Christmas approached, and with it came a little wintry sunshine. Christmas at the parsonage was a traditional one with preparations afoot for a customary family dinner. The goose had been plucked, the ham cooked, and the puddings boiled well in time, and the house was adorned with garlands of holly, while at the church, the choir practised relentlessly for their biggest annual performance. Edward, who was not particularly musical, had surrendered the choice of hymns and carols to his wife and the verger, who had chosen well; none were too difficult for the choir nor too esoteric for the congregation to sing with the usual degree of enthusiasm.

Into the midst of these preparations, Margaret arrived, laden with presents for them all and plenty of stories about her sojourn in France and the very special delights of Provence. She was welcomed with warm affection by both Edward and Elinor and then hugged again and again by their two sons, John and Harry, for whom she had brought many special treats.

Having left her friends Claire Jones and Nicholas Wilcox to spend Christmas together, Margaret was glad indeed of the familial warmth and kindness that surrounded her in her sister's home; it took away some of the chill of loneliness she had endured since being back in England, leaving Daniel Brooke behind in France.

In the weeks since her return, she'd written him two letters and received one; they had all crossed in the post, which meant nothing they wrote related to anything they had written to one another before. Her first had been for the most part an expression of thanks for all he had done and the time he had spent helping her learn and love the delights of Provence; her second had been short and simply said how much she missed him and how she hoped to see him again, soon.

When his had arrived a few days later, she had hoped it would be a response, but he had not received hers, so it was a somewhat disconnected series of paragraphs, about one thing and another, of which the line that meant most to her was a sentence at the end recalling with pleasure their journey to the abbey at Le Lac du Sainte Germaine in the mountains. If he remembered it so well, she thought, he must also remember what they had said to each other. It was very small consolation, but it was all she had. He had concluded by wishing her a blessed and peaceful Christmas with her family, and Margaret had read and re-read it and carried it around in her pocket like a talisman.

On Christmas Eve, as Edward went to the church to prepare for the Christmas vigil, Margaret sought out her sister. Elinor was wrapping up the presents for her servants and preparing hampers of food for their families. She carried on with her work, chatting happily, regaling her sister with the tale of Colonel Brandon's accident and the arrival of Miss Williams and her daughter to stay at Barton Cottage. "It is typical of Sir John, of course; Mama says he had simply told Colonel Brandon that Eliza and her child would be safer in the country and offered them the cottage. Do you not think that is very generous of him?" she asked, and Margaret had to agree that it certainly was.

Seeing her sister busy, contented, and obviously happy in her home, Margaret could not help the little pinpricks of envy that assailed her. Why, she wondered, had she not been able to fall in love as Elinor had done with a man who was free to love and marry her? Why was her love to be thwarted by cruel circumstances neither she nor Daniel could have foreseen or controlled? With these thoughts came uncharacteristic tears, and Elinor, seeing them, asked in some alarm, "Why, Margaret, my dear, whatever is the matter? Have I said something to upset you?" at which the tears fell faster and Margaret had to retreat to her room, where Elinor followed her soon afterward, bringing with her a most welcome cup of tea.

Elinor had sensed not long after her sister's arrival that all was not well. Even though Margaret had appeared cheerful and ready to participate in their celebrations with her usual enthusiasm, her sister had noted a certain lack of *joie de vivre*. She had put it down initially to weariness after the journey in a vehicle that Margaret had declared was full to overflowing with people and their animals! "I counted three geese, two ducks, and a sack of rabbits—I could not say how many," she had told them, "all travelling happily, unaware that they were soon to be a part of someone's Christmas dinner."

But this morning, she had been rather pensive at breakfast and now this. Elinor was concerned. Margaret was the most stable member of her family; she was dependable, warmhearted, and for the most part predictable in a way that Marianne had never been. To find her in tears was exceedingly discomposing, and Elinor hoped to discover what had caused it. She had noted that no mention had been made of Daniel Brooke and wondered if there had been a falling-out, perhaps? She waited until Margaret had finished her tea and asked, "What is it, my love? Is it about Mr Daniel Brooke?" and that brought on a veritable flood.

It was a random question, asked only because Elinor could think of no other person who could have been the cause of her tears. From Margaret's letters Elinor had gathered that Mr Daniel Brooke had become quite important to her sister; she wrote of him in special terms, admired his learning and his great knowledge of the history of France, and marvelled at his willingness to spend time with them guiding them through so many places, which, without him, they would never have appreciated fully. She had written of his kindness and his humour and other estimable qualities besides, all of which had ensured that Elinor regarded him as a special person for whom Margaret had developed feelings of gratitude and affection. And yet, in the last two days since her arrival, though she spoke often of Claire Jones and her engagement to Mr Wilcox, she had said nothing about Daniel Brooke.

Fearing that their friendship may have ended, Elinor asked, "We had hoped to meet him one day; did he not return to England with the rest of your party?" Margaret shook her head violently and blew her nose before replying, "He did not, and I do not know when he will."

"But why?" asked Elinor and was stunned into silence when she replied, "Because he has stayed on in Nice, where his wife is in the care of an order of nursing nuns. She is dying of some dreaded disease—tuberculosis, I think—and he will not leave her there alone."

Margaret saw her sister's face drain of colour, her eyes fill with tears as she put a hand to her mouth as though to stop herself from crying out. It was as if she was thinking, "Not another case of deception... not another false lover," and Margaret, reading her thoughts, cried out, "No, Elinor, you must not think that—he did not deceive me, he told me himself of the true circumstances of his life. He is not to blame, I am. Even after I knew, it did not stop me falling in love with the only man for whom I have ever felt anything deeper than passing friendliness."

Silently, Elinor put her arms around her sister and held her close. "My darling girl, I am sorry. And yet, I am glad too that you can say that he did not deceive you, for there is nothing that brings greater anguish, as we know with Marianne. I am grateful that you have been spared that, at least." Then looking at her, she asked, "What will you do?"

Margaret took a little time to answer, and spoke softly when she did, not because she was unsure of her response, but because she wished to spare her sister's feelings. "I am not entirely certain when he will return, to England, but whenever he does, probably in the new year when he must return to his college at Oxford, I shall go to him. He has suffered much, Elinor, and needs some comfort. He knows how I feel; I hope he will let me comfort him."

Elinor did not respond as Margaret had expected; she was shaken, certainly, but she expressed no outrage. Instead she asked, "Are you quite sure Margaret?" and Margaret replied with a degree of certainly that surprised her sister, "Indeed I am. Ever since he told me—and he did so with the clearest objective of warning me not to fall in love with him—ever since then, I have known that I must go to him. I have never felt so deeply nor cared so well for any person before, apart from my own family, and knowing how much he has suffered, I must go to him."

Seeing her determination, Elinor, rather than censure or dissuade, asked a practical question, "Where will you stay?"

"He has a cottage in the Cotswolds," Margaret said simply, as though that was all that mattered, and in truth it was, for apart from her determination to go to Daniel when he returned to England, she had made no other plans. It was plain, Elinor thought, that her young sister's feelings were so deeply engaged, she had paid no attention to any other consideration. The practical realities of life in the community appeared to have faded into insignificance.

Elinor's eyes were full of sympathy, but her voice was grave as she strove to counsel her. "You do know it will not be easy, Margaret; there will be those who will gossip and others who will condemn you, once it is known. Do you think you are prepared for that?" Margaret's usually gentle face was stern as she responded, "I am. I have no fear of the censure those others, who mean nothing to me, may bring against me. My only fear is that he, in some noble act of renunciation, will send me away and try to endure this pain alone, as he has done for years already. I fear he will say that I must not sacrifice myself to care for him." Elinor, understanding her feelings yet dreading the consequences of her sister's impending actions, held her hands but could find no words to console her. She wondered how well prepared Margaret was for the kind of condemnation she would surely face in a small rural community.

But it seemed that Margaret was not seeking consolation; her mind was made up, she had decided upon her course of action and was ready to face the consequences. She spoke reasonably and without emotion. "Elinor, I cannot ask you not to tell Edward, I know you have no secrets from him; but please do not say anything to Mama or Marianne. It would kill me to have them ask me questions and give me the benefit of their opinions. I will tell you my plans and send you word of where I am, when the time comes."

The sisters clung together, and when they broke apart, Margaret said, "Thank you for not preaching at me, Elinor, or berating me for what I plan to do. It would not have changed my mind, I love him too much, but it would break my heart to have you turn against me."

Elinor kissed her cheek and said, "I could never turn against you, you know that. But I will admit that I am very afraid of what you may have to face. Please promise me that you will think very carefully before you take such a step. I should hate to see you throw away all you have achieved from study and hard work—you, with all your life ahead of you, more than Marianne or myself, have much to lose."

Margaret promised and thanked her sister again; but Elinor could not but feel a deep anxiety for her. Spirited and intelligent, Margaret had been the one who combined both good sense and a gentle sensibility; Elinor would pray that it was not all to be squandered on a passionate affair. Without the advantage of knowing Daniel Brooke, she could not judge if Margaret's love would bring her happiness or misery.

The sound of carol singers at the gate took them to the window, and seeing the children with their lanterns and candles, the sisters went downstairs together to greet them. Harry and John ran out to join them, and the housekeeper brought out a basket of goodies for the singers, who crowded into the hall, glad of the warmth and the welcome.

It was Christmas, and Margaret was determined that her problems would not spoil the special celebrations of her sister's family. With a bright smile that belied the sadness that filled her heart, she joined in the singing. This time it was Elinor who could not hold back the tears.

～∽～

On the morning after Christmas, they all slept late, following what was generally agreed to be an excellent Christmas dinner. Cook had excelled herself, and Margaret claimed that she could not recall a better pudding since they had left Norland Park!

While they were at breakfast, there was heard a great commotion outside the parsonage and, on looking out of the sitting room window, Edward saw the large carriage from Barton Park standing in the road and Sir John Middleton, attired like some explorer bound for the Arctic, alighting from it. He marched to the door and banged upon it, calling out for the family of Ferrars to wake and prepare to celebrate Boxing Day at Barton Park.

He had travelled all this way, he declared, to take them to his home so they could all be together, and he had organised a great celebration with food, fun, and fireworks for the entire family. Amidst cries of delight from Harry and John and groans from most of the adults, Sir John proceeded to rouse and ready the entire party, pack them into his carriage, and drive away, all within the hour, assuring them that everyone at Barton Park awaited their arrival, determined to have what he termed "a jolly good time on Boxing Day!"

END OF PART FOUR

EXPECTATIONS OF HAPPINESS

Part Five

Chapter Twenty

A FEW DAYS AFTER their return from Barton Park, choosing a quiet
moment of the day, Margaret sought out Elinor in the nursery,
where she was helping her sons solve a picture puzzle they'd received
for Christmas.

There had been no mention of Daniel Brooke between them since
Margaret had revealed the circumstances of Helène's health. Wishing to be
certain that her sister had not changed her mind about inviting him to dine
with them, she asked, albeit a little tentatively, "Elinor, when you wrote me in
France about inviting Daniel to dinner, I did mention it to him at the time; do
you still wish to meet him?"

Surprised at being asked, Elinor replied, "Of course I do."

"And Edward?" Margaret persisted. "Would he, do you think?" Elinor said,
"I have said nothing of Daniel's situation to him yet; I shall not, until your plans
are more certain and you advise me of them. But I have no reason to suppose that
Edward will not be just as pleased to see Daniel again; as I said in my letter, he
recalls meeting him at Dr Grantley's rooms and speaks highly of him as a historian.
When Daniel returns to England, we shall decide on a day when you can ask him
over to dinner. I am looking forward very much to meeting him, Margaret, especially since he means so much to you." Elinor spoke with such transparent honesty
that Margaret had no doubt at all of her sincerity. She had been both surprised and

pleased by the calm manner in which Elinor had received the news about Helène; knowing her sister's high standards of personal morality, Margaret had feared her censure above anything. For Margaret, inexperienced in love, still struggling to impose a degree of rationality upon her feelings for Daniel Brooke, Elinor's genuine solicitude and understanding, however qualified, meant everything to her.

Before she said her final goodbyes, Margaret spoke again to Elinor of her plans. "It will probably mean giving up my work at the school; it will not do to have a teacher of young girls setting such an example. But it is no matter, I can teach privately; there are many families who cannot afford the fees for a place in a school or the cost of a governess. They are happy to have their daughters taught at home. I have seen many notices in the papers seeking such services; I shall write to a few of them and see what eventuates. They do not pay as well as the school does, but I live fairly simply, I do not need a great deal of money."

Elinor looked worried; it was hard for her to accept that her young sister was making these difficult decisions alone. "How will you manage? I could give you something to tide you over... I have some savings..." she began, but Margaret laughed and said, "Thank you, dear, dear Elinor, but I do not need to take your money. I have some savings, too; remember that I have always planned to be a writer when I tire of teaching and I've been putting a part of my income away. So I shall be all right, you must not worry about me."

Elinor could not help but be concerned. "But will you promise me that if you do need help, at any time, you will ask?" she pleaded, and Margaret promised. The sisters embraced then and wept a little, each conscious of the other's pain, though unwilling to speak of it. Since Marianne's marriage to Colonel Brandon, Margaret, then just a girl, had grown closer to Elinor, and theirs was a warm, supportive affection; however, they dried their eyes, smiled at one another, and Margaret went away to finish packing her trunk.

The following morning, the small carriage from Delaford Manor would take Margaret to meet the coach at Dorchester. There were still a few days before her friends would return and she had much to do.

The coach from Dorset was late and it was almost dusk when Margaret arrived at the cottage she shared with Claire Jones. She put down her luggage, lit the lamps, and started the fire before she saw the letters propped up against a vase on the mantelpiece. One was a note from Claire and the other was from Daniel Brooke. There was also a nondescript brown envelope, with the direction to Miss M. Dashwood inscribed in perfect copperplate but with no indication who it was from.

During the last hour on the coach, Margaret had longed for a cup of tea; she had planned to put the kettle on the moment she got inside the door, but those thoughts fled as she found her letters and began to open them. She read Claire's note first, which said simply that the letter from Daniel Brooke had been addressed to Nicholas Wilcox's rooms in Oxford and he had brought it round. She added that Nicholas had also had a note from Mr Brooke, who had written that he would be back at Oxford in the new year.

Margaret then opened and read Daniel's letter to her, and try as she might, she could not restrain her tears. It was not that there was anything shocking or tragic in the news it brought, it was just the stark, painful truth she confronted that hurt so grievously. After a few brief words of greeting and expressions of hope that she had enjoyed Christmas with her family, he wrote of his efforts to spend some time with Hélène at Christmas.

> *I was permitted by the kind nuns who care for her to see her for about an hour each morning and again on Christmas day for a short period in the evening, while the nuns went to chapel. On both occasions I took her flowers and little gifts, which she clearly liked; she smiled and thanked me, but said very little else that was coherent. I saw her on several occasions thereafter, but I am certain she has no recollection of me at all. She is very frail now and grows weaker by the day. The senior nun, who has had much medical experience, advised that Hélène was too ill to be moved back to Provence; they felt it was best that she be cared for at the hospice in Nice at least until the spring, when they would make a decision depending upon her condition.*
>
> *I can do no more for her here and must return to my work at the college by mid-January, when I hope I will see you again. I have just received your last letter and can only say in response that not a single day passes that I do not think of you, dear Margaret. I should not have to say it, because I am quite certain you know it already. I miss you and long to see you again.*
> *Yours very sincerely,*
> *Daniel Brooke.*

Margaret read the letter over many times before she folded it and put it in her pocket. She wondered at the strange mixture of intense sadness and joy it had brought her and thought again of the resolution she had made to go to him when he returned to England. "Well, at the very least, I think I know that I will not be unwelcome," she thought, as she opened up the unfamiliar brown envelope.

It contained a single sheet of note paper bearing the letterhead of a publisher, Fielding and Armitage, on which were two brief paragraphs written in the same precise hand.

> *Dear Miss Dashwood,*
>
> *Thank you for sending us your manuscript of* A Country Childhood, *which we are happy to accept for publication and offer a payment of twenty pounds, on the condition that you agree to certain editorial changes that we may advise.*
>
> *As to your proposal to write* A Provençal Journal *based on your travels in that part of France, we should be pleased to review it on completion and decide if it is acceptable for publication. I might add that we are impressed with the quality of your first composition, and if this standard is maintained in the rest of your work, we foresee a promising future for you as a writer.*

The letter concluded by inviting her to call on them at the address above, if she was willing to accept their offer, and it was signed by someone called Armitage, who wrote his name with a great flourish. Margaret could not quite make out his first name from his signature, but she did not care; so delighted was she that for fully five minutes she laughed and wept alternately, unable to control the feelings that completely overwhelmed her. This was indeed unexpected and joyous news!

Unbeknownst to anyone, even her friend Claire, some months ago Margaret had sent the manuscript of *A Country Childhood* to a publisher in a small town near Oxford. It was a compilation of pieces she had written over the years; simple and evocative, they recounted the experiences of a young girl growing up at Norland Park in Sussex and later transplanted against her will and at very short notice to Barton Cottage in Devonshire. Having told the stories to her pupils and been pleased with their response, Margaret had supposed that the anthology might make pleasant reading for young ladies. It seemed the gentlemen at Fielding and Armitage agreed.

In her letter accompanying the manuscript, she had mentioned her extensive travels in France and her intention of spending some weeks in Provence this autumn. She expected to keep a detailed journal, which she hoped could form the basis of a travelogue, she'd said, and asked if they would be interested in reading the manuscript when it was ready.

Thereafter, Margaret had given it little thought, expecting to receive a polite letter of rejection. Not in her wildest dreams had she anticipated this response. She wished someone had been there with her to share her joy; then again, she was glad there was no one to see how totally silly she looked as she threw cushions into the air, rolled on the rug in front of the fire, laughed and wept without reason, and finally collapsed exhausted on the sofa, where she fell asleep, clutching both her treasured letters to her heart.

❧

It was late when Margaret awoke, rather stiff and uncomfortable, realising that she was both cold and hungry, but nevertheless feeling weirdly, deliriously happy. Opening a window, she noted that the weather had cleared, with bits of blue sky showing through the clouds. She recalled that she had eaten nothing last night, and this time, she did put the kettle on and was preparing to get some eggs from the larder, when there was a loud knocking at the door. When she opened it, there, to her immense relief, was Mrs Muggle, the woman who came regularly to "do" for the two young ladies, by which she meant clean, cook, and shop for them, which jobs, despite her uninspiring name, she did very satisfactorily.

Margaret greeted her like a long-lost friend, and confessed that she was hungry and would give her life for a pot of tea. "No need for that, miss," said Mrs Muggle, who put down her basket of fresh bread, butter, and eggs on the kitchen table and got to work at once, getting tea and breakfast ready in less time than it took Margaret to go upstairs, clean her teeth, and brush her hair.

As Margaret ate hungrily, feasting on the plate of ham and eggs, Mrs Muggle continued working around her, dusting, washing, and putting things away, all the while plying her with food and giving her the neighbourhood news. Margaret heard, without paying much attention, that the butcher's wife had had twins on Christmas Eve, the grocer's daughter had been married on Boxing Day, the fishmonger had been in a fight with a traveller from another village and he had been locked up by the local constabulary, which meant no one had any fish that week. And of course, she added with a twinkle in her eye, everyone in the village knew by now that Miss Jones was going to be married very soon to that lovely young gentleman from Oxford, Mr Wilcox.

This last piece of information did alert Margaret, and she stopped Mrs Muggle in midsentence to ask who had told her and did she know how soon the couple were to be wed. Mrs Muggle declared that she had had it from Miss Jones herself, before Christmas, and indeed, she thought the wedding would be in February, because she believed they'd want to get it done before Lent. Margaret didn't quite comprehend why this was so, but said, "Ah yes, of course," and continued eating, as Mrs Muggle produced more buttered eggs and refilled her tea cup, while adding that she anticipated there'd be a bit more work for her at the cottage once the couple were married and settled there.

Margaret was pensive. In the euphoric mood of the previous evening, this was one situation she had not anticipated. If her friend Claire and Nicholas Wilcox were to marry in the next month or two, where would they live? She knew Wilcox had rooms at a boarding house in Oxford, which probably meant he would move into the cottage when they were married. The cottage, though perfectly comfortable for two young women, was small and not constructed to offer much privacy and, thought Margaret, this must mean that she would have to find somewhere else to live. While not particularly frightening, it did add some uncertainty to the picture and cloud the bright prospect to which she had awakened an hour ago.

But this was not a morning on which Margaret was going to be disaffected; she had in her pocket two letters that had brought her the best news she could have asked for. Daniel Brooke, the man she loved, missed her and was returning to England within the week, and a certain Mr Armitage was happy to publish her book and had offered to pay her twenty pounds for it! Nothing else mattered at the moment.

She decided to take a good look at the clothes in her wardrobe and choose an appropriate gown to wear when she went to meet the perceptive Mr Armitage. If only Claire were here, she thought, she'd know what I should wear to a meeting with my publisher; but moments later she set that thought aside, as realisation came that henceforth, she would have to make most of her own decisions in matters of far greater import. She selected a simple gown in a soft cream fabric with an overcoat in deep green wool. It had been a gift from Elinor, who'd said it suited her well, and that was sufficient for Margaret. The colours certainly set off her striking honey-gold hair.

Leaving Mrs Muggle to continue with her chores at the cottage, Margaret left to take the coach into town. She had decided that she needed a new hat, one that would impress Mr Armitage and please Daniel Brooke as well. If such a hat might be found somewhere in Oxford, then Margaret was in the right mood to purchase it.

The milliners in town had hats aplenty, but they were all very expensive and some, replete with ribbons and plumes, were rather daunting; but, when she saw the pretty straw bonnet adorned with a cream rose and a wisp of silk, she had to go in and try it on. Once she had done that and the woman in the store had let her look in the mirror, there was no turning back. She paid up and returned with her prize, hoping, as she held the hat box on her lap, that both Daniel Brooke and Mr Armitage would be impressed by her choice.

The return of Claire Jones and Mr Wilcox a few days later provided Margaret with an opportunity to obtain her friend's advice before setting out for the offices of Fielding and Armitage. Claire, who had alternately encouraged her to submit her work and berated her for not doing so, was delighted when she read the publisher's letter.

"You will accept, of course?" she said, and when Margaret nodded, she assured her that twenty pounds was a very reasonable sum, considering that many publishers would not even contemplate publication of a lady's work unless it was specifically for the edification of young wives or the education of small children. "They appear to believe that we are incapable of mature thought and feeling," Claire grumbled, "and that our imagination is limited to domestic and childish matters." Margaret said she hoped that Mr Armitage had not been misled by the title of her manuscript into thinking it was a children's story, because if he had, he was in for a big surprise. Claire urged her not to be intimidated by Mr Armitage. "He is probably a fusty old fellow, with a large moustache, who will try to overwhelm you with facts and figures; just let him see you are not afraid of him. If they have offered you twenty pounds, it is because they know they can make a profit with your work," she advised.

Despite some misgivings, Margaret's frame of mind, as she went to meet Mr Armitage, was optimistic. Fielding and Armitage were an old firm of modest but well-regarded publishers situated in the main street between the offices of a solicitor and the popular tea shop on the corner. Her Mr Armitage turned out to be the son of one of the partners, responsible mainly for what might be termed the lighter side of the publishers' list. Mr Samuel Fielding and his partner Nathaniel Armitage ran the business and handled the weightier tomes, which consisted of heroic translations from the Greek and Latin classics, some academic and philosophical treatises, and similar momentous works.

When Margaret walked in through the glass front doors, a supercilious-looking young man appeared and asked whether it was Mr Nathaniel or Mr Mark Armitage she wished to see. Since she was unable to say, she had to take out her letter and show it to the gentleman, who said in a patronising tone, "Ah, that would be Mr Mark Armitage, come this way." Margaret followed him down a long corridor and was shown into a tiny office at the back of the building, where, behind a huge desk, piled high with bundles of paper tied up with string, sat a fresh-faced young man, who rose to greet her with the brightest smile she had seen in years. He was dressed in a rather informal fashion, sporting a floppy cravat tied in the style affected by many writers and artists of the day, and when he spoke, his voice was particularly pleasing. As for his words, they were music to her ears.

"Miss Dashwood? I am delighted to meet you and even more delighted that you have agreed to accept our offer for your charming manuscript," he said, and Margaret thought she had never met such an agreeable young man. He was certainly a pleasant change from the superior sort of person who had met her at the door.

When they were seated, he began by asking her about Sussex, where he had never been, inviting her to tell him of its delights, adding that he had enjoyed very much her account of life at Norland Park. He then proceeded to explain the terms under which they would publish her book. She asked a few pertinent questions about payments, which he answered precisely, they signed a couple of documents, witnessed by his clerk, and their business was settled. Thinking they were done, Margaret rose to leave, but was surprised that Mr Armitage seemed keen to meet again to discuss the actual design and production of her book. She had not expected to receive this degree of attention and agreed to return on another occasion; however, she said, she would soon begin work at her school and might not be free to see him for a while.

At this, he looked disappointed and said, "Miss Dashwood, if it is too inconvenient for you to come to us, I could arrange to meet you at a place and time convenient to you," which Margaret found quite astonishing. She did not know quite how to deal with this unexpected suggestion and used the excuse that she could not make an appointment immediately, since it would depend on her working hours at the school, whereupon he wanted to be told what subjects she taught. Having satisfied his curiosity, Margaret promised to advise him when and where she could meet him. He bowed and agreed, promising to bring her their plans for the publication as soon as they were ready. He then accompanied her up the long corridor to the front door and out into the street, where he insisted on waiting until a vehicle arrived to convey her, handed her in, and closed the door, before waving her on with the cheeriest of smiles.

It was an altogether unusual encounter for Margaret. Far from being a fusty old publisher with a great moustache, who would try to intimidate her, young Mr Armitage had proved a very pleasant surprise. Never before had she met such a genuinely cheerful young man.

Returning home in time for tea, she found a letter from Elinor, with news of Colonel Brandon. She wrote:

Mama writes to say that Doctor Richards is very pleased with Colonel Brandon's recovery; his leg is healing very well and he is in excellent spirits and so, I believe, is Sir John Middleton, who is exceedingly happy to have both the colonel and Marianne for company. Mama says it is like old times again: Marianne sings or reads to them after dinner, and Sir John tells everyone he meets how fortunate he is to have such good relations and friends around him.

Mama says that Colonel Brandon and Marianne plan to go to Europe in the spring, which will be very good timing indeed, because the most recent gossip from Mrs Palmer is that Willoughby's wife's application for a divorce is expected to come up for hearing before the Consistory Courts at about the same time and will no doubt be a subject of much gossip. His wife's parents are influential in church circles, we are to understand, which should favour her cause. I am told his exposure here has meant that he has no friends left in this part of the country. My friend Mrs Helen King has also had some similar information from his cousins, the Clifts, who are far from pleased with his recent behaviour, so it does appear that he is about to reap the whirlwind both socially and financially. There is even talk of Combe Magna being put up for sale!

My dear Margaret, we must be very thankful that Marianne was saved, by the merest chance, from being drawn back into his nasty web. It would have been a disaster from whose consequences none of us would have been spared.

Margaret took her letter up to her room and re-read it slowly. She was relieved too, although she had not been as fearful as her elder sister. She had known before Elinor of Marianne's meetings with Willoughby, and while she'd had concerns about her sister's propensity for self-delusion, she had been far less certain that Willoughby had it in him to do more than indulge in the ephemeral pleasures of dalliance with her. He was no Casanova, she had decided. Writing in her notebook, Margaret was quite candid in her estimation of both.

Now that it has come out that he kept a tawdry mistress, who followed him around the country, it seems even more certain that Marianne was in greater danger of doing her marriage harm by her own precipitate behaviour, than being led down the primrose path to perdition by Willoughby. I cannot see him as some Regency rake—more a petty deceiver of gullible young women, like poor Eliza Williams and our foolish Marianne, who are taken in by his false charm. Had Marianne been once again deceived into trusting him, the person most injured by her conduct would have been Colonel Brandon, and we must indeed be thankful that it did not eventuate. There would have been a tragedy and much undeserved suffering.

Margaret was pondering albeit in a whimsical manner, whether it might not make an interesting plot for a novella—a cautionary tale of romance and intrigue that might interest Mr Armitage—when Mrs Muggle struggled up the steep stairs to advise that a gentleman was at the door asking for her. "Who is it, Mrs Muggle?" she asked in a whisper; Margaret was not in a mood to meet strangers. Mrs Muggle did not know. "He did not say, miss, he's very tall and dark, looks foreign... He has a beard..."

She did not get much further, for Margaret had leapt out of her chair and raced down the stairs and into the arms of Daniel Brooke, who was still standing in the open doorway with a brisk breeze blowing through the hall. Breaking out of his embrace, she shut the door, dragged him into the parlour, and stoked up the fire. "You're freezing, how long have you been standing out in the cold?" she asked and was appalled to learn that he'd been walking up and down the street for the best part of an hour, trying to decide whether he should call at the cottage, wondering if she would be alone or whether Miss Jones would be home and his sudden appearance might be an embarrassment to her.

Margaret went to the kitchen to get a pot of tea, which she brought in and dispensed, lacing it with brandy, insisting that he drink it before she would let him speak another word. She was shocked to see how gaunt he looked, and the beard made him seem older and even more serious than before. It was clear to her that he had endured a great deal of anguish.

As he finished the tea, she re-filled his cup and asked, "Why did you not send word that you were back in England?" and he, cradling the cup between his palms to warm them, replied, "I did, when we reached Dover. I had to travel overland to Calais and cross the channel on the packet; I could not get a place on the boat at Marseilles. I was fortunate enough to meet a colleague, who was travelling direct to Oxford and offered me a seat in his vehicle. We arrived yesterday; my letter is probably still on its way to you."

When Daniel had finished his second cup of tea, she was eager for news, but afraid to ask. Seeing the unspoken question in her eyes, he said quietly, "Hélène is very weak; they are not confident that she can return to the convent in Provence. She will probably remain in Nice, but they have promised to send me word if she worsens. When they do, I shall have to go at once." His voice was strained, as though it hurt to speak, and she felt tears sting her eyes.

"Of course, I understand," she said softly. "And are you staying at the college?" she asked. He replied, "Just for a day or two, but I am going to the

Cotswolds and I think I will stay there until the new term begins. I have shipped a lot of my things and need to arrange for their collection and storage when they arrive." He was silent for a moment, then his voice quickened suddenly and he asked, "Margaret, would you like to come down to the cottage for a few days? I should like very much for you to see it. It is peaceful and quiet, I enjoy working there… Perhaps you might like to bring some of your work along, too. Have you started your new school term?"

Before she could give him an answer, Mrs Muggle knocked and put her head round the door; it was time for her to leave and she had to be paid. Margaret went out of the room and took some time paying Mrs Muggle and shutting the front door.

When she returned, Daniel was standing beside the fire. It was no use at all to deny how much they had needed one another; she went to him and was enfolded in his arms and held as though he never wanted to release her. For herself, she wished he never would let her go. When he spoke, his words were unequivocal. "You know how dearly I love you, Margaret, so you must also know that I will do nothing to offend you, I give you my word. But I do long to have you with me, to hear you talk and laugh and see you smile, as you did in Provence, where you brought me new energy and spirit, when I was feeling drained of life and hope. I have missed you these long weeks and longed for your company; will you come with me?"

She waited only to catch her breath before saying, "Of course; when do you wish to go?" and was delighted to hear him say, "Tomorrow, if that suits." When she smiled and nodded, he asked, "What about your friend Miss Jones? What will you tell her?" Margaret replied, "Claire and Nicholas are planning to visit her parents in Wales, she will not worry if I say I have gone to visit a friend in the Cotswolds for a few days."

A thought struck her and she asked, "Do either of them know of your cottage?" and his answer fixed her resolve. "No, nobody does but my good friend Francis Grantley. He spent a week there on some kind of retreat, working on a theological dissertation, and said it had helped him clear his mind and work wonderfully well."

"Well, perhaps it will help me work better too, I have been distracted somewhat of late," said Margaret with a coy smile, whereupon he pretended to be disappointed and asked if she would have some time to spare for him.

She matched the lightness of his tone with her own response, "I may, if I am permitted to love you; am I?"

"Of course, did you doubt it?" he replied and she asked in a voice somewhat more serious than he was accustomed to from her, "You do not reproach me then for saying it, Daniel?" This time he was surprised and she feared she may have hurt his feelings when he said, "Reproach you? Why, my dear Margaret, do you take me for a hypocrite that I, loving you as I do, should reproach you for your honesty?" The expression in his eyes and the tone of his voice told her she had hurt him, and relenting at once, she apologised and embraced him, reassuring him with such warmth as surprised them both. "I could never do that Daniel, not when you have been so honest with me. But I do want you to know that my feelings are unchanged."

Never having been in love before, nor knowing how deeply such emotions could affect her, Margaret was ill-equipped to feign more or less than she actually felt, and Daniel understood and loved her for it. Clearly she had no wish to hide her feelings and yet he had resolved never to take advantage of the artless honesty that characterised her dealings with him and almost everyone she met. She had a freshness combined with clear-sighted intelligence that had intrigued him when they first met in France; meeting her again, he knew it was one reason he loved her so well.

After a while, Margaret suggested that perhaps Daniel should leave, because it was best that her friend Claire did not discover that he was back. They arranged to meet at an appointed place and parted reluctantly, each longing for the moment when they would be together again. He left, and within minutes she regretted having sent him away and wept, annoyed with herself, because she had hurt his feelings and she had not even told him the news about Mr Armitage and his offer to publish her book.

Chapter Twenty-One

MARGARET SPENT A SLEEPLESS night, but not on account of her decision to accompany Daniel to his cottage in the Cotswolds. On that matter, she had no reservations; she loved him and trusted him implicitly. She knew, without a shadow of a doubt, that she would be completely safe with him and nothing would happen between them, unless she wished it. And if, perchance, she did wish it, she thought, she would deal with that prospect when it happened.

Her discomposure arose from the troubling question of having to leave her work at the school. They had been good to her and she had enjoyed teaching the children, but she knew full well that once her relationship with Daniel became generally known in the village, questions of propriety would arise. The dilemma had kept her from sleep until the early hours of the morning and she slept late, so that by the time she came downstairs, Claire Jones had already left for work. Mrs Muggle had her breakfast ready, but Margaret ate very little, making the excuse that she was in a hurry, because she was going away for a few days to stay with a friend who was ill and needed caring for. She left a letter for Claire on the mantelpiece saying much the same thing, and adding her good wishes for their journey to Wales and her compliments to her parents.

Margaret, dressed for travelling, left the cottage, walked down the street carrying a small valise, and found Daniel waiting for her in a hired vehicle around the corner from the inn. He helped her in and they set off along the road travelling west to the town of Burford. It was a journey of some twelve miles, he told her, and the cottage was a short distance from the town. As they left the main street, taking the road to Burford, Margaret looked out; she loved travelling and always hoped to enjoy the sights and sounds of the countryside through which they drove. But there was little here to excite her enthusiasm, for the scene was still rather cheerless; winter had not loosened its grip on the land. The grey stone walls seemed unfamiliar and cold, unlike the friendly little hedgerows she had grown up with, and the trees, great elms and ancient beeches, appeared like phantoms in the lingering mist, their ghostly bare arms hung with long swathes of climbing ivy and mistletoe, while the occasional evergreen fir or pine stood out like stiff sentinels in the grey landscape. Catching a glimpse of hills in the distance, she thought even they looked unfriendly and bleak.

"Are those hills on the horizon the Cotswolds?" she asked, and Daniel, hearing the disappointment in her voice, said, "They are only the foothills—we are still in Oxfordshire, remember. One must travel much farther west into Gloucestershire to see the heartland of the Cotswolds," he explained and then taking her hand in his, said, "I am sorry, Margaret, it is not the best time of year to introduce you to my favourite part of England, is it? Nowhere are there prettier spots to see than in the Cotswolds in spring, summer, and autumn, but I will admit that even I can find little to praise in this dismal winter landscape. But I am determined that you shall not be disappointed, so let me tell you of its history, which is colourful and busy enough to satisfy even the keenest scholar."

She laughed then and sat back, declaring that she was prepared to be entertained with tales from the history of the Cotswolds, if he was sure they were going to be as diverting as the tales he had told them in France. Assuring her that it would prove even more exciting, he proceeded with an amusing narrative of the history of the area known as the Cotteswold, dating back to Saxon times, with tales of ancient battles and the totem dragon banners of Uther Pendragon, father of the fabled King Arthur, and many other wondrous things besides.

Margaret, who could never resist a really good story, listened keenly, her eyes shining as he told of the battle between Cuthred of the Saxons and Aethelbald of the Mercians, in a field near the present town of Burford, at which the Mercians prevailed. "It is a victory celebrated in Burford to this day with great enthusiasm, around midsummer," he said, and when Margaret said she would love to see the celebrations, added, "So you shall, if you will come back later this year. I'll take you down to the field where it happens and you shall see the triumph of the golden dragons."

With such tales he kept her engaged and entertained until they reached the town of Burford, which had been built in Norman times at a ford in the river Windrush. They alighted and went across to the inn, so Margaret could rest and take some refreshment, while he purchased stores for the cottage from the market stall across the road. Later, they stood on the banks of the Windrush, which ran down from the Cotswolds. It wasn't a very impressive sight now, but with the spring thaw it would swell into a stronger river rushing through the reed beds on its banks, through towns like Burford and Witney, to join the Thames. Daniel told her that one of the little tributaries of the Windrush trickled through the orchard behind his cottage, and promised that she would love waking up to its sound in the mornings. Seeing the stream running busily over the stones and under the bridge, she heard his words and blushed at she thought of waking up in his cottage. She had not stopped to think precisely what that could mean for her; she had not asked about their sleeping arrangements.

They got back in the vehicle and proceeded out of the town up a road that narrowed into a rutted country lane with bare trees bordering a field on one side and box-hedged gardens on the other. A mile and a half on they arrived at the gate—and Margaret almost cried out as she saw what was the most perfect cottage built of the warm yellow Cotswold stone, with that patina of age that lends much more honesty to a building than a coat of paint. She could not wait to leap out of the cart and run to the door and stand in front of it as though it would open at her command.

Daniel followed her, having unloaded their luggage and paid the driver, and when he asked, "Well, do you like it?" even he was surprised at the fervour of her response. "I love it, Daniel, it is quite perfect. How do you leave it? If I had a place like this, I wouldn't dream of living in town." He laughed at her then and once they were inside, mocked her enthusiasm. "And would you also keep ducks and grow beans and cabbages?" She had to laugh, even as she said, "I would love to try," because she knew he was teasing her.

They spent an hour wandering around the garden and the orchard, where with great delight she collected mushrooms growing around the roots of apple trees and early snow drops pushing up out of the long grass. There were still some old apples left on the gnarled trees and shrivelled blackberries hiding from the cold. He watched with amusement as she picked and ate them like a child enjoying a treat, then laughed as she pulled a face at the tart taste on her tongue. It had been many years since there had been a visitor at the cottage, and Margaret's candid responses delighted him.

When the sun disappeared they went indoors, and Daniel lit the fires in the kitchen and the parlour, made them tea, and carried hot water up to her room. She went upstairs and found her room, with its window that overlooked the orchard. It had a bed and a book case, a dresser with a mirror, and a large, comfortable armchair in front of the fire. She changed out of her travelling gown, washed, rested a while, dressed, and came downstairs to find Daniel preparing dinner.

Margaret insisted on helping him, and he let her lay the table and slice the bread, making her feel comfortable and at home. They talked cheerfully as they worked and then as they ate, he asked if she was tired and she admitted that she was, a little. "It's probably the long drive—you need a good night's sleep," he said, and she agreed. She was beginning to feel the strain of everything that had happened in the last twenty-four hours and hoped that he would not be annoyed because she was quiet.

In fact, far from being disappointed, it seemed he had anticipated her situation and made certain that her room was warm and comfortable. There was another, larger bedroom at the front of the house, and Margaret assumed that Daniel would sleep up there; when she said good night, she took her lighted candle and went upstairs.

But, having slept for some hours, she awoke as the clock struck two and was disturbed by a sound downstairs. Pulling a robe over her nightgown, she went to the landing and looked down into the parlour and saw Daniel lying on the couch in front of the fire.

A log had burned through and fallen into the fireplace. She waited only a few seconds before running down the stairs, and as she reached him, he sat up and, looking rather confused, said, "Margaret, what are you doing here? You should be in bed, asleep."

"And so should you," she said. "I thought you were going to sleep in your room upstairs. It is so cold, why are you down here?"

She stood over him, small, irate, and demanding to be told. He had no answer for her; he looked somewhat foolish and smiled as she stood there, unable to put into sensible words the awkward reasons that had prompted him to remain downstairs, rather than use his bedroom and perhaps cause her some trepidation about his intentions. When he said nothing, she persisted, "Why, Daniel? Had I known that you were to suffer such discomfort on my account, I would never have come." He had to say something then and began by trying to reassure her that he was not in any real discomfort. "Margaret, I am not uncomfortable, believe me, this is an exceedingly comfortable couch and I am very warm here beside the fire. I have often slept here."

She shook her head. "I don't believe you," she said and then when he added, "I had hoped you would be asleep and not notice. I did not wish to alarm you," she interrupted him. "Alarm me! Oh Daniel, how can you say that?" It was an argument he could not win and presently, he gave in and agreed to go upstairs to his room, which he did, having doused the fire and given her another lighted candle for her room.

The next day was near perfect; the weather was cold but dry, and they spent it following the little stream into the woods, where they walked beside it through the stands of beech and elm, still gaunt and bare, until it tumbled hurriedly over rocks into a shallow pool and flowed on thence to join the Windrush. Later, they explored some of the old churches in the district and one in particular moved her to tears, an ancient abbey that had been deliberately vandalised when Henry the Eighth dissolved the monasteries.

She knew little of that era, and recalling the many similar places they had visited in Provence, all lovingly preserved, Margaret could not comprehend that here in England, they had been so ruthlessly destroyed. Looking at the mutilated images, she asked, "Why?" and he tried to explain, without much success, the irrational brutality of the period. "It was a hard, cruel time, Margaret, unlike anything you and I have known; powerful kings ruled like gods, by decree. It was as much as your life was worth to question their orders," he said and saw her shudder with disgust.

Warm and companionable, their affection for one another acknowledged, but neither paraded nor hidden, they achieved a degree of intimacy very like that they had enjoyed during those last two days in Provence. He promised her that he would bring her back in the spring so she could enjoy the wealth of wildflowers and apple blossoms and again in autumn, to taste the sweet ripe berries and crab-apples that grew in profusion everywhere.

"I shall not rest until you have seen the Cotswolds at their best; winter has to be the very worst time of year," he said ruefully, but she shook her head. "I don't agree, because unless one has seen the bare bones of the land in winter, how can one appreciate fully the new life that rises in it in spring? No, Daniel, I am glad I have seen it as it is now, cold and bare on the surface, but with everything waiting impatiently underground to burst into life with the return of the sun."

He clapped his hands and praised her poetic account of the changing seasons, and she thought it was the right time to tell him of Mr Armitage and his offer to publish her book. This brought on a clamour of congratulations with Daniel putting his arms around her and kissing her, which made her shy, but seemed to please her very well, especially when he told her he was very proud of her.

A sudden gust of wind from the north cut through the bare woods and hit them; he took off his coat and wrapped it around her and they hurried back to the cottage, which was warm and welcoming. After dinner, they were seated together on the couch in front of the fire, and she was telling him of her intention to use the material she had gathered in Provence for a travelogue, when, with lightning and thunder, a storm broke over the valley of the Windrush.

As the doors and windows rattled and shook and the wind blew out their candles, Margaret looked apprehensive; she had been terrified of storms since childhood. She hated the thought of going upstairs and trying to sleep in total darkness with the wild sounds of the storm outside. When he lit the candles again and asked if she wanted to go to bed, she said quietly, "I hate storms, Daniel, may I stay down here with you?" He smiled then and said, "Of course."

It was simply said and done with no fuss at all; she tucked herself into a corner of the sofa and said, "You were right, it is a very comfortable couch." He covered her up with a warm rug, put more wood on the fire, and as the storm abated, she fell fast asleep.

He awoke early the next morning and gently moved her so he could extricate himself from his corner of the couch. When he brought her tea, she awoke, smiled, and thanked him as she reached for her cup. She knew there would never be any question of trust between them ever again.

They returned to Oxford that afternoon and reached the cottage well before Claire and Nicholas arrived. A letter from Elinor awaited Margaret, and on opening it, she found a reminder about inviting Mr Daniel Brooke to dinner. Elinor wrote:

> *Should Mr Brooke wish to stay overnight, it can be arranged because Mama's room has not been used in many months. It may be more comfortable than rooms at the inn and tramping around in the cold at night. And do please tell me, Margaret, if he has a favourite dish—or on the other hand, if there is something he particularly dislikes which we should avoid. I do recall that Edward had a distinct aversion to pig's trotters, which we all loved, except Marianne, who was much too dainty to try them. You must write directly and let me know a date that suits, so I can order the fish and poultry.*

The timing was perfect and Margaret conveyed the message to him at once, obtaining an immediate acceptance. "Please thank your sister and brother-in-law and say I am delighted to accept," he said, and they arranged to meet and travel down to Dorset together on the following Saturday. When he left her, reluctantly and after much affectionate leave-taking, Margaret wrote to her sister to advise her of their visit. She was feeling a good deal more confident now of her situation. The days spent at the cottage had not only confirmed her strong feelings for him, they had demonstrated how completely she trusted him and how entirely worthy he was of that trust.

As for Daniel, she had not failed to notice that much of the strain that had marked his countenance, when he had first returned from France, had faded over the past three days.

Margaret decided to wear the same outfit she'd worn to meet her publisher, and Daniel's delight with her pretty new bonnet was particularly pleasing. They took the morning coach and arrived in the early afternoon, just in time to see Edward and Elinor waving off the Palmers and Mrs Jennings, who together with their entire entourage had called in at the parsonage on their way back into town. Of course, when Charlotte Palmer saw Margaret, whom she had not met in many months, she had to scream for the carriage to be halted and for Margaret to come to the door to be kissed and hugged and told how very pretty she looked.

Nor could Mrs Jennings resist joining in with a little speculation about the handsome gentleman with a beard, who had been seen alighting from the hired vehicle. "And who is that handsome person you've been hiding from us all, Miss Margaret? Does your dear mama know about him? Come along now, tell me, I promise I shall not say a word," and hearing a loud snort emanating from her son-in-law, she added indignantly, "Nor shall I, I give you my word, my dear—I believe young women are entitled to make their own choices. Tell me, is he your latest beau?"

Margaret shook her head. "No, Mrs Jennings, he is a friend of Edward's from Oxford; we travelled down together."

Poor Mrs Jennings looked rather deflated, but Charlotte Palmer was not to be denied her fun. "But that is ideal, Miss Margaret, a friend of your brother-in-law—just the ticket, do you not agree, Mama?"

Margaret was beginning to think she was never going to get away, when Mr Palmer growled that Miss Margaret was probably going to catch her death of cold if they kept her standing out there, and ordered that the carriage move on. With much waving and cries of goodbye, they were finally gone and Margaret escaped indoors, where she found Edward had already placed their guest in the best seat by the fire with a drink in his hand, and the maid had brought in a large tray of refreshments.

Elinor embraced her sister. "It is so good to see you, Margaret—and looking so well, isn't she, Edward?" she asked, to which her husband agreed, but urged her to get closer to the fire and keep warm, after standing out in the cold so long. "I thought they would never leave; you know how it is with Mrs Jennings and Charlotte," said Margaret, making herself comfortable on the sofa, "they have no conception of time at all." Elinor remarked that it was a good thing they were to break journey at Barton Park. "No doubt Sir John and Mama will enjoy all the news."

It seemed to Margaret that her brother-in-law and Daniel Brooke had a lot to talk about; their mutual friend Dr Grantley provided an excellent link, since the three men were keenly interested in similar subjects, albeit in differing ways. Daniel's study was mainly historical, while both Edward Ferrars and Dr Grantley, being clergymen, had a theological interest as well. Edward and his friend Dr Bradley King had very recently visited Dr Grantley at his college in Oxford, Elinor said, and Margaret heard Edward say, "Yes, we were fortunate to catch him, he was preparing to leave for Derbyshire that very day, where, I understand, his wife's family has a great estate." To which Daniel replied, "Indeed, she was a Miss Darcy, and I believe the Darcys of Pemberley are one of the most highly respected families in the county. Francis Grantley is recently married to Mr Darcy's sister, Georgiana, a very handsome and accomplished lady, I am told," he explained.

"Have you not met her?" asked Elinor, to which he replied, "No indeed, Mrs Ferrars, I was in France at the time of the wedding and have not called on them at home since my return." Then, turning to Edward, he asked, "Was Dr Grantley able to assist your friend with his enquiry?" Edward shook his head and said, "Sadly, he did not have the information to hand. Dr Bradley King was interested in some historical information about the old priory at Burford—and here's the coincidence," Edward added with a smile. "Dr Grantley declared that he knew one man who would have all the information we need, but he was away—probably, he said, at his cottage in the Cotswolds. Now, can you ladies possibly guess who that knowledgeable man might be?" and as all their eyes met, Daniel broke into a laugh, as Edward continued, "He sits right there by the fire. Now what do you say to that?"

Elinor was laughing, but Margaret had her eyes fixed on Daniel as her sister asked, "And was Dr Grantley right? Were you at your cottage in the Cotswolds, Mr Brooke?" to which Daniel, who carefully avoided meeting Margaret's eyes, laughed and said, "Indeed I was, and Dr Grantley is perhaps the only one of my colleagues who knew where I was." Thereafter Margaret had to make some excuse to get out of the room and go upstairs; she prayed they would pursue the matter of the cottage no further, for she feared her flushed face would soon betray her.

By the time they were sitting down to dinner, the conversation had veered around to the serious subject of the historical research that Dr Bradley King was involved in, and Edward had succeeded in persuading Daniel Brooke to meet with his friend and help him discover the information he sought. It was, thought Margaret, a most auspicious beginning and the very best way for Daniel to be introduced into her family.

Then, there was the exciting story of Margaret's book to be told, which brought many congratulations, taking up more of the evening. Mr Brooke stayed the night at the parsonage and on the morrow, after church, they went over to call on the Kings, whose delight at seeing Margaret again was doubled when it turned out that Edward had brought along the very man who could assist Dr King with his study. The three men spent the rest of the morning in Dr King's workroom, while the ladies wandered around the house and garden and admired Mrs King's beautiful collection of porcelain miniatures, before sitting down to dinner.

Returning to the parsonage in the afternoon, it was quite clear that it was too late for the travellers to leave. The night coach was not to be recommended for ladies, Edward said—not only would it be freezing cold, there were too many inebriated travellers aboard—so they were easily persuaded to stay over and take the coach in the morning.

That night, Elinor went to her sister's room, and to Margaret's surprise she had tears in her eyes. "Oh my dear Margaret, he is such a wonderful man; I hope and pray that it comes right for you. I can see that you love him and best of all, he loves you dearly—it's very plain to see, even Edward saw it as soon as you arrived. Can you tell me how things are?" she asked.

Margaret wept as she told her how things stood now and what the future might hold for them. "But Daniel knows I love him and will not leave him, no matter what happens. He is a good man, Elinor, I cannot leave him," she said.

Elinor could not hold back her tears as she held her sister close, understanding how she must feel and willing her to find the happiness she deserved. Elinor knew that Margaret's youth and inexperience of the world would make it hard for her to accept that pain, in one guise or another, was always a part of loving. She would pray that this young sister of hers would be spared the anguish that had afflicted and almost destroyed Marianne.

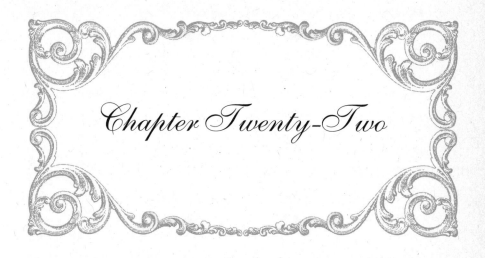

Chapter Twenty-Two

Spring 1820

WITH THE ARRIVAL OF spring, Margaret went back to teaching at the school, and Daniel returned to his rooms at his college in Oxford. His sabbatical year was almost coming to a close, and he had hoped for some degree of certainty in his life, which might enable him to complete work on his book. Margaret's interest and encouragement had increased his desire to bring it to a conclusion, but he had felt neither the imperative nor the will to do so.

With the warmer weather, the pace of life quickened in the woods and fields of England, as well as in the towns and villages, as new crops were planted and the cycle of country life began anew.

In London, only one notable event had occurred; at the end of January, the old king, George the Third, delusional and sad, had finally died at Windsor, leaving his son the Regent ready to assume the throne. However, a coronation was not immediately forthcoming, because the new king refused to be crowned together with his legal wife, Caroline, and months of machination and bitterness followed. While the antics of the king, his wife and mistresses, together with the wasteful expenses of his court, continued apace, the people of Britain were to suffer a good deal more scandal and stupidity before that particular question was resolved.

Meanwhile, Claire Jones and Nicholas Wilcox were married in Oxford and left to spend their honeymoon in France, whither Colonel Brandon—well recovered from his accident—and his wife had gone also, persuaded by Sir John Middleton that nothing could surpass the pleasures of Paris in the spring.

Short letters had arrived for Mrs Dashwood at Barton Park and the parsonage at Delaford, in which Marianne enthused in glowing terms about all the "exciting places" they had visited and the "beautiful things" her loving husband had showered upon her, in gratitude for her devoted care during his weeks of enforced inactivity following his accident. Marianne, clearly bewitched by the beauty and spirit of Paris in the spring, appreciated his generosity in taking her there.

Perhaps as an even more significant consequence of those momentous events, Colonel Brandon had taken Sir John's advice and appointed a manager to overlook his Irish estates, so he would have more time to spend at Delaford, keeping his wife happy and contented—a development that brought Elinor considerable relief.

Letters from Mrs Dashwood also reported that Eliza Williams and her daughter had been satisfactorily settled at Barton Cottage, and the young woman had shown an interest in needlecraft and tapestry, in which she was acquiring some skills. She wrote:

> I intend to ask Sir John if Eliza may be permitted to practice her craft by restoring some of the worn pieces of tapestry around Barton Park; if she could master it, it would prove a useful occupation, which could allow her to earn some money as well. I have also persuaded Eliza to let Alice help in the school room, when the new governess Miss Dalton takes the children through their lessons. I think it may create an interest in the girl for learning her letters and numbers and surely, that can do no harm.

Both Edward and Elinor thought these were exceedingly sound propositions, and Elinor wrote to congratulate her mother on her plans. At the same time, she suggested that Mrs Dashwood might like to join them for a fortnight in summer when they travelled to Weymouth again. She wrote:

> We had such an enjoyable fortnight there last year, but it was all too short,

and both Edward and I would like to make a return trip. If you should care to join us, I am sure you will enjoy it just as well.

Daniel and Margaret's friendship continued, free of some of the constraints of concealment, now that her sister Elinor and their friends Claire and Nicholas Wilcox were privy to their secret, even though Margaret had said nothing to her friend about Helène. Margaret's own fears were gradually eroded by the gentle tenderness of Daniel's affection, letting her enjoy the mature relationship that had developed between them, despite the ever present anxiety of Helene's deteriorating health.

The publishers had already begun the process of production that was to bring to fulfilment Margaret's childhood dream. Mr Mark Armitage had arranged regular meetings to which he would bring along the designs for her book and its covers and spend time discussing the progress of what he called "my most favourite project." Naturally, Margaret was exceedingly gratified, pleased with his diligence and the quality of the work.

As the reach of spring extended deeper into the valley of the Windrush, Daniel and Margaret spent more time at the cottage, enjoying the return of the birds and blossoms and attending to the maintenance of the cottage and its garden. Here, in the quiet tranquillity of the Cotswolds, they found their deepest levels of contentment together.

Walking in the woods among the great trees now clad in bright spring garb, many carrying scarves of fine green vines, their roots deep in the rich soil from which rose clumps of crisp white meadowsweet and blue geranium, Margaret could scarcely believe the change that the new season had wrought here. She would have wished, if Daniel would let her, to collect wildflowers until her arms were full and bring them into the house. But he would caution that they would only last a day or less, since their best would be past even before she got them home. "They are best left and loved in the woods, where they grow as they please. Pick the daisies or roses if you will; they are culti-vated plants and their blooms will last longer indoors," he counselled, and she, having once tested his thesis and found it to be sound, did as he advised. There were plenty of roses and daisies in the cottage garden at the front of the house and she loved to fill a vase or two and carry them into the parlour or her bedroom, where their scent would fill the room. Clearly, he enjoyed seeing her performing these little chores, for she often caught him watching her with a thoughtful smile.

Since the night of the storm, whenever they had been at the cottage she had slept in her bedroom, parting from him each night with such affection that concealed little of their feelings but allowed the lines of decorum to be drawn. Margaret had resolved that though she loved Daniel dearly, she would not sleep with him while his wife still lived, and he had accepted her unspoken decision without question. While they enjoyed the many pleasures of an affectionate and companionable relationship, neither moved to invoke the more passionate indulgence of feelings that lay beneath its surface.

Should situations arise that could have taken them down such a path, they were adroitly circumvented. Margaret was very clever at anticipating them and avoiding the consequences.

One such event took them completely unawares, when they were caught in a sudden shower while walking in the woods and she was drenched. Returning to the cottage, Margaret knew she should change out of her clothes immediately, else she would catch a chill. Practical as always, she used the laundry, adjacent to the kitchen, while he went to fetch towels and a robe from her room. When he returned he found her still struggling to get out of her long cotton petticoat, which, with the water, mud, and forest litter that adhered to it, was heavier and more unwieldy than when she had put it on.

Perhaps it was the exigency of the moment, but the swiftness of his response in helping her out of it and wrapping a large towel around her alleviated her embarrassment and allowed her to regain her composure. By the time she emerged, modestly robed, towelling her wet hair, he had lit the fire and made a pot of tea. She thanked him then and reached for her tea, grateful indeed for his sensibility.

A practical consequence of the incident followed that afternoon, when the sun came out and Margaret washed her muddied clothes and hung them out to dry. Daniel was standing in the garden, watching her, and she said very casually, "A thought occurred to me today, whilst I was in the laundry; why do I not take my bath in there every evening?" and when he looked surprised, she added, "It would mean that you do not have to carry hot water up to my room; I feel very guilty letting you do that. Using the laundry instead would make it so much simpler, would it not?"

Daniel seemed astonished; he had not known a woman who would choose to have a bath in a cold laundry instead of her own warm bedroom or dressing room. "Will you not be very cold?" he asked, and she smiled and said, "Not if I had plenty of hot water and nice warm towels." He laughed then and said that would not pose a problem and added, "Perhaps we should convert the laundry into a proper bathroom, with a boiler for heating the water. That would keep the room warm, too. What do you think?" When she declared it an excellent scheme, he promised to start work on it directly. He would need to engage a tradesman for some of the work, he explained, but it seemed he was quite amenable to the idea.

It was not long after Easter, which they had spent at the cottage enjoying the bounty of spring, that the message came; it had been both expected and dreaded. Helène had died, peacefully, in her sleep. Daniel came to the house to tell Margaret he was leaving directly for France and would probably be away for some weeks. She had wept, and though he wanted very much to hold her and comfort her, and she would have wished to do likewise, neither seemed to know what to do, and in the end, he had left her, having held both her hands in his for a while and gently kissing her cheek.

Before leaving, he gave her a key to the cottage, saying she should feel free to use it while he was away, if she wished to be on her own. They had talked often of the need for her to find lodgings in the village so she could move out of her present accommodation when Claire and Mr Wilcox returned, but there being no urgency with the Wilcoxes away, Margaret had given the matter little serious thought.

Closing the door after him, she went to her room, lay on the bed, and wept inconsolably, unable to explain even to herself why the news they had both known was coming had hurt so deeply when it came. She had seen the agony in his eyes as he told her and knew that he had loved Helène and had suffered as she did, more especially because he could do nothing to help her. Margaret loved his honesty and longed for the time when she could ease his pain.

She awoke the following morning and, seeing her red eyes and pale face in the mirror, decided she could not possibly face the pupils and teachers at school. She sent a hurried note to her superior claiming she had just received information of a sudden illness in her family, dressed quickly, walked into town to catch the coach to Dorchester, and arrived at the parsonage in Delaford late that afternoon.

With Edward away on parish duties, Elinor was reading in the front room when she heard the hired pony cart stopping at the gate. Seeing Margaret alight, she knew right away that something was amiss and rushed out to meet her. The sisters embraced as Margaret wept, and they went quickly indoors. Elinor asked for tea to be brought upstairs as they repaired to the relative privacy of the spare room, which was always kept ready for Margaret.

Elinor did not need to ask; it was clear to her from Margaret's distress that Daniel's wife had died and he had gone to France—that much was obvious. However, since this tragic event had been long anticipated, ever since Daniel had returned from France, she wondered what could have precipitated such a fierce outpouring of grief. A woman of both sensibility and compassion, Elinor did not press her sister for an answer, waiting instead for Margaret to reveal it herself. And when it was told, it was not difficult to comprehend the source of her sorrow.

Through the last six weeks of spring, Margaret had let her mind slip out of its constant awareness of the perilous circumstances in which she and Daniel lived from day to day. It had not seemed right to spend each day contemplating, even anticipating, the death of an innocent if unfortunate young woman, who, through no fault of her own, had been destined never to enjoy the simple pleasures of a happy marriage with a loving husband and children. "Which is why I allowed myself to live each day as it dawned and go to bed each night giving thanks for the day," she explained, "trying to ignore the melancholy circumstances of our lives, disregarding the fact that I knew the news would come one day and we would have to face it."

Elinor tried to comfort her. "But, my dearest girl, you had both faced it already; Daniel in explaining it to you when he told you in Provence about Helène, and you when you told him you loved him and would stay with him; you both knew what was to come. Of course when it did happen, it was going to be a shock; but it is not something you were unprepared for."

Margaret agreed that it was not; yet she could not bring herself to admit that as she had waited these months since he had returned from France, it had been always in the knowledge that no matter how deeply they loved one another, nothing could come of it until Helène was dead. "We never spoke of it, but we both knew it; each time we met, each time we confessed that we loved one another, we knew. The sadness was always there, even on the best days, and though I never met her, I knew he had loved her dearly and it was unbearable to contemplate her death," she said, and the tears came again.

There was something Elinor needed to know, yet was reluctant to ask. It could account for the inordinate degree of grieving that was afflicting her sister. She feared that asking might distress or even anger her, yet decided she had to know. "Margaret, you may tell me to mind my own business and refuse to answer, but I recall you told me that Daniel had suffered much and needed comfort and that when he returned to England, you would go to him. Did you?"

Margaret did not resile from her words; she looked at Elinor directly and said, "He came to me; and yes, I did tell him I love him and would not leave him—he needed to know that. And, yes, before you ask, we have been to the cottage in the Cotswolds, which I love. But, if you mean have I made love with him, then the answer is no, I have not. I do not say that to pretend that I am some pure spiritual creature, who feels no passion, because I am not. I admit I have desired it, because I love him dearly, but I was not comfortable with it, while his wife lived. And, to be fair to Daniel, he has never attempted to draw me into such a situation, either. Indeed, he has been even more particular about it than I am."

Elinor breathed a quiet sigh of relief and gave thanks in her heart, for she had feared that Margaret's excessive grief had signified a deeper anxiety. To learn that this was not the case, to be assured that her sister had taken a decision that Elinor could, in her own right, defend and support, in a manner that would not have been possible for her to do had they been living together as lovers while Helène lived, was a source of deep comfort to her.

Pouring out a cup of tea and seeing Margaret dry her tears eased some of the strain and she said, "You have been strong, Margaret, strong and compassionate, and no one could ask more of you. Now, I would ask you to think only of the future; think only of how you must help Daniel restore his life—which has indeed been held in abeyance for many years while he dealt bravely and mostly alone with the consequences of a tragedy that was not of his making. If your love can help him regain his enthusiasm for a full and happy life, I think you can be well satisfied. Do you not agree, my dear?"

Margaret looked a little uncertain, "Do you believe I could?" she asked, and her sister's response was unequivocal, "My dear, of course I do. I have no doubt that you, who have dealt so creditably with the most painful part of this situation, will have little difficulty in convincing a man whom you love, and who loves you dearly, that despite the grief he has suffered in the past, the future is well worth striving for. As for you, my dear sister, you are not yet twenty-two years old. Most of your life is ahead of you; with your book coming out soon, your work, and Daniel beside you, what more can a bright young woman ask? Sir John always said you were the most promising Miss Dashwood, because you were intelligent and keen to learn. Come now, when shall I see that optimistic young sister of mine smile again, eh?"

Margaret smiled then and recalling that her brother-in-law Edward knew nothing of Helène, she asked, "What shall we tell Edward? Will he not wonder why I am here?" Elinor was dismissive. "Of course not, why would he? He will assume you are visiting us. Will you stay a few days?" Margaret nodded. "The school believes I am visiting a sick relative, so I can stay a day or two." Elinor laughed and hugged her. "One of those little white lies you used to worry about when you were a little girl! Never mind, this one at least is in a good cause," she said as Margaret washed her face and tidied her hair, before they went downstairs together to await Edward's return.

Two days later, Margaret returned to Oxfordshire to find that Claire and her husband, Mr Wilcox, had returned and were setting about moving his things into the cottage. Before Claire's wedding they had spoken briefly of it, and Margaret had been left with the impression that they would have no objection if she stayed on, since there were two large bedrooms upstairs. But Margaret had always felt that she would be in the way of the newly wedded pair, and besides, she knew that her own desire for privacy would soon make the arrangement less agreeable. Unwilling to jeopardise her friendship with Claire on account of some petty domestic inconvenience, Margaret had determined that she would look for another place to stay.

She began by asking other teachers at the school and soon discovered that there were several householders who took in lodgers, but there was always a price to be paid, in that most of them were widowed or single women, whose curiosity about their lodgers often got the better of them. Some had strict rules about visitors, while others were inveterate peddlers of gossip into whose care Margaret was not prepared to deliver her life.

It was on a day when she was beginning to worry whether she would ever find a suitable place that Mr Mark Armitage had arrived bearing suggestions for a new cover design for her book. She had to tell him that she would not be at the cottage much longer and was looking for new lodgings. They were by now on sufficiently friendly terms to allow her to ask if he knew of a respectable family, who might have room for a lodger who would give no trouble at all and would pay well for the service. He promised to make enquiries, and indeed, he returned on the very next day with what appeared to be an ideal solution.

His sister was married and lived a mile out of town along the Cheltenham road, he said, and she had two rooms which might be used together as a bedroom and study. She was happy to let them to a lodger, but it had to be a lady, because she would not consider having a man in the house on account of the fact that her husband often went away on business. "A single lady, who would be no trouble and could pay regularly, would suit her very well," he said. Pleased to be so easily suited, Margaret agreed to go with him that evening to meet his sister, Mrs Hopkins, who turned out to be a pleasant young woman with a couple of well-behaved little girls.

She gave them tea and crumpets and took Margaret upstairs to see the rooms, which were themselves very neat and comfortable, and when she named the price she expected, Margaret was surprised indeed at how reasonable it was. Not wishing to waste any more time, she paid for a week in advance, thanked Mrs Hopkins and her brother, and returned feeling she had done very well indeed.

On the Saturday following, she moved her things in with the help of Nicholas Wilcox, who obtained for her the services of a carter. Her friends were sorry to see her go but understood her need to find a more permanent place to stay. "Promise you will come and visit?" Claire pleaded, and Margaret promised. She did not know for how long she would need to stay with Mrs Hopkins, but she was glad to have a place of her own.

Mrs Hopkins, who had her own children to care for, proved far more easygoing and less inquisitorial than most landladies, which suited Margaret well. She needed time and space in which to think and work, and she felt

Mrs Hopkins would surely provide that. She was grateful, too, to young Mr Armitage for his help and said so.

Daniel Brooke's absence gave Margaret an opportunity to work on her book, and with the enthusiasm and energy that Mr Armitage brought to the work, it was proceeding very well indeed. They would meet once or even twice a week, he to consult and suggest changes where they were needed and she to approve or resist them. Unfamiliar with the workings of the publishing industry, Margaret was not aware whether all this to-ing and fro-ing was a regular part of their processes or not, but she was exceedingly pleased to be so well served.

Mr Armitage would even turn up on a Sunday occasionally, and since it was his sister's house, there was nothing particularly surprising about it, Margaret thought, until one day, when after he had left late on a Sunday evening, Mrs Hopkins remarked that they had been seeing a great deal more of her young brother recently. "We have you to thank for that, Miss Dashwood; since you came to stay, we see him far more often than before. He thinks the world of you, I know; he regards you as one of the best writers he has met and a fine young lady as well," she said with a funny sort of a smile that seemed to suggest that young Mr Armitage was developing a partiality for his client, which his sister appeared eager to encourage.

Initially, Margaret was not inclined to take the hint too seriously, for Mr Armitage could not have been much older than herself. He was of an age when young men are susceptible to such afflictions but are equally able to shake them off like a cold in summer, without serious damage. Nevertheless, she did feel the need to take some precautionary measures against a sudden surge in his interest, if only to ensure that she did not lay herself open to a charge of encouraging his youthful ardour.

She wondered about the wisdom of hinting to Mrs Hopkins, in the hope that it would be tactfully conveyed to her brother, that there was already another gentleman in her life, but decided against it. She was disinclined, on two counts, to do so. There was her reluctance to do or say anything to anyone about Daniel without his knowledge, and she also feared that admission of the existence of another man might lead to a guessing game as to who it might be. Averse to being the subject of such speculation, she believed it would probably be simpler if she were to absent herself on Sundays, when Mark Armitage came to pay his sister what was primarily a social call.

Apart from a short letter following the funeral, in which he had declared his intention to visit the nuns at the convent in Provence where Helène had been cared for, there had been no word from Daniel, and it was now three weeks since he had left for France. She decided to visit Claire and Nicholas Wilcox on Saturday morning and found them planning a picnic—not an occasion on which Margaret wished to impose upon the couple.

Unwilling to be outwitted again—Mark Armitage had spent all of last Sunday at the Hopkins's home, during which time he had paid her very particular attention—Margaret made an impulsive decision. Returning quickly to her lodgings, she packed a change of clothes, announced that she was going to visit her sister, and went, not to catch the coach to Dorchester, but the one that left soon after noon for Burford.

Arriving in Burford some hours later, after what had been a particularly pleasant drive through the now verdant landscape of West Oxfordshire, Margaret purchased some provisions and walked the rest of the way to the cottage. She was by now familiar with the lanes and landmarks, and taking a convenient route which left the road and cut through the beech wood, she arrived at the house around five o'clock, when the oblique rays of the setting sun were striking the windows and setting fire to the bunches of yellow blossoms that cascaded from the lattice on the western wall of the house. It was such a pleasing prospect, she sat awhile on the stone seat inside the gate and gazed upon it before rising to go indoors. Here at last, she could hope for the solitude she craved.

She had learned from Daniel that one should bring in the wood for the fires and prepare them well before dark, which she proceeded to do at once. That done, she heated up the water for her bath, which she now took regularly in the laundry, changed into her nightclothes, and put the kettle on for tea.

It was a long evening, with the twilight hours lengthening as summer approached, and although she was tired after her journey, Margaret did not wish to retire upstairs and spend sleepless hours in bed. She carefully locked both doors, read until the candles were exhausted and the fire was ready to be doused, and fell fast asleep on the couch. She remembered thinking just before she fell asleep that Daniel was right, it was a very comfortable couch indeed.

When she awoke, it was dark and, struggling to light her candles, she gave up and decided to spend the night on the couch. Her bedroom would probably be too cold for comfort anyway, she thought, as she snuggled under the big knitted rug that held pleasant memories for her and went back to sleep.

❧

Margaret was awakened early on the morrow by the dawn song of hundreds of birds, calling in the woods and in the trees around the cottage. One in particular, a blackbird, whose singularly melodic aubade belied his dour appearance, always brought a smile to her face and she rose and went to look for him in the garden. It was a picture of Nature's bounty, with every tree and shrub growing in such profusion, laden with blossoms and new fruit, which would swell and ripen through the year to provide a bountiful harvest. The blackbird sat atop the clothesline, singing his heart out. If only, she thought, if only life could always be like this.

But she was sensible enough to know that it could not, and having had breakfast, she set to work to get the rest of her tasks done. She knew Daniel's routines well and followed them exactly; cleaning out the fireplace and tipping the ash into the vegetable patch, letting the water out of the boiler and filling it up with fresh water from the well at the bottom of the garden, and collecting sufficient kindling to light the fires again at night. She worked cheerfully, weeding and clearing out the rows where she hoped they could plant beans, conscious of the sense of freedom the cottage had given her and grateful that Daniel, even in a moment of great strain, had been thoughtful enough of her needs to give her a key before he left. It was a gesture typical of his considerate nature, she thought.

Several times through the morning, she had stopped to think of him, and wonder what he might be doing. She recalled, with a little personal bravado, that last night she had slept at the cottage alone for the first time, but had felt no fear at all. Indeed her feelings had been of singular security and contentment.

Toward afternoon, she grew a little weary with the work and lay on the couch, the tiredness together with the quietude of the time, when the birds seemed to rest their voices too, caused her to fall asleep. When she awoke, it was unusually dark. She went to the window to look out and saw that the sky had clouded over; the blue expanse of the morning had been replaced with a mass of low-hanging clouds that completely hid from sight the hills on the horizon. She made herself a cup of tea, and before she could finish it, a low rumble of thunder began in the mountains and gradually reverberated around the valley. There was lightning too, still at some distance, but it was a sign that a storm was on its way.

Racing to get her linen off the clothesline, she almost tripped and cried out, "Please, God, not a thunderstorm—it's the one thing I cannot cope with alone." Putting down her basket in the kitchen, she ran upstairs to close the bedroom windows; it had been such a beautiful morning, she had opened them all to let in the fresh air. She shut and bolted them, rushing from one to another, recalling Daniel's dire warning that, if you left a window open in a storm, you would have a flood, because the water would beat in at the window and trickle down the walls and through the floor boards! She was not going to let that happen.

Another clap of thunder, much nearer this time, gave her such a shock, she stopped in her tracks and had to take a deep breath before leaning out to pull the shutters of the big window in Daniel's bedroom. As she did so, she noticed that large drops of rain had begun to fall and remembered that she had thrown the straw mat from the front porch onto the paved path to dry in the morning sun. She had to get it in before it was soaked by the rain.

Running down stairs, she opened the front door and there, coming in the gate, his head bowed against the rain that was heavier now, was Daniel. Margaret called out his name, and as he came up the steps, he looked up, saw her, and dropped his things in the porch.

Stepping inside the door, he reached for her and embraced her as she wept with relief. They said little, but released from the restraints they had placed upon themselves for months, they could at last express their deepest feelings and the sweetness of the moment was beyond imagining.

Daniel had been so astonished to see her in the doorway, he followed her around as though he expected her to vanish from his sight, and each time she stood near him, she would put out her hand and touch him as if to reassure herself he was really there. The rain came down heavily and completely ruined the old straw mat, but no one noticed its untimely demise.

That night, as they sat before the fire on the couch, saying all those things that lovers suddenly discover they have to say to one another, things which had been hitherto left unsaid, Margaret's spirits rose to a new level of lightness as she told him of young Mark Armitage and her reason for escaping to the cottage.

He laughed then and teased her. "You could have put him out of his misery. Why did you not tell him you were already spoken for?" he asked, to which she replied quietly, "How could I? I was not sure that I was; we had not spoken of it," to which he replied, "Because, my darling, I could not speak of it, I could not ask you, not morally, not legally; I had no right while Helène lived to make you an offer of marriage. Nor did I wish to invite you to participate in what would have been an adulterous relationship." A little startled by his forthright words, she was silent and he thought he saw tears in her eyes, which required some very particular reassurance on his part, reaffirming his love for her, that occupied them for quite some time, albeit very pleasantly.

It wasn't difficult then for him to say what he had meant to ask her later that night, "Margaret, if I were to tell you now how very dearly I love you and ask you to be my wife, what would you say?" She sat up and smiled at him as if she thought he was teasing her, but seeing the serious look in his eyes, she said, "I would have to say, 'thank you, yes, I think I would like that very much, Daniel.'"

They pledged their love even as the lightning continued to dance on the mountains and the storm raged around the valley.

Later, Daniel asked, "Now, my love, I know you are afraid of storms and dislike sleeping alone in the midst of one. You told me so the last time we had one of these and decided to sleep down here. So where do you propose to sleep tonight?" This leading question she answered without equivocation, "I think I should like to sleep in your room tonight, Daniel, if I may." There was never any doubt of his response. "Of course you may, if you are quite certain?" he said, to which she replied, "I am, yes, absolutely certain."

In the days that followed, Margaret thought often about the decision she had made that night; a decision she knew would change utterly her life and her relationship with Daniel. Yet, the more she thought about it, the more certain she was of her feelings and the rightness of her judgment, that it was time to let Daniel see how she felt and to learn what his love could mean for her.

Awaking on the morrow and looking at him, she had seen the delight in his eyes as he regarded her. Her vivid recollections of his gentle tenderness as he matched her passion and his strength as he let her feel how deeply he loved her, filled her with a rich sense of sharing love and belonging together; it was an experience such as she had never known nor could have imagined before.

Over the days they spent together, the love they had shared became part of everything they did; as they talked and laughed and loved each other in many tiny ways, Margaret recognised that it had transformed their relationship and enriched her life.

Chapter Twenty-Three

I T WAS TIME TO tell her family, Margaret and Daniel agreed, and decided they would travel to Delaford parsonage on the Friday following. Margaret wrote to her sister to advise her of their visit, but first, she insisted, they must tell Claire and Nicholas. Thereafter, she wished to have Daniel meet her landlady, Mrs Hopkins.

Mr and Mrs Wilcox were delighted with the news that their friends were engaged. They admitted that they had hoped, right from the first days when they had all met in the south of France, but could not be certain. "You were both so good at concealing your feelings; we did suspect something was afoot, and we spoke of it, but we had no notion of your intentions," Claire complained, and Margaret was quick to explain it away by saying, "That was because we were not quite sure ourselves." The couple were pleased indeed that their secret had been so well concealed.

While they had not fixed a date for the wedding, since Margaret's family had yet to be consulted, they were already making their plans. Margaret revealed that she had resolved to conclude her teaching at the school by midsummer, and they would take a house on the outskirts of Oxford, which would enable Daniel to work at his college, while she taught pupils privately and continued with her writing. With her first book, *A Country Childhood*, being published at the end of summer, Margaret was already working on a second—about the many pleasures of travelling in Provence.

The Wilcoxes were happy to be assured that these plans would mean that Daniel and Margaret would remain in their neighbourhood and the intimate association between them could continue into the future, of which they were given many assurances, for were it not for Claire and Mr Wilcox, the pair might never have met. "We owe as much of our happiness to you and Nicholas, as we do to the magic of Provence," said Margaret to her friend, setting a seal upon their friendship.

As to Mr Mark Armitage, he was yet to learn from his sister Mrs Hopkins that Miss Dashwood was engaged to be married to a gentleman from Oxford. Mrs Hopkins appeared both honoured and delighted to meet Daniel Brooke when he called at the house; it was, she insisted, a very special pleasure to have not only a soon-to-be-published writer lodging with her, but to discover that she was engaged to a distinguished gentleman of learning from Oxford. Her pleasure, which extended to inviting both Mr Brooke and Miss Dashwood to take afternoon tea with her in her best parlour, seemed not to be diminished by the possible disappointment that her young brother might suffer on hearing the news of Miss Dashwood's engagement to Daniel Brooke. Doubtless Mrs Hopkins, like Margaret, had assumed that her brother was of an age when the pain of disappointment would not outlast the spring.

While dispensing tea and some small cakes, Mrs Hopkins did manage to extract the information that the wedding was still some months away and likely to be in Dorset, where Miss Dashwood's family lived, and she would continue to lodge with her until the end of the school term, about which she seemed very gratified.

When Margaret's letter arrived by express at the parsonage, Elinor's rising excitement prevented her from opening it for a few minutes, whilst she considered what news it might possibly contain. But, when she had it open and read, her pleasure was too much to be contained and she rushed into her husband's study to tell him all about it.

Edward Ferrars took his position as parson at Delaford seriously, but not to the extent of letting the composition of his Sunday sermon get in the way of his wife's desire to communicate what was obviously important news. When Elinor rushed in, her face reflecting the level of excitement she felt, he put down his pen, pushed aside his notes, and leaned back in his chair. "Elinor, my dear, I see you have had a letter and I assume it brings news that cannot wait to be told. Am I right?" he asked, and his wife agreed immediately. "Indeed, Edward, it is from Margaret and she writes that Mr Daniel Brooke and she are coming to visit on Saturday. While she does not say it in so many words, the clear implication is that they are engaged and wish to consult us about arrangements for the wedding." Seeing his raised eyebrows, she added quickly, "Oh Edward, I am so happy with this news. I have been anxious about Margaret for a little while now..."

"Have you, my dear?" he interrupted. "On what grounds? With your sister Marianne, I know you had quite legitimate concerns, which are thankfully resolved now, but was not young Margaret a rock of virtue and sound common sense?" he asked. Elinor had to explain without giving too much away that Margaret had confessed to falling in love with Mr Brooke during their holiday in Provence, but had not been certain of his feelings. However, now it seemed as though everything was going to be all right, she said.

But Edward had another question; did Elinor not think that it was Mrs Dashwood who should be applied to by Mr Brooke for permission to marry Margaret, he asked, and was quite surprised to hear her say, in a very matter-of-fact voice, "Mama? No indeed, I doubt that Margaret would stand for that. She is almost twenty-two years old, Edward, and entitled to decide whom she will marry. No doubt they will inform Mama, as a matter of courtesy, but I do not believe that Mr Brooke is coming here to ask for my consent; most likely they both wish to ask you to marry them at Delaford church and to fix upon a suitable date."

Edward was quite incredulous. "Do you really think so? Would not Mr Brooke wish to ask his distinguished friend Dr Grantley to officiate at his wedding? He is, after all, a most eminent theologian and they could be married by him at St John's in Oxford, rather than our little parish church," he said, but his modesty was misplaced and his wife was to be proved right.

When Margaret and Daniel Brooke arrived, they were received with congratulations and warm affection and, as they celebrated the news of their engagement with a glass of wine, the couple revealed that they did wish to be married at Delaford by Edward, with just a few friends and family around them. Edward, mightily pleased to be so distinguished, declared that he would be more than happy to marry them, and the date was fixed for the last Saturday in July.

"Have you written to Mama? Do you not intend to call on her?" asked Elinor, a little concerned that Mrs Dashwood, when she heard of their plans, might blame her, Elinor, for not keeping her mother informed of developments in Margaret's life. The fact that she had neither met Daniel Brooke nor knew of his intentions might well prove to be a shock, she thought, and advised Margaret to write directly to their mother and possibly arrange to call on her with Daniel without further delay.

"You do not want to upset Mama, which I know she will be, were she to learn of your engagement from someone else," she warned. But Margaret was quite sanguine about it. "I shall write to Mama right away, Elinor; we have not the time to travel to Devon just now. But, if it were at all possible for you to invite Mama to Delaford, we could certainly call on her here. There's plenty of time, since the wedding is not until the end of July," she said. Daniel Brooke added that he intended to write to Mrs Dashwood anyway, as was proper, so she would not be left in ignorance. "I had already decided to communicate with Mrs Dashwood, and since I have not had the pleasure of meeting her, I have waited only to ask your counsel, Mrs Ferrars, before putting pen to paper," he confessed, and Elinor assured him that would be quite appropriate.

It was while they were thus engaged in discussing wedding plans and Elinor made a note of Margaret's favourite hymns, that a large carriage drew up at the gate, and on looking out they saw alighting Mrs Jennings, her daughter Mrs Charlotte Palmer, and her two children, together with their governess and Charlotte's maid. "Good heavens!" Elinor exclaimed. "This is a most unexpected visit. I wonder what on earth could have happened? Something very extraordinary has either occurred or is about to occur. Mrs Jennings and Charlotte look very agitated indeed!"

Before anyone could say anything more, the maid had opened the door and admitted the ladies and their entourage, and Mrs Jennings and her daughter burst into the sitting room in a state of high excitement. Ignoring the presence of Margaret and Mr Brooke, who had withdrawn discreetly to the alcove at the far end of the room, they made straight for the large sofa by the fireplace, and Mrs Jennings announced in strident tones, "Mrs Ferrars, you will not believe a word of this and I shall not blame you if you do not, but I must tell you it is absolutely true, for I have it on the best possible authority: I understand Sir John Middleton is to marry again."

"What?" Elinor's exclamation did not adequately express the sense of shock she felt at hearing Mrs Jennings's words; she was left speechless because nothing they had heard before or since the death of Lady Middleton had suggested such a possibility. Sir John, a bluff, hearty sportsman with a kindly disposition and a well-known partiality for wine and good company, had no reputation as a ladies' man, nor had any lady been mentioned in that connection, who might be a possible candidate as the next Lady Middleton.

But both Mrs Jennings and Charlotte Palmer were quite adamant. When Edward asked, "How do you know this, Mrs Jennings?" both women answered almost together, "We are absolutely certain, Mr Ferrars," and Mrs Jennings continued, "We had it from the wife of the clerk of Sir John's lawyer, who has been summoned to Barton Park, presumably, to make changes to Sir John Middleton's will."

"Mama fears that he may be about to deprive her two dear grandchildren of their inheritance, the poor little things," said Charlotte, dabbing at her eyes, and Elinor, who had never been able to regard the spoilt Middleton children as "poor little things," realised what it was that had got Mrs Jennings and her daughter so upset. The prospect of a second Lady Middleton stepping in between Sir John's estate and the two Middleton children must be disturbing to their aunt and grandmother, she thought.

But she was unwilling to enter the controversy, and let Edward carry the argument, which he did, logically and calmly. "But you cannot be certain of that, Mrs Palmer," he argued reasonably. "Sir John may wish to make some innocuous alterations to his will that have nothing to do with marriage at all. Besides, why would he disadvantage his own children? Come now, Mrs Jennings, if that is all the evidence you have, I for one would be most reluctant to believe that Sir John, who is an exceedingly sensible gentleman, is about to do anything as rash as you suggest."

"Oh but, Mr Ferrars, I assure you that is not all," said Mrs Jennings, in the tone and manner of one who is possessed of a trump card and is about to play it. "We have also learned from another source, one who must remain nameless, that Sir John has had all my late daughter's jewellery placed in a safety deposit box at his bank." Edward laughed, "Has he? Well, I would have to say that is certainly the act of a very sensible man who is conscious of the need to store such valuables in a safe place, do you not agree?"

At this point Elinor found her voice and said, "Mama did say, when we were last there, that Sir John had been very concerned about reports of burglaries in some parts of the county. Perhaps he only wished to ensure that Lady Middleton's jewels were safely stored in the bank and thereby not at any risk from burglars."

Mrs Jennings harrumphed, clearly unimpressed, and Charlotte Palmer dabbed at her eyes again before declaring, "Mama thinks he is getting all my sister's jewels valued, prior to giving them to his second wife as a bridal gift!"

Edward realised that this was a battle he was not going to win; it was getting far too complicated and the two ladies would produce arguments, however illogical, to counter every sensible proposition he made. He did, however, indicate that nothing he knew of Sir John Middleton's character would indicate that he was likely to act in such a way and urged the ladies not to be overanxious.

Elinor had slipped out to order tea, and only then did Charlotte Palmer stand up and notice Margaret and Daniel seated quietly in the alcove. She gave a little shriek. "Miss Margaret! Oh my Lord, you did give me a start, sitting there so quiet. Why didn't you say something?" and before Margaret could even open her mouth to utter a single word, Mrs Jennings had turned around and, regarding them with a look of astonishment, said, "Miss Margaret? Oh my goodness! I had no idea there was anyone there—you sneaky little thing! Well, I am happy to see you looking so well, and who, pray, is your handsome gentleman friend? You modern young women are quite beyond me!" at which Margaret came forward to greet both women and Edward had the presence of mind to introduce Mr Daniel Brooke as "a friend of mine from Oxford." The mention of Oxford may have intimidated the ladies somewhat, for they said no more, and when Daniel stepped forward and bowed politely, they looked him over and both ladies appeared to lose interest in him thereafter. Doubtless they did not believe that Margaret could have any connection with a gentleman from Oxford.

Tea was served and, having partaken of it, they left, still shaking their heads about the activities of Sir John Middleton, although just before they entered the carriage, Mrs Palmer did say, in a complaining sort of voice, "I shall tell Mr Palmer that you don't agree with Mama and me, Mr Ferrars; he won't mind, he probably doesn't believe a word of it either, but then he is always so droll about such matters!"

Edward returned wearing a huge smile. "I knew that Mr Palmer had a good deal more sense than his wife or his mother-in-law," he said, and both Elinor and Margaret said in unison, "But, Edward, he is always so droll!" and they all exploded in laughter.

❧

Daniel Brooke had been a little nervous when he approached Elinor the next morning as she sat reading in the sitting room; he had arranged to consult her about the letter he planned to write to Mrs Dashwood, and she had appeared perfectly agreeable. Yet, he could not help a certain degree of discomfort when he went in to see her, even though she looked up and greeted him cordially. "Ah Daniel, do come in," she said, putting away her book, and added, "Edward and Margaret have gone into the village with a donation of books for the parish school. They do appreciate it very much at this time; they are preparing for the new term."

Daniel indicated that he had thought it might be a good time to talk about that letter he intended to write to Mrs Dashwood and she agreed, "Of course; and what do you want to know from me? I can tell you, and I am sure Margaret will support me, that our mother is perhaps one of the most easygoing women I know, and once you say that Margaret and you love each other, you will have little difficulty convincing her that you should be married."

He laughed softly and said, "That is certainly very comforting, but are you quite sure? I do not know how much Margaret has told you about me, but—" Sensing his embarrassment, Elinor stopped him in midsentence. "Daniel, Margaret has told me everything I needed to know to understand the unhappy situation in which both of you were placed. I know of your marriage and the sad loss of your children that caused your wife's long illness, and that you loved and supported her through it for many years. I am deeply sorry for your tragic loss and understand your feelings. I know also that when Margaret and you met in Provence last year, and you revealed these matters to her, Margaret accepted it, despite her feelings for you. It is to your great credit that you were honest and open with her from the start."

Daniel said, almost as if he were talking to himself, "That is true, but would your mother see it in the same light? How would I convince her that I was worthy of her daughter…" and Elinor intervened, "Mama does not have to know, Daniel. Margaret tells me that only your close friend Dr Grantley knew your situation. I would advise that you let it remain so. Margaret and you met in France and fell in love; that is all my mother needs to know. For the rest, your reputation as a scholar and a historian, not to mention a tour guide *par excellence*, will soon be known to her and will inform her judgment of you," she said with a smile, clearly hoping to reassure him.

Regarding her with some concern, he asked, "And you do not feel constrained to question any aspect of my conduct?"

To which she smiled and replied, "Which part of your conduct must I question? That you were faithful and caring toward your ailing wife for several years? Or that last autumn you fell in love with my sister? I am aware from what Margaret has told me that throughout her tour of Provence, you made no direct approach to her—"

This time it was his turn to interrupt, "Indeed I did not; I tried at first to discourage her interest in me, but Margaret is very hard to resist, and when it became apparent that she was developing a particular partiality for me, I had to tell her the truth, so she should not be hurt later. I admit I had already fallen in love with her and it was too late for me, but, Mrs Ferrars, please believe me, I did not encourage her affection, nor make her an offer of marriage that I had no right to make while Helène lived. It would have been unpardonable!"

Elinor nodded. "I know and I commend you, even though I know it was very difficult for Margaret. She is young and knew only that she loved you; it was entirely right that you made her no offer of marriage until you were free to do so. But, since circumstances have changed and you are both free to do as you wish, I cannot see any impediment."

He had one more question. "May I ask—and forgive me, this may seem an impertinence—does Reverend Ferrars know?" he asked, and Elinor read the anxiety in his eyes and answered kindly, "He does not, not at the moment; but I will explain the circumstances to him, in time, and knowing my husband to be a compassionate man, I am sure his view will not be very different from mine. But no other member of my family will hear of it from me. I give you my word."

He thanked her then and left to write his letter.

Later that afternoon, Daniel and Margaret walked in the Delaford woods, where she showed him some of the places she had frequented as a young girl, often spending many hours alone among the splendid stands of trees that were the pride of Colonel Brandon's estate. In a particularly beautiful grove of oaks, which stood beside a clear running stream, they spent some quiet hours together while he told her of his conversation with Elinor.

"Your sister is one of the wisest people I have met and perhaps the kindest, as well," he said, and she agreed as he went on, "I had to confess that I had fallen in love with you, but could say nothing because I had no right to do so and indeed, I tried to discourage you because I feared—" She put her hand up to his lips to stop him then and said gently, "I know, Daniel, and that is why I knew I could trust you and love you without reservation. Elinor knows that, too, because I told her many months ago, before you returned from France." It was the kind of innocent sincerity that he had found irresistible.

He told her then, how very early in their acquaintance he had been attracted to the spirited young lady with the lovely open countenance and an insatiable thirst for learning.

"It was hard to believe that you were real! I had not met anyone with so much energy and such a genuine desire to learn, much less a charming, intelligent young lady with such a passion; there are no ladies at Oxford, you know, and to a scholar and a teacher like me, it was quite seductive," he admitted, opening himself to her inevitable question.

"And when did you discover that you wanted to love me as well as teach me?" to which he answered without hesitation, "Almost at once; you were such a delight to teach, Margaret, and very easy to love," which declaration pleased her very well.

She told him then of her plans to use even more of what he had taught her in her new book. On his return from France, Daniel had brought her a gift: a beautifully illustrated little book of the songs of the medieval troubadours of Provence, who were credited with writing some of the most poignant and sensual love songs ever written. Since they were almost all written in the Provençal dialect, which was the language used by troubadours of the era, Daniel had translated them into modern French for her and Margaret had been deeply touched by their exquisitely moving lyrics. It had stimulated her own interest in the troubadours, and she planned to include them in her book on travels through Provence.

But, curious as to why he had not spoken of them when they were travelling in Provence last autumn, she asked, "Why did you not mention them? Did you not think I would be interested in the troubadours' songs?" He looked directly at her and said, "I think, Margaret, you know the answer to that question." And when she looked genuinely puzzled, he said, "How should I have introduced you to the love songs of the troubadours, while trying to pretend that I was not in love with you? It was hard enough when we were only visiting abbeys and churches and talking of sacred music." She smiled then and said, with an unusual archness of tone, "And were you trying also to keep me from falling in love with you?"

His voice almost broke as he replied, "Indeed, I was, although I was not so vain as to believe it was the case; you are so much younger than I am... nevertheless, there was a risk and it would have been quite unconscionable, in the circumstances, to promote it."

Margaret said softly, "I do understand and I am delighted that now you have given me a whole book of these beautiful love songs; but, Daniel, if I am to write about them, I shall need you to read them to me and tell me more about them and show me where they were composed and by whom. Will you?"

"It will be my greatest pleasure, and I shall read them to you as often as you wish," he said and promised that when they returned to Provence, after they were married, they could spend as much time as she wished on the troubadours and their exquisite lyrics, a pledge that brought tears—tears that could now be swiftly countered with the promise of happiness to come.

After a few more splendid days at Delaford, spent in the happiest way possible, with the family at the parsonage and their friends Dr Bradley King and his wife, Daniel and Margaret returned to Oxford to make their plans, leaving Edward and Elinor to ponder a number of interesting propositions. It had been a special pleasure for them to see how well Daniel Brooke was accepted by Dr King and his wife. Helen King had congratulated Elinor on her brother-in-law to be, saying that Dr King had declared him to be a most remarkable scholar in his field. To Elinor he was all those things, but most importantly, he was the man with whom she hoped her sister would find true contentment.

As they retired to bed that night, Elinor turned to her husband and said,

"I do like Daniel, don't you?" to which he replied, "I do indeed, my love—he is an authority in his field, but, happily, he is also a thoroughly modest, amiable fellow. But you do realise they are already lovers, do you not?" Completely taken aback, she said nothing for a minute, then asked, "However did you deduce that?" He laughed and replied, "It wasn't difficult. They hardly leave each other's side, if it can be helped, and I did observe a particular closeness between them, which must signify a level of intimacy in their relationship. Do you not agree?"

"Do you disapprove?" asked his wife, a little nervously, and Edward put away his book before responding, "It is not for me to approve or disapprove; Margaret and Daniel are mature enough to make such decisions for themselves. I asked if you had noticed, because I had hoped Margaret had confided in you and that you had counselled her," he said, and she realised how deeply he had considered the matter, with Margaret's interest at heart. Elinor admitted that she had advised her sister, but had tried not to be overbearing or censorious about it, which her husband assured her she could never be.

But Elinor too had a question to resolve. "I did wonder why it was that I was willing to accept Daniel so readily, to believe the best of him on such short acquaintance, and yet I was always wary of Willoughby. Even when he was presenting himself at his best, visiting our home at Barton Cottage and wooing Marianne like a gentleman of honour throughout that summer, I had certain reservations about him, for which I was severely censured by Mama and Marianne. Why do you suppose my responses were so markedly different, Edward?" she asked and his answer gave her the explanation in simple terms.

"Because, my dearest, as you have correctly judged, Daniel Brooke is quite clearly a man one can trust; he is open and forthright, a man who is a gentleman and a scholar. Whereas Willoughby—well, as we have seen many times over, he is a fraud, a pretentious nobody, a contemptible deceiver."

There was no more to be said.

Two letters brought more surprises for Elinor the following week.

One from Marianne, posted in Paris, informed her sister that Colonel Brandon and she were extending their tour to take in a couple of other cities in France and would therefore not be back at Delaford until the middle of June.

In a brief paragraph, Marianne said again that they were both enjoying their holiday in France very much and declared that she was happier than she had been in years.

Relieved, Elinor turned to her other correspondent, whose exceedingly expensive perfumed note paper was quite new to her. It bore a London postmark, and the writing was unfamiliar, too. "Who can it be?" she thought as she broke the seal and opened up two sheets of paper, closely written in a very cultivated hand. Turning swiftly to the second page, Elinor looked for the writer's name and was bewildered to see that it came from Fanny Dashwood, wife of their half brother, John.

Elinor's reaction was due chiefly to the fact that in all the years that Fanny had been married to John Dashwood, she had never found it necessary to write to her or her sisters. She recalled a very brief formal note written on black bordered notepaper, received by her mother on the death of her husband, but no more. Any further communication between them had been through Fanny's husband, John, or Edward, who was Fanny's younger brother.

This sudden compulsion to write a letter two pages long must have been provoked by some quite portentous event, thought Elinor, as she began to read. Fanny wrote:

Dear Elinor,

I trust that Edward and you are well and enjoying the benefits of country life, albeit in a county far removed from where you grew up and many miles from London. We remind ourselves daily of our great good fortune that we live in salubrious Sussex and can travel to London within a couple of hours if we choose.

However, it is not to discuss such trivialities that I write, but to ask if you can either confirm or deny a most disturbing rumour that has been circulating in London this last week. I had it first from my brother Robert, whose wife, Lucy, had heard it when they were dining with Mrs Jennings and the Palmers, and if the truth were told, I gave it no credit at all. Both Mrs J and Lucy are wont to listen to any story and repeat it ad nauseam, without ascertaining its veracity.

However, two days later, to my amazement, my husband, John, returned from his club with the very same tale, which caused me to take some notice. It concerns Sir John Middleton of Barton Park—who, I recall, is related to your mother's family—he is a widower now since the untimely death of his wife last year. Well, the news around town is that he plans to marry again, although no one knows who the lady is. Elinor, it really does not signify whether Sir John Middleton remarries or not, but we are from time to time invited to receptions at his house in London and occasionally to a weekend shooting party at Barton Park. If we are to continue the acquaintance, I should very much wish to have some information about the person who is to be the next Lady Middleton, before I am called upon to accept or refuse the next invitation. I wonder if I could prevail on you or perhaps on Mrs Dashwood, since she lives on the estate, to undertake some discreet enquiries and discover the details of the lady's name, age, family antecedents, etc., etc.

I often find that butlers and valets are usually well informed on such matters.

The writer carried on for another sentence or two, but Elinor could not be bothered to continue reading. She put it down, still puzzled by the rumour, but far more disgusted by the snobbery and furtive curiosity of her sister-in-law, who had hoped to recruit her or her mother to obtain information about Sir John Middleton's private affairs from members of his household staff.

When Edward returned, she showed him his sister's letter and was gratified to hear him roundly condemn her. "I cannot imagine why Fanny is concerned; Sir John is nothing to them, and whom he chooses to marry is entirely a matter for him. As for trying to get you to discover his secret, I hope, my dear, that you have given her short shrift. It is none of our business, nor should it be of hers," he said and threw the letter down on the table in the study before going upstairs to change for dinner.

"My sentiments exactly," said Elinor as she followed him up the stairs, pleased at his response, "and I do not intend to do anything at all about Fanny's request. If she wishes to discover whom Sir John plans to marry—and I suppose there may be some truth to this story, seeing that it is gaining currency in London, where Sir John has many friends—Fanny can ask him herself."

Edward laughed. "And I must admit that I would not put it past her to do so. Fanny has become so consumed with matters of family prestige and social status, she fails to see how ridiculous she looks. You are right, though, the story, which sounded rather farfetched when Mrs Jennings talked about it the other day, does appear to have gained some ground. I wonder who the lady could be. But, whoever it is, as I said before, it is none of our business," he concluded.

"Amen to that," said his wife, and that, they thought, would be that.

On the very next day, however, it became their business in no uncertain terms.

Edward Ferrars, when he was a very young man, had often had cause to wonder whether he belonged at all in the strange mix of characters that constituted his family. He'd had very little knowledge of his father, having been sent away to school at a very early age; his mother had always seemed remote and unfeeling; his sister Fanny was recognisably grasping and uncharitable; while his brother Robert had grown up spoilt and selfish.

That Edward had never satisfied his family's ambitions for him, refusing to consider careers in the military or in Parliament and insisting on becoming a clergyman had set him apart from them, and with his marriage to Elinor Dashwood, that separation had been complete.

A letter received from his brother, Robert, was not therefore as astonishing to him as it might have been had their relationship been closer. In it, Robert disclosed that his wife, Lucy, had heard of the imminent remarriage of Sir John Middleton from Mrs Jennings and had been somewhat put out by the news, because there had been plans afoot (Edward assumed these were plans initiated by either Lucy or Mrs Jennings or both) to promote a match between Sir John and Lucy's elder sister, Anne, who was as yet unmarried and well on the way to being a regular old maid. Mrs Jennings had been angling for some time to obtain an invitation for Miss Anne Steele to Barton Park, and while none had been forthcoming, she was hopeful it could still be arranged for next Christmas. Robert asked if Edward knew or could discover through the good offices of his wife or his mother-in-law, Mrs Dashwood, who was Sir John's cousin, whether there was any truth in the rumour. He wrote:

> *If you could, my dear brother, I would consider it to be a great favour, since it would enable me to extricate myself from the unending chatter that this*

tale has aroused in the family and enjoy some peace and quiet, which at present I can only find at my club.

Greatly diverted by this request, Edward was about to take his letter out to the garden, where Elinor had spent most of the afternoon, attending to her roses. He was sure she would be as entertained by Robert's concerns as he had been, but before he could share it with her, he saw the carriage from Barton Park coming up the road and stopped to alert Elinor, who stood up and brushed twigs and leaves from her skirts and took off her gardening gloves, as she prepared to receive their welcome though unexpected visitors.

Alighting from the carriage was Sir John Middleton himself, who then assisted Mrs Dashwood out and ordered his servant to attend to the luggage. As Edward and Elinor looked on, uncomprehending, the man unloaded two trunks and carried them into the house, where they were placed in the hall, while Sir John—who seemed to be in remarkably good humour—and Mrs Dashwood greeted them with great affection.

As they went indoors, Elinor was still wondering what it was all about; she'd had no message from her mother about their intention to visit, nor had Edward heard from Sir John. And what of the two trunks? They obviously contained her mother's belongings; could it be that all the stories were true? Sir John *was* getting married and he'd brought Mrs Dashwood back to them, because she was no longer needed to manage his household at Barton Park? As the thought crossed her mind, Elinor glanced at her mother and discarded it instantly, for Mrs Dashwood did not have the appearance of one who had been summarily evicted from her preferred accommodation at all—indeed, she was all smiles.

They had moved into the sitting room, and Elinor was about to send for the maid to order tea, when Sir John said, "I think we must have something a little stronger than tea, Edward—a glass of sherry, perhaps, if you do not have any champagne to hand."

Edward and Elinor exchanged glances, Sir John laughed heartily, and Mrs Dashwood smiled. There being no champagne to hand at the parsonage, Edward was quick to get out the best sherry, and when they had their glasses filled, Sir John said, "Well now, Edward and Elinor, you are the first to know that my dear cousin Mary, your beautiful mama, has done me the great honour of accepting my proposal to become my wife."

He smiled and continued, "Needless to say, this has made me very happy indeed, and we thought we had to come over directly and tell you ourselves, because it just would not do if someone read it in *The Times* tomorrow and told you of it. Besides, we had to bring some of her things over, because, as I am sure you would agree, it would not be seemly, now we are engaged, for the lady to remain under my roof, as it were, until we are married."

Amazed, Elinor hesitated only a minute or two before embracing her mother and turning to Sir John, with whom Edward was shaking hands as though in a dream. "Of course I am delighted, but when did this happen?" she asked, and Sir John laughed and Mrs Dashwood blushed and said it had come about over the last few weeks and they had hardly been aware of it because they had been so busy.

Sir John explained further, "But a few days ago, when we were at dinner, your mama mentioned a letter from you, Elinor, inviting her to travel to Weymouth with you in the summer, and suddenly it struck me that one of these days, she could decide to leave Barton Park altogether and I realised how very much I would miss her if she went. Our lives have been so much more enjoyable with her there; I simply could not imagine how I would get on without her. So, I gave it some thought and I decided to ask her to marry me." Sir John looked across at the lady then, and it was obvious from her countenance that she was completely satisfied with his version of the events that had led to their engagement. Mrs Dashwood wore the perfectly serene smile of a contented woman.

While neither Elinor nor Edward had much understanding of how this had come about, what was plain was the obvious satisfaction of the couple. Both Sir John and Mrs Dashwood had the look of people who had done exactly as they had pleased.

Later that evening, after they had dined, Sir John left to return to Barton Park, and Elinor took her mother upstairs to the spare room. Believing she was tired and would welcome an early night, Elinor was about to leave, when Mrs Dashwood asked a little tentatively, "You are not displeased with me, are you, my dear?" Elinor swung round, "Displeased with you? Of course not. Mama, what right have I to be displeased with you? You are as entitled to find happiness as Marianne or I have, and I am very pleased for you. But, Mama, are you quite sure this is what you want?" she asked.

Mrs Dashwood smiled and said, "Of course I am. Sir John is a dear, kind, generous man; he is my cousin and I have known him all my life, we get on together like the best of friends. Besides, Marianne and the colonel are happily settled now, and I believe our dear Margaret has had an offer from a very nice gentleman from Oxford—he has written me a most charming letter—and she plans to accept him. So, I did feel it was time I thought of my own future; and Elinor, my dear girl, only think, it will be just like being at dear old Norland again, except of course, I shall be Lady Middleton."

She said it with such genuine glee that Elinor was startled for a moment, before she laughed and hugged her mother. She could not wait for the morrow, when she would write to John and Fanny and break the news of the impending marriage of Sir John Middleton and Mrs Dashwood.

Despite the fact that the notice would have already appeared in *The Times*, she intended to write to John and Fanny herself. Elinor had but one regret: She would not be present to see Fanny's face when she read the letter.

END OF PART FIVE

An Epilogue...

THROUGHOUT THE SUMMER, THE consequences of the announcement
in *The Times* of the engagement of Sir John Middleton of Barton Park in
Devonshire to his widowed cousin, Mrs Mary Dashwood, continued to rever-
berate like rolling thunder around the various families: the Ferrars, the Steeles,
the Dashwoods, Mrs Jennings and Mrs Palmer and their coterie of friends and
relations, all of whom felt the need to make some comment, mostly adverse,
about the couple.

It caused such a storm in the household of John and Fanny Dashwood, they
even attempted to dissuade the pair from proceeding with their marriage plans
by suggesting in a most foolhardy manner that they had "rushed into it without
due consideration of their responsibilities to look after the interest of the next
generation" and warning of the possibility of "bad blood between members of
the Middleton clan" were the marriage to take place.

It was clearly Fanny's relentless nagging that had driven her husband to
write. While Mrs Dashwood paid very little attention to a note from John,
suggesting that she would be blamed by Sir John Middleton's relations for
intruding into his family, a similar missive addressed to Sir John himself,
pointing out his "responsibilities to his family," caused him to laugh uproari-
ously and declare in his reply to John Dashwood that *"the next generation of
my family is so well looked after that they will soon have forgotten how to look after*

themselves," adding that he was now *"fast approaching that age when a man had to consider how best to ensure that he would be well looked after for the rest of his life."* To this vital question, he said, he had *"given due consideration and reached the conclusion that marriage to his amiable cousin Mrs Dashwood, whom he had known and had regarded with affection for many years, would best secure that object."* And he was *"delighted and honoured that she had agreed and accepted his proposal."* That riposte silenced the glum John Dashwood, but not his loquacious wife, Fanny, who would continue to tell anyone and everyone she met how shocking it was that Sir John had abandoned his duty to his family and married an impoverished widow, who must have taken her chance to get her hands on his money. Between Fanny and her mother, Mrs Ferrars, the reputations of both Sir John Middleton and his prospective bride were well shredded.

Robert and Lucy Ferrars, who had been involved in a plan initiated by Mrs Jennings to ensnare Sir John for Lucy's sister, Anne, were disappointed, more on account of the fact that Lucy and Robert feared they would have to be responsible for looking after Miss Steele into the future, if she remained forever unwed.

For Lucy, there would also have been the advantage of another large country estate to visit, apart from those of her mother-in-law, Mrs Ferrars, and her sister-in-law, Fanny, who never failed to remind her of her great good fortune in marrying Robert Ferrars and thereby getting her feet on the rungs of the social ladder, although she was constantly warned never to assume that she would reach their elevated situation.

As for Miss Anne Steele, she had very little knowledge about Sir John Middleton, and though she would certainly have liked to have the distinction of being "Lady Middleton" and thereby a cut above her sister, Lucy, she had never quite believed that the plan would actually come to pass. She'd seen many similar schemes proposed and fall apart before. Her disappointment was therefore qualified by her lack of confidence in the proposition, and not quite as profound as that of her sister.

The outrage of Mrs Jennings and her daughter Charlotte Palmer was perhaps the most comprehensible; the sudden death of Lady Middleton had deprived them of their place in the world of the titled class, with all the rank and prestige that it added to mere money, of which Mrs Jennings had plenty. If Sir John had remained a widower or married Anne Steele, they would have been guaranteed their share of his hospitality and status, but his marriage to Mrs Dashwood, who was no relation of theirs, would, they feared, rob them of that advantage. It would be a serious blow to their social standing as well as an irritating setback to their plans to spend Christmas in Devonshire that year, enjoying the convivial atmosphere of Barton Park.

Only Mr Palmer, who claimed to have met the happy pair shopping in Exeter, made light of all their complaints and grievances, with the genuinely droll observation that if marriage was an institution meant to make people happy, then it was surely a pleasure to see one in which both parties seemed so thoroughly pleased with each other, their felicity was assured. He reported also that several of Sir John's friends, who had met Mrs Dashwood, had pronounced her to be a most charming and amiable lady, and declared that Sir John had been singularly fortunate in his choice of a second wife.

While the groans of the malcontents resounded through the social scene, the people primarily concerned went on with their lives, unperturbed. Sir John Middleton himself, blissfully ignorant of the machinations of some in his circle, maintained a cheerful countenance whenever he met any of these disgruntled parties, content to bask in the certain pleasure of marriage to a mostly compliant and agreeable woman, whom he had known all his life.

Mrs Dashwood was not only well pleased with her forthcoming union to Sir John, a man she had regarded with gratitude and genuine affection for several years, she was happy too because she no longer feared that in the onset of what might be termed her "advanced years" she would become a burden upon her daughters and their husbands. While she knew well that neither Edward Ferrars nor Colonel Brandon would ever begrudge her any assistance or comfort, nor did she fear any disquiet from her daughters, she did feel a good deal better knowing that she would never have to call on them for such support in the future.

She enjoyed very much making plans for her own wedding but also looked forward to assisting with Margaret's. Once she and Sir John had met Daniel Brooke, neither had any doubt that Margaret, of all the Dashwood girls, would have the most eminent husband, for though neither Sir John nor Mrs Dashwood could boast of any academic achievement, they had great respect for learning, and a learned gentleman from Oxford was worthy of their highest regard.

Margaret, on learning the news of her mother's engagement, had experienced a great sense of relief, for she had always been concerned that her mother might, on an impulse, do something she would later regret Margaret knew her mother would never regret marrying Sir John Middleton; they had a great deal in common, including an ability to live in the present and enjoy its bounty, which their generous natures enabled them to share with others. It was clear to her that her mother was as happy as she had ever been since they lived at Norland Park and a good deal happier than she had been at Barton Cottage, where Mrs Dashwood had struggled to maintain the social position her family had lost with the death of her husband and the loss of his estate.

Now, with the prospect of being the mistress of Barton Park, her dignity and sense of self-worth had been restored, nay enhanced, with the addition of a title as well. Margaret contemplated the prospect of her mama's elevation to being "Lady Middleton" with a good deal of amusement, which she was able to share with Daniel.

A keen observer of the human condition, Daniel had found both Mrs Dashwood and Sir John Middleton quite agreeable, if a little eccentric, while his response to the bizarre behaviour of Mrs Jennings and Charlotte Palmer had been one of complete bewilderment. "I had almost forgotten that people actually held such views," he had said, and Margaret had laughed and assured him that there were those among her family connections, such as Mrs Ferrars and Fanny Dashwood, whose opinions were far more ludicrous than those of Mrs Jennings. "They are both women with high notions of their own importance and if entertainment is what you wish for, there is much to be had at very little cost, in observing them," she had said, causing Daniel to declare that he was unsure whether he should look forward to the experience or strive strenuously to avoid it.

When, in mid-June, Marianne and Colonel Brandon returned, having heard the happy news from both Sir John and Mrs Dashwood, they persuaded her to move to live with them at Delaford Manor until the wedding, which suited everybody exceedingly well. It meant that Marianne and her mother could share their mutual happiness uninterrupted, while Sir John was free to visit his friend Colonel Brandon, shoot on his manor, and see his bride-to-be at the same time—a most convenient arrangement, indeed. That he could so happily combine his preference for sport and companionship with his romantic inclinations was a matter of great satisfaction to him.

Marianne and the colonel were even more delighted to discover that in their absence, Margaret had become engaged. Although they had no knowledge of Mr Daniel Brooke, when they met him, they approved of him without question. Marianne saw in him the kind of learned intellectual she esteemed, and the colonel found him to be a man he could engage easily in conversation and whose opinions he could respect. Both agreed that Margaret and Daniel, whose intellectual curiosity and love of learning had brought them together, were well suited.

They decreed, therefore, that their wedding, no matter how small their guest list, must be celebrated at the manor house at Delaford and, despite some earlier misgivings, Margaret was persuaded by Elinor to agree.

"It will make Mama and Marianne very happy, Margaret, and just think how pleased Colonel Brandon will be. He is such a warmhearted, generous man, he will enjoy hosting your wedding, as though you were his own daughter," she had said, and Margaret—who had earlier asked the colonel if he would give her away at the church, and seen the expression of immense satisfaction that had suffused his countenance at her request—had agreed. It meant she could be married from the manor at the Delaford church by her dear brother-in-law Edward. "It was," she declared, "quite perfect."

Margaret and Daniel had, in the intervening weeks, set about looking for a suitable house in the environs of Oxford, where she could continue her work on her next book and the instruction of her private pupils, of whom she already had five.

Despite the fact that Daniel had assured her that his income would be quite sufficient for them to live in comfort, Margaret had determined that she would not permit her study and practice of teaching to be wasted by disuse. She pursued various enquiries, was interviewed by the parents of prospective students, and made her plans, so that when they did find a house that suited them, she was able to make the arrangements necessary to begin work with them in the new year.

Margaret had set her heart on a large old house in the village of Kidlington, but Daniel had convinced her that a town house no further than two miles from the university would be more practical, pointing out that her students would also find it more convenient for travelling. Consequently their search continued until a satisfactory house was found, which suited both their purposes. "I know you love the ambience of the countryside, my love, which is why we have the cottage and can always return to the Cotswolds to restore our spirits," said Daniel, "but we both need a place conveniently situated from which to work." She agreed, and when they found it, the house they leased had the distinct advantage of a back parlour, which was ideally situated to be used as a school room for her new pupils.

If Provence was where their love had begun to grow, the cottage in the Cotswolds was where it was nurtured, blossomed, and matured. The times spent there had brought them a deeper understanding of each other and greater happiness than either had thought possible. For Daniel, Margaret had brought a freshness and vitality that he had thought he had lost forever, while the extent of his learning no less than the depth of his love for her had opened up an entirely new world of experiences for Margaret.

In all of her life so far, no other person had ever unlocked her mind or touched her heart as Daniel had done. He had added a new dimension of intellectual excitement to her existence. Always curious, always eager to learn, she had come recently to understand the kind of knowledge that Daniel could open up for her and she was profoundly grateful for it.

But Margaret had a practical streak too, which served them well. She had insisted that one of the prerequisites to her happiness was an undertaking that Daniel would work seriously on completing his book on the historic abbeys and churches of Provence.

"While I am very confident that we will be happy together, I think I shall not be truly happy, Daniel, unless I know that you intend to complete what is your life's work. Besides, I know it was one of the reasons you were in Provence last autumn, and that is what brought us together. I should like to think we could see the fulfilment of that hope. Will you give me that promise?" she asked seriously, and Daniel's fond response that he would promise her anything she asked did not satisfy her.

"Do be serious, my love, I know how much it means to you and how hard you have worked on collecting the material; I want only to see you fulfil your ambition," she pleaded.

He surrendered then and produced his plan; they would return to Provence after the wedding and he would work on the final chapters of his book, with her help. "I have the singular advantage now of a published writer to assist me," he said. When they returned to England, he would present his work to his college for review, and if they approved, it would be submitted for publication.

That seemed to please her more, especially since it was combined with the assurance of that journey by boat down the Rhône from Lyon to Avignon, which he had promised she could take, if she returned to Provence in the summer. "Did you really mean that?" she asked and was reminded that he was a man of his word. Margaret could not think of anything that would give her greater pleasure than the fulfilment of those two promises.

※

When the time came for their wedding, they insisted on the smallest possible gathering of friends and family, but were happy to have the occasion celebrated at the manor house, with a degree of style and extravagance that Colonel Brandon's generosity of spirit and Marianne's sense of occasion deemed essential.

"My dear Margaret," the colonel had said solemnly, "your mama will not be happy, nor will we be, your sister and I, if you were not to have your own wedding celebrated in proper style. Besides, it is the best possible reason for a family celebration, and since I have the highest regard for your Mr Daniel Brooke, I believe it is incumbent on us to welcome him into our family in the proper manner. Do you not agree?"

Margaret agreed completely, delighted that her Mr Brooke had been so warmly accepted by everyone who mattered to her. Sir John, with his talent for overstatement, had declared that they were honoured indeed to have a scholar of such distinction in the family, adding, "Well, I always said that Margaret was the brightest one, did I not? So it is no surprise that she has got herself the cleverest husband." Prompted by his wife to clarify his preference, lest he offend her other sons-in-law, he had assured them that he admired Edward and loved his dear friend Brandon unreservedly as well.

On their wedding day, Dr Francis Grantley and his elegant wife, Georgiana, attended, and Dr Grantley spoke most eloquently of his friend and colleague Daniel Brooke, while Edward Ferrars conducted the marriage service.

The beautiful young bride was the centre of attention, and all the traditional ceremonies of the old Dorset village were in place when the bride and groom walked out of the church, man and wife, to the cheers of the gathered guests, who included Nicholas and Claire Wilcox and some of the teachers and pupils from the seminary, to which Margaret owed so much.

After a splendid wedding breakfast, at which Margaret, seeing her family and her husband mingle happily together, was unable to restrain her tears, while her mother and both her sisters did not even try to hide theirs, the family watched with pride as the youngest Miss Dashwood departed with a degree of style and élan that could not have been anticipated those many years ago, when the death of their father had left them homeless and bereft.

Daniel and Margaret were driven away in Colonel Brandon's carriage, bound for Plymouth, from where they were due to sail on the morning tide for Marseilles and Provence.

Postscript

Winter 1820

CHRISTMAS FOUND THE DASHWOOD women together again; this time at Barton Park, for Sir John had insisted that he should be permitted to host the happy occasion of their reunion.

Despite the gloomy prognostications of certain persons in his circle, Sir John's marriage to Mrs Dashwood had been celebrated amidst much goodwill, for they both had many friends and neighbours who had reason to be grateful for the generosity of one or the cheerful kindness of the other.

Mrs Dashwood, never one to hold a grudge, had forgiven Mrs Jennings and Charlotte Palmer for their lapse in manners, and in view of the exemplary conduct of the very droll Mr Palmer, they were all invited to spend Christmas at Barton Park, where they could make amends for their past errors by praising both Sir John and his lady to excess. Besides, as Elinor whispered to her husband, she was quite certain that there was a twinkle in her mother's eye each time someone addressed her as "Lady Middleton."

But the new Lady Middleton's charitable nature did not extend to John Dashwood and his wife, Fanny, who had been seen and heard at the wedding, sniggering at the bride's elegant gown, said to have been selected from one of the best dress salons in London. Fanny had claimed it cost twice as much as her own wedding gown and was a wasteful extravagance, a remark that soon made its way back to the happy bride.

The Dashwoods' disappointment at not being invited to Barton Park at Christmas, had to be borne with patience at a far less entertaining function hosted by Fanny's mother, Mrs Ferrars, at which she spent much of her time bemoaning the fact that her son Robert's wife, Lucy, had produced not the grandson she had hoped for but a rather weak-looking little girl, whose features owed nothing to the Ferrars family and who was to be named not Constance, after her grandmother, but Clarissa, after the heroine of some romantic novel!

Clearly, Mrs Ferrars was disinclined to change her will to favour the child—a fact that pleased Fanny beyond measure. As she had done on a previous occasion, when she had dissuaded her husband, John, from materially assisting his sisters, despite a pledge made at his father's deathbed, she had argued against her mother's initial plan.

"Why would you do it?" she had asked. "Why would you impoverish our dear boy by reducing the funds available for his inheritance and handing them out to all and sundry? It makes no sense at all." Needless to say her husband agreed completely, while Robert and Lucy Ferrars felt so aggrieved, they turned down the invitation to Christmas dinner with Mrs Ferrars and elected to spend it with friends in Dawlish on the other side of the country!

Meanwhile, Edward and Elinor, Colonel Brandon and Marianne, and Margaret with Daniel Brooke had come together to celebrate Christmas in what was without doubt the most hospitable household in the county, possibly in England, for Sir John was determined that all his tenants and servants should also share in his happiness.

Among the many friends who joined them at Barton Park on Christmas Eve were Dr Bradley King and his wife, who brought apologies from their daughter, Dorothea, together with the happy news that she was spending Christmas day with the family of the young guardsman—who had finally summoned up the courage to ask her to marry him. No one was in any doubt that Dr and Mrs King were thoroughly delighted.

Also there that evening was a young woman who was known only to a few in the party: Eliza Williams, with her nine-year-old daughter, Alice. Mrs Williams, as she called herself, soberly dressed and quietly spoken, was accorded by both Sir John and Lady Middleton the same degree of attention and cordiality as all their other guests, and Elinor noted with pleasure that her sister Marianne and Colonel Brandon had brought gifts for the little girl and her mother—something that would have been unthinkable a year ago. Eliza, who had lost most of the rather petulant expression that had long blemished a pretty face, was seen accepting them with smiles and thanks that augured well, Elinor thought, for her future, as well as Marianne's peace of mind. Of Colonel Brandon's satisfaction there was no doubt, since the question of the welfare of Eliza and her daughter had been so happily settled, without in any way disconcerting his wife. Once again it was something he owed to the generosity of his friend Sir John and the genuine kindness of his wife.

Elinor had recently ascertained from her mother that Sir John was adamant that young Eliza Williams was not—contrary to the piece of petty calumny put about by Mrs Jennings—the natural daughter of Colonel Brandon. She was, he had declared emphatically, the child of the colonel's brother's wife, also Eliza, who had been monstrously mistreated by her husband and others, leaving her destitute. Colonel Brandon had been the only member of his family who had been willing to help her. It was something for which he should have been honoured, Sir John had said, not pilloried, as some stupid folk had tried to do.

Since this account confirmed that which Colonel Brandon had related to her several years ago, when Willoughby's duplicity had been first exposed, Elinor had consulted her husband and, on his advice, proceeded with some delicacy and not a little trepidation to convey this information to her sister Marianne, intending that it would quiet her previous suspicions about her husband's involvement with Eliza Williams.

To her delight, she discovered that while on their extended tour of France, following the colonel's recovery from his accident, Marianne and he had rediscovered the art of communication, and the matter of Eliza and her child had been discussed between them. Marianne, having been assured of the facts by her husband, whom she trusted implicitly, no longer harboured any suspicions or grievances against the hapless Miss Williams and her daughter.

"She has been the victim of great misfortune and cruelty, Elinor, as was her mother, and Colonel Brandon and I are determined to assist her and little Alice as best we can," Marianne had told Elinor, explaining that the colonel had planned to pay the rent for Barton Cottage and make an allowance to Eliza to enable her to live respectably and educate her daughter. It was a decision that her sister applauded.

Returning to the parsonage, Elinor had found her husband waiting for her in a state of some anxiety, but her smiling countenance had reassured him even before she spoke. "Oh Edward, it is quite the best news I have heard in many months. It is such a significant change for both Marianne and Eliza Williams. I had been afraid even to hope, because my sister was so set against the girl; this means Marianne is more confident of her own place in Colonel Brandon's affections and no longer regards Eliza with suspicion. Indeed, it's like a little miracle," she cried, and he was relieved and pleased.

Many things had changed in the course of that year.

On Christmas night, as they sat around the great dining table at Barton Park, each one had something to be grateful for. Sir John, with his wife beside him, regarded his friends and family gathered there, and was ready to admit that he was happier than he had ever expected he could be. His marriage to Mrs Dashwood had brought a different kind of felicity to that which he had enjoyed before, one that took more pleasure in the company of a loving wife and a comfortable family home, than in the pastimes of galloping around the countryside hunting and shooting and counting the number of birds in his bag.

His lifelong friend Colonel Brandon and his beautiful wife were now happily settled at Delaford and so were Edward and Elinor, who were very dear to him. But, as he had said when he raised his glass to welcome them to Barton Park for the first time as Mr and Mrs Brooke, he was proudest of the achievements of young Miss Margaret. "I always knew," he said, confident that he would not be contradicted, "that the youngest Miss Dashwood would surprise us all. And she has—in the most delightful way."

Margaret and Daniel had been married but a few months, and after some magical weeks spent in Provence, they returned with much to celebrate.

Margaret's first book, *A Country Childhood*, had been well received and her publishers had been happy to accept the manuscript of *A Provençal Journey*, but her greatest reward came from helping her husband complete his work on the ancient abbeys and churches of Provence, which was to be published by the university in the new year. Their lives were now fulfilled and in the closest harmony.

The familiar sounds of a party of carol singers in the porch caused several of the guests to leave the table and rush to the front door; Mrs Williams, the housekeeper, and her staff had brought out refreshments for the singers, who were in good voice, and many of the guests joined in the singing, led by Sir John himself. But for Edward, Elinor, and Lady Middleton, who had remained seated at the table, Margaret and Daniel had some very special news. Confirmed only this week, they were delighted to share their secret: Margaret was expecting their child next spring.

The ecstatic response with which this happy piece of news was received was almost drowned out by the hearty singing of "God Rest Ye Merry, Gentlemen" in the hall, but no matter, for there would be time enough to tell the others.

For now, they were content to share the felicity of the moment just with those they loved the most.

Appendix

A list of the main characters in *Expectations of Happiness*:

Readers familiar with the original Austen novel will realise that most of the main characters in this sequel come directly from Jane Austen's *Sense and Sensibility*.

Mrs Dashwood and her three daughters—Elinor (now Mrs Edward Ferrars), Marianne (now Mrs Brandon), and Margaret. Margaret is a teacher in a ladies' seminary in the neighbouring county of Oxfordshire.

Edward Ferrars (Elinor's husband)—parson at Delaford parish

Colonel Brandon (Marianne's husband)—owns the estate of Delaford in the county of Dorset

Sir John Middleton—of Barton Park in the county of Devonshire; Mrs Dashwood's cousin

Mrs Jennings—his mother-in-law (mother of Lady Middleton and Charlotte Palmer)

Mr Palmer—Charlotte's husband

John Dashwood—stepson of Mrs Dashwood and stepbrother to her three daughters

Fanny (his wife)—daughter of Mrs Ferrars and elder sister of Edward and Robert Ferrars

Lucy Steele (Mrs Robert Ferrars)—once secretly engaged to Edward, jilted him to marry his brother

Mr John Willoughby—a young man who courted Marianne when she was seventeen, but jilted her and married a rich heiress, Sophia Grey

Eliza Williams—a young relative of Colonel Brandon, who was seduced and abandoned by Willoughby, leaving her with an illegitimate daughter, whom I have named Alice

❧

From the imagination of Rebecca Ann Collins, some new characters:

Miss Claire Jones—a close friend and confidante of Margaret Dashwood

Mr Nicholas Wilcox—an Oxford tutor and friend of Claire Jones

Mr Daniel Brooke—an Oxford historian and colleague of Mr Wilcox

Dr Francis Grantley (from the Pemberley Chronicles, husband of Georgiana Darcy)—an Oxford theologian and close friend of Daniel Brooke

Dr and Mrs Bradley King—close friends of Elinor and Edward

Dorothea King—their daughter

Mr and Mrs Perceval and their daughters, Maria and Eugenie—friends of Marianne

Misses Harriet and Hannah Hawthorne—friends of the Percevals

Miss Henrietta Clift—a cousin of Mr Willoughby, known to Mrs Helen King

Mr Mark Armitage—a publisher

Acknowledgments

The author wishes, above all, to acknowledge her debt to Miss Jane Austen, whose original work, *Sense and Sensibility*, provided the inspiration for this novel. Miss Austen's characters and values have been treated with understanding and respect and in the sincere hope that, by continuing their stories into the second decade of the nineteenth century, the pleasure they have brought many thousands of readers already will be further enhanced.

Thanks are due to her friends and family for their encouragement, to Ms Claudia Taylor, librarian, for assistance with research and editing, and to Deb Werksman, Susie Benton, and their team at Sourcebooks, whose enthusiasm and understanding has been invaluable.

Many thanks too, to all those readers of the Pemberley novels, whose appreciative letters and emails since the conclusion of that series have encouraged the author to take up her pen again.

Rebecca Ann Collins / February 2011
www.rebeccaanncollins.com

About the Author

A lifelong fan of Jane Austen, Rebecca Ann Collins first read *Pride and Prejudice* at the tender age of twelve. She fell in love with the characters and since then has devoted years of research and study to the life and works of her favorite author. As a teacher of literature and a librarian, she has gathered a wealth of information about Miss Austen and the period in which she lived and wrote, which became the basis of her books about the Pemberley families. The popularity of The Pemberley Chronicles series with Jane Austen fans has been her reward.

With a love of reading, music, art, and gardening, Ms. Collins claims she is very comfortable in the period about which she writes, and feels great empathy with the characters she portrays. While she enjoys the convenience of modern life, she finds much to admire in the values and world view of Jane Austen.

The Pemberley Chronicles

A Companion Volume to Jane Austen's **Pride and Prejudice**
The Pemberley Chronicles: Book 1

REBECCA ANN COLLINS

"A lovely complementary novel to Jane Austen's *Pride and Prejudice*.
Austen would surely give her smile of approval."
—**BEVERLY WONG, AUTHOR OF** *Pride & Prejudice Prudence*

The weddings are over, the saga begins

The guests (including millions of readers and viewers) wish the two happy couples health and happiness. As the music swells and the credits roll, two things are certain: Jane and Bingley will want for nothing, while Elizabeth and Darcy are to be the happiest couple in the world!

Elizabeth and Darcy's personal stories of love, marriage, money, and children are woven together with the threads of social and political history of England in the nineteenth century. As changes in industry and agriculture affect the people of Pemberley and the surrounding countryside, the Darcys strive to be progressive and forward-looking while upholding beloved traditions.

"Those with a taste for the balance and humour of Austen will find a worthy companion volume."
—*Book News*

978-1-4022-1153-9 • $14.95 US/ $17.95 CAN/ £7.99 UK

The Women of Pemberley

The acclaimed Pride and Prejudice *sequel series*
The Pemberley Chronicles: Book 2

REBECCA ANN COLLINS

"Yet another wonderful work by Ms. Collins."
—BEVERLY WONG, AUTHOR OF *Pride & Prejudice Prudence*

A new age is dawning

Five women—strong, intelligent, independent of mind, and in the tradition of many Jane Austen heroines—continue the legacy of Pemberley into a dynamic new era at the start of the Victorian Age. Events unfold as the real and fictional worlds intertwine, linked by the relationship of the characters to each other and to the great estate of Pemberley, the heart of their community.

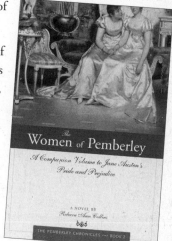

With some characters from the beloved works of Jane Austen, and some new from the author's imagination, the central themes of love, friendship, marriage, and a sense of social obligation remain, showcased in the context of the sweeping political and social changes of the age.

"The stories are so well told one would enjoy them even if they were not sequels to any other novel." —*Book News*

978-1-4022-1154-6 • $14.95 US/ $17.95 CAN/ £7.99 UK

Netherfield Park Revisited

The acclaimed Pride and Prejudice *sequel series*
The Pemberley Chronicles: Book 3

REBECCA ANN COLLINS

"A very readable and believable tale for readers
who like their romance with a historical flavor." —*Book News*

Love, betrayal, and changing times for the Darcys and the Bingleys

Three generations of the Darcy and the Bingley families evolve against a backdrop
of the political ideals and social reforms of the mid-Victorian era.

Jonathan Bingley, the handsome, distinguished son
of Charles and Jane Bingley, takes center stage,
returning to Hertfordshire as master of Netherfield
Park. A deeply passionate and committed man,
Jonathan is immersed in the joys and heartbreaks
of his friends and family and his own challenging
marriage. At the same time, he is swept up in the
changes of the world around him.

Netherfield Park Revisited combines captivating
details of life in mid-Victorian England with the
ongoing saga of Jane Austen's beloved *Pride and
Prejudice* characters.

"Ms. Collins has done it again!"
—BEVERLY WONG, AUTHOR OF *Pride & Prejudice Prudence*

978-1-4022-1155-3 • $14.95 US/ $15.99 CAN/ £7.99 UK

The Ladies of Longbourn

The acclaimed Pride and Prejudice *sequel series*
The Pemberley Chronicles: Book 4
REBECCA ANN COLLINS

"Interesting stories, enduring themes, gentle humour,
and lively dialogue." —*Book News*

*A complex and charming young woman of the Victorian age, tested
to the limits of her endurance*

The bestselling *Pemberley Chronicles* series continues the saga of the Darcys and
Bingleys from Jane Austen's *Pride and Prejudice* and introduces imaginative
new characters.

Anne-Marie Bradshaw is the granddaughter
of Charles and Jane Bingley. Her father now
owns Longbourn, the Bennet's estate in
Hertfordshire. A young widow after a loveless
marriage, Anne-Marie and her stepmother
Anna, together with Charlotte Collins, widow
of the unctuous Mr. Collins, are the Ladies
of Longbourn. These smart, independent
women challenge the conventional roles of
women in the Victorian era, while they search
for ways to build their own lasting legacies in
an ever-changing world.

Jane Austen's original characters—Darcy, Elizabeth, Bingley, and Jane—anchor
a dramatic story full of wit and compassion.

"A masterpiece that reaches the heart." —**BEVERLEY WONG, AUTHOR OF** *Pride
& Prejudice Prudence*

978-1-4022-1219-2 • $14.95 US/ $15.99 CAN/ £7.99 UK

WILLOUGHBY'S RETURN

JANE AUSTEN'S *SENSE AND SENSIBILITY* CONTINUES

JANE ODIWE

"A tale of almost irresistible temptation."

A lost love returns, rekindling forgotten passions...

When Marianne Dashwood marries Colonel Brandon, she puts her heartbreak over dashing scoundrel John Willoughby behind her. Three years later, Willoughby's return throws Marianne into a tizzy of painful memories and exquisite feelings of uncertainty. Willoughby is as charming, as roguish, and as much in love with her as ever. And the timing couldn't be worse—with Colonel Brandon away and Willoughby determined to win her back...

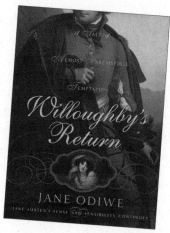

Praise for *Lydia Bennet's Story*:

"A breathtaking Regency romp!" —Diana Birchall, author of *Mrs. Darcy's Dilemma*

"An absolute delight." —*Historical Novels Review*

"Odiwe emulates Austen's famous wit, and manages to give Lydia a happily-ever-after ending worthy of any Regency romance heroine." —*Booklist*

"Odiwe pays nice homage to Austen's stylings and endears the reader to the formerly secondary character, spoiled and impulsive Lydia Bennet." —*Publishers Weekly*

978-1-4022-2267-2

$14.99 US/$18.99 CAN/£7.99 UK

Eliza's Daughter

A Sequel to Jane Austen's Sense and Sensibility
JOAN AIKEN

"Others may try, but nobody comes close to Aiken in writing sequels to Jane Austen." —*Publishers Weekly*

A young woman longing for adventure and an artistic life...

Because she's an illegitimate child, Eliza is raised in the rural backwater with very little supervision. An intelligent, creative, and free-spirited heroine, unfettered by the strictures of her time, she makes friends with poets William Wordsworth and Samuel Coleridge, finds her way to London, and eventually travels the world, all the while seeking to solve the mystery of her parentage. With fierce determination and irrepressible spirits, Eliza carves out a life full of adventure and artistic endeavor.

"Aiken's story is rich with humor, and her language is compelling. Readers captivated with Elinor and Marianne Dashwood in *Sense and Sensibility* will thoroughly enjoy Aiken's crystal gazing, but so will those unacquainted with Austen." —*Booklist*

"...innovative storyteller Aiken again pays tribute to Jane Austen in a cheerful spinoff of *Sense and Sensibility*." —*Kirkus Reviews*

978-1-4022-1288-8 • $14.95 US/ $15.99 CAN

Mansfield Park Revisited

A Jane Austen Entertainment

JOAN AIKEN

"A lovely read—and you don't have to have read
Mansfield Park to enjoy it." —*Woman's Own*

It's not so easy to keep scandal at bay...

After Fanny Price marries Edmund Bertram, they depart for the Caribbean, and
Fanny's younger sister Susan moves to Mansfield Park as Lady Bertram's new
companion. Surrounded by the familiar cast of characters from Jane Austen's
original, and joined by a few charming new characters introduced by the author,
Susan finds herself entangled in romance, surprise, scandal, and redemption.

Joan Aiken's diverting tale vividly imagines
how the Crawfords might have turned
out, and Jane Austen's moral tale takes
new directions—with an unexpected and
somewhat controversial ending.

"Her sense of time and place is
impeccable." —*Publishers Weekly*

"An excellent sequel...remarkably
effective and very funny."
—*Evening Standard*

978-1-4022-1289-5 • $14.95 US/ $15.99 CAN

Darcy and Anne

Pride and Prejudice continues…

JUDITH BROCKLEHURST

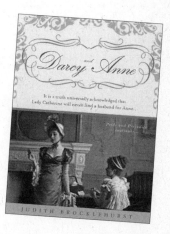

"A beautiful tale." —*A Bibliophile's Bookshelf*

Without his help, she'll never be free…

Anne de Bourgh has never had a chance to figure out what she wants for herself, until a fortuitous accident on the way to Pemberley separates Anne from her formidable mother. With her stalwart cousin Fitzwilliam Darcy and his lively wife Elizabeth on her side, she begins to feel she might be able to spread her wings. But Lady Catherine's pride and determination to find Anne a suitable husband threaten to overwhelm Anne's newfound freedom and budding sense of self. And without Darcy's help, Anne will never have a chance to find true love…

"Brocklehurst transports you to another place and time." —*A Journey of Books*

"A charming book… It is lovely to see Anne's character blossom and fall in love." —*Once Upon a Romance*

"The twists and turns, as Anne tries to weave a path of happiness for herself, are subtle and enjoyable, and the much-loved characters of Pemberley remain true to form." —*A Bibliophile's Bookshelf*

"A fun, truly fresh take on many of Austen's beloved characters." —*Write Meg*

978-1-4022-2438-6
$12.99 US/$15.99 CAN/£6.99 UK

The Plight of the Darcy Brothers
A TALE OF SIBLINGS AND SURPRISES

Marsha Altman

*"A charming tale of family and intrigue,
along with a deft bit of comedy."* —Publishers Weekly

Once again, it falls to Mr. Darcy to prevent a dreadful scandal...

Darcy and Elizabeth set off posthaste for the Continent to clear one of
the Bennet sisters' reputations (this time it's Mary). But their madcap
journey leads them to discover that the Darcy family has even deeper,
darker secrets to hide. Meanwhile, back at Pemberley, the hapless
Bingleys try to manage two unruly toddlers, and the ever-dastardly
George Wickham arrives, determined to
seize the Darcy fortune once and for all. Full
of surprises, this lively *Pride and Prejudice*
sequel plunges the Darcys and the Bingleys
into a most delightful adventure.

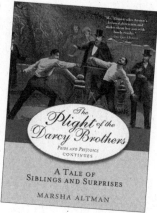

"Ms. Altman takes Austen's beloved characters and
makes them her own with lovely results."
—*Once Upon A Romance*

"Humorous, dramatic, romantic, and
touching—all things I love in a Jane Austen
sequel." —*Grace's Book Blog*

"Another rollicking fine adventure with the
Darcys and Bingleys...ridiculously fun reading."
—*Bookfoolery & Babble*

978-1-4022-2429-4
$14.99 US/$18.99 CAN/£7.99 UK

Mrs. Darcy's Dilemma

DIANA BIRCHALL

"Fascinating, and such wonderful use of language."
—JOAN AUSTEN-LEIGH

It seemed a harmless invitation, after all...

When Mrs. Darcy invited her sister Lydia's daughters to come for a visit, she felt it was a small kindness she could do for her poor nieces. Little did she imagine the upheaval that would ensue. But with her elder son, the Darcys' heir, in danger of losing his heart, a theatrical scandal threatening to engulf them all, and daughter Jane on the verge of her come-out, the Mistress of Pemberley must make some difficult decisions...

"Birchall's witty, elegant visit to the middle-aged Darcys is a delight." — **PROFESSOR JANET TODD, UNIVERSITY OF GLASGOW**

"A refreshing and entertaining look at the Darcys some years after *Pride and Prejudice* from a most accomplished author." —**JENNY SCOTT, AUTHOR OF** *After Jane*

978-1-4022-1156-0 • $14.95

A Darcy Christmas

AMANDA GRANGE, SHARON LATHAN, & CAROLYN EBERHART

A HOLIDAY TRIBUTE TO JANE AUSTEN

Mr. and Mrs. Darcy wish you a very Merry Christmas and a Happy New Year!

Share in the magic of the season in these three warm and wonderful holiday novellas from bestselling authors.

Christmas Present
BY AMANDA GRANGE

A Darcy Christmas
BY SHARON LATHAN

Mr. Darcy's Christmas Carol
BY CAROLYN EBERHART

978-1-4022-4339-4
$14.99 US/$17.99 CAN/£9.99 UK

PRAISE FOR AMANDA GRANGE:

"Amanda Grange is a writer who tells an engaging, thoroughly enjoyable story!"
—*Romance Reader at Heart*

"Amanda Grange seems to have really got under Darcy's skin and retells the story with great feeling and sensitivity."
—*Historical Novel Society*

PRAISE FOR SHARON LATHAN:

"I defy anyone not to fall further in love with Darcy after reading this book."
—*Once Upon a Romance*

"The everlasting love between Darcy and Lizzy will leave more than one reader swooning." —*A Bibliophile's Bookshelf*